# THE REVEALING

## JEFFREY RUSH

Cover design by: Alexander Killabrew
Published by: Revealing The Times

Printed in The United States

HARDCOVER ISBN: 979-8-9892558-0-1
PAPERBACK ISBN: 979-8-9892558-1-8
E-BOOK ISBN: 979-8-9892558-2-5

Contact the author for information about permission to reproduce selections from this book.

First Edition: 2023

# FORWARD

I met Jeffrey as a young man while on staff as an Associate Pastor in the 1990's. It was my great pleasure to become reacquainted with him as he researched the material that was the foundational background for this book. He began to share some of the biblical concepts at our church and with me personally. We all found ourselves digging deeper into the word of God for understanding. I highly recommend this book for the intriguing aspects, but even more for the scriptural references that will motivate you to think deeply about the correlations to the modern age. I know Jeffrey's heart is to help you see our world through the lens of biblical prophecies and to encourage each of us to prepare for when our Lord, Jesus Christ, returns. Get ready for an adventure that might change your view of the future and set you on the path to God's preferred future for you.

- Dr. Bob Dickerson

# SYNOPSIS

Is it possible that there are concealed messages within the scriptures?  Hidden mysteries concerning particular years of deliverance from ancient times to mysteries concerning what John both saw and heard when he wrote Revelation?  Is it possible the timing of the baptism of Jesus is concealed within the gospels and even concerning the two witnesses and their timeline when they begin to give their testimony?  Could there be more to discover about the two witnesses throughout other places in the scriptures?  Is it possible there is a concealed message from the Red Heifers to even the recent shaking of Syria and Turkey?  Could the time of the revealing be now for such a time as this?  Some revealed by dreams, others revealed by Divine guidance.  Is it possible there is more to what has happened with Russia and Ukraine to China and Taiwan?  Is there something to search out?  What has been concealed.... The mysteries.... The time is now for....
The Revealing.


The story between characters is fictional, though the events throughout the book are real.

# DEDICATION

I first and foremost dedicate this book to the Lord.  Without His guidance, this book would not have been possible.  Secondly, I dedicate this book to the prophets found in the scriptures.  I thank them for their boldness to speak and write what they both saw and heard, given to them by God.  May this book act as a Shofar that will sound around the world to reach those who have ears that they may hear and wake.  May they return to the Lord and stand watch together, especially as we see the Day approaching.


I would also like to dedicate this book to my Esther, she knows who she is.

# CONTENTS

**Welcome to THE REVEALING!**

In this book, we've incorporated an interactive feature to enhance your reading experience. Throughout the chapters, you will come across QR codes that link to additional content, such as chapter images, calendars, or more in-depth information. These QR codes provide a unique opportunity to delve deeper into the subject matter, view visual aids, or explore related multimedia resources.

**How to Use QR Codes:**

1. Look for the QR code symbol at the end of select chapters.

2. Using your smartphone or tablet, open the camera app or a QR code scanner app.

3. Align your device's camera with the QR code. It will automatically recognize the code.

As you scan the QR codes, you'll unlock a wealth of supplementary material designed to enrich your understanding and engagement with the book's content. Whether it's a visual illustration, a video demonstration, or an extended discussion, these additional resources are here to provide a more immersive and comprehensive reading experience.

Feel free to explore the world beyond the printed page by scanning the QR codes or typing in the attached link for your web browser to see the additional content in a much fuller way from your computer. We hope this interactive element adds depth to your journey through the chapters as you embark on this adventure!


May you have eyes to see and ears to hear as you come into...
THE REVEALING


Many Blessings,

Jeffrey Rush

# CHAPTER 1
# THE APPOINTMENT

"David will see you now."

The receptionist escorts him to the front door of David's office. He watches as the door opens, thinking, "Could this be it?  Could this be the moment chosen to open this up before the whole world?"

David stands at the other side of the doorway as he reaches out his hand to greet his newly welcomed guest.

"Welcome.  I am glad you were able to make it.  Thank you, Penny."

The receptionist smiled and said to David, "You're very welcome 007." She looks to the welcomed guest, then looks back to David and says, "He has shared some amazing things with me as he waited here in the lobby, and I look forward to hearing more or perhaps reading more about this." She smiles again.

"Well, we shall see." David looks at Penny, then looks at him and says, "After all, that is why you are here, right?  To see about publishing your book?"

All he could do at that moment was nod his head "Yes." Unlike him, it was like he was at a loss for words.  He almost always had something to share, a word, a message to give.  Though at this moment, he was nearly overwhelmed, thinking that this could very well be the time appointed for sharing with the world.  It was not about him.  It was not about making a name for himself.  He did not care about that.  He was overwhelmed by the weight of the message that seemed closer to being shared with the world following David opening the door.  The reality of it for him was standing there at that moment.

Penny looks at them both before walking back to her desk and says, "If you need anything, don't hesitate to let me know."

They walk further into David's office and sit in two chairs directly in front of David's desk, a coffee table between them.

"Would you like a cup of coffee?"

"Not at the moment, thank you though." He would have liked a cup of coffee then, though he could not bring himself to say "yes" as Penny had just sat back at her desk. He did not want to make her get up again.

"So, you come recommended by one of our very well-known Authors. He tells us that you have some information people should know about."

"That's right."

"Well, I must say that we don't normally bring in someone to accept unsolicited material. However, because someone we love and trust brought you to our attention, we thought it best to arrange this meeting. I trust that you found your way here okay?"

"Yes, I did. GPS does wonders." He smiled and said, "All I had to do was follow the way that it took me, look at my surroundings while looking at the map, and before you knew it, I was here."

"Very good. I take it that what you shared with Penny out in the lobby is some of what is in your book, is that right?"

"It is what would be shared in the book."

"By the way, Penny, that is not her actual name. I call her Penny as she sometimes calls me 007 as we are both big fans. We like to think of ourselves on a mission, and sometimes the mission may seem to be a mission impossible, though we know that with The Lord, all things are possible. So, we look to Him to guide us on the next mission. I trust you can relate to this from what I have heard about you?"

"Yes, that's right. Just like the GPS. All I had to do was follow the way He took me, look at what has been happening or has happened while looking at the map."

"I like that. So, what is the map you look at?"

"The map is His Word, The Bible, written by man though inspired by The Holy Spirit."

"Yes. Amen to that."

"I actually call that GPS as God Points Straight. It doesn't matter what I have gone through in this life; some of the trials I have been through were meant to mold me and shape me into the person I am today. Though I may plan in my heart, God directs my steps. We get so lost in the ways of the world that if we take the time to look to Him, we will find out that He is still talking to us, even now and in a time like this."

"I love that, so true. So, you said what you shared in the lobby would be in the book? Do you have the book with you?"

At that moment, he took out of his Jacket pocket a device too small to be a book. It looked like a phone. He touches his finger to a button with the word "Stop."

"What is that?" David asked.

"I should tell you that I have been recording this from the moment your receptionist told me that you would see me now. If you would trust this and permit me to hit start again, I can explain why I am recording this. You can ask any questions you want. We can record for as long as it takes."

David nods his head, permitting him to continue recording.

He puts his finger on the start button as the recording continues right as David says, "So why the recording?"

"Because this recording is to become the book."

"We were told that you have a book, that we should meet with you and hear what you have to share with us. That was the whole purpose of this meeting."

"I do have something to share with you, and that is the reason for recording this. I also brought with me a book, many books to be exact, about sixty-six in total."

David saw only a leather bag on the floor beside where he was sitting. The bag had writings on it. On the strap, the words read, "God's Peace + His Beloved = God Remembers." On the side of the bag, read the names of the original twelve disciples. To the other side of where his guest was sitting was a Shofar with a dark leather strap attached to it.

"How could you have brought sixty-six books with you when all you have here is a leather bag and a Shofar? I see the names of the original twelve disciples written on the side of your bag. Do you have anything written on the other side of your bag?"

"As a matter of fact, something is written on the other side of the bag."

He reached down to pick up the leather bag beside him and turned the bag around so David could read what was engraved on the other side of the leather carrying case. It was the names of the 12 Tribes of Jacob, Jacob's 12 sons, beginning with the order of their birth. He then looks to David and says, "As for the 66 books I have brought, let me show you."

He begins to unlock the straps that were wrapped over the leather carrying case. As he opens it, he pulls out a large dark leather book with Hebrew letters written on the back. When he turned the book around, a large red Templar Cross was on the front. The book was bound in leather with its own strap bearing the name "Jerusha." The book was also held closed by two straps equally spaced apart to either keep the book closed or bring the book to be opened.

"Is that the Bible?"

"It is."

David then smiles as he says, "Sixty-six books of the Bible, why didn't I think of that? Now, it makes sense. You brought sixty-six books with you. What are the Hebrew writings on the back?"

"The word Shalom, meaning peace."

"What about the name 'Jerusha' on the strap?"

"That is a name that means 'Married or a possession.' It can also mean 'Inheritance.' It is a unique variation of the masculine name Jebediah with connections to Jerusalem."

"Why did you choose that name to be on the strap?"

"Because the name contains the first two letters of my first name, and the middle of that name contains the letters of my last name. The name 'Rush.'"

"I see. So, do you prefer to go by Jeremiah, Jeremy, or Mr. Rush?"

"Jeremy is fine, though Jeremiah is fine too, just not Mr. Rush." He begins to smile.

"Okay Jeremy, I'll call you Jeremy. Is that okay?"

He laughed, saying, "I already told you that would be fine."

"Very good, so Jeremy, you have brought the Bible, not your own book, and we are recording this conversation between us now, and you are saying that our conversation will be the book?"

"That's right."

David laughs a bit as he says, "I must say that I have never met with a potential Author who has never even written a book, let alone agree to publish a book that has not yet been written."

"The book has been written." He places the Bible on the coffee table while putting his hand on it.

"You're referring to the Bible?"

"Yes."

"I am not following. We are in the business of publishing new books. The Bible is 'The' Book and has been in existence for a very long time and is even the most bought book. That book, The Bible, will always be the number 1 seller."

"Yes, and as so it should be."

"So, where is the book you have written?"

"I have not written it yet, and for the sake of time, that is why we are recording this conversation. Why spend all the time writing a book when I can share with you now some of the things I have shared with the very one who recommended me to you? Things that I have shared with your receptionist in the lobby before our meeting. Things that the one who recommended me to you has said needs to be shared with people around the world. As you shook my hand, your receptionist even said she wants to hear more and perhaps read more about this. The recording of our conversation during this meeting would become the very words to be printed on a number of pages that would then come to be bound as a book."

"Wow, so what is the book to be about? What would be in it?"

"What if I told you that some of the very things we read in the Bible are happening now? That some of these things have already happened. We can read about them by looking at our history, even over the past one hundred years, and yet long before these events of our time happened, they were written down more than 2,000 years ago in our very Bible. The things I would share with you are some of those events marked in our history books. I would also share with you the dreams I have had. Dreams that contained visions that led me to truths I searched out when I woke, only to find those truths were real, and some of the dreams gave clues to things that had already happened before, some long ago, though for the purpose of revealing what has been hidden and some to reveal what was to come to pass. I would share with you things within the Book of Revelation, the Book of Daniel, the Book of Zechariah, and even some of the Psalms and various other places within the Scriptures that tell of the times in which we have lived and are now living. We do not know the day or the hour of His Return. Only the Father knows. We are to be watchmen though. Watchmen on a wall. As a Watchman, based on what I have been shown and what I share with you today, would tell us that we don't have long."

"Even the disciples said that the days they were living in were the last hour."

"Yes, that's true, and they were.  Though God's time is not our time, and our time is not God's time.  As you know, a day is as a thousand years, and a thousand years is as a day."

"So, what is the purpose of this book?  This book that is being written as we speak here and now?"

"Jesus said to His disciples that He would tell them of things before they come to pass, so that when they do come to pass, they may believe.  He was saying that He would tell them of things before they came to pass so that when they do come to pass, they may believe that He is the Son of God and that The Father has sent Him."

"Okay, I understand that.  Though, why this conversation between us?  Why make what is shared today into a book?"

"Because, just as Jesus told His disciples of things before they would come to pass, this same thing can be found and discovered throughout the Bible, which is His Word to us.  He is the Word.  What was written in the Old Testament was given to man inspired by Him.  He is God in the flesh.  What Jesus gave to John as he wrote the book of Revelation almost 2,000 years ago was meant to tell us of things that had not yet happened so that when they do, those who are alive during that time when they do come to pass may believe that He is the Son of God and was sent by The Father.  What is to come to pass is found in the Book of Revelation and many other books within the Bible.  Some things that have already happened. Some things that have always been hidden in plain sight as we read the Gospels while joining together the writings of historians who lived around the time Jesus walked the earth would reveal hidden truths that have always been there waiting for us to discover in a time like this."

"Interesting.  I must say that I am intrigued."

"Your choice of using the word 'intrigued' is appropriate for a time like this.  Part of Daniel 11:34 says this, 'Many shall join with them by intrigue.'"

"Who is 'them?'"

"Those of the people who understand which shall instruct many."

"The people who understand?"

"Yes, the watchman on the wall. The ones who have been looking at their surroundings, what has happened and been happening, the ones who have not been focused on the distractions of the world and have looked to Him while at the same time holding close the map, His word, the Bible. They shall instruct many."

"Back to this unwritten book. What would you call this book? What would the title be?"

"The book would be called or known by the very purpose of what is to be found within it. The book would bring people to search out the Scriptures for themselves just as the Bereans did in the time of the Apostle Paul. By those reading the words of what would be shared during our time today, while those same people search out the Scriptures for themselves, may they come to see that the very One, Jesus Himself, told us of things before they would come to pass, so that when they do come to pass, we may believe that He is the Son of God and that The Father sent Him, that He is coming again. This book would be for the hope they would come to believe in Him, in Jesus, and be saved before the time of tribulation, before the time of His return."

David picks up his phone from his desk and pages the receptionist.

"Yes, 007."

"Penny, cancel the rest of my appointments for today. Jeremy and I are going to be here for a while."

David asks Jeremy, "Would you like that cup of coffee now?"

"Yes, David, thank you."

"How do you take it?"

"Black, with one of those sweetener packs if you have it."

"Penny, could you bring us some coffee with some sweetener packs."

"Sure thing David, and I will call your other appointments. When would you like for me to reschedule them?"

"As today is Friday, just let them know we will get back to them first thing Monday morning.  I will have some time over the weekend to think about times to reschedule them and can let you know as well on Monday."

"Very well, I will tell them.  Let me get your coffee first."

She comes into David's office with the coffee.  David and Jeremy both took their coffee the same way.  Black with one sweetener packet.  David and Jeremy prepare their coffee, knowing they will be in for a long day, perhaps even a long night.  As David finishes stirring his coffee, he looks to Jeremy and says, "So, the title of the Book?"

Jeremy taps his spoon at the edge of his cup before laying his spoon on the napkin in front of him, taking a sip of his coffee as he looks at David and says just two words.

"The Revealing."

# CHAPTER 2
# THE DREAMS

The Revealing?"

"Yes, The Revealing.  That's right David."

"So, the purpose of this book would be to reveal something?"

"Yes."

"Like what?  To reveal things that relate to what is in the Bible?  I assume that since you have brought your Bible here today."

"Yes David.  To reveal things that relate to what is in the Bible. Things that have always been there awaiting the time to be discovered and revealed for such a time as this."

"How have they been revealed to you?"

"In many ways.  Some through dreams.  Others by seeing something and feeling that I needed to look in a particular place or search something out only I had no idea what I was searching for though yet, the feeling guided me to truth that I would have had no possible way of discovering on my own."

"That is amazing.  Are there any other ways things have been revealed to you?"

"Yes.  Someone I had met.  Who was a stranger.  The meetings seemed to be by chance, though looking back on it now, I know the meetings could not have been chance.  They were divine appointments."

"Does he have a name?  What did he share with you?"

Jeremy could tell that David was anxious to know and hear as much as possible, though Jeremy knew that everything that would be shared would have to be shared with such precision as others would one day read the very words spoken in this meeting. He wanted to make sure everything was clear among those who read the words spoken and wanted to leave little room for the upcoming mockers as he knew regardless of how precise he would be, there would still be some who would struggle with unbelief and choose to mock instead. While choosing to be precise, all he could do was focus on the road ahead, to reach as many as possible that may have doubts, in hopes they may come to believe that Jesus is the Son of God, that He was sent by The Father, in hopes they come to be saved. To repent, to return before the time of His Coming.

Jeremy looks at David and says, "He did not give me his name. He told me that his name was not important, only the message that he had to give was important. He told me to call him 'Messenger.' As for what he shared with me, I will share with you as well."

Jeremy took another sip of his coffee, then sat it down on the coaster on the coffee table in front of him. As he sat back in his chair, he looked at David and said, "Where would you like for me to begin?"

"I am looking forward to hearing what the Messenger shared with you, though I suppose I would like to hear about the dreams you had first. How do you know the dreams were God-given dreams?"

"Because the dreams, the visions I had within the dreams lead to truth that I had no way of knowing on my own, and yet when I woke and searched out what I saw in the dream, the truth was there waiting to be found."

David picked up his coffee and began to take a sip, then looked to Jeremy and said, "Whenever you would like to begin, I am all ears."

## The Coming Pope

"It was October 2012 when I had this dream. In the Dream, I was looking at a hill, and there was nothing on the hill except for a man who was wearing a suit. I look at the man and hear a voice that says, "Here is a beginning." I look away from the man in the suit and look back to the hill again, only the hill is not just a hill anymore, I now see The Capitol Building on it and what looks like construction going on with it.

I then look back to the man wearing the suit, who is no longer wearing a suit, instead, the man is dressed in a Pope's clothing. I then woke up from the dream. I knew the dream was not like a regular dream. I knew there was something to it. So, I asked myself, 'Why did I see a man wearing a suit on a hill, to then seeing The Capitol Building on that Hill, to then seeing the man no longer wearing a suit, but dressed like a Pope.' I started searching for answers as I looked up information on Capitol Hill, and what I found was shocking as it directly related to the dream. What I found out was that there was a man who once owned the land that the Capitol Building was built on. The man had a vision that a house of parliament would be built on the land he owned. The man ended up selling the land to the Government, and sure enough, The Capitol Building was built on it. The man who owned the land, his name was "Francis Pope." In October 2012, I told one of my Chaplain friends about the dream, and after I had understood the meaning of the dream, I told him, 'Mark my words, the current Pope will resign, and another Pope will take his place, and he will choose the name "Francis" and he will be a 'First of Firsts.'" Surely enough, Pope Benedict resigned in February of 2013, and a New Pope was selected on March 13th, 2013, and chose the name "Francis." When this happened, my Fellow Chaplain asked me how I knew, and he said, "Do you remember telling me what you told me in October?" I said, "Yes, I remember." He then asked how I knew. I then reminded him of the dream I had shared with him in October of 2012 and told him that I was able to understand the meaning. It was during this time when Chaplain Dexter asked me if I had ever heard of a Rabbi by the name of Jonathan Cahn. I told Chaplain Dexter that I had not heard of him. Chaplain Dexter then tells me about the book (The Harbinger) that Jonathan Cahn had put out only months ago, in 2012. A few years later, in 2015, Pope Francis spoke in the Capitol Building while Construction was going on. He was the first Pope to speak in the Capitol Building and the first Pope to Speak at the United Nations on September 25th, 2015. Pope Francis spoke in the Capitol Building on the land once owned by "Francis Pope." He is also the first Pope to choose the name "Francis." I find it interesting as well that this very dream is what led Chaplain Dexter to tell me of Jonathan Cahn and that the day that Pope Francis spoke in the United Nations in 2015 was on September 25th, which, as you know, is Jonathan Cahn's birthday, which confirms yet again the Divine ordinance. It was Pope Francis' Speech at the United Nations that made me realize something else. It was Pope Francis' opening address, just the first few lines he spoke as he said, "In my own name and on behalf of the catholic church." When he said, "In my own name," that was enough for me as I had watched Pope Francis go from Country to Country and be well received by everyone, and when he came to the United States, how so many just wanted a chance to touch him, I was reminded by what Jesus said 2,000 years ago. John 5:43 "I have come in My Father's name, and you do not receive Me; if another comes in his own name, him you will receive.""

Jeremy looks to David and says, "Do you have any questions, or would you like for me to continue?"

"Have you had other dreams?"

"Yes.  I can share more of them with you if you'd like."

"Yes Jeremy.  Just give me a moment." David picked up a notepad from his desk and began writing down a few notes to himself.  He then looked at Jeremy and said, "I can ask my questions later.  Please continue."

"Very well."

## The Ruinous Heap

"Also in the year 2012, I had a dream that I was looking at the Statue of Liberty, and at the base of the Statue of Liberty, a door opens, and bright light is shining through the door, and I hear a voice beside me that says, "Lazarus Come Out."  There was no one beside me, only a voice. Then I hear what sounds like planes behind me, and I turn to look, and I see the planes hitting the Twin Towers.  I then see the Twin Towers Fall and a bunch of rubble.  However, the images of the Rubble of New York had changed to a different location.  I started seeing news Headlines/Snapshots of Bashar Al-Assad, and no longer the Rubble of New York from 9-11, but the Rubble of Damascus.  When I woke from the dream, I knew again that it could not be a regular dream but something prophetic, something of Divine origin.  So, I began doing some research, and this is what I found.  In the dream, I dreamt that the base of the Statue of Liberty had a door that opened and a bright light shining through with a voice at my side that said, "Lazarus, Come Out." I found out that at the base of the Statue of Liberty there is a poem written that says, "Give us your poor and your oppressed." The poem at the base of The Statue of Liberty was written by: Emma Lazarus.

Now, as far as seeing 9-11, granted, this was a dream in 2012, so 9-11 in New York had obviously already happened, but I asked myself, 'Why was I seeing 9-11, the Rubble of 9-11 in New York to then change to seeing snapshots of Bashar Al-Assad and Rubble of Damascus.' Again, I started to do research, and we know the scriptures say that in the later days, Damascus will be a ruinous heap, never to be built up again.  That was already something I knew.  What I didn't know though as I looked up information on Bashar Al-Assad, is that he was born on September 11th, 1965.  The fact that the dream was connecting me to things that I simply did not know, yet there were still things about that dream that I had not fully understood at the time, so I just kept the matter in mind until a future time.

Jeremy looked at David as he was still writing in his notepad and said, "Would you like for me to go on to the next one?"

"Yes please.  Continue."

## The Eclipses

"In the Fall of 2020, right before going to Washington D.C. for "The Return," I had a dream that I was at the Church that I used to Minister at in Carterville, IL.  In the Dream, I was outside in the Parking Lot of the Church watching a Solar Eclipse, and others were there watching the Solar Eclipse as well.  Then suddenly, I was no longer at the Church, I was then standing on the other side of a Bridge looking at the other side of the bridge into Key West, Florida.  In the dream, I then was back at the Church in Carterville, IL. watching a Solar Eclipse, only this time, everyone wore different clothes.  While watching the Solar Eclipse, I heard someone say the number 1,260.  I then went inside the Church and saw etched in big numbers across a wood table the number 1,260. It was then that I woke up from the dream.

In real life, I did actually watch the August 21st, 2017, Solar Eclipse at the Church in Carterville, IL. which just so happened was the area of the center of the Solar Eclipse.  In the dream, I was there at the Church again, watching a Solar Eclipse.  When I woke, at first, I thought that maybe I had just dreamt of something I had already done a few years ago; however, I was Wondering why, in the dream, I was looking on the other side of a bridge into Key West, Florida. Was it just because I was born in Key West, Florida, and therefore was just part of the dream? After Key West, Florida, being back at the Church Watching a Solar Eclipse and seeing everyone was wearing different clothes told me that this was a different Solar Eclipse than the first one, and the mention of 1,260 and seeing 1,260 etched in big numbers across a wood table. I knew that 1,260 is mentioned in the Book of Revelation, talking about the 3 1/2 years of the Tribulation. I knew this must have been something of God, but I didn't fully understand it at the time. I asked myself what the significance was of Key West, Florida, other than myself being born there. Why see one Eclipse at the Church in Carterville, IL. to then standing on the other side of a Bridge looking across to Key West, Florida, to then being back at the Church in Carterville, IL. watching another Solar Eclipse with the number 1,260 being heard and seen?

I thought to myself, 'I wonder what the distance is from the Church in Carterville, IL. to Key West, Florida?' I looked it up on Google Maps. The address of the Church in Carterville, IL. is 1025 South Division Street Carterville, IL. 62918 to Key West, Florida. The result was mind-blowing. The distance is exactly 1,260 Miles. So, the distance from the Church to Key West, Florida, and then back to the Church is a total of 2,520 Miles. I then asked myself why I was standing on the other side of a bridge looking into Key West, Florida, rather than just looking at Key West, Florida. Why did I have to be on the other side of a bridge that led to the Island? I then thought more about that, so I went to Google and asked the question of the bridge leading to Key West Florida, and the 7-mile bridge came up. I already knew about the 7-mile bridge though, my dad ran across the Seven Mile Bridge back when they had opened it when my dad was stationed down there in the Navy. I asked myself, was there something more to it though? Sure, I knew that 1,260 and 1,260 is a total of 2,520 which is a total of 7 years on the Biblical Calendar and here I was faced with 1,260 miles from the Church in Carterville, IL. to Key West, Florida and 1,260 miles from Key West, Florida back to the Church in Carterville, IL. and the 7 Mile bridge. I then thought about the other number in Revelation that talks about a 3 1/2-year period, which is 42 months. So, there are 1,260 days and 42 months. I think again about the Bridge. I go to Google search, and I ask the question, "How many bridges are there from Miami Florida to

Key West, Florida?" The answer, there is a total of 42 Bridges that connect from the mainland of the United States to Key West, Florida."

## The 'Swamp Fox' Connection

"This next dream I had a week after coming back from the Return in Washington D.C. in 2020.  In the dream I was seeing what looked like the Revolutionary War, men were wearing the blue coats and red coats, their rifles looked like that of the Revolutionary War and their hats were like those worn during that time.  I see men from both sides in the middle of a wooded swamp area firing across this swamp at each other.  I look to an opening between the trees at a small hill where a Fox was looking right at me.  The Fox was away from the men, on a hill, yet close enough to the swampy waters.  I look back at the men on both sides as they sat behind the trees reloading their rifles and the dream ended before I saw the men fire their rifles again.  When I woke up, I wondered if I had dreamt of what seemed like the Revolutionary War because I had just come back from Washington D.C. Though I didn't understand the reason for seeing the soldiers in a swampy area and seeing a fox in the dream.  I wasn't sure at the time if the dream was a God-given dream or if it was just a dream.  I didn't know for sure because I didn't understand the dream.  Still, I kept the dream in mind, not knowing if I could understand it in the future.

Instead of going over the eclipse dream with you again, I will show you what led me to find a connection to both dreams I had the week before and the week after 'The Return.' I will just share with you what I felt led me to look further into the Solar Eclipse of August 21st, 2017.  I felt led to look further into the Solar Eclipse of August 21st, 2017, simply because I lived in the Marion/Carterville, IL.  area at the time of the Solar Eclipse on August 21st, 2017.  I was serving as a Chaplain at the Marion VA Hospital in Marion, IL. and was serving at Christian Covenant Fellowship in Carterville, IL.  I felt led to look further into the Solar Eclipse of August 21st, 2017, because 1.  I Watched it in real life. 2. I Had a for sure God-given dream regarding the Eclipse. 3. Knowing the area was the center of the Solar Eclipse.  All this information led me to believe there must be something more to the Eclipse of August 21st, 2017."

Jeremy then reaches down to his leather carrying case and pulls out a few pages that he hands to David as he says, "Here is a list of details of things I had found that relate and connect both of the dreams I had the week before and the week after 'The Return.' I also wrote some additional things below the list of details for you to read."

David looks at the pages and begins reading silently to himself. Jeremy then reminds David, saying, "For the sake of the recording, could you read what I have handed you out loud?"

"Oh yes, of course." David then begins to read the detailed list and what followed out loud.

## The Connecting List

1.  As the Sun was setting in Jerusalem, the Sun was being Eclipsed in Salem, Oregon.

2.  The Eclipse entered the United States at Salem, Oregon.

3.  The August 21st, 2017, Solar Eclipse path across the U.S. from Northwest to Southeast crossed over 7 Salems.  They are: Salem, Oregon.  Salem, Idaho.  Salem, Wyoming.  Salem, Nebraska.  Salem, Missouri.  Salem, Kentucky.  Salem, South Carolina.

4.  The longest period of the Solar Eclipse was in Marion, IL.  area.

5.  The County of Salem, Oregon, where the Eclipse started in the United States, is Marion County.

6.  There is a news clipping from South Carolina before the Solar Eclipse of August 21st, 2017, where the people of South Carolina thought they would have the longest period of totality.  The area was at Lake Marion, South Carolina.  They were the second longest in duration, however.

7.  The Solar Eclipse of August 21st, 2017, began in Marion County Salem, Oregon.  Lasted the Longest in Marion, IL.  area known as Little Egypt and Exited in South Carolina with the second longest duration around Lake Marion, South Carolina.

8.  We get the name "Salem" from "Jerusalem," which as you know, "Jeru" means "City" and "Salem" means "Peace."

9.  "Marion" in Hebrew means "From the Family of Mary" and also means "Wished-for Child."

10.  I then looked up the areas of Marion County in Salem Oregon. The County was named after "Francis Marion" who fought in the Revolutionary War.

11.  I then looked up Marion, IL.  Marion, IL. was also named after "Francis Marion" who fought in the Revolutionary War.

12.  I then looked at Lake Marion in South Carolina.  Lake Marion was named after "Francis Marion," who fought in the Revolutionary War.

13.  I then looked up "Francis Marion," who fought in the Revolutionary War, and he was known as "The Swamp Fox." Under his relations on Wikipedia, the first name listed of one of his relatives was "Julia Rush Cutler Ward." Julia's Grandmother was "Francis Marion's" Sister, his only sibling.

14.  My Great, Great, Great, Great-Grandfather was Benjamin Rush, one of the signers of the Declaration of Independence.  He was the first person in this Country to do a mass printing of The Bible.  He was the founder of public education; he believed the people should have a free education.  He was also the one who started Sunday School/Bible Study in this Country.

I still don't understand it completely, though I ask myself what the odds are that the dream I had before I went to 'The Return' of the Solar Eclipse and the Dream I had a week after 'The Return' about The Revolutionary War, in what looks like a Swamp to seeing a Fox looking right at me connect somehow.  I have come to understand that both dreams do indeed connect.  All three Marion's are named after "Francis Marion," who fought in The Revolutionary War and was known as "The Swamp Fox."

15.  I then consider the Solar Eclipse of April 8th, 2024.  It just so happens that April 8th is the exact anniversary of the Month and Day that Jesus was Resurrected.  Jesus was Crucified in 30 AD during

Passover on April 6th. He rose again on the Day of First Fruits, which was on Sunday. Sunday, the Day of First Fruits, was April 8th, 30 AD, and at Sundown became April 9th.

16. So, the time of Jesus' Resurrection was on April 8th. I will ask you, "What shape was the stone that had closed the Tomb?" It was round, that's right. Can you imagine, His light shines in the Darkness. Can you imagine, as the round stone still covered the tomb, the moment of His Resurrection, imagining the Glorious Light shining around the rim of it before it rolled away? What would it have looked like? It would have looked like a Solar Eclipse.

17. Back to the Eclipse of August 21st, 2017, again lasting the longest in the Marion, IL. area. Marion, IL. just happened to be founded on August 21st, 1879, the exact Month and Day. All I have shared with you is too much to be a coincidence.

I looked up Julia Rush Cutler Ward and came to find out she was a poet. I will quote the end part of the poem, "Soon to illume those threatening skies, The Sun of Righteousness shall rise, and on my soul His glories pour: Securely then my bark I'll moor Within that port where all are blest--The haven of eternal rest. Shine onward, then, and guide me through, Si je te perds, je suis perdu."

(SI JE TE PERDS, JE SUIS PERDU.) Is the title of the poem she wrote. In the poem she mentions the Star of Bethlehem as well.

I looked up "Sun of Righteousness," however. "Sun of Righteousness" can be found in Malachi 4:2 "But to you who fear My name The Sun of Righteousness shall arise with healing in His wings; And you shall go out and grow fat like stall-fed calves." This blessing is promised to those who fear the Lord and are ready for His return."

David finished reading the detailed list that seemed to connect both dreams and read what followed the list. He was amazed by it all. He had so many questions he wanted to ask. Questions like "How were you able to understand the meaning of the dreams? How did you know where to look once you woke up? Why do you think God is giving you these dreams? When do you think you will understand them fully?" The list of questions David had about this could go on and on the more he thought about it all. One thing David did know was that this was too much to be random chance.  This was Divine.  He knew that questions could come later though he didn't want to ask them now.  Afterall, David knew the recording was still going.  He did not want this future book to be full of his questions to Jeremy.  As a Publisher, he knew the book would need to focus on its main objective.

David hands the papers back to Jeremy and says, "This is amazing.  I have my questions, though that can wait until afterward." David laughs a bit as he looks down at his notepad and says, "I have been taking notes to ask when we are done."

"Okay David, that sounds good.  Sounds like a plan." Jeremy smiles.

David took another drink of his coffee.  The coffee had cooled down, no longer hot enough to be sip-worthy.  He was completely locked into what was being shared with him that he had not thought about his coffee during all that time.  He looks to Jeremy and says, "One thing I do know is that this is Divine.  There is too much here to be a bunch of chance, too much that connects."

"Yes David.  Too much to be chance, not to mention this would be like looking for a needle in a haystack to bring all this together.  This would be impossible without guidance."

"That's right.  I agree completely.  So, what's next?"

"What's next is I would like to use the restroom if that's okay."

"Oh yes, of course.  I may need to take a break myself."

Jeremy begins to laugh as he looks at David and says, "Coffee will do that to you.  Not long after drinking a cup, the urge comes along for needing to use the restroom."

"Yes.  I can relate there."

As Jeremy begins to walk out of David's office to use the restroom, David says, "I will get us a fresh cup of coffee for when you get back."

"Okay, thank you David."

David pages the receptionist, "Yes David."

"Can you bring us another cup of coffee?"

"Yes, of course.  How are things going?"

"Great, everything is going great.  Thank you.  If I happen to be out of the office, just leave it on the table."

"Will do."

David starts to look down at Jeremy's Shofar that laid on the floor beside where he was sitting.  He can see five etched marks on it, like five tally marks, and wonders what that could be.  What could it mean?  He walks over to pick it up to look at it more closely.  He always liked the sound of the Shofar; he had tried to sound a Shofar in the past, though he never could figure out how to make the sound it makes.  Whatever the trick was, he didn't know.  He sat the Shofar back down while thinking to himself, "I hope Jeremy tells me about the five tally marks on his Shofar, maybe that will be one thing I do ask him when he gets back.  After all, the focus of the book is to reveal.  I am sure there is something to be revealed with these marks on his Shofar."

Explore this chapter's photos/calendars mentioned by scanning the QR code or visiting the link:

https://www.revealingthetimes.com/chapter2

# CHAPTER 3
# THE MESSENGER'S SHOFAR

Jeremy returns to David's office, and right as he entered the door to David's office, he pushes record from his phone. He didn't want his recorder to miss one word from their time together.

David looks to Jeremy and says, "I have a fresh cup of coffee there for you on the table."

"Thank you David."

"You are very welcome."

David watches Jeremy begin to sit down where he had been sitting before. He couldn't keep his eyes off of the Shofar on the floor beside him. David wanted so much to ask about the markings, the five tallies on it. He sits across from Jeremy, picking up his coffee to take a sip as Jeremy also began to sip his coffee. David still glancing down at the Shofar.

"Are you okay David?"

"Oh yes, why do you ask?"

"Because I notice you keep looking at something." Jeremy sits his coffee back on the table and leans to his side to pick up the Shofar. "Is this what you are looking at?"

"Yes, it is. I picked it up and looked at it while you were in the restroom. I hope you don't mind."

"No, not at all. I can imagine you have questions."

David laughs as he says, "I have questions about a lot of things."

Jeremy points to the five tallies on the Shofar and says, "And questions about this?"

"Yes, how did you know?"

"Because David, that was my question when I first saw these five markings."

"When you first saw them?  Didn't you put them there?"

"No David.  I did not put them there.  They were put there by someone else."

"By someone else?  Why would someone else put these markings on your Shofar?"

"This was not always my Shofar.  It belonged to another and was later given to me."

"Given to you by who?"

"By the one who called himself 'Messenger.'"

"Did he tell you what the five markings meant when you asked him what they were?"

"Yes David, he did.  Though he did not tell me what they meant right as I asked him.  He shared with me other things first."

"Like what?  What did he share with you?"

"He first shared with me the purpose of what the Shofar was and is used for."

"And…go on."

Jeremy begins to look down at the Shofar while it rests across his lap. Looking at it in such a way of honoring both its beauty and the significance of its purpose.  He then looks back to David and says, "The Shofar is meant to sound an alarm."

"An alarm?"

"Yes David.  An alarm of an approaching enemy, the coming of war. The Shofar would be in the hands of a Watchman.  In ancient times, the Watchman would stand on a high place, sometimes a mountain, or a tower, even a high fortress wall near the corners and the entrances of their gates.  They would watch from a high place to see out far distances. The further they could see out, the sooner they could see the approach of an enemy.  If they spotted the enemy approaching, the Watchman would blow the Shofar."

"In ancient times, wouldn't the enemy often come at night in the hopes of not being seen?"

"Yes, that's right.  The enemy knew there would be Watchman looking out across the distance from a high place so the enemy would sometimes approach at night making it more difficult for the Watchman to see further out.  The enemy would also sometimes send out excellent marksman who would attempt to approach close enough to where the Watchman would stand and strike the Watchman with their arrows."

"Why would they shoot at the Watchman with their arrows?"

"Because David, if the enemy was approaching at night, that meant that many in the town or city were sleeping, though not the Watchman. The Watchman was awake, always watching, always waiting.  If the enemy came at night and visibility was bad, this meant that the Watchman also had to be very attentive to what he heard.  He not only had to perceive what he saw, he also had to have ears to hear.  If the enemy sent only a few with their bow and arrow to strike the Watchman, a few would be more difficult to spot in the night and more difficult to hear in the night as well.  If the Watchman would be hit with an arrow in the night before sounding the alarm, the enemy would have the advantage on a sleeping town, village, or city as they approach to seize and take plunder."

"So, the Watchman was meant to warn the people?"

"Yes, and if people of the town or city were sleeping.  The sound of the Shofar was meant to wake the people up, to put on their armor, to assemble and be ready for a soon approaching battle or war."

"Was the Shofar used for anything else?"

"Yes, the Shofar would also be blown by the Watchman when the Watchman would see the King approaching, to let the people know the King is coming.  It would also be blown during the coronation of a King. It would be blown even in acts of celebration."

"Celebration?"

"Yes David.  Celebration as in perhaps celebrating deliverance. Deliverance from bondage, deliverance from slavery, from prison. Deliverance from the enemy, from the enemy's land and returning home."

"That is amazing.  I never knew this.  The Shofar seems to have been very important."

"It was and it is.  Though the Watchman is just as important as the Shofar.  Without the Watchman, the shofar is unable to sound."

"That's right.  The Watchman is just as important."

"And do you know what is more important than the Shofar and the Watchman David?"

"What?  What is more important?"

"The people.  The people David.  The Watchman stands watch for the people.  The Shofar sounds as the Watchman blows it to awaken the people."

"Yes, the people."

"The Watchman may stand watch, they may be the ones to sound the Shofar, though the focus of the Watchman is not on themselves but on the people, hence the reason for blowing the Shofar.  The sounding of the Shofar is meant to bring the people together as one.  The people are to come together to prepare for battle, the people are to come together in victory with shouts of deliverance, the people are to come together as the King approaches.  The sounding of the shofar brings the people together."

"Thank you so much for sharing this with me."

David takes a sip of his cold coffee and decides just to drink the rest of it.  As he places his coffee cup back on the table, he begins to laugh and says, "I just can't seem to keep a cup of coffee hot long enough.  What ends up being 30 minutes to an hour only feels like 5 minutes as you've been here sharing all this with me.  Time sure flies."

Jeremy laughs and says, "Yes David.  Time sure flies by quickly."

David begins to look at the markings again, the five tallies and says, "About the five tallies, will you tell me what they are now, what Messenger told you they are?"

Jeremy looks at the five markings again as he brushes his finger across the grooves of their imprint.  He then looks back up to David and says, "Before I share with you what they are, let me share with you what 'Messenger' shared with me next."

"Does it relate with the Shofar?"

"It does.  It relates to one of the other purposes of the Shofar.  To sound it in celebration of deliverance."

"Messenger shared with you a message of deliverance?"

"Yes David.  Though what he shared with me required him to take me back in time as he talked with me.  It was like he took me on a journey through significant times marked within the Scriptures.  These times he shared with me have always been there for the reader to see for themselves, from the people who read the words when they were first written to the people of today.  As Messenger shared with me these times, he also shared a mystery that connects some of the significant times of that deliverance.  Times of deliverance from prison, from bondage, times of deliverance from the enemy, from the enemies land, to return home, even the deliverance that was paid by the Son of God, Yeshua….Jesus."

"A mystery that connects them?"

"Yes, a mystery.  Though as Messenger shared the mystery with me, it no longer was a mystery, but a revealing."

David looked at his watch to see the time.  He pages the receptionist and says, "Penny, are you there?"

"Yes, I am here.  More Coffee?"

"No, I think I have had my fair share of coffee." David looks at Jeremy and asks, "Would you like more coffee?"

Jeremy laughs and says, "No David, I too have a cup full of cold coffee that I need to drink."

"I can have it heated up for you."

"That would be nice, thank you."

"Penny, can you heat Jeremy's coffee for him and bring us both some water and perhaps a few cookies from the breakroom?"

"Of course.  I will be in there in just a moment."

"Thank you, Penny."

Jeremy waited until David was off the phone then said to David, "I must tell you that my time with 'Messenger' was not the first- and only-time meeting with someone who had such insight into the Scriptures and the things happening around us.  There had been others before him, the first one, many years ago, though that is for another book."

"I see.  Well Jeremy, I would be very interested in hearing about the others who met with you before.  Why would you not want to mention them in this book?"

Jeremy smiles and says, "David, I just now mentioned them in this book."

"You know what I mean.  Why do you not want to share what the others shared with you in this book?"

"Because what I have to share with you now is for such a time as this. What the others shared with me is important.  However, what will be shared in this book is meant to reach as many across this nation and the world, in hopes that those who have had doubts concerning God and the Scriptures may come to believe that He is and that He sent His Son

Jesus, that He died on the Cross, rose again on the third day and is coming back again. The hope is that they come to be saved."

"I understand. Not everything can be shared in one book."

Jeremy looks to his Bible and says, "Actually, everything has been shared in a book, in 66 books to be exact. Some things have been hidden within these Scriptures, waiting to be shared for such a time as this, though they have always been there. This and more, is what I plan to share with you."

David walks back to his chair to sit down and asks Jeremy, "So, when would you like to begin sharing this mystery that Messenger shared with you?"

Jeremy places the Shofar back on the floor beside him and then says to David, "How about after we have our water and Penny has gone back to her desk. I will then first share with you how 'Messenger' brings me to the year of the flood and how he shows me the mystery of the connection concerning significant years of deliverance."

"The flood, as in Noah's flood?"

"Yes David."

"And 'Messenger' showed you how to discover the year of Noah's flood?"

"He did, though let's wait for Penny."

"Yes, I understand." David was looking forward to hearing about this. With anticipation and excitement David said, "Then you will share the mystery that connects certain years of deliverance already within the Scriptures?"

"Yes, though remember, it is no longer a mystery, but a revealing."

"Yes, that's right, a revealing." David stands back up and says to Jeremy, "If you'll excuse me, I need to step out to my car. I just remembered I left some fruit in there that I need to put in the breakroom. They are probably ruined from the heat by now."

"No worries. I will just wait here."

Penny comes into the office to get his coffee from him and says, "Would you like me to heat this up for you or would you prefer a fresh cup?"

"Heating it up will be just fine, thank you."

"You're very welcome.  Do you need anything else?"

"I don't think so." Jeremy says with a smile, "Thank you."

Jeremy is able to see David through the glass wall as David walks towards the breakroom with his bag of fruit.

Penny also saw David walking towards the breakroom.

"Let me heat this coffee for you, I'll see if David needs any help.  I will come back with some cookies as well."

"Thank you Penny."

As Penny approached the breakroom, David was already walking back towards the office.  David comes into the office with two bananas in his hand and says, "Well, the fruit is still good.  The heat didn't ruin them, though I thought these bananas will not be good by Monday." David then hands one of the bananas to Jeremy.

"Thank you, David."

"You're very welcome.  I don't want them to go to waste.  Not sure why I had bought bananas to sit in our breakroom over the weekend and with the heat from the car I just know they would not be good by Monday."

Penny walks back into the office with a push tray that had a plate of cookies, some water, and Jeremy's coffee.  "Here you go David.  Jeremy the cookies with the jelly filling are my favorite, you will have to try one."

"Thank you, Penny, I will do that."

"If either of you need anything else, let me know."

Once Penny walks back out of the office, David sits back down, looks at Jeremy, and says, "Okay, I believe we have everything we need."

"Perhaps."

David had a look of confusion on his face when he said, "What else do we need?"

"Not we, but you.  You will need to have eyes to perceive and ears to hear what 'Messenger' shared with me.  You will need to have this throughout what I share with you that will be in this book."

"Okay, I understand."

"To start, I will take you back to that day when 'Messenger' arrived as I was standing at the river's edge.  On that day, 'Messenger' showed me through scripture how to find the year of the flood and then showed me the revealing of the mystery that connects certain years of deliverance."

"Okay," David sits back in his chair.  "I am ready."

"Then let's begin."

# CHAPTER 4
# MESSENGER'S ARRIVAL: THE TRAIL OF YEARS TO NOAH'S FLOOD

It was Spring of 2021. The warm days were here and there. During one of the nice days, I had decided to go to the Arch in St. Louis, Mo. Just to walk around, get a chance to be out and about for a while. It was there during that walk when it happened. I walked down by the riverbank of the Mississippi looking down at the cobblestones when I heard the voice of one behind me say,

"How odd is it to find you here standing on the side of a riverbank, and the Arch, the Gateway to the West behind you."

I turned around to look at the man. He looked to be in his mid-sixties. The man smiled and said, "Don't let me stop you, look back to the East....tell me....do you think the waters will part for you?"

I was taken back by what this man said to me. This reminded me of the first conversation I had almost 17 years ago with a man who told me a story about a man who had come to a body of water and saw there was no way to cross, until another man had built a bridge and once the man crossed that bridge, he realized his journey had just begun. The man from almost 17 years ago went by the name Mr. Bell. I remember Mr. Bell saying, "Remember the bridge Mr. Rush...Mr. Rush...the bridge." It has sure been a journey since I had crossed Rush Bridge. My only thought though was... "how much longer will this journey be?"

I turned around to look at the man as he said, "Well, my friend, do you think the waters will part for you?"

I was not sure whether he was trying to test me or not. I thought to myself, "I will answer his question, as they have answered mine so many times in the past." I looked to him and said, "Only time will tell."

"Good answer," said the man.

I waited for a moment to see if the man would introduce himself and give me a name.  I knew that whatever name he would give me, would not be his actual name.  He would be like all the others before him.  He would give me a name that would somehow serve a purpose, to reveal something that had been hidden in some way and would relate to our current conversation or relate to something that would follow after, or even relate to some person perhaps.  Still, moments of silence as I watched the man only look at me and smile back.  I had to break the silence.  "So, do you have a name?"

"You can call me, 'Messenger.'"

"Okay, and why Messenger?"

"Because I have a Message, news to bring, information to give."

"Okay, and do you know who I am?"

"I wouldn't be here if I didn't know who you are." Messenger smiles.

"So, what's the message?" I anticipated being left with nothing but clues or riddles that would leave me still waiting for more information, yet something seemed different about this man.  He had this look on his face as if he had been holding something within himself for so long, something so secret and you could sense it seemed the man had been given permission to finally share what had been held back for so long.

Messenger said, "The message is of many things, the message is a 'Revealing' within the Scriptures written thousands of years ago, and within those Scriptures connect many places, events, and people."

"Other places?  What events?  What people?"

"Other places in time, some from a time of about 2700 years ago, to the place of time of the Birth of Yeshua known also by many by the name Jesus, to the place of time when Yeshua was Baptized by John the Baptist, to the place even long before 2700 years ago and even to the place in time of which you now live."

"The time of Jesus' Birth?  The time of His Baptism by John the Baptist?"

"Yes, this I will share with you in time, though first join me here on this bench and I will share with you of a time long before 2700 years ago."

Messenger motions to a bench in front of us.  Messenger was dressed just like the others in the past years.  He was in all black with a long black coat that went almost to his ankles.  He had a leather case to his side connected to a strap that went over his shoulder and at his other side was a Shofar that hung by a leather strap also across his shoulder. He had both straps crossed over him making like an 'X' on his back.

As we walked toward the bench I noticed a tall clay vessel, like a vase sitting beside the bench.  As we sat down, Messenger reaches over to the clay vessel beside him and pulls out what looks like an old ancient scroll.

Messenger then looks to me and says, "First let me take you on a journey going back in time through the scriptures to show you of the time when the world was flooded."

"Flooded?  As in the Flood during Noah's time."

"Yes."

"You are telling me that we can discover the time of the flood by reading through the scriptures?"

"Yes.  That's right."

"How?"

"We must first go to a place in time in the scriptures that is known. Think of it as a reference point."

Messenger then starts to open the scroll.  I begin to notice, there are no chapters or verses found on the scroll.

I look to Messenger and say, "Are these scriptures from the Bible? There are no chapters or verses."

"Yes, this is one of the scrolls from the Bible. Long ago, they did not have chapters or verses. If you must know Chapter and Verse of what book we will be looking at, I will tell you as we come to it."

"Okay." I look at the Scroll and see that the writings are in another language. "How will I be able to follow along with what you are reading?"

Messenger then reaches for the leather case hanging between himself and the clay vessel. He begins to open the leather straps that had kept the case closed. Once he opens it, he pulls out this large leather book with Hebrew writings on it. When he turned the book around, the other side had a red templar cross covering the book's length. He hands it to me and says, "Here you go, here is a Bible for you, written in your language so you can follow along with me as I share with you what is to be revealed."

"Thank you."

Messenger then begins to look back to the open scroll and says, "Once again, as we begin this journey of discovery through the scriptures, we must start at a place in time that we know, as a reference point in order to reveal what comes before it. The clues are there waiting to be discovered, are you ready?"

"Yes, I am."

Messenger then says, "No, you are not ready, first, begin with Prayer, ask that you have eyes to perceive, ears to hear, for understanding. That His Spirit guide you through His word as we look at it together. Also, to thank Him for the time that He has given us to explore His word and pray that others may benefit from what is shared, that others may come to be saved and that God alone gets the Glory."

After I prayed the prayer, Messenger then says, "Now you are ready, the first place in time we will look to is **1Kings 6:1** would you like to read it from yours?"

I open and begin to read **1Kings 6:1** *"And it came to pass in the four hundred and eightieth year after the children of Israel had come out of the land of Egypt, in the fourth year of Solomon's reign over Israel, in the month of Ziv, which is the second month, that he began to build the house of the Lord."*

Messenger then says, "We know that Solomon became king in the year 970 BC. That is our place of reference. The coronation of Kings began at the time of the Feast of Trumpets. The fourth year of his reign would have begun in the fall of 966 BC, though scripture says it was in the second month known as the month of Ziv. The month of Ziv would fall during the month known to you as around May. The fall months of 965 BC would begin the fifth year of his reign, so the month of May before the fall months of 965 BC would still be considered as during the fourth year of his reign which means that the time being observed in **1Kings 6:1** is referring to the month of May in the year 965 BC. The scriptures here say that four hundred and eighty years before that, the children of Israel had come out of the land of Egypt. It is simple math, others may try to complicate it, though it is simple math left for us to discover. 965 BC back 480 years from there brings us to the year 1445 BC, the time the exodus out from Egypt took place."

"Interesting, I had never thought to look there to discover that before."

"We are not finished though." Messenger rolls up the scroll, places it back into the clay vessel and begins to pull out another scroll. He begins to open the scroll then says, "Open your Bible to **Exodus 12:40-41**. You may read it, when you come to it."

I turn to it and began to read **Exodus 12:40-41** *"Now the sojourn of the children of Israel who lived in Egypt was four hundred and thirty years. And it came to pass at the end of the four hundred and thirty years—on that very same day—it came to pass that all the armies of the Lord went out from the land of Egypt."*

Messenger then says, "Now that we know the Exodus was in the year 1445 BC by looking at **1Kings 6:1**, by now looking at **Exodus 12:40-41**, we know then to go back 430 years from 1445 BC which will then bring us to the year 1875 BC. 1875 BC would be the year when Jacob, known as Israel and his Children, came into the land of Egypt."

Messenger begins to roll up the scroll. He places it back into the clay vessel as he pulls another scroll from the clay jar. He opens the scroll and says, "Now turn to **Genesis 45:4-7**. When you come to it, you may begin to read."

As I came to it, I read **Genesis 45:4-7** *"And Joseph said to his brothers, 'Please come near to me.' So they came near.  Then he said: 'I am Joseph your brother, whom you sold into Egypt. But now, do not therefore be grieved or angry with yourselves because you sold me here; for God sent me before you to preserve life.  For these two years the famine has been in the land, and there are still five years in which there will be neither plowing nor harvesting.  And God sent me before you to preserve a posterity for you in the earth, and to save your lives by a great deliverance.'"*

Messenger looks to me and says, "1875 BC was the year Jacob and his children come into the land of Egypt, though before Jacob comes to Egypt, first were his children who Jacob sent to buy grain.  What you just read was the moment when Joseph reveals himself to his brothers. He tells them that there have already been two years of the famine which means the famine began in the year 1877 BC, then going back seven years from 1877 BC will bring you to the year 1884 BC the year the seven years of plenty began which would also be the year that Joseph was released out of Pharaoh's Prison and made second to Pharaoh in all of Egypt. Joseph also says there are five years left of the famine.  Five years later from the year 1875 BC brings us to 1870 BC which would be the year the famine ended.  However, we want to know whether we can still travel on this journey of discovery?  Knowing that Jacob and his children enter the land of Egypt in the year 1875 BC, can we still travel back in time from there to discover precise years?"

"Are you asking me this question?"

"Yes, I am."

"I have no idea."

"The answer is yes.  If you just go on two chapters ahead to **Genesis 47:7-9**.  You may read it when you come to it."

**Genesis 47:7-9** *"Then Joseph brought in his father Jacob and set him before Pharaoh; and Jacob blessed Pharaoh.  Pharaoh said to Jacob, 'How old are you?' And Jacob said to Pharaoh, 'The days of the years of my pilgrimage are one hundred and thirty years; few and evil have been the days of the years of my life, and they have not attained to the days of the years of the life of my fathers in the days of their pilgrimage.'"*

After I finished reading, Messenger says, "So the year was 1875 BC when Jacob and his children entered the land of Egypt and Jacob has just told Pharaoh that he is one hundred and thirty years old. 1875 BC going back 130 years brings us to the year Jacob was born, not just Jacob, also Esau his brother, as we know that Jacob and Esau were born the same day. Going back 130 years from 1875 BC brings us to the year 2005 BC, the year Jacob was born. Now go to **Genesis 25:26**. Let me know when you get there."

I turned back to **Genesis 25:26**. Once I got to it, I looked to Messenger and said, "I am here."

"Go on and read it."

**Genesis 25:26** *"Afterward his brother came out, and his hand took hold of Esau's heel; so his name was called Jacob. Isaac was sixty years old when she bore them."*

Messenger then says, "2005 BC would have been the year Jacob was born and what you have just read tells us that Isaac was sixty years old when Jacob was born. 2005 BC going back another 60 years brings us to the year 2065 BC. 2065 BC would have been the year Isaac was born. Now go back a few more chapters to **Genesis 21:5**. You can read it when you get there."

**Genesis 21:5** *"Now Abraham was one hundred years old when his son Isaac was born to him."*

"Now just go back one hundred years from 2065 BC. That will bring you to the year 2165 BC. 2165 BC would have been the year Abraham was born."

"This is amazing. I never knew all of this could be found this way."

"There is still more, we are not finished yet. Do you remember how old Abraham was when he departed from Haran? He was actually known by the name of Abram at the time before God changed his name to Abraham."

"He was 75 years old right?"

"Yes, that's right.  So that would have been in the year 2090 BC.  We discover how old Abram was by reading **Genesis 12:4**. Go ahead and read that."

**Genesis 12:4** *"So Abram departed as the Lord had spoken to him, and Lot went with him.  And Abram was seventy-five years old when he departed from Haran."*

"Now look at **Genesis 11:32** and that will tell us how old Abram's father Terah was when he died.  You may read it when you're there."

**Genesis 11:32** *"So the days of Terah were two hundred and five years, and Terah died in Haran."*

"There is reason I wanted you to be able to see how old Abram was during the time his father Terah died.  Knowing that Abram was seventy-five years old and his father was two hundred and five years old at that time tells us that Terah was 130 years old when Abram, known as Abraham, was born.  Why is this important, you may ask.  It is important to know this because of where we will look next.  Turn to **Genesis 11:10-26**."

"Okay, I am here."

"From **Genesis 11:10-26** we will not start at verse 10, instead we will start at verse 26 and go back from there to verse 10.  We will only focus on the age that each of the fathers were at the time of the birth of each child and will then go back from there.  By doing this we will come to a discovery."

"Okay, I am ready.  Verse 26 you said?"

"Yes, that's right, start there."

**Genesis 11:26** *"Now Terah lived seventy years, and begot Abram, Nahor, and Haran."*

"Here it says that Terah was seventy years old when he begot Abram, Nahor, and Haran.  We know however that Terah was 130 years old when Abram was born.  So, is this a mistake?  Not in the least.  Verse 26 simply states how old Terah was when he fathered his first child.  Terah was seventy years old when he fathered his first child.  Once a father always a father, his children are grouped together at the age he was when he fathered his first.  Do you understand?"

"Yes.  I understand what you are saying."

"Let us proceed then.  Since we know that Abram known today as Abraham was born in the year 2165 BC and that his father Terah was 130 years old when Abram was born.  2165 BC going back 130 years brings us to the year 2295 BC. 2295 BC would have been the year Abram's father Terah was born.  From **Genesis 11:26** we will read back every other verse to see the age each father was at the birth of each child.  With that, continue with **Genesis 11:24**."

**Genesis 11:24** *"Nahor lived twenty-nine years, and begot Terah."*

"2295 BC the year Terah was born.  Nahor was 29 years old.  2295 BC going back 29 years brings us to the year 2324 BC.  2324 BC was the year Nahor was born.  Continue on."

**Genesis 11:22** *"Serug lived thirty years, and begot Nahor."*

"2324 BC the year Nahor was born.  Serug was 30 years old.  2324 BC going back 30 years brings us to the year 2354 BC.  2354 BC was the year Serug was born.  Keep going."

**Genesis 11:20** *"Reu lived thirty-two years, and begot Serug."*

"2354 BC was the year Serug was born.  Reu was 32 years old.  2354 BC going back 32 years brings us to the year 2386 BC.  2386 BC was the year Reu was born.  Please Continue."

**Genesis 11:18** *"Peleg lived thirty years, and begot Reu."*

"2386 BC was the year Reu was born.  Peleg was 30 years old.  2386 BC going back 30 years brings us to the year 2416 BC.  2416 BC was the year Peleg was born.  Go on, continue."

**Genesis 11:16** *"Eber lived thirty-four years, and begot Peleg."*

"2416 BC was the year Peleg was born.  Eber was 34 years old.  2416 BC going back 34 years brings us to the year 2450 BC.  2450 BC was the year Eber was born.  Continue."

**<u>Genesis 11:14</u>** *"Salah lived thirty years, and begot Eber."*

"2450 BC was the year Eber was born.  Salah was 30 years old.  2450 BC going back 30 years brings us to the year 2480 BC.  2480 BC was the year Salah was born.  Only a few more left to go, please carry on."

**<u>Genesis 11:12</u>** *"Arphaxad lived thirty-five years, and begot Salah."*

"2480 BC was the year Salah was born.  Arphaxad was 35 years old. 2480 BC going back 35 years brings us to the year 2515 BC.  2515 BC was the year Arphaxad was born.  One left to go.  Continue please."

**<u>Genesis 11:10</u>** *"This is the genealogy of Shem: Shem was one hundred years old, and begot Arphaxad two years after the flood."*

"2515 BC was the year Arphaxad was born.  Shem was 100 years old. Did you catch that verse 10 says that Shem begot Arphaxad two years after the flood?  This means the year Arphaxad was born was 2515 BC, if you go back just two years it will bring you to the year of the flood. The year of the flood was in the year 2517 BC."

"This is absolutely amazing.  Though this was a lot to cover to get us to this point."

"Yes, it was, though you see the importance of it don't you?"

"Yes, I do."

"Many people do not like to read the Book of Numbers chapter 26 for the very same reason, though the Book of Numbers 26 serves a purpose.  It gives the people a history concerning the Census of the people of Israel who are of the age of 20 years old and above who are able to go to war in Israel.  The people who would read that would know the history is true as it is so precise.  For the same reason, I have just shared with you this.  The account from the scriptures from where we began to where we ended up here is so precise that it brings you right to the year of the flood.  But that's not all.  Do you want to know what else we learned by going through this?"

"What?  What else have we learned?"

"You now know the year Joseph was released from Pharaoh's Prison; you know the year the seven years of plenty began. Both happened in the year 1884 BC. You now know that seven years later, in the year 1877 BC was the year the famine began, and two years into the famine in the year 1875 BC was when Jacob and his children came into Egypt. You know there were five years left of the famine at that point, which means the famine ended in the year 1870 BC. Though going back to 1875 BC when Jacob and his children entered the land of Egypt, you know that 430 years later, the people of Israel and a multitude made their exodus out of Egypt in the year 1445 BC, and 480 years from 1445 BC brings you precisely to the year 965 BC in the second month known as the month of Ziv which would be the same as your month of May when Solomon began building the temple. Everything that has been shared with you at this moment has a purpose, there is a reason. To show you and others that what is here is true, an actual account through time and history."

"I can understand that, though why is it important to know the year Joseph was released from prison? Or why is it important to know the year the seven years of plenty began and the year the seven years of famine ended?"

"Let's do one question at a time, shall we?"

"Yes, of course."

"As to why it is important to know the year the seven years of plenty began and the year the seven years of famine ended, that I will share with you at a later time. As for the importance of knowing the year Joseph was released from prison, remember what Joseph said to his brothers when he revealed himself to his brothers?"

"He said a lot to his brothers. He told them how long they had been in the famine and not to be grieved or angry for selling him into Egypt."

"Yes, that's right, though specifically look at **Genesis 45:7**."

"Do you want me to read it?"

"Yes."

**<u>Genesis 45:7</u>** *"And God sent me before you to preserve a posterity for you in the earth, and to save your lives by a great deliverance."*

"By a great 'deliverance.' Wouldn't you say that the year Joseph was released from Pharaoh's prison was a time of great deliverance for Joseph?"

"Yes, being released from Pharaoh's prison and doing what he did after would be a great deliverance, absolutely. Still though, why is it important to know the year that happened?"

"What if I told you a mystery that connects a time through history and found within the scriptures of other key years of deliverance for God's covenant people, the people of Israel. A mystery that when revealed, would not just be meant for the people of Israel, but for all people. All those who would have eyes to see and ears to hear. For all people who would not mock, but come to believe, to be saved. The word posterity in **<u>Genesis 45:7</u>** means 'remnant.' What if I told you that a remnant was preserved through history in times past, and in times such as in the days you now live, a remnant is being preserved? What if I could show you this mystery? To reveal to you without question God's hand through some of the significant years of deliverance recorded in history, within the very scriptures you read? Times of deliverance from prison, from bondage, times of deliverance from the enemy, from the enemies' land, to return home, even the deliverance that was paid by the Son of God, Yeshua…. Jesus."

"A mystery that connects them?"

"Yes, a mystery that connects them. Though after I share this with you, it will no longer be a mystery, but a revealing."

"I would say, please share, please tell me, show me that I may know."

Messenger rolls up the ancient scroll and places it back into the clay vessel. He stands as he reaches for his Shofar, pressing it to his lips, he begins to sound it. Again and again, the sound of the Shofar was heard.

"Why did you just do that?"

"Why did I just sound the Shofar?"

"Yes, why did you just sound the Shofar?"

"In hopes that others may hear and come?"

"I am sure others probably heard, but why would you want others to come?"

"Because what I am about to share with you is not just meant for you, but for all who may hear and come, for the mystery I am about to share with you will no longer be a mystery, but a revealing."

# CHAPTER 5
# A FEW SIGNIFICANT YEARS OF DELIVERANCE: THEIR CONNECTION

I looked around to see if anyone who had heard Messenger blow the Shofar would start walking this way. There were people who were walking as they began to look in our direction as Messenger blew the Shofar, though no one else came, they just looked at us and walked on in the direction they were heading.

I looked to Messenger and said, "Why do you suppose no one else is walking this way?"

"Not everyone knows what the Shofar is used for." Messenger then begins to tell me what all the Shofar was used for. Messenger said, "Even if there were those who did know what the sound of the Shofar meant, there are those who still would not come. People in your day are not as approachable as they once were."

Messenger begins to sit down and places his Shofar between us. As he laid the Shofar down, I saw five distinct markings on it, like five tally marks. I looked at him after pointing to the markings and said, "What are these? These five markings?"

"I will tell you about them in due time, though first, let me tell you about another time. A time of a few significant years of Deliverance and their connection over the course of a thousand years and others, hundreds of years between them, yet still there is a connection."

"Okay, that's fine, as long as you promise to share with me what these five markings mean."

"I will share much more with you, beyond what those five markings mean. I will, however, share what these markings mean after this."

"Okay then."

"Let me first take you back to one of the years I had shared with you already. Do you remember what I had shared with you about the year 1884 BC?"

"Yes, I remember." Messenger then says, "Very well, let's start there, shall we."

## 1884 BC
## Joseph's Release from Pharaoh's Prison
## & The Seven Years of Plenty

Messenger begins to look around, then looks to me and says, "As I had shared with you, Joseph was released from Pharaoh's Prison in 1884 BC. You remember how we discovered that right?"

"Yes, I remember. 1875 BC was when Jacob and his family came into Egypt. Joseph had told his brothers they had been in the famine for two years and had five years left until the seven-year famine would end."

"That's right. So, two years before 1875 BC was 1877 BC when the seven years of famine began. Seven years before that was when the seven years of plenty began, bringing us to 1884 BC."

"Yes, I remember you sharing that with me."

"Do you know how Joseph knew when his brothers arrived that there was only five years left for the famine?"

"Yes, because at the time, right before Joseph was released from Pharaoh's Prison, Pharaoh was troubled by some dreams of seven fat cows and seven lean cows."

"Correct. The butler who had been restored to Pharaoh's service and spent some time in Pharaoh's Prison, had told Pharaoh about Joseph's ability to interpret dreams because Joseph had accurately interpreted the butler and the baker's dreams. What Joseph said would happen to the butler and the baker based on the interpretation of their dreams was exact to what happened."

"I remember reading about that."

"So, as you know then from reading. Joseph was sold by his brothers when he was just 17 years old. He then worked for Potiphar as a slave, was falsely accused by Potiphar's Wife, and sent to Pharaoh's Prison as a result. After Joseph interpreted the butler and baker's dreams, when the butler was being released from Pharaoh's Prison, Joseph said to the butler to remember him when he is restored to his service, though the butler doesn't mention Joseph to Pharaoh until another two years later once Pharaoh began being troubled by the dreams he was having."

"Yes, that's right. I remember this well. I enjoy reading about Joseph. It is a beautiful story of redemption."

"Do you know how old Joseph was when he was released from Pharaoh's Prison?"

"He was 30 years old right?"

"That's right, and the year I have shared with you was the year 1884 BC."

Messenger paused for a moment as if he was in deep thought, then said, "Now 1884 BC was not just a year of deliverance for Joseph, it was the beginning of a deliverance for Jacob and his family, as well as for others in Egypt."

"How was it the beginning of a deliverance for Jacob, his family and others in Egypt?"

"Do you remember Joseph telling his brothers that it was not them, but God who sent him ahead of them to preserve a posterity, to bring a great deliverance?"

"Yes, I remember that."

"Well, what kind of deliverance would there have been for Jacob, his family and the people of Egypt had they not begun to store the grain? Had they not stored the grain during the seven years of plenty, there would have been no grain to deliver them through the seven years of famine."

"I see, I understand."

"Therefore, their deliverance began in 1884 BC at the start of the seven years of plenty, as Joseph was released from Pharaoh's Prison and began to store grain. Even though Jacob and his family had no idea that grain was being stored, even though Jacob and his family had no idea there would be a severe famine to come in the years ahead, God saw it fit to send Joseph ahead of them to store the grain, to bring his father Jacob, his brothers and the people of Egypt through a great deliverance."

"I can see what you are talking about now. Yes, a deliverance not just for Joseph being released from Pharaoh's Prison, but also the start of deliverance in the working by storing grain at the start of the seven years of plenty, happening in 1884 BC. So, I understand the importance of that year, though what about some of the other times of significant deliverance you mentioned earlier? You said that some were more than a thousand years apart and others hundreds of years apart."

"That's right." Messenger begins to reach towards the clay vessel to his right and pulls out from it another ancient scroll. He looks at me before he opens it up and says, "Do you know what happened in the year 538 BC?"

"Yes, I do actually."

# 538 BC
# The Cyrus Decree

Messenger begins to open the scroll and says, "Tell me then, what happened in 538 BC?"

"That was the year when king Cyrus issued the decree that allowed the Jewish people to return to Jerusalem."

"That's right. You have been spending time in the scriptures, haven't you?"

"When I can, yes I have."

Messenger then says to me, "Open your Bible to the book of **Ezra 1:1-4**. You may begin to read when you come to it."

**Ezra 1:1-4** *"Now in the first year of Cyrus king of Persia, that the word of the Lord by the mouth of Jeremiah might be fulfilled, the Lord stirred* *up the spirit of Cyrus king of Persia, so that he made a proclamation throughout all his kingdom, and also put it in writing, saying, 'Thus says Cyrus king of Persia: All the kingdoms of the earth the Lord God of heaven has given me. And He has commanded me to build Him a house at Jerusalem which is in Judah. Who is among you of all His people? May his God be with him, and let him go up to Jerusalem which is in Judah, and build the house of the Lord God of Israel (He is God), which is in Jerusalem. And whoever is left in any place where he dwells, let the men of his place help him with silver and gold, with goods and livestock, besides the freewill offerings for the house of God which is in Jerusalem."*

Messenger says, "The first year of Cyrus king of Persia was 538 BC. Even before Cyrus issued the decree, his name was spoken by Isaiah about 150 years before Cyrus lived and became king of Persia. Turn to the book of **Isaiah 44:28**. You may read it when you're there."

**Isaiah 44:28** *'Who says of Cyrus, 'He is My shepherd, and he shall perform all My pleasure, saying to Jerusalem, 'You shall be built,' and to the temple, 'Your foundation shall be laid.'''*

"Now the foundation of the temple had been laid in the year 536 BC. Then construction halted and was not resumed until the year 520 BC. It was in the year 520 BC that the temple started being built. The temple was finished in the year 516 BC. All that was there from the year 536 BC to the year 520 BC was the foundation."

"Why are you sharing this time with me? I thought we were talking about the year 538 BC?"

"There is reason I have brought up these years with you concerning 520 BC and 516 BC, though I will share more on these particular years at another time. I wanted you to know however, that this building would not have happened without first the decree from king Cyrus in the year 538 BC. More importantly, king Cyrus would not have issued such a decree had it not been for God touching his heart. All credit and glory goes to God. How did Isaiah know to name Cyrus by name 150 years before Cyrus's time? Because God, who sees the end from the beginning, who knows all things, knew that there would one day be a king whose name would be Cyrus. God knew that when He touched the heart of king Cyrus, that king Cyrus would respond the way he did by issuing the decree for the Jews to return to Jerusalem."

"Yes, and just like Joseph being released from Pharaoh's Prison, the seven years of plenty having to happen first, a time of deliverance, so too did the decree from king Cyrus in 538 BC have to happen first, a time of deliverance for the Jews to be allowed to return to Jerusalem following their Babylonian captivity."

"That is exactly right. You are beginning to catch on."

"So, what is the next one? Is there another year?"

"Yes, there is. The next year of a significant deliverance happened in the year 473 BC. Do you know what happened in the year 473 BC?"

"That one I am not quite sure about. You will probably need to share this one with me."

"Very well." Messenger rolls up the scroll, places the scroll back into the clay vessel, and pulls out yet another scroll. As Messenger begins to open the scroll, he looks at me and says, "Open your Bible to the book of Esther."

## 473 BC
## The 13ᵗʰ Day of the Month of Adar

"Okay, I am here. I am in the book of Esther."

"How many chapters do you see there are in the book of Esther?"

"Ten. There are ten chapters. Is there a certain place you would like me to read from?"

"No. I just wanted you to look at how many chapters there are."

"Okay, why?"

"Because within those ten chapters covers a lot. From king Ahasuerus showing people the glory of his kingdom for about six months, to Queen Vashti refusing to come before the king as he had sent for her, to Queen Vashti being removed from the palace never to be in the presence of the king again. Then, there was a beauty contest if you will, for the king to choose for himself a new Queen. It was during this time that the king then chose Esther to be Queen. Queen Esther is a Jew, though the king doesn't know this. The king had someone who was second to him, a man who wore the king's signet ring, and with the king's signet ring, this gave him authority to make laws and issue decrees as if given by the king himself as he would seal documents with the signet ring of the king. That man's name was Haman. Haman did not like the Jewish people, and there was one particular Jew that he absolutely didn't like. The Jew's name was Mordecai, who would never bow down to Haman. This made Haman furious. Mordecai was Esther's cousin who practically raised her as his own daughter as Esther's parents were both deceased."

"I remember this from the book of Esther, though where is the deliverance you are referring to? Are you referring to when Esther becomes Queen?"

"No. Not when Esther becomes Queen. I will tell you the deliverance I am referring to."

"Okay."

"Because Haman did not like Mordecai and did not like the Jews, he wanted to be rid of them for good, to annihilate the Jews. Haman ends up creating a document that he then seals with the king's signet ring and posts it on the 13th day of the 1st month, known as the month of Nisan. This was around the time of the month of April and was right before Passover. The document was put up on the 13th of the first month basically to let the Jews know that on the 13th day of the month of Adar, which would be 12 months later to the exact day, the Jewish people would be destroyed, no more. The month of Adar was the 12th month and usually was the month of March."

"I remember reading about this in the book of Esther. Mordecai read the document after it had been posted, puts on sackcloth, and begins to wail. Mordecai sends word to his cousin Esther, who is Queen, and informs her of this."

"Yes, that's right. After being informed of this, she fasts for three days and nights. She then went before the king even though the king had not called for her. Walking into the court of the king when he has not called for you would mean death unless the king would point his golden scepter towards you, then you would be spared and live. Esther knew that she would be risking her life to go before the king without having been called, though she had to take that chance. It was either going to be her life or the lives of her people. She chose to risk her life for the sake of her people. When she approached the king, he pointed his golden scepter towards her. She ends up having two banquets with the king and Haman on two different days. It was during the second banquet that Queen Esther informed the king of Haman's plot to annihilate the Jews. When the king was made aware of this, the king had Haman hung on the very gallows that Haman had built to hang Mordecai on. Do you remember how this turn of events took place?"

"I remember that Mordecai had once saved the king by reporting an assassination attempt on the king's life, and this account was recorded in their book of chronicles. One night, the king was unable to sleep, and one came in to read their book of chronicles to the king, which spoke of Mordecai having saved the king's life. The king had asked Haman how he should honor a person whom he wanted to honor. Haman thought the king was referring to himself, that he would be honored, though it turns out the king wanted to give honor to Mordecai. Instead of Haman getting to hang Mordecai on the gallows, Haman was given the news by the king that Mordecai was to be honored."

"That's right. What the enemy meant for evil, God meant for good."

"How do you mean?"

"The book of Esther never mentions God or even mentions the presence of God, however, you can see His guiding hand throughout it. The men who plot an assassination attempt on the king's life were evil, though Mordecai reporting such an attempt brought him to be written in their book of chronicles. Haman wanting to hang Mordecai on the gallows that one day was evil, though the king being unable to sleep and having their book of chronicles read to him brought the account of what Mordecai had done back to the king's attention, so instead of Mordecai being hung by wicked Haman that day, Mordecai was instead honored by the king that day. Queen Esther, who is a Jew, becomes Queen for such a time as this, as the enemy, wicked Haman sets a plot to annihilate the Jews, her position helps to aid in her people's deliverance. Mordecai, who once wore sackcloth before the gate, who wailed from the news that he and his people would be destroyed on the 13th day of the Month of Adar, turns out by that time, Mordecai is no longer wearing sackcloth, he is dressed in a position of honor, wearing the signet ring of the king and given the house of Haman."

"When did the deliverance happen though?"

"It happened on the very day the Jews were set to be annihilated by the enemy. The 13th Day of the Month of Adar that was once set to be the day of their destruction turned out to be the day of their deliverance as they defeated their enemy that day."

"And when did this happen?"

"It happened in the year 473 BC on the 13th day in the Month of Adar. Queen Esther set up a time following that day of deliverance for a celebration on the two days that followed. They would feast and send gifts to one another as they celebrated the death of those who had tormented them. This time is known as the Feast of Purim."

"So that was the year of their deliverance from their enemy? 473 BC?"

"Yes." Messenger rolls up the scroll and places it back into the clay vessel. He doesn't pull out another scroll, instead he says, "Would you like to hear about the year of The Deliverance now?"

"The Deliverance, as in another time of deliverance?"

"Yes, and not just for the Jewish people, not just for the people of Israel, but for all who may come to believe. A time that happened hundreds of years later, after 473 BC."

"Are you talking about Jesus?"

"Yes, Jesus, known also by the name Yeshua."

"His crucifixion?"

"Not just His crucifixion, His resurrection as well. Do you know what year this happened?"

"Please tell me, do you know?"

## 30 A.D.
## The Crucifixion of Jesus and His Resurrection

"It was in the year 30 A.D."

"How do you know that it was in the year 30 A.D. Some say that it was in the year 31 A.D. others say 33 A.D. others may even say a different year than those. So, how do you know that it was in the year 30 A.D.?"

"Because His ministry began in the fall of 26 A.D. and His ministry was for 3 ½ years. His crucifixion was at the time known as Passover. Passover was in the Spring, as I have said before, around the month of April. What is 3 ½ years from the fall months of 26 A.D.? The answer is the Spring at Passover in the year  30 A.D."

"I see."

"There are many other reasons why we know that His Crucifixion and Resurrection happened in the year 30 A.D., though we won't go over those at this time. This should be enough for now."

"Okay." I pause for a moment, then look to Messenger and say, "I don't think you need to share with me how His being on the cross, His death and resurrection are in fact, the deliverance. I know that His death on the cross was the way for my salvation and that His resurrection is the hope that we too will one day be resurrected and be where He is. Just about everyone knows that right?"

"You would be surprised at how many do not believe. Some who have read the Bible think of what is in it as just stories. Some people do not believe there is a God. Some people do not believe in Heaven or Hell. Some believe you live, and you die and that's it. Many will not believe, others have not heard, and then there are those who have had doubts and needed a little more convincing to know these scriptures are not just stories, they are history, they are true, they happened."

"What do we do about those people?"

"We share what we know. Now, at such a time as this. This time of revealing."

"Revealing what?"

"God's presence, His guiding hand. Even when He is not mentioned in the book of Esther, we could see so much evidence that He was there guiding with His hand. All that happened was not coincidence or mere chance."

"And Joseph, his release from Pharaoh's Prison, the start of the seven years of plenty? God's presence, His guiding hand was there too?"

"Absolutely. Though God is mentioned in the account of Joseph, whereas in the book of Esther, God is not mentioned once, still though we see His working among them in both the book of Esther and during that time with Joseph."

"And the decree of king Cyrus, there too?"

"Yes."

"So that is how all these connect? Because of God's presence? Because of His guiding hand during these years of deliverance?"

"That is one way of seeing their connection, yes. Though remember, God's presence is all around us, He is still guiding with His hand even today. The connection I am about to share with you is a hidden connection, though it has always been there waiting to be discovered and revealed for such a time as this."

"What is it?"

## The Hidden Connection

Messenger opens the leather case that once held the bible he handed me. He pulls out some pages. I couldn't see what was on the pages as he held them close to his side between us.

"What is that?"

"I will show you, though first, turn your bible to the book of **Proverbs 25:2**."

**Proverbs 25:2** *"It is the glory of God to conceal a matter, but the glory of kings is to search out a matter."*

"Do you understand what is being said here?"

"That the ways of God are unsearchable, some things are concealed, meaning kept secret or hidden, and it is the glory of kings to search it out, searching for answers, to find what is hidden in the unsearchable ways of God."

"If the ways of God are unsearchable, then how could kings search the matter out?"

"I am not sure."

"I will give you a clue. Read the next verse, **Proverbs 25:3**."

**Proverbs 25:3** *"As the heavens for height and the earth for depth, so the heart of kings is unsearchable."*

Messenger looks to me and says, "The ways of God are unsearchable, and the heart of kings are unsearchable. What does this mean then?"

"I don't know."

"It means since both are unsearchable, for kings to search out a matter of God that is concealed, that is hidden, he cannot do this on his own, and it requires God Himself touching the kings' heart, speaking to it. The feeling one gets to look here or there even though they may not know where or why they are looking, yet they unveil something that had been hidden, something they could not have discovered on their own, the Holy Spirit guided them."

"Okay, yes. God speaks to our hearts."

"Yes. So, are you ready to see what I have here to show you?"

"Yes, I am."

Messenger begins to turn the pages toward me where I can see them. They were calendars. Calendars that showed the calendar we use, as well as the biblical calendar. There was a large number at the top left of the page indicating the Hebrew Month, and in each box for each day on the month's calendar, there was a number showing what day of the month it was during that Hebrew month, below that number was written how that day corresponds to our Solar Calendar of 365 days whereas the

Biblical Calendar is 360 days. Then, below that showed the year each of these calendars represented.

Messenger points to these areas within each of the calendars and says, "Do you see these days? Do you see these years?"

"Yes, I see them."

"Do you see the connection?"

"I am not sure. Can you explain?"

"The biblical calendar and our calendar are not the same. The biblical calendar is 360 days a year, and yours is 365 days a year, which means that one year, the 13th day of the Month of Adar may fall on what corresponds to your calendar as March 16th, and the next year, the 13th day of the Month of Adar may fall on what corresponds to your calendar as March 6th. Each passing year would be different."

"Okay, so what are you showing me here? What is the significance here?"

Messenger then has me hold two of the pages from the calendar for the Hebrew month of Adar. I look down at the page and see that one represents the year 473 BC, and the other represents the year 30 A.D. I then look at the two Messenger is holding up. The two he is holding are also for the month of Adar, though one of his represented the year 538 BC and the other the year 1884 BC.

"Look at the 13th day of the month of Adar. Do you see what day it corresponds to?"

I look at each of the pages during their years and am suddenly shocked and amazed by what I saw.

I look to Messenger and say, "For the year 1884 BC, 538 BC, 473 BC and 30 A.D., the 13th day of the Month of Adar corresponds to March 6th."

"Yes, that is correct. Not only does that match." Messenger then begins to show the month for Passover for each year, the day of first fruits even. Passover corresponded to April 6<sup>th</sup> for each of the years, and first fruits corresponded to April 8<sup>th</sup> for each of the years.

"This is amazing!!"

"From 1884 BC to 538 BC is more than 1300 years difference, from 538 BC to 473 BC is 65 years difference and 473 BC to 30 A.D. is hundreds of years difference, yet over all this time, the calendars match. I have already shown you that from year to year, the biblical calendar and your calendar are different in their corresponding years. So, do you believe this is chance or coincidence? Or do you now believe this is God's guiding hand throughout history and time?"

"This is God's guiding hand. There is no question."

Messenger shows me one more month for all four of the years. He shows me the 7<sup>th</sup> month of the Hebrew calendar, known as Tishrei. The tenth day, known as the Day of Atonement, fell on what corresponded to September 25<sup>th</sup>.

"Do you see the Day of Atonement?"

"Yes, I see it, but I just thought about this, the day of Passover and even the Day of Atonement did not exist until the time of the Exodus, so how could there be Passover and Atonement in the year 1884 BC?"

"You are right, there would not have been Passover or the Day of Atonement in the year 1884 BC. However, we know that Passover is the 14<sup>th</sup> day of the first month known as Nisan and happened to fall on that particular day in April that I had already shared with you. The Day of Atonement we know is always on the 10<sup>th</sup> Day of the 7<sup>th</sup> month known as Tishrei and happened to fall on that Particular Day of September 25<sup>th</sup> for each of those years."

I was still stunned and in awe by what I saw. I handed the pages back to Messenger. He then turns to place the pages back in the leather case. While he was turned, I looked down at his Shofar between us and focused my attention on the five markings on his shofar that looked like five tallies. Messenger then turns around as he notices where I have my gaze.

"I suppose you would like to know about these five markings on my Shofar now, wouldn't you?"

"Yes, I would. If you have the time."

"Of course, I have the time. Each of these five markings represents a specific time within your history that spans over the last hundred years to even times within your own lifetime."

"Each marking, each tally mark represents a time?"

"Yes, that's right. I suppose the best way to share each of them with you would be to describe them one at a time, starting with the first one."

"Is this going to be another revealing?"

"Yes, a revealing of something written in the scriptures almost 2,000 years ago before it ever happened so that when it would happen, those who would see it, those who would read of it in their history books may one day look back to those very scriptures and come to believe."

"Believe what?"

"That Jesus is the Son of God and that the Father sent Him. To believe and be saved. To understand the revealing is now, for such a time as this."

"And you said you would start with the first one?"

"Yes, let us start with the first one."

Messenger pulls a scroll out from the clay vessel. He places the scroll on his lap and then says, "Turn your bible to the book of Revelation."

"The book of Revelation?"

"Yes, the Book of Revelation, the very book of revealing."

Explore this chapter's photos/calendars mentioned by scanning the QR code or visiting the link:

https://www.revealingthetimes.com/chapter5

# CHAPTER 6
# THE FIRST TRUMPET

I turn to the book of Revelation, and once I get there, Messenger says, "Begin to read **Revelation 1:1-2**."

**Revelation 1:1-2** *"The Revelation of Jesus Christ, which God gave Him to show His servants—things which must shortly take place. And He sent and signified it by His angel to His servant John, who bore witness to the word of God, and to the testimony of Jesus Christ, to all things that he saw."*

Messenger says, "As you just read, Jesus gave this to John. John wrote down what he both saw and heard of things that had not happened yet. The book of Revelation was written by John around 95 A.D. while he was on the island of Patmos. This was written almost 2000 years ago. Do you know why John wrote such a book? Why he was given things to write down, both of what he saw and heard?"

"Why?"

"For the people who would be living when these things begin to come to pass, as they may see what is happening around the world, they may look here in the book of Revelation and see that this was written down almost 2000 years ago before they happened in hopes that others may believe that Jesus is the Son of God and that He has been sent by the Father. In hopes that others are saved and return to Him."

"Verse 1 says that these things would shortly take place. Since this was written almost 2000 years ago, wouldn't the things written within the book of Revelation already have happened back during that time?"

"You must remember God's time is not like our time. Remember, a thousand years are like a day, and a day is like a thousand years to the Lord. Our time is not like His time."

"Though God knows all things, He sees the end from the beginning. Since He knows exactly when these things will be, why does He say they will shortly take place since He would know those things would not take place at the time the book of Revelation was written?"

"Haven't you read concerning the coming of the Lord that no one knows the day or the hour, only the Father knows. Why do you suppose the exact day and hour is not revealed?"

"I am not sure."

"If everyone knew the exact day and hour, would others be watching as they should? If your brother was traveling to you from out of state and your brother told you that he would be at your house at 5:30 pm on Friday, what would you do?"

"I would make sure to be at the house right before that time to let him in."

"Precisely, instead of you going out or meeting up with others, you would make sure you were home around that time. You would check your calendar, maybe even call others to let them know your plans with your brother that Friday. You were able to do all of that because your brother told you the day and time he would be there."

"Okay, though what does that have to do with God saying these things will shortly take place?"

"Imagine those who were living 2000 years ago were told exactly the day and time of when Jesus would return, that it would be 2000 or so years beyond their time. Do you suppose they would have been ready or even watching for His coming? God wants His people to always be watching, to be ready, to make disciples."

"I heard a Pastor say once, 'Plan your life as if Jesus may not come for another one hundred years, but live your life as if He is coming tomorrow.'"

"Yes, that is exactly right." Messenger then tells me, "Now, if you will, turn your bible to **John 14:29**."

**John 14:29** *"And now I have told you before it comes, that when it does come to pass, you may believe."*

"What Jesus is saying there is He is telling of things before they come to pass, so when they do come to pass, we may believe."

"Believe what?"

"That He is who He says He is. That He is the Son of God and was sent by His Father." Messenger then says, "Now look at **John 6:28-29**. You may read it when you get there."

**John 6:28-29** *"Then they said to Him, 'What shall we do, that we may work the works of God?' Jesus answered and said to them, 'This is the work of God, that you believe in Him whom He sent.'"*

"He made it that simple, just believe in Him and believe His Father sent Him."

Messenger picks up his shofar and places it on his lap along with the scroll of the book of Revelation. He then looks to me and says, "Within the book of Revelation, there are many symbols and other places one should read to get a better understanding of what is written in the book of Revelation. Going to places like the book of Daniel, the book of Ezekiel, some of the Psalms and even the book of Zechariah, to name some of them."

"Yes, that's right. I have been told that before."

"Then there are things John wrote down that he both saw and heard, things that had not happened yet. Some of the things that John described did not exist in his day, so when describing a war taking place, he may mention horses simply because he is unable to describe the weapons and machinery that are used in your time, so he describes the machinery as horses because that is how wars were fought back in his day. They were fought on horses. However, I assure you, there will not come a day when everyone will be riding horses again to fight a war like they did in the Revolutionary War. John is describing as best as he can how wars were fought back in his day."

"I can understand that."

"What you may not understand is what I am about to share with you. Your first couple thoughts will be: "But I thought these things happen during the seven-year tribulation, not before it?" You will also think something like this: "But I thought the seven seals, the four horsemen, happen before the things you are sharing with me?" These will be your questions."

"Why do you think that?"

"Because this is what you have been told, this is what you have been taught growing up, though what I am going to share with you is so spot on, so precise, you will be left with asking the question, could this just be a bunch of coincidence, could this just be random chance, or could this very well be the very things that Jesus gave to John to write both what he saw and heard, in order for those of us who are watching can know and blow the shofar, to awaken the people from their sleep, in hopes others may know, to share, in hopes that others may come to believe that Jesus truly is the Son of God and the Father sent Him."

"And you said that you are going to start with the first marking, the first tally on your Shofar? You were going to share what it means?"

"Not what it means, what it represents."

"What it represents?"

"Yes, it represents something that has happened should you choose to accept it. Something that has happened a little more than one hundred years ago." Messenger then opens the Scroll on his lap as he says, "Open your bible to **Revelation 8:7**. You may read it when you find it."

**Revelation 8:7** *'The first angel sounded: And hail and fire followed, mingled with blood, and they were thrown to the earth. And a third of the trees were burned up, and all green grass was burned up.'*

Messenger says, "The first marking on this Shofar represents the first trumpet."

"And you are saying that it has already happened?"

"Yes, should you choose to accept it."

"That it happened more than one hundred years ago?"

"Yes." Messenger rolls up the scroll while still keeping the scroll on his lap, then he looks to me and says, "It happened during World War I."

"During World War I? I don't remember seeing any history reports of a third of the trees being burned up, let alone all green grass of the earth being burned up."

"When John reported what he saw as a third, he was not reporting a third of the whole world. He was reporting a third of the area that he saw." Messenger began to reach down under where we were sitting, and he pulled out a plastic bag that had some tomatoes in it. He started to take out one tomato at a time until he had a stack of 12 tomatoes sitting on the ground in front of us. He then looks at me and says, "I want you to imagine that this stack of 12 tomatoes was sitting on your counter in your kitchen at home."

"Okay."

"Now I want you to imagine that a third of those tomatoes were smashed, destroyed. Your report would be that a third of the tomatoes were destroyed, and your report would be true, though is it a third of the tomatoes of the entire world? The answer is obviously no, however, it is a third of the tomatoes destroyed from the area you observe. This is the same as what John reported when he saw a third of the trees being burned up. He was reporting the area he was observing."

"Okay, I can understand that, but what about the hail and the fire falling to the earth mingled with blood?"

"World War I was the first war where planes were introduced. During the night and even during the day, as planes would fire rounds of bullets from the air down to the people below, it would look like hail falling to the earth on fire, and once those very bullets hit others below, they would then be mingled with blood. Remember again, John is reporting things he saw that did not exist during his time, so he is doing his best to describe it."

"What about the trees burned up and green grass burned up? You are saying that happened during World War I?"

"Yes. It was during World War I when a particular policy was in place. It was a policy known as 'The Scorched Earth Policy.' During World War I, some fought in the War who had flame throwers, and these men, as they crossed through enemy land, they would torch all trees and all grass so the enemy would be unable to utilize the resources of the land."

Messenger then pulls out a page from the leather case. It was a picture of the front cover of a book. The picture showed a few soldiers standing who were from WWI. Behind them were all trees and all green grass burned up.

After looking at the picture, I looked at Messenger and said, "I don't know, this could just be a coincidence. What if others say you are just reading into this and making it fit?"

Messenger then says, "Others may say that, and others who don't may think that, though we have only mentioned the first trumpet."

"There is more? Are you saying that the second trumpet has already happened as well?"

"If you choose to accept it?"

"Why do you keep saying, 'If you choose to accept it?'"

"Because not everyone will accept this, not even you perhaps, though you will be left with a choice of asking yourself, 'is all this mere coincidence and random chance, or is this perhaps something much more, meant to be a warning for those living in such a time as this. To help you better answer that question, let us look at the second marking on the shofar to see what this marking represents, or tally as you put it. Let us look to the second trumpet."

Explore this chapter's photos/calendars mentioned by scanning the QR code or visiting the link:

https://www.revealingthetimes.com/chapter6

# CHAPTER 7
# THE SECOND TRUMPET

Messenger begins to open the scroll on his lap as he says to me, "Turn to **Revelation 8:8-9** in your bible. You may read once you're there."

**Revelation 8:8-9** *"Then the second angel sounded: And something like a great mountain burning with fire was thrown into the sea, and a third of the sea became blood. And a third of the living creatures in the sea died, and a third of the ships were destroyed."*

After reading, I looked at Messenger and said, "So, you're telling me this has already happened? I know, I know, if I choose to accept it right?"

"Yes, that's right."

"And you are going to share with me each piece of what I just read, just like you did with the first trumpet?"

"Yes." Messenger then rolls up his scroll, again leaving the scroll placed on his lap. He reaches into the leather case and pulls out a couple of pages. I couldn't see what they were as he held them close to himself just as he did with the calendars before he revealed them to me. Messenger says, "John said as the second trumpet sounded that he saw something like a mountain. He doesn't say it was a mountain, it was something like a mountain. After all, a mountain is not thrown into the sea, is it?"

"Could it have been a meteor or an asteroid? That would have been on fire as it fell, giving the appearance of being thrown in the middle of the sea?"

"Perhaps others could think that. We must understand that the second trumpet comes after the first trumpet. As I have already shared with you, the first trumpet happened during WWI. This would mean that the second trumpet happened at some point after WWI. We then need to look at everything within the second trumpet to see if the time that John is seeing all connects."

Messenger then handed me the first page in his hand. It was a picture. He says to me, "Do you know what this picture is of?"

I looked at the picture, and I couldn't believe it. It looked like a mountain on fire in the middle of the sea, and I knew what it was. Anyone who knows history would know what this picture was of. While still looking at the picture, I said to Messenger, "Yes, I know what this is. This is the dropping of the Atomic Bomb, the bombing of Hiroshima."

"That's right. August 6th, 1945, was the day of the bombing of Hiroshima. This was after WWI and was during the next major War known as World War Two."

"John says that a third of the sea became blood. I don't recall from history at that time where a third of the sea became blood."

"Remember what I shared with you about the tomatoes?"

"Yes. I remember."

"You must realize that John was seeing bits and pieces of each period of time. Some things that John saw, like the bombing of Hiroshima, there was nothing in his day that could have given such a visual, so he describes it as best as he could as looking like something like a mountain on fire in the middle of the sea. What John ends up seeing during the time of the second trumpet are bits and pieces of things that happened during that time, during WWII."

"So, the part about a third of the sea becoming blood?"

Messenger then hands me eyewitness accounts from soldiers who had survived WWII. Soldiers who were on the beach of Normandy. Messenger then says, "The water was turning red with blood. The water coming up the shore was red with blood. This is what John saw should you choose to accept it."

"If this was what John was seeing, the beach of Omaha would not be considered a third of the area that he would have been looking at though."

"The beach of Omaha was not the only beach invasion. It is the most known because of how many lost their lives during the taking of Omaha Beach. The other beach invasions in other areas also left the water red with blood. The picture is the water coming up to shore filled with blood. John seeing this would give the appearance that the sea became blood, and the areas that he saw, he would say a third. Anytime you read where John says a third, just keep thinking of the example I showed you with the tomatoes. When John says a third, it does not mean a third of the whole world. It is of the area he is seeing."

"I understand. I will keep what you said about the tomatoes in mind."

Messenger then pulls out another page from the leather case. It was an eyewitness account of a man who lived during the time of the bombing of Hiroshima. The man had gone to see the aftermath of the bombing. This was some of what I read, *"He walked down to the river and saw numerous mullets and rainbow runners floating down the river surface. Fish in the water too seemed to have died from the impact of the explosion. He picked up some and brought them home, but couldn't get himself to eat any."*

Messenger then said, "John also saw that fish had died from the aftermath."

I looked to Messenger, then back at the pages he had handed me. I handed the pages back to Messenger, then said, "And the ships? What about the ships? John said that a third of the ships were destroyed."

Messenger then says, "Remember, it is not a third of the ships of the entire world. As I have shared with you, the second trumpet is WWII should you choose to accept it. Since this was during WWII, we must look at the ships from all over the world that had participated in WWII."

Messenger then hands me another page. It was a picture of a ship used during WWII that was on the Ocean's surface, while below showed a picture of a ship sunk at the bottom on the ocean floor. Next to the picture was written a detailed account of the ships of WWII. This was what it said, *"There were 105,127 ships that participated in WW2. 36,387 ships were destroyed at the end of the war."*

I then said to Messenger, "This is right at a third. A third of the ships."

"Yes. Not a third of the ships of the whole world. A third of the ships that had participated in WWII were sunk, destroyed."

I handed the page back to Messenger and said, "I am still not convinced that this could in fact be the second trumpet. I mean don't get me wrong. This does make sense, though how are we to know what John saw?"

"Remember what I have said to you all this time. I have said to you, should you choose to accept it."

"Why couldn't everything just be spelled out for us? Why does it have to be a mystery?"

"Should you choose to accept it, this will no longer be to you a mystery, it will become a revealing. To answer your question though, why everything is not spelled out, God still wants His people to act on faith. If everything was told to you and shown you, where would your faith be?"

"I understand. Though this could also bring a person to have doubt."

"The very opposite of faith is doubt, and with doubt comes fear. Think of the disciples when they were on the boat with Jesus. The storm had come crashing against their boat, Jesus had already told them before the storm, before they even started their journey, that they would come to the other side, though when the storm came, they had doubt, and with doubt came fear, fear they would perish. When they look to Jesus, what do they see?"

"They see Him at the back of the boat sleeping."

"Yes, and what did they do then?"

"They woke Him up and asked Him if He cared that they were about to perish."

"That's right. Jesus was not only sleeping at the back of the boat. The back of the boat was also where one would steer the boat in the direction it was to go. Since Jesus was asleep, who was steering the boat?"

"No one, no one was steering the boat."

"You're wrong."

"Who was steering the boat then?"

"Not who, but what."

"What was steering the boat?"

"The storm, the storm was steering the boat. The storm had the disciples in doubt and fear. They ask Jesus if He cared they were about to perish, though were they about to perish? The answer is 'no' they were not about to perish. And how do we know they were not about to perish? Because Jesus had said they would make it to the other side even before they started on the journey to the other side. Jesus slept and rested not because He didn't care, but because He knew they would all make it to the other side. Sometimes the Lord allows for a storm to come into your life to steer your boat, to teach you something. One may think that He isn't there or that He doesn't care, just as the disciples thought while they were in the middle of the storm. However, rest assured that He is still the one who can calm that storm, who will steer your boat if you let Him have that position in your life. All one needs to do is rest in Him and trust they will make it to the other side. Have faith."

"That is beautiful. I never thought of it that way, that He allows some storms to come into my life, as the storm will steer me in a direction or teach me something, though He is still the one guiding me if I let Him. That is beautiful."

"More than beautiful. This is true. You will find though, with what I am sharing with you, those who continue in doubt, those without understanding, will speak against what I am sharing with you. They will speak evil against what they do not understand."

"Are you referring to the trumpets again?"

"Yes, along with other things I have already shared with you, as well as what I will continue to share with you, to reveal to you."

"I still am not convinced what you shared with me concerning the first and second trumpet is in fact the first and second trumpet."

Messenger then says, "I understand, this is a lot to take in. To see what I am showing you, you will need to take it with faith."

"I do see what you are showing me, and like I said, it does make sense. Though again, how do we know this was what John was shown? What John was seeing?"

Messenger pauses as he places his hand up to his chin as if in deep thought. Messenger then says, "I suppose the next thing to do would be to go over what the third marking on the shofar represents. To go over the third trumpet. Then maybe you will begin to have faith in knowing this is what John had been shown, what John was seeing."

"You're saying the third trumpet has also already happened?"

"Yes, and you already know what I am about to say, don't you?"

"Yes, I do. Should I choose to accept it."

Messenger places all the pages back into the leather case, saying, "Let us look to the third trumpet then shall we."

Explore this chapter's photos/calendars mentioned by scanning the QR code or visiting the link:

https://www.revealingthetimes.com/chapter7

# CHAPTER 8
# THE THIRD TRUMPET

essenger begins to open the scroll of Revelation on his lap as he says to me, "Look at **Revelation 8:10-11**. Will you please read it?"

**Revelation 8:10-11** *"Then the third angel sounded: And a great star fell from heaven, burning like a torch, and it fell on a third of the rivers and on the springs of water. The name of the star is Wormwood. A third of the waters became wormwood, and many men died from the water, because it was made bitter."*

Messenger then says, "Since we know that the second trumpet was WWII, that would mean that the third trumpet would happen sometime after."

"And you are saying that it has?"

"Yes."

"When? How? I don't recall a great star falling or the waters being made bitter due to a star falling. Besides, stars are stationary, right? They don't move, so how could a star be falling?"

Messenger smiles at me and then says, "You certainly have a lot of questions. Rest assured, I will address each of them for you." Messenger pauses for a moment, he then rolls up the scroll he has on his lap, reaches into his leather case, and pulls out more pages like the other ones before, keeping them close to himself until he is ready to show me. He then looks at me and says, "You are right concerning stars, they are stationary. During the times when the scriptures were written, you had what people knew as wandering stars. Today, you know them as planets. Wandering stars during that time are known today as planets."

"Why did they call them Wandering stars?"

"Because the people of that time noticed they moved."

"So, what was this great star that fell?"

Messenger then says, "Remember what I have told you before. John was writing what he both saw and heard. John saw and heard bits and pieces during particular times in our history. When he wrote what he saw and heard, he was doing so during a time when much of what he saw did not exist in his time."

"So, it is history for us, though for John, it was something that had not happened yet."

"That's right. What John wrote concerning the trumpets had not happened, nor would happen for almost 2000 years after John wrote what he both saw and heard."

"I still don't recall what is described in the third trumpet as something that happened in our history after WWII."

"It did though. It happened many years after WWII. Precisely a little more than 40 years after WWII."

"That would have been in the 1980's."

"Exactly, and believe it or not, you had already been born during the time of the third trumpet."

"How old was I?"

"You were 3 ½ years old during the time of the third trumpet."

I began to add up the years and months in my head from the time I was born. Once I discovered the time, I told Messenger, "That would have been April of 1986."

"Yes, that's right."

"You're saying that the third trumpet happened in April 1986?"

"Yes. Not only I, there are many who lived in the area where trumpet three occurred that also believe and say that what happened during that time was in fact the third trumpet." Messenger hands me one of the pages. It was a picture of an Angel. It was a sculpture of an Angel with a trumpet to its mouth. I said to Messenger while still looking at the picture, "Where is this? Where is this Angel?"

"The Angel is in the place where the third trumpet happened. The Angel is in Ukraine, in a place known as Chernobyl. They call it the 'Third Angel Monument.'"

"What happened there? What happened in Chernobyl?"

"The fourth nuclear reactor at a nuclear powerplant exploded. When this happened, it caused massive amounts of radiation to go out into the area. Many had died who worked around the clock to clean up and close the site of the explosion."

"When did this happen?"

"It happened on April 26, 1986."

"What about the rivers? The springs of water? The third trumpet said many men died from the waters because they were made bitter."

"When it rained in the area of Chernobyl, the rainwater soaked up radiation from that area. When the rainwater on the ground evaporated back into the atmosphere, a nuclear cloud spread across areas of Europe. Even the radiation from the initial blast pumped massive amounts of radiation into the atmosphere. When the rainwater fell across areas of Europe, the radiation from that rain fell into rivers, lakes, streams and waters."

"And you are saying many men died from the waters because they were made bitter?"

"Yes. Though I am not the only one saying this. Remember, John wrote this down almost 2000 years ago. This is what he saw, and he is giving the account of what he saw and heard."

"Only men died from the waters made bitter?"

"No, people, many people died from the waters made bitter. John says 'men' to group men and women together. Think of it as when one says 'Mankind,' is it only 'man' one refers to when saying 'Mankind?'

Certainly not, 'Mankind' is grouping men and women together as people. This is what John is doing as well. Many people died from the water made bitter. Though many did not die immediately from the waters made bitter. Their life was shortened, and death came in time to them as a result of the waters made bitter."

"I don't understand. Their life was shortened? What do you mean?"

"Many who drank from those waters did not know at the time that there were levels of radiation in that water from the rain, from the nuclear cloud that spread over many parts of Europe from Chernobyl. When the people drank that water, water from rivers, lakes, streams, and springs of water, a rise in cancer developed in many men, women and children. Their lives were shortened due to the cancer. The cancer developed due to the radiation in the water and atmosphere at the time."

"What about Wormwood? John wrote that the waters were made bitter because of wormwood. John doesn't say the waters were made bitter because of radiation."

Messenger starts to hand me another page, though he waits. Before he hands me the page, he looks at me and says, "The people of Ukraine, before they had their independence from Russia, they had it approved that what they read, such as books, even their bibles, could be written in their language."

"The Ukrainian language?"

"Yes, right around the time of WWII."

"Okay. What does that have to do with what I had just asked about Wormwood?"

Messenger then hands me the page. It was part of an article written three months after the Chernobyl Nuclear Disaster. The article was written by Serge Schmemann on July 26th, 1986, as a Special to the New York Times. This is what was in the part of the article I read:

*"A prominent Russian writer recently produced a tattered old Bible and with a practiced hand turned to Revelations. "Listen," he said, "this is incredible: 'And the third angel sounded, and there fell a great star from heaven, burning as it were a lamp, and it fell upon the third part of the*

*rivers, and upon the fountains of waters; and the name of the star is called wormwood: and the third part of the waters became wormwood; and many men died of the waters, because they were made bitter.' "*

*In a dictionary, he showed the Ukrainian word for wormwood, a bitter wild herb used as a tonic in rural Russia: chernobyl.*

*The writer, an atheist, was hardly alone in pointing out the apocalyptic reference to the star called chernobyl. With the uncanny speed common to rumor in the Soviet Union, the discovery had spread across the Soviet land, contributing to the swelling body of lore that has shaped the public consciousness of the disaster at the Chernobyl atomic power plant in the Ukraine.*

*In the three months since an explosion ripped open the fourth reactor at the plant, Chernobyl has become an indelible part of Soviet life, whether as an inevitable topic in kitchen conversation, as a daily subject in the national press, as a source of rumor, sensation and threat, or as a direct influence on daily life.*

*The dangers of radiation, at first played down in the press, have finally become a topic of open discussion. On July 17 the official youth league newspaper Komsomolskaya Pravda published a long and detailed article on the various radioactive elements and their characteristics, including the threat of cancers."*

*https://www.nytimes.com/1986/07/26/world/the-talk-of-moscow-chernobyl-fallout-apocalyptic-tale-and-fear.html*

I could not believe what I was reading. Wormwood……..Chernobyl. They are the same word written in a different language. The article also mentioned the threat of cancer due to this, just as Messenger had said. I look at Messenger almost with a look of fear. I was beginning to believe that what Messenger had been sharing with me was in fact what was shown to John almost 2000 years ago. Messenger then says to me, "Do not be afraid. What was given to John almost 2000 years ago was not meant to frighten you or cause you to fear. It was meant to warn the people who would be living during such a time as this, to bring many to believe, to be saved by knowing and believing that Jesus is the Son of God and was sent by the Father. That the Father is in Him and He is in the Father. Only God knows the end from the beginning, and God the

Father gave this to Jesus, His Son, to show His servants—things which must shortly take place."

"So, Chernobyl is the Ukrainian word for Wormwood?"

"Yes. Now do you understand why so many in that area believed this to in fact be the third trumpet? As this happened, the people of Ukraine who had a bible written in their language, when they read the description of the third trumpet, in your English language, the word is wormwood, though the people who this happened to, and the very place of where trumpet three occurred, the Ukrainian people read their Ukrainian bible reading the word Chernobyl."

"This is amazing. This is just too much to be random coincidence or chance." I took a moment to think about the two previous trumpets that Messenger had shared with me. I then said, "Knowing this makes what you shared with me about the previous two trumpets make even more sense, even more believable even to those who may have doubts. This is so spot on, so precise. The very things John says about the waters being made bitter because of wormwood, John is saying the waters were made bitter because of Chernobyl. It all makes sense. With all of this too, what are the odds that the very place this occurred, the very place that caused the waters to be made bitter would have occurred from the very place that bares the name Chernobyl that means wormwood. The very place where the people are reading about it from their bible in Ukraine, in their language….it is called Chernobyl."

"Now you believe what I have been sharing with you is true?"

"Yes. I do. Though there is just one other thing about the third trumpet that I don't fully understand."

"And what is that?"

"The star. John said he saw a star falling from heaven, burning like a torch."

Messenger had another page in his hand that he had yet to hand to me. For some reason, I felt that what Messenger held in his hand was the answer to what still puzzled me. Messenger then says, "As I have shared with you already, John wrote down what he both saw and heard. As John was writing down what he saw concerning a star falling from heaven burning like a torch, John then heard the word, the word you know as wormwood, the Ukrainians know the word as Chernobyl. John then writes down what happened to the waters because of Chernobyl and that many died because the waters were made bitter." As Messenger begins to hand me the last page in his hand, before he does, he says, "What would look like a star falling from heaven?"

"A meteor? An Asteroid perhaps?"

Messenger says, "As you have already said, stars are stationary, they don't move, so what would cause John to think this was a star falling from heaven?"

"I suppose because John saw that it was out in space."

"Yes, that's right. Space, as you call it, was known to the people of John's Day as the heavens. What then would give John the appearance that this bright object was falling?"

I thought for a moment, though the more I thought, still I didn't know. I looked at Messenger and said, "I am not sure. I don't know."

Messenger then hands me the page. It was another picture. A picture of what looked like a bright star from space, though it wasn't a star. The bright object had a tail of light behind it. "What is this?" I asked.

"That is a picture of Halley's Comet. Do you see the bright tail of light behind it?"

"Yes. I see it. This was the first thing I noticed from the picture."

"The bright object from space looked to John as a star in the heavens. The bright tail behind it gives the look as if it were falling. Halley's Comet could be seen from earth with the naked eye."

"When? When could Halley's Comet be seen from earth with the naked eye? Isn't Halley's Comet far away?"

"Halley's Comet passes by earth about every 70 or so years. Halley's Comet was the first comet to be studied by spacecraft back when the Comet came close to earth."

"When did Halley's Comet come close to earth?"

# THE REVEALING

"Halley's Comet came closest to earth on April 10<sup>th</sup>, 1986."

I was shocked. Yet, here was the other piece to the puzzle that gave clarity to me because I didn't know what this supposed star that John saw was. Though now, after Messenger shows me the picture and tells me when Halley's Comet came closest to the earth, that the naked eye could see it, now it all makes sense. I looked to Messenger and said, "April 10<sup>th</sup>, 1986, the same month and the same year as the Chernobyl Nuclear Disaster."

"That's right. John saw Halley's Comet in space, the star as he puts it, from the heavens. The tail behind Halley's Comet gave the appearance to John that it was falling, this is where John writes what he saw, then he writes down what he hears. It wouldn't be but days later, only 16 days later to be exact, you then have the Chernobyl Nuclear Disaster. John writes down what he hears. The very article I shared with you even mentions the word wormwood. John hears the word and writes, 'It is called Wormwood.' John then writes what happens to the people, writing that many died from the water because they were made bitter. What you all now know, is that many developed cancer and died because of the water from the aftermath of Chernobyl or, as you all know it....Wormwood."

"As you said, John wrote this from the bits and pieces he saw and heard. He then put them together."

"Yes, that's right. Though what will really bake your noodle is what I will share with you now." Messenger then looks to me and says, "Remember why Joseph was sold into slavery by his brothers?"

"Yes, because of the dreams he was having. He shared The dreams with his brothers and later what he shared with his father Jacob concerning his dreams."

"And do you remember what the dreams Joseph had were of?"

"Joseph said that he dreamt that he and his brothers were binding their sheaves in the field, that his sheaf stood upright, and his brother's sheaves stood around his and bowed down to his sheaf. Is that right?"

"Yes. And what about the other dream?"

"Joseph said that his other dream was that the sun, the moon and the eleven stars bowed down to him."

"And what did sharing this with his brothers do?"

"It caused his brothers to resent him even more."

"What about his father Jacob? What did he do?"

"He rebuked Joseph, though he did not have resentment towards Joseph. Instead, he kept the matter in mind. He pondered what the dreams could mean."

"Exactly."

"So why are you saying this would bake my noodle?" I couldn't understand why Messenger used the term 'bake your noodle,' why didn't he just say 'mind-boggling' something hard to wrap my mind around?

Messenger then said, "God gave these dreams to Joseph, letting him know that one day in the future, his brothers would bow down to him. God was showing Joseph in his dreams something that had not yet happened. Joseph then shared these dreams with his brothers. His brothers sought to kill him, saying, 'Here comes the dreamer of dreams, let's kill him, then we'll see what will become of his dreams.' Though his brothers could not have their brother's blood on their hands, so instead of killing him, they sold him as a slave to merchants who happened to be traveling through. This very act Joseph's brothers did in an attempt to make Joseph's dreams not come true was the very thing that would pave the way to a series of events that Joseph would face and experience as a slave, to then being in prison, to then being freed from prison, to being the right hand to Pharaoh, to later seeing his very dreams fulfilled as his brothers bow down to him, not recognizing Joseph after all those years when they traveled to Egypt to buy grain. The question is, 'Would any of this been fulfilled had God not first given Joseph these dreams?' Had God not given these dreams to Joseph, Joseph would have had no dreams to share with his brothers and his brothers then would not have sold him into slavery, thus fulfilling the very dreams that God gave him."

"I can see how this is mind-boggling."

"It is indeed. Though God was simply showing Joseph through the dreams what would happen before it happened. What Joseph's brothers did as a result, what man meant for evil, God meant for good. Joseph recognized that later in his life when he saw his brothers before him, when he revealed himself to his brothers. God meant it for good, to preserve a posterity, to save many through a great deliverance."

"Why did you just share this with me?"

Messenger reaches for the pages from my hand as he places the pages back into his leather case. He then says, "Because just how I shared with you about Joseph and his dreams given by God, can also be applied to John and what he wrote down almost 2000 years ago."

"How do you mean?"

"John wrote down the word wormwood as he heard the word wormwood. The people who would be alive during the time the third trumpet occurs mention the word wormwood as they read it in their bibles. Would the people be saying the word wormwood had John not written down the word, and would the word wormwood not have been written by John had he not first heard it?"

"Wow, my gosh. Yes, this is indeed mind-boggling. Like the question, 'Which came first, the chicken or the egg?'"

"Precisely. Though what one needs to understand is that, like the dreams given to Joseph, so too is what was given to John to write down both what he saw and heard. God gave both. As Joseph stored the grain to preserve a posterity, to save many by a great deliverance, so too did John write down the words of what God showed him of what would shortly take place, given in order to preserve a posterity, to save many by a great deliverance."

"How would what John wrote down almost 2000 years ago preserve a posterity, to save many by a great deliverance?"

"The people who experienced Chernobyl, the people who lived in that area, who spoke the Ukrainian language, the people who would have read their bibles written in the Ukrainian language who would have read 'it is called Chernobyl.' Many of those people would come to believe that God's word is true. Many of those people would then turn to Jesus. Many would then believe that Jesus truly is the way, the truth and the life. They would believe that Jesus is truly the Son of God, that He was sent by the Father, and they would be then saved. They would then know as they continue to read that Jesus is coming again, and because they are now saved by faith in Him, they are now delivered and shall also one day be the Great Deliverance."

I was amazed, in awe by what Messenger was sharing with me. I was in awe of God's word and His love for us. Having now eyes to see, to perceive. I now understood in a much fuller way the meaning of **Hebrews 10:14-15**.

**Hebrews 10:14-15** *"How then shall they call on Him in whom they have not believed? And how shall they believe in Him of whom they have not heard? And how shall they hear without a preacher? And how shall they preach unless they are sent? As it is written: 'How beautiful are the feet of those who preach the gospel of peace, who bring glad tidings of good things!'"*

As I pondered this, I would not have known this had it not been for Messenger sharing these things with me and revealing them to me. I then think about those out there who have doubts, for those who just walked by when Messenger blew the shofar. How will they believe in Him of whom they had not heard, without a preacher, one to proclaim? Messenger was proclaiming, he was sharing these mysteries, which now to me was no longer a mystery. As he said, should I choose to accept it, they would no longer be a mystery, they would become something that has now been revealed. I can now see; I have now heard. Messenger has been sent for such a time as this. I shared with Messenger the scripture of **Hebrews 10:14-15**. Messenger reaches into the clay vessel and brings out another scroll. He begins to open it while still having the Revelation scroll on his lap. He looks at me and asks, "Do you know where part of that verse is quoted? From what scripture?"

"No. I don't think so."

Messenger then says, "Turn your bible to the book of **Isaiah 52:7**. Please go on and read it once you find it."

**Isaiah 52:7** *"How beautiful upon the mountains are the feet of him who brings good news, who proclaims peace, who brings glad tidings of* *good things, who proclaims salvation, who says to Zion, 'Your God reigns!'"*

As I finished reading, Messenger said, "Who proclaims salvation. The Hebrew word for salvation is Yeshua. Who proclaims Yeshua." Messenger then says, "Now read **Isaiah 52:3-6**."

**Isaiah 52:3-6** *"For thus says the Lord: 'You have sold yourselves for nothing, and you shall be redeemed without money.' For thus says the Lord God: 'My people went down at first into Egypt to dwell there; Then the Assyrian oppressed them without cause. Now therefore, what have I here,' says the Lord, 'That My people are taken away for nothing? Those who rule over them make them wail,' says the Lord, and My name is blasphemed continually every day. Therefore My people shall know My name; therefore they shall know in that day that I am He who speaks: 'Behold, it is I.'"*

Messenger looks to me and says, "As I have shared with you, there is a great deliverance to come. The events that I have shared with you that have been recorded in your very own history books, which have happened even in your lifetime, had first been written by John almost 2000 years ago given by the Lord, and they shall know in that day that it is He who speaks. As the people of Israel experience deliverance from worldwide dispersion, the people will realize the fulfillment of prophecies through Isaiah and others as they will then enjoy the assurance the Lord had indeed spoken and fulfilled His promises of deliverance. What I have shared with you here brings not only warning and awareness to God's people. What I have shared with you brings the good news that He is indeed coming soon. No one knows the day or the hour, only the Father knows, though by what you now have perceived with your eyes, what you have now understood by hearing, you should hold all the more to that good news even in the midst of the storms, He is coming soon!! Jesus is coming soon!! Amen and Amen."

I fully agree with Messenger as I say, "Amen."

Explore this chapter's photos/calendars mentioned by scanning the QR code or visiting the link:

https://www.revealingthetimes.com/chapter8

# CHAPTER 9
# THE INTERMISSION

David didn't know where to begin. Everything that Jeremy had just shared with him had him almost speechless. From the time going back to Noah's flood to the connection on the calendars for each of the years shared that would mark a deliverance and to the first three trumpets. To think all of this has always been there in the scriptures. Some things mark the past, others connect through time, and speak of the future. As David also now sees it, there are things that speak of the very time he has lived and is now living. What was once a mystery has now become revealing.

David grabs a bottle of water from the food cart and decides to stand. He begins to pace the office while opening his bottle of water. Once he takes a drink, he looks at the bottle of water and thinks of the third trumpet. The water was made bitter, and all the people who have developed cancer in that area because, at the time, those waters were made bitter because of wormwood or Chernobyl, as has now been revealed. While standing there, he looks at Jeremy and says, "So, Messenger came to you near the spring of 2021?"

"Yes. Messenger shared more with me during that time as well."

"I figured he did. I just needed to take a moment to ask you how you felt through all of this?"

"How I felt with what Messenger shared with me?"

"Yes."

Jeremy grabbed a bottle of water from the food cart. He didn't want to share more about other things Messenger had shared with him, at least not yet. He thought back to what he had already shared with David and said, "At first, when Messenger began sharing with me the timeline that brought us to Noah's flood, I thought to myself, 'Where is he going with this?' It almost felt like a math lesson."

Both of them laugh as David says, "And after? Once you reached the time of Noah's flood, what did you think then?"

"I was amazed by the discovery. To think that this has always been there within the scriptures. Like Messenger had said, all one needs is a reference point, a time to start with, that we would know, then all we have to do is follow what the scriptures say. If the time says 480 years, then it was 480 years. One doesn't need to add or take away years to fit their own conclusions. We know that with the genealogies being accurate as they were recorded and written down, so too would be the years. What I found to be even more amazing was all the other timeframes of discovery while Messenger took me through this journey back to Noah's flood."

"That is amazing. It's almost like being on an Indiana Jones adventure. You and Messenger looked back in time, followed the clues that lead to a treasure of knowledge, and you both did it while sitting on a bench."

"Yes. That is the beauty of God's word. With the bible, you could be anywhere. All one has to do is open it and begin to read. Before you know it, you are there standing beside David as he places the stone in the sling, and you watch him sling the stone, hitting Goliath in the head. You join in the celebration with David. I only mention David because that happens to be your name."

David laughs, then says, "Or walking through the Red Sea with Moses. While reading it, you could imagine seeing the waters of the Red Sea part right before you."

"Exactly."

"So, the exodus was in the year 1445 BC?"

"That's what the math says. 480 years back brings you exactly to the year 1445 BC. There is also another way to know that 1445 BC was the year of the exodus."

"Oh, how's that?"

"Something else Messenger shared with me later. I will share it with you too, just not yet."

"Why not now?"

"When Messenger shared the other part with me, it was like he was taking me on another adventure. When I share it with you, I want to be able to do as he did, to take you on an adventure."

David throws his fist in the air as if victorious and says, "A quest."

"Yes David. That's right. A quest."

"What about when he shared with you the connections on the calendars with each of those years through time? What did you think when he showed you that?"

Jeremy takes a drink of his water and then says, "Well I must say that up until that point, I wasn't sure of the mystery Messenger would share with me. I didn't understand why he had spent so much time sharing each of those years with me and their significance, though once he showed me the calendars and how each of them, through all that space of time, matched and connected, I was in awe. Amazed by the discovery, or as Messenger put it, a revealing that God's hand, His presence was truly guiding the very history from the very scriptures we were reading."

"Yes. I was in awe too, as you shared this with me. I felt as if I too was sitting on that bench with you while Messenger was sharing all of this with you."

"That is what I was hoping for. As I have shared this with you, I wanted you to feel as if you were there with us as Messenger shared these things with me."

David walks by the window to look out at the city. It was already dark. The city was aglow from the streetlights and all the city's surrounding buildings. Penny had already left for the day. The office was closed, still they were both there recording all that was said as the book was being made as they were both talking. From the questions David asked, to what Jeremy had to share, including all that Messenger had shared with Jeremy before. All was being recorded. David looks to Jeremy and says, "Come and look out at this view of the city."

Jeremy gets up, walks to David by the window, and says, "You have quite a view from here. Looks peaceful."

David nods his head in agreement, though, while still looking out at the city, David says, "Yeah, as if the town is sleeping."

"The people are sleeping."

David looked at his watch, it was almost 8:30 at night. David then says, "I doubt many are sleeping at this hour, not this early."

"I don't mean that kind of sleeping."

"I see what you mean." David then thinks about the first, second and third trumpet Jeremy had shared with him as he says, "To think that we now know the very trumpets you have mentioned have already happened. Two of them during WWI and WWII and one of them while the two of us have been alive."

"Are you saying that you too, believe this to be true?"

"How could I not believe this to be true. There is too much that lines up too well. Too much to be coincidence or left to chance. The statistical odds that any of this is just random chance or coincidence is too high to be so. Of course, I believe these trumpets have happened. Though now, as you have said, 'the people are sleeping.' The people don't know. They are oblivious to even seeing it, of noticing. Even though they may have read about WWI and WWII in their history books, still the people did not see or connect it with what has been here in Revelation for almost 2000 years."

"There are few out there who have noticed. There are few who are awake, some more awake than others. Though many are still sleeping."

"As Messenger shared with you, the people who lived in Ukraine around Chernobyl recognized that was the third trumpet. They even have an Angel Monument out there as you said, to show that what happened at Chernobyl during that time was the third trumpet."

"Yes, that's true. Though believe it or not, some still live in Ukraine, who lived during that time in that area and still have doubts of that being the third trumpet."

"How? How could anyone doubt that?"

"For a few reasons. One, some may never come to believe no matter what you tell them or what they are shown. Two, many who are believers, who are Christians, have always been taught that all of the seals and trumpets happen during the seven-year tribulation. Because Christians and the people know that we are not yet in the seven-year tribulation, they have as a result, become oblivious to it. The third reason is that even those who may have realized that Chernobyl was in fact the third trumpet, some of them choose to ignore it because they are more concerned with the cares of this life, while others choose to have their 'wow moment' of discovery and not share it with others, they choose to just keep it to themselves."

"So, what can we do about this?"

"All we can do is Pray, test what we know with scripture and then share with others. We cannot remain silent out of fear of those who may choose to attempt to do us harm. We cannot worry about those who will mock or continue in their unbelief. Our purpose is to share what we know in the hopes that those who may have had doubts, who may not be saved, may come to have eyes to perceive and ears to hear that Jesus truly is the Son of God and the Father sent Him. What Messenger has shared with me and what I am now sharing with you could very well be the extra nudge that the unbeliever or doubter needed in order to come to the Lord to be saved. That is why I am here with you today. To share this first with you and then the world."

"This for sure needs to be shared with the world. People need to know." David takes a moment to walk by his desk as he says, "Excuse me for a second." David looks at his calendar to see if anything is scheduled or planned over the weekend. He then looks to Jeremy from across the office and says, "Since it is already pushing 8:30, would you like to meet tomorrow? We could even meet tomorrow and Sunday if you would like."

"Sure thing. That would be nice. Where would you like to meet?"

"How about I have you come to my house? My family is gone for the weekend, and I have this bench out in my backyard overlooking the lake. I think it would be nice sitting out there, to feel even more like I am sitting with Messenger as you share more of what he has shared with you."

"Absolutely. That sounds like a great idea."

"Did Messenger ever tell you his name?"

"No, I only knew him as Messenger. After he shared with me all he had to share, I found out that what he told me from the beginning was true."

"And that is?"

"That his name was not important. Only the message was important, to call him Messenger because he had information to share, a message to give."

"Did you ever wonder who he was?"

"I had my thoughts as to who he was, and sometimes I think he even hinted at who he was, though he never openly shared that information with me."

David looked down at the floor where the Shofar was sitting. He again sees the five tally markings on the Shofar. He then looks to Jeremy and says, "I suppose now that I know what Messenger shared with you concerning the five markings on the Shofar that it would be safe to assume that each marking represents one of the trumpets, is that right?"

"Yes, that's right."

"Since there are seven trumpets mentioned in the book of Revelation, though only five markings on the Shofar, does that mean only five trumpets have already happened?"

"Yes." Jeremy paused for a moment as he thought back to what Messenger would say to him. He then looks across the room to David and says, "Should you choose to accept it."

David laughs. He then says, "What's not to accept? I already believe that three of the trumpets have happened from what you shared with me. What's two more, right? Messenger shared these two with you as well?"

"He did."

David walked back over to Jeremy near the window as they began looking at the city. David then looks to Jeremy and says, "You know, just because I said we could continue this tomorrow, there is no reason you couldn't share one more with me tonight."

Jeremy thought for a moment as he looked out at the night sky above the city, thinking about how the night seemed to get darker sooner and last longer. He thought about the fourth trumpet, though for the sake of time, he thought about going right to sharing the fifth trumpet with him. He looked at David and said, "For the sake of time, I would like to share the fifth trumpet with you."

"Really, why not the fourth trumpet?"

"We have already lost light of the Sun, and now we have also lost light of the moon. I would like to share other things with you tomorrow besides the trumpets, so since we still have tonight, I would like to share the fifth trumpet with you as the fifth trumpet is so very detailed. The fifth trumpet not only gives you a time frame in months, John also mentions names as well as giving a description of something that didn't exist during his time. Still, John does his best to write down what he saw and heard."

"Very well. That is fine with me. Did Messenger share this with you that same day you both were sitting on the bench together?"

"Yes."

David motions towards where they had been sitting before and says, "Would you like to sit down again?"

Jeremy and David walk back over to their seats. As they sit down, Jeremy picks up his Shofar and places it on his lap, saying, "I suppose I should be holding this since I will be sharing with you the fifth trumpet, the last marking here that represents it."

David smiles and says, "Very well. You have my full attention."

Jeremy looks down at the markings once again. He looks to the fifth marking as he goes back to that day with Messenger, remembering all of what Messenger shared with him about that dark time during the fifth trumpet, dark for those who saw it and lived it. He then looks back up to David and begins to share with him just as Messenger had shared with him detail for detail concerning the fifth trumpet.

104

# CHAPTER 10
# THE FIFTH TRUMPET

**M**essenger opens the scroll of Revelation and says, "Turn your bible to **Revelation 9:1-12**. Think about it carefully as you read it. You can read it when you get there."

**Revelation 9:1-12** *"Then the fifth angel sounded: And I saw a star fallen from heaven to the earth. To him was given the key to the bottomless pit. And he opened the bottomless pit, and smoke arose out of the pit like the smoke of a great furnace. So the sun and the air were darkened because of the smoke of the pit. Then out of the smoke locusts came upon the earth. And to them was given power, as the scorpions of the earth have power. They were commanded not to harm the grass of the earth, or any green thing, or any tree, but only those men who do not have the seal of God on their foreheads. And they were not given authority to kill them, but to torment them for five months. Their torment was like the torment of a scorpion when it strikes a man. In those days men will seek death and will not find it; they will desire to die, and death will flee from them. The shape of the locusts was like horses prepared for battle. On their heads were crowns of something like gold, and their faces were like the faces of men. They had hair like women's hair, and their teeth were like lions' teeth. And they had breastplates like breastplates of Iron, and the sound of their wings was like the sound of chariots with many horses running into battle. They had tails like scorpions, and there were stings in their tails. Their power was to hurt men five months. And they had a king over them the angel of the bottomless pit, whose name in Hebrew is Abaddon, but in Greek he has the name Apollyon. One woe is past. Behold, still two more woes are coming after these things."*

Messenger then says, "As you can see, there is much to cover here. Though we will be able to. You will need to pay close attention to each detail as I describe what is within the fifth trumpet. Can you do that?"

"I think so. I have more of an open mind now, especially after what you shared concerning the third trumpet."

Messenger rolls up the scroll, reaches into his leather case, and pulls out another set of pages. Messenger then says, "It is good that you have an open mind, though you will not need an open mind when it comes to what I share with you concerning the fifth trumpet."

"Why would I not need an open mind."

"Because the fifth trumpet is so very detailed. As I share with you each detail, by the time I am finished, there will be no denying that this is the fifth trumpet."

"Okay, how would you like to start?"

Messenger picks up his shofar that was between us. He places the pages face down on the space between us and rests his shofar on top of them to prevent them from blowing away. Messenger then looks to me and says, "I first need to help you in your understanding of the word 'angel.'"

"Angel? As in an Angelic being."

"An Angel is at times an Angelic being, as you may read about in the scriptures. At other times when you read the word angel, it is simply referring to the word's meaning."

"I am not sure I understand what you mean."

"The word 'angel' in the Greek is 'angelos.' It means 'Messenger.' As John was writing the word 'angel,' he was not referring to an Angelic being. He was simply writing the word that means 'messenger.'"

"So, you are saying that the angel in the fifth trumpet is not meant to be an Angelic being as many would see it? You are saying that John is simply referring to a 'Messenger.'"

"Yes, that's right."

"Okay, I follow what you are saying. I understand."

"John says as he describes the fifth trumpet, that this messenger is a king, meaning that he is a leader, he is in charge, over the people, ruling over them. John says, 'And they had as king over them the angel of the bottomless pit.' In other words, they had this leader over them, the messenger of the bottomless pit. Do you understand?"

"Yes, I understand what you are saying. Though John writes that this messenger had a key to the bottomless pit. It was a key right?"

"As I have shared with you before concerning the previous trumpets, John was writing down what he both saw and heard. He was doing this as best as he could from the time in which he lived. What John saw was the bottomless pit was not open. This messenger did something to open the bottomless pit, causing smoke to come up out of the pit. The smoke blotted out the sun. The smoke blotted out the sky. John saw that at first the bottomless pit was closed, then suddenly the messenger opened it, so John says this messenger had a key to the bottomless pit to open it."

"So, John saw that this ruler, this messenger of the bottomless pit, had a way of opening it to cause smoke to come out of it, not a literal key, but a way to cause the smoke to come out of it as if now opened."

"Exactly." Messenger begins to pull out one of the pages from under the shofar. Before he hands it to me, he says, "In order for you to understand more concerning this bottomless pit, you will need to understand what it actually is. In your translation, you read the words 'bottomless pit.'"

"Yes, that's right. My translation reads 'bottomless pit.'"

"Have you ever read other translations where instead of using the words 'bottomless pit,' the translation will use the word 'abyss?'"

"Yes, I have. I recall some Pastors who have read the word 'abyss' as they preach a message."

"Why do you suppose that is?"

"I am not sure."

Messenger then hands me the page and says, "The original was written in Greek, so one translation says, 'bottomless pit,' another translation says 'abyss.' Both translations come from the original Greek word. Read this and tell me what it says."

I look at the page. I was surprised to see there was only one word that filled the page. "Phrear. It says Phrear."

Messenger then takes the page back from me as he says, "That is the Greek word. The New Testament was first written in Greek. Do you want to know what the word 'Phrear' means?"

"Yes, of course."

"The word 'Phrear' means Shaft, Abyss, Pit, and Well."

"Okay, so what is your point?"

"Each of these words can be taken from the original Greek word 'Phrear' though only one word better describes what John was seeing."

"Which word is that?"

"The word 'Well.'"

Messenger pulls out another page from under the shofar and hands me the page. When I saw the picture, I saw a lot of areas on this plot of ground with pillars of smoke rising into the sky. I looked at Messenger and said, "What is this? What are these pillars of smoke?"

"Those are 'Wells.' They are oil wells that had been lit on fire by a certain ruler. The oil wells were as they were until a certain ruler lit them on fire, giving the appearance that these bottomless wells had been opened as smoke arose out of them."

I continued to look at the picture. The smoke was blotting out the sun, blotting out the air, the sky, just as John had described from what he saw. While I could see the definite connection here, especially since knowing the word 'Well' comes from the very word used in the original Greek. These were indeed wells. And smoke arose out of them, blotting out the sun and the sky. Though I thought to myself, 'What about this king, this ruler? Who is he?' I look at Messenger and ask him, "Who is the ruler? The messenger that lit these oil wells on fire?"

"Not who is this ruler? Who was this ruler?"

"Who was he?"

"The ruler who lit these oil wells on fire was Saddam Hussein."

"When did he do this?"

Messenger then pulls one more page from under the shofar and hands it to me. He then says, "Read this."

I began to read what was on the page. This is what it said, *"The Persian Gulf War also saw one of the most notable uses of the scorched earth strategy, with the Kuwaiti oil fires. During their retreat from Kuwait in 1991, the Iraqi forces set fire to between 605 and 732 oil wells in the country, to hinder the US-led coalition forces. The last of the fires was put out in November 1991, but not before the Kuwaiti economy lost $157.5 billion USD in oil and many soldiers suffered respiratory issues due to the poor air quality." https://www.warhistoryonline.com/war-articles/scorched-earth-tactics.html*

Messenger then says, "Poor air quality. The air was darkened from the smoke. 1991, The Persian Gulf War. This was when it happened. See what it says at the top? Read the first sentence again."

I look at the first sentence and begin to read, *"The Persian Gulf War also saw one of the most notable uses of the scorched earth strategy, with the Kuwaiti oil fires."*

Messenger points to the words on the page and says, "Do you see it? 'Scorched earth strategy.' What should this tell you?"

"That Saddam was destroying resources just like the people did during WWI when they lit fires to all trees and grass."

"Very good, you are beginning to see well. Though you are missing one important piece of the puzzle, a clue that John leaves for us the readers, to connect the two trumpets, to let us know in more ways than one, that these are in fact the trumpets that John writes about as he writes down what he saw and heard. Do you see the clue?"

I keep looking at the page. Looking for a clue, though I am unable to spot it. I then said to Messenger, "I don't have a clue about the clue."

"You won't find it on that page. You must go back to your bible. Back to what John wrote. Read **Revelation 9:4**."

**<u>Revelation 9:4</u>** *"They were commanded not to harm the grass of the earth, or any green thing, or any tree, but only those men who do not have the seal of God on their foreheads."*

Messenger then says, "Do you see what John wrote? Not to harm the grass of the earth, or any green thing, or any tree. John was giving a clue. The scorched earth policy used in WWI which brought harm to the grass of the earth, the green things and the trees, was not to be harmed during the fifth trumpet, though John is connecting them by giving this clue."

"Yes. I see it. This is amazing. This couldn't be coincidence. Though this was talking about locusts, these creatures, right?"

Messenger begins to laugh and says, "Is that what you think those locusts are? Do you think they are some kind of creatures?"

"Well, John says they have teeth like a lion, breastplates of Iron. John says they have faces of men. From that description, yes, I would say they are creatures of some kind, maybe demonic, coming up out of the earth or something."

Messenger then says, "Mark my words. Remember what I tell you right now because this will happen. The very things I am sharing with you will be ridiculed and attempted to be torn apart by some of the very people who call themselves Biblical scholars. Do not hold it against them, for even they speak evil against what they do not understand. Some of them will test what has been shared with you in the scriptures, and they should do that. All should do that. Though still some may not see or understand. Some of the very people who will ridicule what is being shared with you are the same people who can so easily say the locusts are some kind of demonic creature coming out of the earth. Why do they say that these locusts are some kind of demonic creatures coming out of the earth? Because they are trying their best to come up with what John was seeing. They know there is no such thing as a locust with faces of men, so to them, it must be demonic creatures of some kind coming out of the earth. Some will ridicule you for what has been shared with you as to what these locusts were that John saw because you will be saying what they are, what they were, yet are they not attempting to do the same thing when they tell people they are demonic creatures coming out of the earth?"

"Why would they do this? If some of them are Biblical scholars who would do this. Why wouldn't they rejoice in what is being shared? Why would some ridicule this?"

"For some of the same reasons the Pharisees did what they did during Jesus' time. Some of the Pharisees were puffed up with pride by their knowledge of the scriptures, so much in fact, that their knowledge got in the way of seeing the miracle standing before them. They did not see Jesus as Messiah, as the Son of God, even as He was on the cross as He spoke the words 'My God, My God, why have You forsaken Me.' With all their knowledge of scripture, they should have thought back to the very Psalm written by David. You know it as Psalm 22. Psalm 22 starts off saying, 'My God, My God, why have You forsaken Me.' The same Psalm also reads, 'They pierced My hands and My feet.' As those biblical scholars of Jesus' day, those Pharisees stood there while Jesus was on the Cross, hearing Him say that, with their knowledge of the scriptures and then seeing right in front of their very eyes that His hands are pierced, His feet are pierced. Though the Pharisees of that day didn't make the connection, their eyes were darkened, meaning they didn't perceive what they saw. They were so full of the knowledge of the word that they missed the Spirit of the Word that gave it life. There are some who are puffed up with pride because they can quote scripture left and right. They have verses memorized, though even with all that, some of those very people may lack the understanding of what they just read or quoted."

"You said there would be mockers and those who have doubts even after this is shared."

"Yes, that's true. Though mockers shouldn't be coming from those you know as fellow brothers and sisters in Christ. Still, some will because people speak against what they do not understand. Think about what John said found in **John 9:49** *'Now John answered and said, 'Master, we saw someone casting out demons in Your name, and we forbade him because he does not follow with us.'* Though what do we see that Jesus says in the next verse, **John 9:50** *'But Jesus said to him, 'Do not forbid him, for he who is not against us is on our side.'* Some biblical scholars, as they call themselves, should remember what Jesus told John, people in the church should remember this. This is not the time for the church to be divided but united in Him. You are a believer. You believe that Jesus is the Son of God and that the Father sent Him. The church needs to hold onto that truth, the truth."

"Yes. Amen to that. With all that you have said, though, you haven't shared with me what this locust is. If it is not some demonic creature coming out of the ground, what is it?"

Messenger pulls out another page from under the shofar. While still holding the page close to him, he looks at me and says, "First of all, John doesn't say that it is coming up out of the ground. He says that he sees it coming out of the smoke. John is describing what he saw as best as he could of something that did not exist back in his day. He could see that it could fly, so he describes it as a locust, then he sees faces of men, so he just writes down what he sees." Messenger then hands me the page.

I couldn't believe what my eyes were seeing. There were even teeth painted on the front of it. I looked at Messenger and said, "This is a helicopter."

"Yes. That's right. You can see the breastplates of Iron at its' bottom, you see the teeth painted on the front, you see the faces of men as you see them in their cockpits, their wings on top are long like a woman's hair, their tail swoops up like a scorpions tail, and while the helicopter is in flight, if you have ever been near a helicopter in fight, it sounds like horses on chariots running into battle. The color of this particular helicopter used during the Gulf War, during Desert Storm was even the color of a locust, and even in this picture, what do you see?"

"It is appearing out of the smoke."

"Exactly. It is coming out of the smoke."

"Okay. What about the time? John says that it was a period of five months."

"Saddam Hussein left Kuwait in January 1991. Do you know when he invaded Kuwait?"

"No. When?"

"Saddam Hussein invaded Kuwait on August 2nd, 1990. Do the math. How long was he there?"

I began to count from August to January. Again, I was in awe as I said to Messenger, "Five months, he was there for five months."

"And Saddam Hussein was this ruler that John is mentioning? He says he has two names though. John said in the Hebrew is Abaddon and in the Greek Apollyon."

"When John is giving you these two names, it is meant to be giving you the meaning of those two names. The Greek name Apollyon means 'Destroyer.'"

"Saddam the Destroyer. I remember the people would call him that. In news headlines, people would call him Saddam the Destroyer."

"Yes. Even his own people, the people in Iraq nicknamed him Saddam the Destroyer. John is hearing the word 'Destroyer' affiliated with this man and attached to part of his name, so he writes that in the Greek, it is Apollyon to say 'Destroyer.'"

"What about the other name, 'Abaddon?'"

"Did you know that Desert Storm was the first war you could watch live from your living room?"

"No, I didn't know that. I was like nine years old at the time. I would have been outside playing or at school. I wouldn't have been watching the news or watching a war at this age."

"Well, what I can tell you is that when Saddam Hussein lit these oil wells on fire in 1991, news reports began coming out looking back to what he had done to a particular city and oil refinery a little more than 10 years before that in 1980. The news reports from that time even say that he brought 'Destruction' to that city in Iran and the oil refinery in Iran back in 1980. The oil refinery and the city in Iran share the same name, the name is 'Abadon.' The Hebrew name Abaddon means 'Destruction.' The news reports from that time said he brought 'Destruction.'"

"The spelling of Abadon, the city of Iran, and Abaddon that John wrote in Revelation is spelled differently though."

"Take out your phone."

I reach into my pocket to pull out my phone. I begin to hand it to Messenger, saying, "Here it is. Do you want it?"

"I want you to go to Google and type in the word 'Abaddon.'"

"Okay."

"Do you see the little sound icon at the bottom?"

"Yes, I see it."

"Press it. This will let you hear the pronunciation of the word."

Once I heard the pronunciation of the word 'Abaddon,' Messenger then said, "Now, clear that out of the search and type in the word 'Abadon.' Press the sound icon at the bottom once you finish typing in the word."

Once I hit the sound icon, I heard that the pronunciation of both words was the same. I then said to Messenger, "They are the same. They both sound the same."

"That's right. And what have I told you? John wrote down not only what he saw."

"He wrote down what he heard."

"Yes, he heard the word 'Abadon.' He then wrote down the Hebrew name 'Abaddon' as the name means 'Destruction.' The very news reports that said he brought 'destruction.' Even though this happened in 1980 concerning the City in Iran and the oil refinery in Iran that share that same name, it came back up in the news during the time of the Gulf War of Desert Storm, during the time of the fifth trumpet.....and so John wrote it down as he heard it."

I hand all the pages back to Messenger, saying, "I do hope others will have eyes to perceive and ears to hear this. There is just too much detail here, too much with all of it, even from the trumpets before this one, too much to be coincidence or chance."

Messenger takes the pages, places them back into his leather case and says, "As I have told you, there will be mockers and still unbelievers, though you still share what you know because there will be many who have had doubts, who were unbelievers that will come to believe that Jesus is truly the Son of God and the Father sent Him."

"Yes. That is our hope. That they come to believe." I think about all Messenger shared concerning the fifth trumpet as I ask him, "Is there anything else?"

"Anything else?"

"Yes. Is there anything else to the fifth trumpet?"

Messenger leans forward, resting his elbows on his knees as he looks out toward the river and says, "Yes, there is." Messenger then looks back at me and says, "One woe is past. Behold, still two more woes are coming after these things."

Explore this chapter's photos/calendars mentioned by scanning the QR code or visiting the link:

https://www.revealingthetimes.com/chapter10

# CHAPTER 11
# THE WELL CONNECTION

Jeremy makes it to David's house. He walks up the stone steps towards the front door. Right as he was about to ring the doorbell, David opens the door and says, "Good morning. Come on in."

"Good morning." They both shake hands as Jeremy walks into David's house.

"I trust you rested well?"

"Oh yes. Thank you so much for your recommendation on which hotel to stay at. I slept very well." Jeremy begins to look around the front foyer of David's home and says, "You have a lovely home."

"Thank you. Yeah, my Wife and I were after this house the moment it came on the market."

"Oh, what about this house made you feel this was the one?"

"We liked the design of it, the stone fireplace in the living room that reached up to the ceiling, the double island kitchen for hosting guests, though what really caught our eye was the view from the back, which is where I wanted us to sit. There is a nice spot out there with a bench overlooking the lake."

They walk straight through the living room towards the back of the house. Once they walk out, Jeremy can see the beautiful landscaping surrounding an inground pool with a fire pit and hot tub. He then sees in the distance a gazebo with a bench inside the gazebo and a bench beside the gazebo facing the lake. Jeremy then says to David, "This is nice."

"We like it. It is a nice spot to relax and unwind from the previous week. Even if my Wife and I are only out here a short while, it makes all the difference."

As they both get closer to the bench, Jeremy can see a small table beside it with a tray of coffee and two cups. He looks at David and says, "I see you have everything prepared."

"Yes, I thought coffee would be good this morning. How was your breakfast at the hotel?"

"It was great."

They sit beside each other on the bench looking out at the water. David then said, "So I first wanted to say that I thought last night on my way home and even this morning about the fifth trumpet you shared with me last night. I must say, there is just so much detail, and for Messenger to give you piece by piece. Looking at it all, there is just too much, and one could not deny that this is in fact the fifth trumpet."

"Though there will be those out there who will deny, no matter what they are shown. Our focus must be on all those who will come to believe in Jesus, and those who have fallen away, in hopes they return."

"I know you said you didn't want to talk about the trumpets today, though when I got home last night, I opened my Bible to the fifth trumpet, there is just one question I have."

"What's that?"

"The part that talks of the men being tormented for five months, who would seek death but not find it. You didn't mention that part last night."

"I left that out on purpose."

"Why?"

"Because the details of how some of the men who Saddam had captured were tortured, not only the men but even their families. It is too graphic to mention for this book. Just know that the men would have wanted to die, though Saddam and his men would not kill these men, only torment and torture them."

"I understand. To think it has been a little more than 30 years since that happened. Since the Gulf War, what has it been, 32 years?"

"Yes, that's right."

"Time sure goes by quickly as you look back on it."

"It sure does."

David looks out at the lake and asks Jeremy, "So, what would you like to share today?"

Jeremy begins to look around as he notices a well on the left side of their yard near the lake resting on top of a small mound. He then looks at David and says, "Is that a well?"

"Yes. Yes it is."

"Is it yours?"

"Yes, though we don't use it. We will normally place a wood cover over it that we made and use it for a table. That has kind of become the place where my Wife and I have a glass of wine with one of those fruit, cheese and meat trays."

Jeremy begins to smile without saying a word. David looks towards Jeremy and says, "What? Why are you smiling."

"Because I had nothing preplanned about what I would begin to share with you this morning. On my way here, I asked the Lord to guide me, to show me what He would want me to start with, and then I noticed the well over there right as you asked me what I would like to share today."

David seemed puzzled as he said, "You would share something about a well?"

"Yes. I call it….. 'The Well Connection.'"

"Why do you call it that?"

"I suppose I will have to share it with you for you to understand why I call it that."

"Did Messenger share this with you?"

"He did. Though I tested what he shared with me, with what was in the scriptures and sure enough, it was there."

"What was? What was there?"

"The Well Connection."

David pours himself a cup of coffee, asking Jeremy if he would like one. He then pours a cup for Jeremy. David begins to sip his coffee and then says, "By all means, please continue. Don't leave me in suspense. I am all ears."

## Meeting at The Well

Jeremy looks at David and says, "How did you and your Wife meet?"

"We met through mutual friends several years ago while a group of us guys went to a football game. The women were together at a friend's house and after the football game, us guys met up with them there at the house. Little did I know my future Wife was there too. We both got to talking, then dating, and the rest is history. Why do you ask?"

"Husbands and Wives in today's time have many different stories to share in how they first met, though during the bible times, many of them had a very similar story as to how they first met."

"Oh, and what's that?"

"Many men in the bible days first met their soon-to-be bride at a well."

"Really? That seems like a strange place to be meeting."

"Not back then, it wasn't, especially if you had animals to care for. The well was a common place where people would gather."

David stands up and says, "Come, walk with me." Both begin walking towards the well. David then says, "So who were some of the men from the bible who met their soon-to-be bride at a well?"

"There were quite a few of them. Abraham sent his servant to find a bride for his son Isaac. Abraham's servant first met Rebekah at a well. Rebekah was Isaac's Wife. Then Jacob first met Rachel at a well. Rachel was the one Jacob loved most. Jacob served seven years for Rachel, though as you may recall from reading about it, Jacob's Uncle Laban tricked Jacob and gave Jacob his oldest daughter Leah during Jacob's Wedding night."

"Why did Jacob's Uncle Laban do that?"

"Because it was their custom that the oldest daughter be given away in marriage first. Laban still let Jacob have Rachel as his Wife as well. Jacob served another seven years for Rachel, though Jacob did not have to wait another seven years for Rachel. Once Jacob fulfilled Leah's week as newlyweds, he was given Rachel and served another seven years."

"Was there anyone else that met their soon-to-be bride at a well?"

"Yes, Moses met Zipporah at a well."

David takes a moment to look down into the well, then as he looks up towards the sun, he says, "You know what I think of when it comes to a well in the bible?"

"What's that?"

"I think of the Samaritan Woman who was at the well."

"Yes, the one whom Jesus spoke with. The one who came to the well to draw water as Jesus was resting there."

"Yes, her." David then asked, "Do you suppose Jesus knew she was going to be coming there to draw water and that is why He chose to rest there?"

"I suppose that would be so. After all, Jesus is God in the flesh. God knows all things. Jesus had told his disciples of things before they had come to pass, so I would suppose he would have known the woman was coming to draw water at about that time. Though there is another mystery to this as well, in fact a few mysteries concerning this time."

"Oh, what's that?"

Jeremy opens his bible and begins to read **<u>Song of Solomon 1:7</u>** *"Tell me, O you whom I love, where you feed your flock, where you make it rest at noon. For why should I be as one who veils herself by the flocks of your companions."*

David then says, "Okay, what is the mystery here?"

"What did Jesus do before he went to the well?"

"I am not sure."

"Jesus sent his disciples away to buy food. After He sent His disciples away to buy food, He went to rest at the well. And what time was it when He rested?"

"It was noon."

"That's right. He sends His disciples away to buy food. His disciples are His flock, and He rests at noon."

"Yes, I see what you are saying, though what is written in the Song of Solomon is between the woman and her beloved Husband-to-be. The woman at the well is a Samaritan woman talking with Jesus. It is not like they are to soon be married."

"Not soon to be married as we would think. However, this Samaritan woman who becomes a believer, would she not be considered part of the church body?"

"Yes, your right."

He then looks at David and says, "And the church is what?"

"The church is the bride of Christ."

"Exactly." Jeremy then says, "And why do you suppose Jesus had His disciples to go buy food?"

"They had stopped there, and that area would have been a good place to get food I suppose. Would there have been another reason?"

"There are a few other reasons. One is what I had just shared with you from Song of Solomon. The woman asks her beloved where do you feed your flocks? Jesus sends His disciples, His flock to buy food. Jesus sending His disciples off to buy food allowed Himself the privacy He would need to meet the woman."

"Ah, so He did know she was going to be there."

"The same as how He knows what you will do tomorrow and who you will meet tomorrow."

David laughs and says, "Well that is easy. You and I both know what I will be doing tomorrow and who I will be meeting. I will be meeting you again tomorrow."

"Fair enough, Jesus knows who you will meet and what you will be doing even a year from tomorrow." Jeremy pauses for a moment, then says, "Jesus was not the one who needed to have privacy with this woman though, it was the woman, the woman was going to need to have that private moment with Jesus, even though she had no idea she was going to be meeting anyone at the well at that time. If any more people had been around at that time other than Jesus, she could have become closed off, so Jesus sends His disciples off to buy food as He rests there at the well at noon time."

"What would she have been closed off from? I don't understand."

"Remember what Jesus asked her to do?"

"Jesus asked her for a drink of water."

"After that, even after He had told her that if only she would ask Him for a drink, He would give her living water."

"Jesus said to her to call her husband and come back."

"That's right. And what was her response?"

"She said that she did not have a husband."

Jeremy then says, "Jesus then says to her that she spoke truly in that she has no husband. He tells her that she has had five husbands and the one she is living with now is not her husband. Had the disciples been there other than only Jesus Himself, do you suppose He would have exposed her shame in front of them so openly? Do you suppose she would have responded as she did so openly in perceiving Jesus to be a prophet had the disciples been there in that moment?"

"I suppose not. Though how do you know she would have needed that privacy?"

"Jesus was resting there at noon. The woman came to draw water during the hottest part of the day. Women would come to draw water from the well in the evening time when it was the cooler part of the day. The woman came during the hottest part of the day as no one else would be there, or so she thought until she met Jesus resting there at noon. The fact that it was only her and Jesus, she felt comfortable being honest in saying that she had no husband. Jesus then can be open with her without exposing her shame in front of others. Once He tells her who He is, that He is the Messiah, what does she do?"

"She goes into the city and tells people to come and see a Man who told her everything she had ever done and then says to them, 'Could this be the Christ?'"

"That's right. And before she had left to do that, she even left her waterpot behind. She had gone there to the well to draw water at the hottest part of the day to avoid people, though after meeting Jesus, having that time with Him, and hearing Him say to her that He is the Messiah, she leaves her waterpot and goes into the city to speak to the very people she used to avoid. Something changed in her at that moment, something radicle. Would you like to know what she could have thought at that moment?"

"Yes, of course."

"This is what she could have thought, 'who am I that the Lord would visit me, that the Lord would speak to me. I have lived a life of shame. I have avoided those who live around me. I told this Man that I have no husband, and I was honest with Him, though He tells me about the fact that I have had five husbands and the one I am living with is not my husband, still knowing now that He knows this about me, this very thing that has had me looked at as an outcast. Still, He is standing here talking with me and sharing with me about the true way to worship God, to worship in spirit and truth, and while He still speaks with me, He openly shares with me that He is the Messiah who is speaking to me.' What do you suppose she could have felt in that moment?"

"I suppose she could have felt full after having received such grace and mercy, not to mention the love for her, that the Lord would visit her, speak to her, and tell her who He is."

"In other words, that veil of hiding herself, she could remove, go out among the men of the city and tell them about Jesus." Jeremy pauses for a moment and then says, "Now back to the disciples when they come back and offer Jesus some of the food they had bought. What does He do?"

"He turns it down. He refuses to eat any of it."

"Yes. And what does He say to them?"

"I don't remember what He said."

"He said, 'I have food to eat of which you do not know.' The disciples didn't understand this and thought someone could have brought Him something to eat. Then Jesus says, 'My food is to do the will of Him who sent Me, and to finish His work.'"

"That's right. I remember now."

"What Jesus said to His disciples when He refused to eat any food lies a mystery, the disciples didn't understand it at the time, though you can discover this hidden mystery of what Jesus was referring to by just opening your bible and going back in time to another account of where a man had met a woman at a well."

"Really? Which one?"

"After Abraham sends his servant to find a bride for his son Isaac, when the servant sees Rebekah approaching the well, there is more to what happens at the well, though I want you to see what follows all of this." Jeremy then begins to read **Genesis 24:32-33** *'Then the man came to the house. And he unloaded the camels, and provided straw and feed for the camels, and water to wash his feet and the feet of the men who were with him. Food was set before him to eat, but he said, 'I will not eat until I have told about my errand.'''*

David then said, "The servant, he too refused to eat."

"He refused to eat and would not eat until he had told them about his errand, which was what?"

"His errand was Abraham sending him to find a bride for his son Isaac."

Jeremy then says, "And like this servant sent by Abraham, Jesus had been sent by the Father to also find a bride. In order to have His bride, He would pay the dowry, the bride price, and the price was His life by His death on the Cross. He died for us that we may live. Those who believed in Him then and those of us who believe in Him now know and believe that Jesus is the Son of God, that the Father sent Him, and those of us who have come to Him in faith, we are His church, His bride."

"So, the will of the Father for His Son Jesus was to find a bride, being what would be known as the church, and to do that, to finish that work, He would give Himself for her."

"Yes. And when He finished the work, He paid the price that we couldn't pay, only He could. While He was on the Cross, His last words He spoke before He died was, 'It is finished.'" Jeremy then pauses for a moment and says, "Still though, there is something that is yet future."

"What is that?"

"The Marriage Supper of the Lamb."

David began walking back towards the bench, and Jeremy followed closely behind. As David walked, he thought about everything Jeremy had just shared. The Well Connection, the mystery, the marriage. As David sat down, he said, "This is so very beautiful. Everything you shared. I don't think I would have ever seen that connection of Jesus refusing the food from the disciples and when Abraham's servant had also refused to eat until he could first speak about what he had been sent to do."

Jeremy then says, "Yes, His word is indeed beautiful. It is a living word that still speaks to us today by His Spirit." Jeremy then says, "And do you know what else is beautiful?"

"What's that?"

"This view. This lake. Absolutely a beautiful view."

"Yes it is." While looking at the body of water, David then thinks of Moses and the people of Israel crossing the Red Sea. He then says, "Can you imagine what the view could have been like when Moses and the people of Israel crossed the Red Sea? What the view would have been like watching the waters' part? A wall of water on both sides as they cross through the middle?"

"One can only imagine."

David then says, "Hey, remember you were going to share the other connection Messenger shared with you about the Exodus. You told me yesterday that you would tell me later. Well today is later." David then laughs.

"About how we know the Exodus took place in 1445 BC? Are you talking about that?"

"Yes, you said that Messenger shared this with you. Will you share this with me now?"

While sitting there on the bench, Jeremy leans forward and says, "I suppose now is as good of a time as any. Would you like me to share it with you as if I was back there with Messenger on the day he shared this with me, or would you like me to just share with you in this moment as we are sitting here?"

David looks out at the lake again and says, "In this moment will be just fine."

"Very well. I will share in this moment with you what Messenger called 'The Egypt Connection: The Sun and the Moon.'"

David then speaks with excitement in his voice. "The Sun and the Moon! Oh, I can't wait to hear this."

# CHAPTER 12
# THE EGYPT CONNECTION:
# THE SUN AND THE MOON

Jeremy grabs his leather case beside him on the ground and places it on his lap. He looks up towards the Sun, then at David, and says, "What do you know about the Sun and the Moon? What has God used the Sun and the Moon for?"

David then says, "For signs and for seasons."

"That's right." Jeremy then opens his bible and begins to read **Genesis 1:14** *'Then God said, 'Let there be lights in the firmament of the heavens to divide the day from the night; and let them be for signs and for seasons, and for days and years.'"*

"I remember that verse," says David.

"The part of that verse I want us to focus on is where God had made them to be for signs. We know about the seasons, days and years. Though let us focus on where they were used for signs. The Sun, Moon and the Stars were used as God's markers. Now, if the Sun and the Moon were used as signs, what type of sign do you suppose the Sun and Moon could be?"

"They could be eclipses. There could be an eclipse of the sun or an eclipse of the moon."

"Exactly right. Do you remember what I shared with you yesterday, the part Messenger shared with me back in the spring of 2021 about a few significant years of deliverance and their connection?"

"Yes, how could I forget that. After Messenger shared all that information with you, he showed you the calendars."

"That's right. There was something else Messenger had shown me concerning some of those years. He had shown me this before sharing the other connection with how we can know the Exodus happened in 1445 BC."

"What did he show you?"

Jeremy closes his bible and sits it between himself and David on the bench. He then reaches into his leather case and pulls out a few pages. He handed two of the pages to David while he kept the other one in his hand. He then says to David, "Hold them up." Jeremy then holds his up as well. He then says, "What do you see?"

David could see the number 8 at the top left corner to show that this was the 8th month on the Hebrew Calendar, known as the month of Bul. He looked at each day and saw at the bottom of each box that represented each day, a year that each calendar represented. He saw that he held the two calendars representing 538 BC and 473 BC. He looked over at the one in Jeremy's hand and could see that he was holding the one for the year 30 AD. It was also for the 8th month of the Hebrew Calendar, known as the month of Bul.

Jeremy then says, "Look closely."

David continues to look at the calendars in his hand. He then notices a couple of circular orbs on a couple of days. He points to them and says, "What are these?"

"Those are lunar and solar eclipses that occurred on those days during those years."

David then saw what day these eclipses occurred and what day they corresponded with regarding the month and day of our calendar. He looked at Jeremy with amazement as he said, "They are the same."

Here was what David saw in his hand with the two calendars:

**538 BC** 14th day of the 8th month corresponded to October 29th. A Lunar Eclipse.

29th day of the 8th month corresponded to November 13th. Solar Eclipse.

**473 BC**   13th day of the 8th month corresponded to October 29th. A Lunar Eclipse.

29th day of the 8th month corresponded to November 14th. Solar Eclipse.

Here is what David saw with the calendar in Jeremy's hand:

**30 AD** 13th day of the 8th month corresponded to October 29th. No Eclipse.

29th day of the 8th month corresponded to November 14th. Solar Eclipse.

David then looks to Jeremy and says, "The year 538 BC has the 14th day of the 8th month, though whereas the other two years have the 13th day of the 8th month."

"What matters though is that both the 14th day of the 8th month in the year 538 BC and the 13th day of the 8th month on the other two years, all three years correspond to October 29th, the day of the Lunar Eclipse."

"Okay, I see what you are talking about there. Though what about the other day with 538 BC? The 29th day of the 8th month corresponds with November 13th, whereas the other two years have the 29th day corresponding with November 14th."

Jeremy begins to laugh as he says, "The same applies to this as well. What matters is that all three fall on the 29th day of the 8th month of the Hebrew Calendar, where there is a Solar Eclipse."

"Okay, I see your point." David then looks closer and says, "Wait, no lunar eclipse fell on the 13th day of the 8th month in the year 30 AD. There is a solar eclipse on the 29th day of the 8th month, though no lunar eclipse."

"You noticed that did you?"

"Does this mean this is not accurate? That this could just be a coincidence that all of the other ones match?"

"This makes what I have just shown you more accurate."

"How is that?"

"Messenger had told me that others could question this as being accurate. Congratulations, you are the first to question this as being accurate." Jeremy then smiles.

"I just want to understand is all."

"Messenger had told me that what makes this even more accurate being this way is that it shows God's hand even more in that He is the one that causes the Sun to eclipse and the Moon to eclipse in order to communicate to us, to warn us, some warnings may be directed to the nations, and others to the people of Israel. Had all the eclipses been there, people could say that it is simple clockwork. People could try to say that it is not something of God. Though knowing there is one eclipse missing shows this is not just simple clockwork. God's guiding hand can be seen here throughout history."

David then notices that one of the years is missing. He hands the pages back to Jeremy and says, "What about the other year? The year 1884 BC when Joseph was released from Pharaoh's Prison. That one should be connected too right, as the others are?"

Jeremy places the pages back into the leather case as he pulls out one page from the leather case. He then hands it to David and says, "Tell me what you see."

David saw that it was another calendar representing the 8th Hebrew month during the year 1884 BC.

Here is what David saw on the calendar:

**1884 BC** 13th day of the 8th month corresponded to October 29th. No Eclipse.

29th day of the 8th month corresponded to November 14th. No Eclipse.

David then says, "The days are connected like the other ones are, though there are no eclipses at all like the other ones from those other years."

"That's right."

"Why not?"

"Again, like what I have already told you. Had there been eclipses on those days in the year 1884 BC, people could say that it is just simple clockwork, though the fact that they are not there tells us something so much more."

"What more does the eclipses not being there tell us?"

Jeremy takes a moment as he sips his coffee, then says, "Remember I told you that sometimes the eclipses could be a warning to the nations and at other times could be a warning to the people of Israel?"

"Yes, I remember you saying that."

"Was there anything that needed to be of warning in 1884 BC?"

David takes a moment to think and then says, "Yes, the warning of the upcoming seven years of famine."

"You are right. Though God had already warned them, He didn't need to use the sign of the eclipse of the sun or the sign of the eclipse of the moon to send them warning."

"Why not?"

"Because He sent warning by giving the dream to Pharaoh of the seven fat cows and the seven lean cows and then gave Joseph the ability to interpret the dreams of Pharaoh. They then understood the message and the warning. There is another reason God would not have used the eclipses for that year at that time."

"Why?"

"Because the Pharaoh and Egyptians were sun worshipers. God at that moment would not have used something like the sun to give warning only to have Pharaoh and the Egyptians worship the sun even more. Instead, God chose to give a dream to Pharaoh, a dream that no one else could make sense of or interpret except for Joseph, the one man who knew who the one and true living God is. Joseph interprets the dream of Pharaoh, that year Joseph is released from Pharaoh's Prison, and that year was the start of the seven years of plenty. Joseph may have been the vessel chosen to save many and bring them through a great deliverance, though God is the One who gets the glory, without God's guiding hand, there would not have been such a deliverance."

David thinks about what was just told to him, then says, "This is amazing, this all makes sense, and as you have said, or as Messenger shared with you, all of this shows even more the evidence of God's guiding hand through history."

"Yes, that's right."

David looks at Jeremy and says, "So what about the Egypt Connection? The part that Messenger shared with you as another way we can know the Exodus happened in 1445 BC."

Jeremy pulled out another page from the leather case and said, "This is what Messenger handed me." He then hands the page to David.

David looks at the page. It was another calendar. At the top left of the calendar was the number 5, representing the 5th month of the Hebrew month known as the month of Av. He looks down at the year. It was the year 2017. He then sees two circular orbs on two different days. The two orbs were eclipses. One is a lunar eclipse, and the other is a solar eclipse.

This was what David saw on the calendar:

**<u>2017 AD</u>** 15th day of the 5th month corresponded to August 8th. Lunar Eclipse.

29th day of the 5th month corresponded to August 21st. Solar Eclipse.

While looking at the calendar, David says, "Hey, this is showing the Eclipse we had in 2017. The one that went from Northwest of the United States to the Southeast of the United States. The one they called the 'Great American Eclipse.'"

"That's right. And you remember everything I had shared with you concerning this eclipse yesterday and the dreams related to the eclipse, right?"

"Of course I do."

Jeremy then begins to pull out one more page from his leather case. He hands the page to David. David could see it was yet another calendar. At the top left of the calendar, he can see the number 5 representing the 5th month of the Hebrew month just as the other calendar had. David notices one difference. This calendar represents the year 1445 BC. He then sees two circular orbs on two different days. The two orbs were eclipses. One is a lunar eclipse, and the other is a solar eclipse.

This was what David saw on the calendar:

**1445 BC** 14th day of the 5th month corresponded to August 8th. Lunar Eclipse.

28th day of the 5th month corresponded to August 21st. Solar Eclipse.

David then says, "The Hebrew days are one day before in the year 1445 BC."

"Yes, and as Messenger had shared with me, the important part to pay close attention to is that both 2017 AD and 1445 BC correspond with our month of August 8th as the lunar eclipse and August 21st as the solar eclipse. Though, that is not all Messenger shared with me. I mentioned part of it to you yesterday."

David seemed puzzled as he tried to remember what Jeremy had said yesterday concerning this eclipse. He then said, "Refresh my memory."

"The solar eclipse of 2017. The one people call the 'Great American Eclipse.' The center of that solar eclipse happened in a place known as 'Little Egypt.' They called the place 'Little Egypt' because there was a bad famine in the year 1824 up around Chicago, and word was that crops were abundant down in the south part of Illinois, so the people loaded ox and wagons and traveled down to the southern part of Illinois. This made the people think of the time of Joseph and Egypt during their time of plenty and time of famine, so they nicknamed the area 'Little Egypt,' and it has been known as that ever since."

"This is amazing. The Egypt Connection."

Jeremy takes the pages back from David to place them back into his leather case and says to David, "Now, do you think this is just coincidence or mere chance this connects so well across thousands of years of time?"

David felt in awe with everything as he said, "There is no way at all this is coincidence or mere chance. We are witnessing God's guiding hand, His presence through history and even the present."

"I am glad you have had eyes to perceive and ears to hear."

David then asks, "So what brought Messenger to share this part with you regarding the eclipses and the Egypt connection?"

"I had shared with him the dreams I had shared with you yesterday. When I got to the dreams about the eclipses, that was when Messenger began sharing with me the other connection of knowing the Exodus did happen in the year 1445 BC."

"You shared with Messenger each of the dreams you shared with me yesterday?"

"I did. I even shared with Messenger a couple of other dreams that I have not shared with you yet."

"What were they? Will you tell me?"

"Yes, of course. Though for this, how about I take you back to the day I shared these two other dreams with Messenger. I won't talk about the ones I have already shared with you. Instead, I will start with the moment I began sharing with Messenger the other two dreams you haven't heard about."

David smiles and then says with excitement, "Absolutely, and did Messenger interpret these other two dreams for you?"

"He did as a matter of fact. I will also share with you what Messenger shared with me following that. He shared with me the time when Jesus was born, as well as the time when Jesus was baptized by John the Baptist. It was very interesting how Messenger could piece it all together and seemed to have been concealed within the scriptures all this time, though it is being revealed for such a time as this. After that, Messenger also shared with me details relating to the Antichrist, certain patterns from long ago that seem to be showing up in the times we are now living."

David looked at Jeremy and said, "I can't wait to hear of all the things Messenger has shared with you. Will I need my bible?"

"We can use mine. I have it here."

"Okay, good." David sits back as he attempts to get more comfortable, waiting for Jeremy to begin to take him back to the day when he spoke with Messenger. He wanted to imagine himself there at that moment as he was sitting on that bench. David then says, "You can begin whenever you're ready."

"Very well. Now, I will share with you the part where the dreams continue."

Explore this chapter's photos/calendars mentioned by scanning the QR code or visiting the link:

https://www.revealingthetimes.com/chapter12

# CHAPTER 13
# THE DREAMS CONTINUE

Messenger stood up from the bench and began to walk by the water of the river. He looked back at me and said, "Walk with me, and bring your bible with you."

As we walked towards the river, Messenger had his leather case and shofar crossed over on each of his shoulders as before. I looked back at where we were sitting and said, "What about the clay vessel beside the bench with all the scrolls in it?"

"They will be fine. No one will bother them." Messenger then begins walking along the river's edge as I follow him. He then says, "So, tell me about these other dreams you have had. You said the dreams have continued since the ones you had just shared with me?"

"Yes. The dreams have continued."

"Tell me of them."

## The Waters Part

As we walked along the river, I began to share one of the dreams with Messenger.

"In the dream, I see someone who had given their life to the Lord. It was the day they were saved. I only see this for a moment in the dream. Then suddenly, I see what looks like Moses and the Israelites crossing the Red Sea. I see the waters part, watching as they cross to the other side. After I saw this, suddenly, I saw another crossing. The waters had parted as they crossed to the other side. They had the Ark of the Covenant in front of them during this other crossing. Then, the dream ended. That was it."

Messenger took a moment to think about what I had just shared with him. He then says, "This person you saw being saved, giving their life to the Lord, do you know this person?"

"Yes. I know the person."

Messenger then says, "And what makes you think this is another dream the Lord has given you?"

"Because I was seeing at the beginning of the dream something that was during the present time to then seeing what looked like the crossing of the Red Sea and the other crossing, seeing the Ark of the Covenant."

Messenger smiles as he says, "You are right. This was another dream the Lord gave. Have you been able to interpret it? What do you think the Lord was showing you when you saw this?"

"I haven't been able to interpret this. I am not sure what the Lord was showing me. I just know this must have been given for some reason."

"Would you like help interpreting the dream?"

"Yes, of course."

Messenger then says, "Open up your bible. Since you saw the crossing of the Red Sea in your dream, let us first look at what day that fell on."

"You're saying that we can know exactly what day Moses and the people of Israel crossed the Red Sea?"

"Yes, that's right. You know as I have shared with you, that the Exodus occurred in 1445 BC. After Moses and the people left Egypt following Passover, they traveled a three-day journey toward the Red Sea, and they camped each of those days. The first place I want you to read in your bible is **Exodus 12:37**. You may read it aloud once you are there."

**Exodus 12:37** *"Then the children of Israel journeyed from Rameses to Succoth, about six hundred thousand men on foot, besides children."*

"That was the first place they had camped. Now read **Exodus 13:20-22**. Please read aloud to me once you are there."

**Exodus 13:20-22** *"So they took their journey from Succoth and camped in Etham at the edge of the wilderness. And the Lord went before them by day in a pillar of cloud to lead the way, and by night in a pillar of fire to give them light, so as to go by day and night. He did not take away the pillar of cloud by day or the pillar of fire by night from before the people."*

"Etham was the second place they had camped. Now read aloud **Exodus 14:1-2**."

**Exodus 14:1-2** *"Now the Lord spoke to Moses, saying: 'Speak to the children of Israel, that they turn and camp before Pi Hahiroth, between Migdol and the sea, opposite Baal Zephon; you shall camp before it by the sea.'"*

"This was the third place they had camped, and they were by the sea. Now, if you will read **Exodus 14:13-14**."

**Exodus 14:13-14** *"And Moses said to the people, 'Do not be afraid. Stand still, and see the salvation of the Lord, which He will accomplish for you today. For the Egyptians whom you see today, you shall see again no more forever. The Lord will fight for you, and you shall hold your peace.'"*

Messenger then says, "Now to see precisely when Moses and the people crossed through the waters and reached the other side of the Red Sea, you would need to read **Exodus 14:21-24**. Please read it."

**Exodus 14:21-24** *"Then Moses stretched out his hand over the sea; and the Lord caused the sea to go back by a strong east wind all that night, and made the sea into dry land, and the waters were divided. So the children of Israel went into the midst of the sea on the dry ground, and the waters were a wall to them on their right hand and on their left. And the Egyptians pursued and went after them into the midst of the sea, all Pharaoh's horses, his chariots, and his horsemen. Now it came to pass, in the morning watch, that the Lord looked down upon the army of the Egyptians through the pillar of fire and cloud, and He troubled the army of the Egyptians."*

Messenger then reached into his leather case and began to pull out a page. He looked at me and said, "I happen to have a calendar that shows the time of Passover in 1445 BC." Messenger hands the page to me and says, "Look at the day that Passover fell on, then look three days beyond that as we have just seen the three places where they had camped each day following Passover. What day do you come to where Moses and the people would have been camped by the Red Sea?"

I looked at the calendar, counting three days from Passover and then I saw the day and said, "Friday. The day was Friday."

"That's right, and what you had just read said that the waters parted at night, and they crossed during the night, when they reached the other side, the scriptures say that it was the morning watch. The morning watch started at about 6:00am as the last of three-night watches went from 2:00am to 6:00am. So, they reach the other side of the Red Sea around sunrise. This, as you know, would be Saturday. Looking at the calendar, what day does that Saturday correspond to on your calendar?"

I looked at the bottom of that Saturday and said, "It corresponded to April 16th."

"Very good, so now we know that Moses and the people crossed the Red Sea and reached the other side on Saturday, April 16th, 1445 BC. We then know if we continue to read that Moses stretched out his hand over the sea to close up the sea on the Egyptians as the Lord had told him to do." Messenger took the page back from me as he placed the page back into his leather case. He then said, "Now let us look at the other part of your dream. You said that you saw the people crossing the waters after they had parted and that the Ark of the Covenant was in front of them?"

"Yes, that's right. I saw the Ark of the Covenant in front of them as they crossed to the other side after the waters had parted in front of them."

Messenger then says, "Okay. Since during this part of the dream, you saw the Ark of the Covenant in front of them, that means what you saw was Joshua and the people crossing the Jordan River out of the Wilderness and into what would be the Promised land as the Ark of the Covenant was in front of them." Messenger pulls out from his leather case yet another page. Before Messenger hands me the page, he says, "We can know the day this happened as well by looking at the scriptures."

"We can?"

"Yes. Chapter 3 of the book of Joshua is all about the crossing of the Jordan. However, to find out what day they had crossed the other side of the Jordan, you would need to read **Joshua 4:19**. Please turn your bible to **Joshua 4:19** and read it aloud to me once you are there."

**Joshua 4:19** *"Now the people came up from the Jordan on the tenth day of the first month, and they camped in Gilgal on the east border of Jericho."*

Messenger then hands me the page. It was another calendar. The top left of the calendar had the number 1 to represent the first month of the Hebrew calendar. Messenger said, "That is for the Hebrew month that you know as the month of 'Nisan,' though before it was known as the month of 'Abib.' This calendar, as you can see, comes from the year 1405 BC, when Joshua and the people left the Wilderness and crossed over the Jordan river. As you have read from the scriptures, Joshua and the people crossed to the other side on the 10th day of the 1st month. Please look at the 10th day on the calendar and tell me what you see."

As I began to look at the 10th day, I looked below it to see what day it corresponded with our calendar. I couldn't believe what I was seeing. I looked up at Messenger and said, "It says April 16th."

Messenger then smiles.

I looked back down at the calendar as I said, "So, you're telling me that the crossing to the other side of the Red Sea and the crossing of the Jordan 40 years later just happened to fall on a day in their month that corresponds with April 16th?"

"Yes, that's right." Messenger took the page back from me and placed it back into his leather case. He then said, "Now, would you like to know something more that will show you that this was of the Lord?"

"Yes, what is it?"

Messenger then says, "This person who was saved, who gave their life to the Lord, do you have their phone number?"

"Yes, I have their phone number."

"Call them."

"Call them now?"

"Yes, call them. When the person answers, ask them what day they were saved, ask them what day they gave their life to the Lord."

Jeremy calls the person. Once they answered, Jeremy said, "Hey there, I have a question for you. Do you know what day you were saved? Do you know what day you gave your life to the Lord?" The person knew what day it was and told Jeremy the day. They did not stay on the phone long, though when Jeremy got off the call, he was stunned as he looked at Messenger in shock from the news.

Messenger then said, "So, what did the person tell you?"

"They said they were saved on April 16th."

Messenger smiles, then says, "You don't say. So, the dream you had of the person who had been saved, to Moses and the people crossing the Red Sea, to the crossing of the Jordan River all happens to land on a day that corresponds with April 16th. Do you think that was a coincidence? Do you think that is mere chance?"

"No, it couldn't be a coincidence."

Messenger then says, "What do you suppose the dream was meant for? What do you suppose the message was for?"

"I am not sure."

Messenger then said, "The person who had been saved on that day on April 16th, they too have had a dream, something that has stayed with them for some time now, of them in a body of water, there are other parts to their dream, however. Their dream and your dream you have had is meant to tell this person that as the people who had crossed the Red Sea had been delivered from bondage, as the people who had crossed the Jordan River had been delivered, so too has this person been delivered when they came to the Lord. There is another message this dream gives as well."

"What is that?"

Messenger then says, "Just as the stones that the people laid down as a memorial for generations after them to know they indeed crossed on dry ground, so too the following verses I will have you read can also apply to the dream you had of Moses and the people crossing the Red Sea as well as when the people crossed the Jordan River, to find out this day, that all of what you dreamt falls on what corresponds to April 16<sup>th</sup>. Read the book of **Joshua 4:23-24**. Will you please read it aloud to me?"

**Joshua 4:23-24** *"For the Lord your God dried up the waters of the Jordan before you until you had crossed over, as the Lord your God did to the Red Sea, which He dried up before us until we had crossed over, that all the peoples of the earth may know the hand of the Lord, that it is mighty, that you may fear the Lord your God forever."*

Messenger turned around, back in the direction of where they came. They had both walked a long way down the river's edge. As I followed beside him, Messenger said, "What about the other dream you had? Share it with me will you, as we walk back."

## The 9-11 Connection

I looked far in front of us, over into the distance at the bench we had been sitting on. As we continued to walk, I said, "In this dream, I had dreamt about 9-11-2001. I saw in the dream the towers began to fall. I saw the rubble, the ruins following the aftermath of the attack. Then suddenly, I was no longer seeing 9-11-2001. I was then seeing what looked like a time back in biblical times. I was standing in the middle of a courtyard, and there was no one in the courtyard except for one man. He was a young man who had a crown on his head, and he looked like a king. He had this look of anguish on his face. I could hear what sounded like many footsteps behind me, so I turned around and saw many people, all dressed in clothing that looked like people from biblical times. All the people were walking away, and there were about 10 of them. As they were walking out, two others were walking into the courtyard. Then, after this, I was no longer standing in a courtyard but on the side of a dirt road as I watched many people walking down the dirt road. Many of them were crying, and they too, were all dressed how people were dressed in biblical times. In front of the many people, I saw 10 men chained to each other, each one in front of the other. They were chained at their wrists, and they had a chain that traveled from their wrist to the man's waist in front of them. The man chained in the very front had a crown on his head, though all the jewels were missing from the crown, and he had a yoke across his shoulders. His hands were up and chained to the yoke. In front of them were men riding on horseback and camels. Those who rode on them looked like ancient warriors. That was the end of the dream."

Messenger then says, "And I take it you dreamt of this after the actual day of September 11th, 2001, right?"

"Oh yes. This was just a couple of months ago, so more than 20 years since 9-11-2001 happened."

Messenger stops walking for a moment, then suddenly starts walking again as he says, "Well, you obviously know what you saw concerning September 11th, 2001. The other two settings you saw in the dream, besides September 11th, 2001, are of two different time periods. The young man you saw wearing a crown standing in the middle of the courtyard was king Rehoboam. King Rehoboam was the son of king Solomon. The anguish you saw on his face was probably due to what you had just witnessed as you turned around and saw the people walking away. You said there were 10 people?"

"Yes, about 10."

"The 10 people represent the 10 tribes of Israel that had left king Rehoboam. What you saw in your dream was the division of the kingdom. The two you saw walking into the courtyard represent the two tribes that stayed with king Rehoboam. The two tribes that stayed with king Rehoboam were the tribes of Judah and Benjamin."

"Why did the 10 tribes of Israel leave king Rehoboam?"

"Because king Rehoboam would not lighten the yoke of his people. So, they became two kingdoms. The Southern Kingdom was known as the Kingdom of Judah, and the Northern Kingdom was known as the Kingdom of Israel. Jeroboam, who was of the tribe of Ephraim, became king of the Northern Kingdom, and the 10 tribes were part of the Northern Kingdom known as the Kingdom of Israel."

"What about the other part I saw when I was standing on the side of a dirt road? You said that represented another time?"

"Yes, it was of another time. What you saw was the northern kingdom, the kingdom of Israel going into Assyrian captivity. The people you saw were the people of that northern kingdom. The 10 men you saw chained in front of the people represented the 10 tribes that made up the kingdom of Israel. The one you saw in front of the others wearing a crown with the yoke across his shoulders represented the king of Israel during the time of the Assyrian captivity. The jewels missing from his crown were to represent his position being stripped from him, and the yoke to represent his new position of imprisonment and slavery. The men on horseback and camels with them represented the Assyrians who were taking them away captive."

"Why the dream of September 11th, 2001, though? That doesn't seem to make any sense."

"Think of it like the last dream you shared with me. The first part was of something of your lifetime, whereas the two times after that represented two separate times during biblical times. Yet, all three were connected by a message of deliverance and connected by the day that corresponded with all three of them on your calendar."

"I'm still not following how September 11th, 2001, relates."

"In this dream, you dreamt of something first that happened during your lifetime, whereas the two time periods that you saw next were of two separate times during biblical times, yet all three are connected by a message of warning, a message of loss, a message of attack. The duties of the Watchman link all three together. In biblical times, the watchman was to keep watch of approaching danger from the enemy. Some of the prophets during those biblical times were watchmen. They warned the king to repent, to turn back to the ways of God, and warned of an approaching attack. Though the kings of their day, the people would not heed the warning or the message. The kingdoms divided, and the northern kingdom later went into Assyrian captivity. There is more that connects all three of these time periods you saw in your dream."

"What's that? What else is there?"

"The kingdom was divided in the year 931 BC, and the northern kingdom, the kingdom of Israel, went into Assyrian captivity in the year 722 BC. A little more than 200 years between both periods you saw in your dream, yet something links both of them. Something hidden. Something that has yet to be revealed until now."

"What? What is it?"

Messenger reaches for his Shofar and begins to sound it. He then says, "What did I just do?"

"You blew the shofar."

"Yes, but why? What did I tell you the shofar was used for?"

"You said that it was blown as the king approaches, and at the coronation of a king. You also said it was blown if the watchman saw the enemy approaching, the threat of war. They would sound it to bring the people to wake up from their sleep in hopes they would come together to prepare for a battle or war. You also said it was blown at a time of deliverance, and the people would be joined together in celebration."

"Very good. You remembered." Messenger then says, "Two years before September 11th, 2001, there was a man who stood where the Statue of Liberty stands, he was blowing the Shofar, a person who was standing behind this man blowing the Shofar took a picture. The picture shows the Shofar touching the spot on one of the Trade Towers where the first plane hit. This happened two years to the day before September 11th, 2001. It was on September 11th, 1999, and September 11th, 1999, was no ordinary day. There was a reason this man was blowing the Shofar on this particular day. September 11th, 1999, fell on what is known as The Feast of Trumpets. And even though the people and the very man who blew the shofar may not have known what was to come, yet, it did come. Do you believe this was just random coincidence? Or do you believe that God is still present, that He guides those whom He has called for such a time as this, to warn His people, that they might return to Him."

"Yes, I believe that God's presence is very much still with us, that He guides with His hand. I believe that He still today uses those whom He has called for such a time as this in hopes that others may repent, to return, that others are saved through faith in believing that Jesus is the Son of God and has been sent by the Father."

We both come to the bench where we had sat before. The clay vessel with the scrolls was still there beside the bench. We sit down as Messenger looks through his leather case and says, "I think I have them here. I know that I have had them before. Ah, here they are." Messenger pulls out two pages and hands both to me. He then says, "Both of these are the calendars for the year 931 BC and 722 BC. Now, do you remember what I told you? 931 BC was when the kingdoms divided. The kingdoms divided because the king of Judah, king Rehoboam wouldn't lighten the yoke of his people. 722 BC was the year the northern kingdom of Israel went into Assyrian captivity. They had gone into Assyrian captivity because of Idol worship and had turned from the ways of God. Look at both calendars."

I looked at the top left of each calendar. Both had a number 7 representing the 7th month of the Hebrew calendar, the month of Tishri. I can see that one represents 931 BC, and the other represents 722 BC. "Okay, I am looking at them. I see they represent the month of Tishri. Wait, I can also see that both of these times in these years corresponded with our month of September."

"Yes. Now look at the first day of the month, the Feast of Trumpets, the day I just finished telling you about. What do you see?"

I felt my heart beating within my chest, and the hairs began to stand up on my arms and the back of my neck as I saw what I saw. I looked at Messenger and said, "They corresponded with September 11th. The Feast of Trumpets for the years 931 BC and 722 BC, more than 200 years between them, both of these years significant within Israel's history corresponded with September 11th."

"Now you see what had been concealed throughout history has now been revealed for such a time as this. Do you think it is a coincidence that two significant years in the history of Israel pertaining to the division of the kingdoms and the kingdom of Israel going into Assyrian captivity, a time spaced between a little more than 200 years, would just so happen to have the Feast of Trumpets correspond with the day September 11th?"

"Not at all. There is no way this could be a random coincidence. Though what is the significance of September 11th for a time back in biblical times? Why is it important to be linked with the division of the kingdoms and the northern kingdom of Israel going into Assyrian captivity? Why or how is it linked with September 11th, 2001?"

Messenger grabs the two pages from me and places them back into his leather case as he says to me, "There you go with all of those questions again. To answer this for you, I will need to take you back to a time a little more than 2000 years ago. You will have questions, I am sure, as I share what I am about to share with you. Though I ask, should you have any questions, try to save them until after I share everything with you. I will show you the evidence of something that has been hidden or, should I say, concealed within the scriptures. I will show you evidence of discoveries that confirm, and I will show you a place in the scriptures that is read on a particular day that proclaims such news that you will be left asking again, 'Is this coincidence or mere chance?' As I share this mystery with you, by the end, what I share, will birth a revealing."

Explore this chapter's photos/calendars mentioned by scanning the QR code or visiting the link:

https://www.revealingthetimes.com/chapter13

# CHAPTER 14
# THE BIRTH

Messenger looked at me and said, "In order for me to show you the time when something very important occurred, such as the birth of Jesus, I will have to first show you what is concealed within the very scriptures that help us to pinpoint when Jesus was born."

"Okay." I had already thought in the moment, 'Where was Messenger going to go with this?' All I could do was listen and go to the places he wanted me to go in scripture. I would embark on the journey of discovery with him as he would share all that he knew. If I had questions, I would wait to ask them later, for the most part anyway. I looked at Messenger and said, "Would you like me to go to a certain place in the bible?"

"Yes, as a matter of fact, I would. Go to **Luke 1:5**. You may read it aloud to me when you are there."

**Luke 1:5** *"There was in the days of Herod, the king of Judea, a certain priest named Zacharias, of the division of Abijah. His wife was of the daughters of Aaron, and her name was Elizabeth."*

Messenger then says, "As you know, Zacharias and Elizabeth were the parents of the one you know as John the Baptist. The clue we have from what you just read is that scripture says that Zacharias was of the division of Abijah. Now go to **1 Chronicles 24:7-10**. Please read it aloud to me when you're there."

**1 Chronicles 24:7-10** *"Now the first lot fell to Jehoiarib, the second to Jedaiah, the third to Harim, the fourth to Seorim, the fifth to Malchijah, the sixth to Mijamin, the seventh to Hakkoz, the eighth to Abijah."*

Messenger then says, "Now there are 24 divisions of the priests, though I only wanted you to read until you could see what division

Abijah was of since Abijah is the one that we need to know. So, the scriptures say that Abijah was the eighth." Messenger then has me hand the bible to him as he begins to read **1 Chronicles 24:19** *'This was the schedule of their service for coming into the house of the Lord according to the ordinance by the hand of Aaron their father, as the Lord God of Israel had commanded him."*

Messenger then says, "Now, each of these priests from these 24 divisions would serve for one week when the time fell on their division. They would serve from sabbath to sabbath, one full week. Because there were 24 divisions, this meant that when the 24th division would finish their week of service, the following week would start with the first division again. This meant that the priests from each division would serve at two different times throughout the year, and all of them would serve during the three high holy days that required all males to be in Jerusalem. Those three high holy days were Passover, Pentecost and Tabernacles. To find which week the division of Abijah was starting, we must know when the first division would begin to serve their week."

"Okay, and so when would the first division begin their week of service?"

"The first division began during the first week of the first month known as the Month of Nisan. This is the Month Passover is on. The first division served from Sabbath to Sabbath for one week. Then, the second division served from Sabbath to Sabbath for one week, and so on. By doing the math from week to week, we can then discover that the division of Abijah fell on the week during Pentecost. Since Pentecost was one of the high holy days when all males were to be in Jerusalem, this meant the other priests were serving at this time also. Still though, the division of Abijah would have been during the week of Pentecost. This means that Zacharias, who was of the division of Abijah, was serving during the week of Pentecost."

"And why is it important to know when Zacharias was serving?"

"I am about to show you. As you know, while Zacharias was serving, while burning incense, the Angel Gabriel visited him, informing him that his wife Elizabeth would bear a son even in her old age, and he shall be called John. Gabriel tells Zacharias that their son John would be filled with the Holy Spirit, even from his mother's womb. Gabriel tells him that their son John will be in the spirit and power of Elijah. Go now to **Luke 1:23-25**. You may read it aloud to me when you are there."

**Luke 1:23-25** *"So it was, as soon as the days of his service were completed, that he departed to his own house. Now after those days his wife Elizabeth conceived; and she hid herself five months, saying, 'Thus the Lord has dealt with me, in the days when He looked on me, to take away my reproach among people.'"*

Messenger then says, "The week of Pentecost was in the month of June that year. Remember what I shared with you. Their division served from Sabbath to Sabbath for one week. When Zacharias returned home following the completion of his service, it was in those days when Elizabeth conceived. Elizabeth conceived in the month of June of that year."

"And what year was that?"

"I will tell you what year it was in a moment, though first let us look at what you had just read from the scriptures. The scriptures say that Elizabeth hid herself for five months. Now, what happens when Elizabeth is six months pregnant?"

"That was when the Angel Gabriel visited Mary."

"Exactly. Go to **Luke 1:26** and read that please."

**Luke 1:26** *"Now in the sixth month the angel Gabriel was sent by God to a city of Galilee named Nazareth."*

Messenger then says, "So this was the time the angel Gabriel visited Mary and gave her the news that she has found favor with God. Gabriel tells Mary that she will conceive in her womb and bring forth a Son. Gabriel tells Mary that His name shall be Jesus. Go to **Luke 1:32-33**. You can read that aloud to me as well."

**Luke 1:32-33** *"He will be great, and will be called the Son of the Highest; and the Lord God will give Him the throne of His father David. And He will reign over the house of Jacob forever, and of His kingdom there will be no end."*

"There is a reason I had you read that. As Gabriel tells Mary that she will conceive and bring forth a Son, whose name shall be Jesus, Gabriel then says what you had just read. They are linked as Gabriel shares this news with Mary. I will tell you more about this later. So, after Mary receives this news and accepts what the angel Gabriel has shared with her, she then goes to see her cousin Elizabeth in those days."

"And this was when Elizabeth was six months pregnant?"

"Yes. From what I have already shared with you, Elizabeth conceived in the month of June, she hid herself for five months, and this is now her sixth month. Do the math. What is six months from June?"

I began to do the math, then said, "December, it would be the month of December. So, Mary went to see her cousin Elizabeth in the month of December, when Elizabeth was six months pregnant. Wouldn't that time have been rough for Mary to go to her cousin Elizabeth's home during winter?"

Messenger then says, "Just because it was the month of December does not mean that the weather was terrible or that winter cold was fully reaching them at that time. Think about it, there have been December months where you have seen snow, there have also been December months where you have seen no snow, and the temperatures were not too bad either, isn't that right? I mean, even during the beginning parts of December are much like how the weather is during the time when you celebrate Thanksgiving at the end of November, isn't it?"

"Yes, you are right. I see your point."

"And the weather cycles you have here are much the same as they are there around Jerusalem. Now, how long did Mary stay with Elizabeth?"

I thought about it, then remembered as I looked at Messenger and said, "Mary stayed with Elizabeth for three months."

"That's right. And there were a couple of reasons for Mary to stay with Elizabeth during those three months. Can you think of why that may be?"

"Elizabeth was six months pregnant when Mary went to see her. Elizabeth would have been full-term three months later, ready to give birth."

"That is right." Said Messenger.

"And the other reason?"

"Because those following few months after December would for sure be the winter months and cold. You have seen the weather you get in January and February, right?"

"Yes, I have."

Messenger then says, "So do the math. Three months after December brings you to what month?"

"The month of March."

"That's right. John, who you know as John the Baptist, would have been born in the month of March. At this same time, Mary is three months pregnant. Mary would have only had six more months until she gave birth to Messiah, Jesus. What is six more months from March?"

I began counting six months from March, then said to Messenger, "It would be the month of September."

"That is exactly right." Said Messenger.

I began to think about something as I then said to Messenger, "Since there were only 24 divisions of priests, couldn't that mean that in Luke's Gospel, the division of Abijah was during the second period of time the division of Abijah was serving which by that calculation would bring Jesus to being born in the Month of late March or early April."

"You have done your math well." Said Messenger. "And you are right. It is possible that could be if we simply stop with the division of Abijah to give us the answer. We cannot only look at one piece. We must look at all the evidence. We must look at all of the pieces to see the right time. Then, once we have all the pieces, we can look back from there and see precisely which time of the year Zacharias was serving in the temple that Luke was referring to. We can then see that it was during his first service for that year. Some have believed Jesus to have been born during late March and early April. However, some who have stated this also state that Jesus was born around the year 5 or 6 BC."

"Wasn't He born around 5 or 6 BC though?"

"What would lead you to believe that?" Said Messenger.

"Because king Herod died in 4 BC and the scriptures say that king Herod ordered the killing of all male children 2 years old and under based on the time he calculated from when the Wise Men had first seen the star appearing in the East."

Messenger then said, "And why do you believe that king Herod died in the year 4 BC?"

"Because that is what my bible commentary says. That is what other Pastors and teachers have said."

"And where do you suppose those Pastors or teachers got that information?"

"From Pastors and teachers before them, perhaps even from their commentaries in their bibles they use for study."

Messenger then said, "Yes, but how do you suppose they were able to come up with saying that king Herod died in the year 4 BC?"

"I am not sure."

"Have you ever heard of the historian by the name of Josephus?"

"Yes actually, I have. His book is one of the resource books I use and even used while I went through my biblical studies in school."

"The book of Josephus is perhaps a resource for many Pastors, teachers and biblical scholars. Why do you suppose that is?"

"Because Josephus was a historian who lived during the first century, and Josephus even recorded things about king Herod."

"Precisely." Said Messenger. "Josephus records that king Herod died after a lunar eclipse and before Passover of that same year. It was the only eclipse that Josephus recorded in his book. This is how people who lived before the Pastors, preachers and teachers of today could discover the year that king Herod died. You see, there was a lunar eclipse that fell on March 13th, 4 BC. This would have been before Passover, so it aligns with what Josephus was writing, saying that king Herod died after a lunar eclipse and before Passover of that year."

"So, then it was 4 BC."

Messenger then says, "It would be 4 BC had that been the lunar eclipse Josephus was referring to. However, the lunar eclipse of March 13th, 4 BC is not the lunar eclipse that Josephus was recording. If only the people would continue reading the history that Josephus wrote following the year of the lunar eclipse that Josephus was referring to. That Passover, there was a rebellion, and about 3,000 Jews were killed. It was then later that spring, and during the early summer months, a particular war took place called the War of Varus. The War of Varus took place in the year 1 BC. The rebellion that took place during Passover that killed about 3,000 Jews took place in the year 1 BC. Though when people were able to see there was a lunar eclipse on March 13th, 4 BC and that it happened before Passover would begin, they simply went with the year 4 BC and did not consider the history that Josephus recorded following that."

"Was there a lunar eclipse that occurred in 1 BC then?"

"Yes, there was. One also must read what Josephus said happened two days before the lunar eclipse took place."

"What? What happened two days before the lunar eclipse?"

"There was a fast held by the Jews. Open your bible to **Zechariah 8:18-19** and please read aloud to me when you get there."

**Zechariah 8:18-19** *'Then the word of the Lord of hosts came to me, saying, 'Thus says the Lord of hosts: The fast of the fourth month, the fast of the fifth, the fast of the seventh, and the fast of the tenth, shall be joy and gladness and cheerful feasts for the house of Judah. Therefore love truth and peace.'''*

Messenger then says, "The other problem with the lunar eclipse that happened on March 13th, 4 BC, is that it was only a partial lunar eclipse and happened in the middle of the night, whereas the one that happened in the year 1 BC was a total lunar eclipse, it happened during the time of night where many would have observed it, and the total lunar eclipse of 1 BC could be seen over Jerusalem. Now let's see if the total lunar eclipse of 1 BC happened to occur two days after a fast held by the Jews." Messenger reaches into his leather case, pulls out a page, and hands it to me. It was a calendar from the year 1 BC.

As I looked at the calendar, I could see there was a total lunar eclipse that happened on a day that corresponds with January 10th on our calendar. I looked two days before that total lunar eclipse, and there was a fast held by the Jews. It was the fast of the 10th month. The fast of the 10th month was one of the fasts recorded in the book of Zechariah. I then looked to Messenger and said, "Okay, I see it, and I see the fast of the 10th month was held a couple of days before the lunar eclipse."

Messenger then says, "Now, we have the accurate lunar eclipse that Josephus had recorded. It was the total lunar eclipse of January 10th, 1 BC. King Herod would have died between that time and before that coming Passover. Then there was the rebellion that took place during that Passover of 1 BC, where about 3,000 Jews had been killed, and then we have the War of Varus that followed that same year in 1 BC. Now everything lines up. Remember, we must bring together all the pieces, not just a few. By bringing together all the pieces, we get the actual month and year of Messiah's birth."

"So, king Herod had ordered the killing of all males of 2 years and under by calculating the time the Wise Men had seen the star in the East. That would bring the year to be around 3 BC."

"Exactly right." Said Messenger. "King Herod ordered that they be 2 years old and under in an attempt to assure that Jesus would be killed among the other male children."

"So, was there a star in the east in the year 3 BC?"

"There was, though we need to know what was this star that the Wise Men saw. Was it some phenomenon, some miraculous star that would just float ahead of them, or could it have been what they knew in their day to be a star?"

"What do you mean, what they knew in their day to be a star?"

Messenger then says, "I guess what I should have said is what they called stars back in their day. They had the stars that we also call stars today, though they also had stars they called Wandering stars because these wandering stars moved."

"Do we have these wandering stars today?"

"You do. Today, you know them as planets, though back during the bible days, they were known as wandering stars because they were in the heavens, meaning space, and they moved."

"And these Wise Men would have seen it?"

"Yes. These Wise Men were known as the Magi. They were astrologers who studied the stars. It is possible that these Magi could have been from Persia as the Magi of Persia would have had a very important scroll that would give them a count down on the Messiah's arrival."

"What scroll is that?"

"The scroll of Daniel, the book of Daniel." Messenger then says, "Open your bible to **Daniel 5:11-12** and please read it aloud to me when you're there."

**Daniel 5:11-12** *"There is a man in your kingdom in whom is the Spirit of the Holy God. And in the days of your father, light and understanding and wisdom, like the wisdom of the gods, were found in him; and King Nebuchadnezzar your father—your father the king—made him chief of the magicians, astrologers, Chaldeans, and soothsayers. Inasmuch as an excellent spirit, knowledge, understanding, interpreting dreams, solving riddles, and explaining enigmas were found in this Daniel, whom the king named Belteshazzar, now let Daniel be called, and he will give the interpretation."*

Messenger then says, "Daniel was chief over the Magi, and Daniel was given the countdown to the arrival of Messiah. So, it is possible these Magi, when they saw the star in the east while having studied Astrology and Astronomy, could have recognized what this was. Now, I do not condone looking into Astrology. Astrology is wrong. I am not talking about Astrology but Astronomy. Astronomy is different. Astronomy is just the study and looking out at God's creation in the heavens. There is nothing wrong with Astronomy. Do you understand what I am saying?"

"Yes. I understand. So, what could this star in the east have been that the Magi were seeing?"

"I can tell you what it was, and you will ask me how I know. All I can tell you is what I have been telling you, and that is you have to have all the pieces."

"What does that mean?"

"It means I will share with you later the other piece that, by its dating, tells us what this star in the east was."

"So, what was it?"

Messenger then says, "It was a Planet, or as they would have called it back in their day, it was a Wandering star, which was to say that it was an object in the heavens, in space that moved."

"Which Planet was it? When did it appear in the east?"

Messenger then says, "On August 12th, 3 BC, the planets Jupiter and Venus rose with the sun in the east. As the Magi would have noticed and seen this, they would have studied and observed its movement."

"The movement of which one? Jupiter or Venus?"

"The movement of Jupiter."

"And why Jupiter?"

"Jupiter was the Wandering star they saw as the king."

"So, as they would have observed it, what did they see? Was there anything significant about August 12th, 3 BC? What day was that on the Hebrew Calendar in that year?"

Messenger then says, "What is interesting about August 12th, 3 BC is that August 12th, 3 BC was the visible Crescent New Moon of the 6th Month known as the Month of Elul. The Sabbath before the New Moon is called "Shabbat Mevarekhin," which means "Sabbath of Blessing." It is the last Sabbath before the New Moon. Shabbat Mevarekhin does not occur in Month 6 as the entire month anticipates the New Moon of Month 7, which we know as Rosh Hashanah or The Feast of Trumpets. In 3 BC, the Magi would have seen the Star Regulus, known as the "King Star," circling Jupiter at three different times from 3 BC into 2 BC, making a crowning effect. This doesn't mean that the moment they would have seen Jupiter Rising in the East with the Sun, they would have traveled right then and there. The Magi could have very well studied it for some time, and let's not forget as well that the Magi would have been under the authority of a kingship, so it is not like they could just leave at will whenever they wanted to. So, Jupiter and Venus Rise in the East with the Rising of the Sun on August 12th, 3 BC, precisely on the very day of the crescent moon of the month of Elul, and all of the Jews anticipating the New Moon of month 7. Then, on June 17th, 2 BC, Venus and Jupiter come so close together that they shine brightly, looking like one big bright star. The Magi, having seen Jupiter and Venus rising in the east on August 12th, 3 BC, to then seeing Jupiter and Venus looking as if they had merged on June 17th, 2 BC, looking like one single bright star would have got the Magi's attention for sure. As Jupiter began separating from Venus days and months later, the path of Jupiter was heading in the direction of Jerusalem and precisely at the moment when Jupiter would have appeared to have stopped was at the time of the Winter Solstice, which back in that day happened to be December 22nd into the 23rd which also happened to be Day one of the Feast of Dedication known as Hanukkah."

"You're saying that Jupiter would have appeared to have stopped."

"Yes." Messenger then says, "This is what happens when a planet goes retrograde. Its motion will appear to slow down, stop for a short while, and start up again."

"So, you're saying that Jupiter, which they called a star, or knew them to be wandering stars, happened to give the appearance of stopping on December 22nd into December 23rd of 2 BC."

"That's right." Said Messenger. "And it happened right as it was directly above Bethlehem. Go to **Matthew 2:9-11** and please read aloud to me when you are there."

**Matthew 2:9-11** *"When they heard the king, they departed; and behold, the star which they had seen in the East went before them, till it came and stood over where the young Child was. When they saw the star, they rejoiced with exceedingly great joy. And when they had come into the house, they saw the young Child with Mary His mother, and fell down and worshiped Him. And when they had opened their treasures, they presented gifts to Him: gold, frankincense, and myrrh."*

Messenger then said, "As you know, the Magi didn't arrive when Jesus was first born. They arrived when Jesus was a toddler. They arrived right as Jupiter, the wandering star to them, had stopped over Bethlehem during the first day of Hanukkah in the year 2 BC. It wasn't many weeks after that you had the total lunar eclipse of January 10th, 1 BC, and sometime between the lunar eclipse and before Passover of that year, king Herod had died. As you know, Joseph was warned in a dream to take the Child and Mary, flee into Egypt, and stay there until the angel of the Lord would bring him word. Would you please read **Matthew 2:14-15** aloud to me."

**Matthew 2:14-15** *"When he arose, he took the young Child and His mother by night and departed for Egypt, and was there until the death of Herod, that it might be fulfilled which was spoken by the Lord through the prophet, saying, 'Out of Egypt I called My Son.'"*

Messenger then said, "They didn't stay in Egypt very long."

I thought about what Messenger had said about the Magi being there when Jesus was a toddler, not when He was first born. I then said, "I always had the notion that the Magi were there when Jesus was a toddler and not when He was first born because when Jesus was first born, they were in a manger and Jesus was laid in a feeding trough, whereas when the Magi arrived, they were in a house and Jesus was a young Child, a toddler."

"Yes, that's right."

"The Shepherds were there at His birth though."

"That's right."

I started to think about the Shepherds keeping watch over their sheep by night. Then I said to Messenger, "I had heard before that Jesus was born around the time of Passover because that was the timeframe of when lambs were born, and this would have been why the Shepherds were keeping watch over their sheep by night because this was 'lambing season' and since Jesus is the Lamb of God, it would only make sense that He would be born during lambing season. Doesn't that make sense?"

Messenger then says, "It does make sense. However, as I have shared with you before, you need to have all the pieces to see the full picture. Remember, there are still a couple more pieces I have not shared yet. To answer your question about 'lambing season,' it is true that would be the time during the year when lambs would be born. However, what some do not know is there is also an out-of-season time when lambs would be born as well. There would also be breeding of lambs during the time around early spring and in the month of April. It only takes five months from the time of conception to the time of birth. Now, what is five months from the month of April?"

I began to count five months from the month of April, then said, "It is the month of September."

Messenger then said, "So there the shepherds were out in the fields keeping watch over their flock by night, as that too was a time lambs were born."

"You're not going to say that Jesus was born during the Feast of Tabernacles, are you?"

Messenger then says, "No, not at all. Jesus couldn't have been born during the Feast of Tabernacles because it was required that all males were to be in Jerusalem during the Feast of Tabernacles, and if Jesus had been born during the Feast of Tabernacles, that would mean that Joseph wouldn't have been able to go to Jerusalem during the Feast. The Feast of Tabernacles was one of the feasts where all males were to be present in Jerusalem. The other two were Pentecost and Passover."

"So, then His birth would have been before the Feast of Tabernacles?"

"Yes." Messenger then says, "Those who have said that Jesus may have been born around late March, or the first part of April before

Passover say that it would have had to be before Passover because all males would have had to be in Jerusalem for Passover. The same applies to the fall months. He would have had to be born before the Feast of Tabernacles because all males were to be in Jerusalem for the Feast of Tabernacles. As I have said, you need to have all the pieces to know which timeframe it is. I have given you the year Jesus was born. I have given you the month Jesus was born. Now, I will give you the other pieces that we need to affirm this."

"What are the other pieces?"

Messenger then says, "In Jerusalem, mosaic flooring has been uncovered showing the signs of the Zodiac. During that time, they were not looking at the signs of the Zodiac from an Astrology standpoint, but from an Astronomy standpoint, His creation among the stars. John was given a clue in the book of Revelation from an Astronomy standpoint when he has the vision of the woman clothed with the sun, with a crown of 12 stars above her head and the moon under her feet. This can be found in Revelation Chapter 12. Please read aloud to me **Revelation 12:1-2**."

**Revelation 12:1-2** *"Now a great sign appeared in heaven: a woman clothed with the sun, with the moon under her feet, and on her head a garland of twelve stars. Then being with child, she cried out in labor and in pain to give birth."*

Messenger then says, "We know that following these verses that it says the male Child was to rule all nations with a rod of iron, so we know this male Child John is referring to is Jesus Messiah. This was a picture of how the heavens looked at the time of His birth. Again, before I go into this, remember this is Astronomy. On September 3 BC, the sun was in the constellation Virgo. Virgo was clothed with the sun, and there were 12 stars above the constellation of Virgo's head, though for the moon to be under her feet, that could only happen during one specific day when the moon was a crescent moon. The moon was directly under her feet on September 11th, 3 BC."

I was amazed by what Messenger was sharing with me. Everything was in such order. All the pieces together. I looked at Messenger and said, "So since August 12th, 3 BC was the 1st of Elul, that would mean that Jesus was born on the 1st of Tishri, which would be the Feast of

Trumpets during that year. So, the Feast of Trumpets was September 11th, 3 BC?"

"Yes, that's right." Messenger then reaches into his leather case and pulls out a page he hands me. It was a picture of a clay tablet.

While looking at the picture, I asked Messenger, "What is this?"

"That is a picture of a clay tablet in the British Museum. It is the tablet of the Magi."

## The Magi's Tablet

"The Magi's Tablet?"

"Yes, this is a tablet that had been discovered and happened to be a tablet that belonged to Magi. The tablet dates the period of the 1st of Elul 3 BC and has also been dated to September 11th 3 BC."

This stunned me as I said, "The 1st of Elul 3 BC, which was August 12th, 3 BC, the star in the East."

"Yes, the Magi's tablet records this, and the reason for the dating on the tablet that corresponds to these dates is precisely to record what they had observed and when. They wrote it on clay so that it would last throughout the ages. I have already shared why those dates are important to note."

## The Kingdom Connection

Messenger paused for a moment as he said, "Now do you understand the importance of why the Feast of Trumpets fell on September 11th, 931 BC, and why the Feast of Trumpets fell on September 11th, 722 BC? Do you think it was just random chance, or is God telling us something even through the years when those things happened to the people of Israel?"

"I don't believe they are chance. I believe God is telling us something, though what is He saying there?"

Messenger then says, "The kingdom divided in the year 931 BC because Rehoboam would not lighten the yoke of his people, and in that year, the Feast of Trumpets fell on September 11th, 931 BC. In the future, their true King, the King of kings and Lord of lords, the Messiah, would be born on the Feast of Trumpets on September 11th, in the year 3 BC, and He has lightened the yoke." Messenger takes the bible from my hand as he begins to read **Matthew 11:28-30** *"Come to Me, all you who labor and are heavy laden, and I will give you rest. Take My yoke upon you and learn from Me, for I am gentle and lowly in heart, and you will find rest for your souls. For My yoke is easy and My burden is light."*

"I see what you are talking about there. Yes, I see the connection. What about with 722 BC when the northern kingdom of Israel went into Assyrian captivity?"

Messenger then says, "The northern kingdom of Israel with the 10 tribes of Israel going into Assyrian captivity in the year 722 BC, since that time, those 10 tribes are known as the 10 lost tribes of Israel, though they are not lost to God. In the year 722 BC, the Feast of Trumpets fell on September 11th, 722 BC. In the future, the very King of kings and Lord of lords, Jesus Messiah, who was born on the Feast of Trumpets on September 11th, 3 BC, will bring all the tribes back together, and they will no longer be divided but united because He has lightened the yoke and He is our true King." Messenger then said, "Read **Ezekiel 37:15-23** when you get a chance and you will see God is talking about bringing all of the tribes back from wherever they have been scattered among the nations and will bring them back into their own land where there will be one kingdom and one King over them, never to be divided again. This will be during the millennial kingdom. This is yet a future time."

"This is amazing. It is like evidence upon evidence through His word, layers upon layers. Things that have been concealed, though now revealed. Why now though?"

"Things which have been concealed are being revealed for such a time as this. There has been a falling away, though a true revival shall spark, many who have had doubts will come to believe that Jesus is the Son of God, and the Father sent Him, that He is coming again. Many who had been lost shall be saved by faith in Jesus Messiah."

"And you're saying for such a time as this?"

"Yes." Messenger then takes the page from me with the picture of the Magi's tablet and places it back into his leather case. He then pulls out a One Year Bible from his leather case, hands it to me, and says, "Turn to the day, September 11th."

I turn to September 11th in the One Year Bible and say, "I know about this. I don't believe this is chance or coincidence either."

Messenger then says, "I am not talking about Isaiah 9:10, that has been made known to many by one who has been chosen for such a time as this, and he has been doing well as the Lord has guided him."

"What are you talking about then?"

Messenger says, "Isaiah 9:10 was discussing the time when the Assyrians had attacked the people of Israel in the Northern kingdom. They had first attacked in the year 732 BC and then were taken away captive, which I have shared with you was in the year 722 BC. This is in the One Year Bible on September 11th. The year 722 BC had the Feast of Trumpets on September 11th, 722 BC. The Feast of Trumpets is the time of blowing the Shofar. The man who blew the shofar at the Statue of Liberty on the Feast of Trumpets on September 11th, 1999, two years to the day before the attack of September 11th, 2001, has seen a pattern from ancient times of how God would warn His people before Judgement. Now, there has been, and still is, that warning. The pattern is that of Israel and the attack from the ancient Assyrians. At the Statue of Liberty, her headdress bears the image of Semiramis, who was the Assyrian Queen. They both share the same headdress. That man has been guided by the Lord for such a time as this, to warn the people in hopes that they return to Him, a message of repentance, and he has been doing well."

"Yes, I agree. It is amazing all that is there. I too, don't believe that it is a coincidence that Isaiah 9:10 is read in the One Year Bible on September 11th, and the One Year Bible was written years before September 11th, 2001, happened. To see this pattern between them as has been shared by that man."

Messenger then says, "Yes, though where there is warning of coming Judgement, there is also a message of hope, and that message of hope happens to also be read on September 11th in the One Year Bible."

"Oh really, and what is that?"

Messenger looks at me and says, "What I have been sharing with you, remember what I told you to remember, what the angel Gabriel said to Mary, that there was a link to what he said to her right after he told her that she would bring forth a Son and call Him Jesus, that He will reign over the house of Jacob forever, of His kingdom there will be no end. I have said, He was born on September 11th, 3 BC."

"Yes, I remember all of this. I do not doubt you there."

Messenger then says, "I am not saying you have any doubt about what I have shared. I am showing you the message of hope that His word has also left all people to read in their One Year Bible on September 11th. Turn back one page in the One Year Bible and read what it says, for this too is read on September 11th."

I begin to read it silently to myself. I began to cry for the beauty of the message. It was overwhelming after hearing all of what Messenger had shared with me and then reading this. An overwhelming feeling of God's presence and His Son Jesus the Messiah, our redeemer, our coming King.

Messenger then says, "Please read it aloud to me."

I began to read aloud **Isaiah 9:6-7** *"For unto us a Child is born, unto us a Son is given; and the government will be upon His shoulder. And His name will be called Wonderful, Counselor, Mighty God, Everlasting Father, Prince of Peace. Of the increase of His government and peace there will be no end, upon the throne of David and over His kingdom, to order it and establish it with judgment and justice from that time forward, even forever. The zeal of the Lord of hosts will perform this."*

After I had read this, all I could say, while tears still filled my eyes, was…. "Amen."

Explore this chapter's photos/calendars mentioned by scanning the QR code or visiting the link:

https://www.revealingthetimes.com/chapter14

# CHAPTER 15
# THE BAPTISM

Messenger paused for a moment as he reached into the clay vessel to pull out a Scroll. He then said, "What treasures are these His Word, that He has left you with these Scriptures, written by man, inspired by God."

I looked at Messenger and said, "I know, I lose track of time when studying the Scriptures. His Word takes hold of me."

Messenger smiles, then says, "My friend, what I am about to share with you now, it is important that you pay close attention as I am going to take you to the places in the Gospels where Jesus turns over the tables of the money changers and I am going to show you something yet again, that has always been there, though people miss the connection. It is a clue, a mystery, though it will be revealed to you this day."

Messenger looked down at the Scroll. He closed his eyes, and his lips began to move, though I was unable to hear any words. I could tell that he was praying. I also took that moment to pray. I prayed for understanding, for eyes to see. He then opened his eyes and said, "It is fitting that we begin with prayer in this house. I want you beside me as I show you these next Scriptures as I want you to be able to follow along with me with your bible and see the words for yourself."

Messenger then says, "I am not going to read to you the entirety of the event that took place when Jesus turned over the tables. Instead, I am going to read to you the place where they questioned Jesus about where His authority came from, then Jesus' response, and then what they said after. I am first going to have you read **John 2:18-20**. You may read it aloud to me."

**John 2:18-20** *"So the Jews answered and said to Him, 'What sign do You show to us, since You do these things?' Jesus answered and said to* *them, 'Destroy this temple, and in three days I will raise it up.' Then the Jews said, 'It has taken forty-six years to build this temple, and will You raise it up in three days?'"*

Messenger then says, "The Jews demanded that Jesus show some sign that would indicate His authority for the actions that He had just taken in regulating the temple's activities. When Jesus answered by saying that He would destroy this temple and in three days He would raise it up, as you know, He was talking about His body, His death, burial and resurrection. Then, a key time stamp happened. Their response was that it had taken forty-six years to build the temple. They are talking about the time when king Herod refurbished the existing second temple. King Herod began refurbishing the temple in the year 20 BC. If we simply add 46 years from there, it brings us to the year 26 AD. Is there anything significant about the year 26 AD?"

"I am sure you are about to tell me," I said with a smile.

"Jesus, as you know had an earthly ministry lasting 3 ½ years. He was crucified in the Spring of Passover in the year 30 AD. Going back 3 ½ years from there brings you to the fall of 26 AD. So, my friend, I will give you something to write with and I want you to write this down."

Messenger hands me a piece of paper and a strange type of writing utensil, then says, "Write this down: Death, burial, resurrection and the fall of 26 AD."

"Okay, I wrote it down, but as you said, Jesus' death, burial and resurrection happened in the Spring during Passover in the year 30 AD. So why did I need to write the fall of 26 AD?"

"Patience, my friend, patience. I will show you momentarily. For now, I will read another Gospel passage to you where they question his authority the  day after He had cleansed the temple yet again following His Triumphal Entry, so this would have been during Passover week."

"Wait a minute, are you telling me that Jesus had cleansed the temple twice?"

"Yes, in the Gospel of John, John recorded the cleansing of the temple at the beginning of Jesus' ministry. The synoptic gospels record a temple cleansing at the end of Jesus' ministry during the final Passover week before Jesus' crucifixion. The contexts of the two temple cleansings differ and attempts to equate the two are unsuccessful. Two cleansings occurring are consistent with the context of Jesus' ministry, for the Jewish nation never recognized Jesus' authority as Messiah. Instead, they rejected His message and His person, making such repeated cleansing of the temple probable."

"So, if these are two different occasions, how can there be some clue or mystery hidden within the responses when Jesus' authority is questioned?"

"I will show you." Messenger then rolls up the Scroll of the Gospel of John and places it back in the clay jar. He then pulls out another Scroll and says, "Turn to **Matthew 21:23-27**. You can read it once you get there."

**Matthew 21:23-27** *'Now when He came into the temple, the chief priests and the elders of the people confronted Him as He was teaching, and said, 'By what authority are You doing these things? And who gave You this authority?' But Jesus answered and said to them, 'I also will ask you one thing, which if you tell Me, I likewise will tell you by what authority I do these things: The baptism of John—where was it from? From heaven or from men?' And they reasoned among themselves saying, 'If we say, 'From heaven,' He will say to us, 'Why then did you not believe him?' But if we say, 'From men,' we fear the multitude, for all count John as a prophet.' So they answered Jesus and said, 'We do not know.' And He said to them, 'Neither will I tell you by what authority I do these things.'''*

Messenger then says, "Now I want you to write this down: The baptism of John."

"Okay, I have it written down."

"So, you should have written there: Death, burial and resurrection 26 AD and the baptism of John."

"Yes, that is what I have here. This is what you wanted me to write down. I still don't understand how this connects."

Messenger then says, "When Jesus was baptized by John the Baptist, what was this a symbol of?"

"Oh, it symbolized His death, burial and resurrection."

"Yes, and John the Baptist did not want to do this as Jesus was and is the spotless Lamb without sin. John said, 'I need to be baptized by You, and are You coming to me?' Jesus said to John, 'Permit it to be so now, for thus it is fitting for us to fulfill all righteousness.' Though Jesus was and is without sin, as The Lamb of God, He came to die for us, to be our sin offering. John the Baptist was of the line of Aaron, meaning he came from a line of priests. The priest from the line of Aaron was to take the lamb as a sin offering to be sacrificed to make atonement for the people. Jesus being baptized by John symbolized atonement through His death, burial and resurrection."

Messenger paused a moment as he looked at me and said, "I now want you to write the word: Atonement."

"Okay, I wrote it down."

"Now my friend, you should have the words: Death, burial and resurrection, the year 26 AD, the baptism of John and Atonement."

"Yes, that's right."

Messenger then smiled almost in a way that said he would finally bring these words together. At least, that is how I took his smile to mean.

Messenger then says, "So the baptism of John, when John baptized Jesus would have happened in the fall of 26 AD, the baptism symbolized His death, burial and resurrection, His making atonement for us. Tell me, what high holy days are there in the fall?"

I answered Messenger by saying, "There are three: The Feast of Trumpets, The Day of Atonement and The Feast of Tabernacles."

"And what was the last word I had you write down?"

"Atonement, you had me write down the word Atonement." I then took a moment to think of all Messenger had me write down, then said, "So you are saying that Jesus was baptized in the fall of 26 AD on the day of Atonement as the baptism symbolized His death, burial and resurrection, His making Atonement for us?"

Messenger soon replied, "Well, I suppose you and others would simply need to take this on faith. What I have just shared with you are the responses. I had you write down those keywords, and I would invite you to think of this as well: Jesus was our Passover, and He died on Passover. Jesus was buried on unleavened bread, unleavened bread symbolizing His body without sin. He rose on the day of First Fruits. As Jesus fulfilled these High Holy days on the very day, do you think that it would be illogical for the day He is baptized by John the Baptist that symbolizes His making atonement for us to not be on the day of Atonement?"

I thought about it for a moment, what Messenger had just said to me, this did make sense. I then said, "No, I don't think it would be illogical for the day He is baptized by John the Baptist that symbolizes His making atonement for us to not be on the day of Atonement. Given the example you just gave, it makes sense."

Messenger then says, "I have more to share with you that will tell you for sure what day Jesus was baptized by John the Baptist. This too has always been concealed within the scriptures, though now shall be revealed for such a time as this."

I couldn't imagine what more Messenger was about to share with me, though as thorough as he was when he shared Jesus' Birth with me, I just knew Messenger would not disappoint in what he was about to show me.

Messenger then says, "As I have shared with you, as you know, Jesus was crucified on Passover in the year 30 AD. This corresponded on our calendar to the Month and Day of April 6th, 30 AD. From April 6th, 30 AD, if you go back 1,260 days, which we know is 3 ½ years, it brings you exactly to October 25th going into the 26th of 26 AD."

I then said, "Is there anything significant to that particular day of October 25th going into the 26th of the year 26 AD?"

Messenger then says, "Yes, though we have to look at the Gospel of Luke to find out why this particular day would be important. The answer has been there all this time, though we have read over it, not occurring to us the significance."

Messenger then pulls out from the clay vessel the scroll of Luke as he says to me, "Open your bible to **Luke 4:9-15**. You may read it when you are there."

**Luke 4:9-15** *"Then he brought Him to Jerusalem, set Him on the pinnacle of the temple, and said to Him, 'If You are the Son of God, throw Yourself down from here. For it is written: 'He shall give His angels charge over you, to keep you,' and, 'In their hands they shall bear you up, Lest you dash your foot against a stone.' And Jesus answered and said to him, 'It has been said, 'You shall not tempt the Lord your God.' Now when the devil had ended every temptation, he departed from Him until an opportune time. Then Jesus returned in the power of the Spirit to Galilee, and news of Him went out through all the surrounding region. And He taught in their synagogues, being glorified by all."*

I then said to Messenger, "So, the Gospel of Luke says that Jesus returned to Galilee following the 40 days and nights that He was tempted by the devil?"

Messenger then says, "Yes, the question I have for you is, where was Jesus during the last temptation?"

I began to look again at the scriptures I had just read, then said, "Luke shares with us that Jesus was in Jerusalem."

"That's right." Said Messenger. "Though do you know that the last two temptations are in a different order than what is written in the other Gospel accounts? Have you ever thought to ask the question why that is so?"

"No, I never thought about why they were in a different order."

Messenger says, "Luke was very detailed as he wrote what we call the Gospel of Luke. By him writing where Jesus was during the last temptation, we as the reader then have a starting point to look from."

"What do you mean a starting point?"

Messenger smiles as he says, "the walk Jesus would have had from Jerusalem to Galilee as Luke shares that Jesus was in Jerusalem when the devil had ended every temptation. Luke then shares that Jesus returned in the power of the Spirit to Galilee."

"Okay. I am still not following where you are going with this."

Messenger then says, "Jerusalem to Galilee is about 80 miles. Look up on your phone how long it would take a person to walk that distance. With a person walking about 3mph seven hours a day, to rest in the evening."

I began to look it up on my phone, and it gave me an answer. I then said, "The total amount of days is about 4 days of a walk from Jerusalem to Galilee."

Messenger still had this smile as if he knew what he was sharing with me was something revealing. He then says, "So again, going back 1,260 days from the crucifixion on April 6th, 30 AD brings us to October 25th, 26 AD, then go back another 4 days as that would be the amount of time to walk from Jerusalem to Galilee and that brings you to October 21st 26 AD. Then, from October 21st, 26 AD, go back another 40 days as Jesus was in the wilderness being tempted by the devil." Messenger then says, "Now turn your bible to **Mark 1:9-12** and read aloud to me when you get there, please."

**Mark 1:9-12** *"It came to pass in those days that Jesus came from Nazareth of Galilee, and was baptized by John in the Jordan. And immediately, coming up from the water, He saw the heavens parting and the Spirit descending upon Him like a dove. Then a voice came from heaven, 'You are My beloved Son, in whom I am well pleased.' Immediately the Spirit drove Him into the wilderness."*

Messenger then says, "We learn that following His Baptism, He is immediately driven by the Spirit into the wilderness. His baptism and going into the wilderness happened on the same day. With that being said, going back 40 days from October 21st, 26 AD brings us to September 11th, 26 AD, which happens to also be the Day of Atonement of that year."

Again, September 11th. I looked at Messenger and said, "You're telling me that the Day of Atonement in the year 26 AD was on September 11th of that year?"

"Yes. On the Hebrew calendar, in the 7th month known as the month of Tishrei, the Day of Atonement is on the 10th day of the 7th month, and the 10th day of the Hebrew calendar of that year corresponds to September 11th on your calendar." Messenger then says, "What have I shared with you about what the baptism represents and the significance of John the Baptist?"

"That the baptism itself represents death, burial and resurrection and John was of the house of Aaron. John was of the Priestly line, and it was the Priest who was to wash and prepare the Lamb for sacrifice."

"And how often did the priest go into the Holy of Holies?"

"Only once a year, the priest was to go into the Holy of Holies on the Day of Atonement."

Messenger soon after says to me, "And what do we know about the Tabernacle that was set up in the Wilderness? What was said about it as it was being made?"

"The Tabernacle was only a shadow of what was in Heaven."

"And what was in the Holy of Holies in the Tabernacle?"

"The Ark of the Covenant."

Messenger then says, "That's right, this is still a shadow of what is in Heaven." Messenger takes a moment, he then takes the bible from my hand as he says, "What does the Apostle John see as he writes in the book of Revelation?" Messenger then turns to the book of Revelation as he is about to read. He then says, "You read it." He then points to the place he wants me to read from.

**Revelation 11:19** *"Then the temple of God was opened in heaven, and the ark of His covenant was seen in His temple. And there were lightnings, noises, thunderings, an earthquake, and great hail."*

Messenger says, "And what does John the Baptist see that day he baptizes Jesus? He saw the heavens parting and the Spirit descending upon Jesus like a dove. It was from year to year that the Priest would go into the Holy of Holies only once a year on the Day of Atonement, this being the shadow. The day that John the Baptist, who is of the house of Aaron of the Priestly line, baptizes Jesus, the heavens open, not the shadow, the actual heavens open. Again, we know that Jesus is the same yesterday, today and forever. Jesus fulfilled Passover, Unleavened bread, Firstfruits and the Feast of Weeks to the very day. Again, would it be unthinkable that Jesus was baptized on the Day of Atonement?"

"No, it wouldn't be unthinkable at all. Everything you have shared here makes perfect sense, and you are right. The clues are there in the scriptures. What was concealed, as you said, is now being revealed for such a time as this."

Messenger then says, "Yes, for such a time as this. Let us look for a moment, going forward instead of backward, from the dates I shared with you. Jesus was baptized on the Day of Atonement in the year 26 AD on September 11th. He is then immediately driven by the Spirit into the Wilderness for 40 days to be tempted by the devil. 40 days from September 11th, 26 AD comes to October 21st, 26 AD. 40 days end on October 21st, 26 AD. Jesus walked from Jerusalem on October 21st, 26 AD, in the Power of the Spirit to Galilee. The walk from Jerusalem to Galilee would be 4 days. 4 days later, from October 21st, 26 AD, Jesus reached Galilee on October 25th, 26 AD. October 25th, 26 AD was a Sabbath, and Jesus taught in the synagogues on the Sabbath as was the custom. October 25th, 26 AD, being a Sabbath, Jesus taught in the synagogue. This would have been day one when Jesus began His Ministry. Then 1,260 days later, from October 25th, 26 AD, brings us to the exact day of His Crucifixion on April 6th, 30 AD."

I looked at Messenger and said, "This seems to be so, and as you said, Jesus' ministry was 3 ½ years, which on the biblical calendar would be 1,260 days, so going back 1,260 days from His crucifixion would bring you to October 25th going into October 26th. As you went backward, first having a starting point, which was the day of His crucifixion, you were then able to find out the rest. You then look at it from the starting point of His baptism to the time of His crucifixion, showing a concise order."

Messenger then says, "Yes, that's right. The first thing Luke mentioned as Jesus entered Galilee is that Jesus taught in the synagogues. The answer is that this discovery has been here in the Gospel of Luke for almost 2,000 years. It is just simple math of going back 1,260 days from the Crucifixion that brings us to day one that falls on a sabbath on October 25th, 26 AD."

"And to think as you shared earlier, that Jesus was born on the Feast of Trumpets on September 11th, 3 BC, and then was Baptized on the Day of Atonement on September 11th, 26 AD. Both were on September 11th. It is not like you are saying it was on September 11th for the sake of September 11th. You have shown thoroughly piece by piece that it was on September 11th."

Messenger hands the bible back to me as he says, "It is not to make the day of September 11th, 26 AD the amazing thing because of September 11th, 2001. It is much more than that. Of all the connections I have just shown you, it is not by coincidence or mere chance but even more evidence of God's presence and His guiding hand among us throughout history and even through the present time." Messenger then said, "And do you want to know what else is revealing of the day when Jesus was born and the actual day Jesus was baptized, being that it was September 11th? Do you know what that will also reveal?"

"What? What else will it reveal?"

Messenger says, "The workings of the principalities. The devil knows the scriptures. The devil knows what day John baptized Jesus because he knows that Jesus was brought into the wilderness that same day. We wrestle with principalities, principalities that we do not see. The devil and his fallen angels know what September 11th, 26 AD was, and they war on that day. Though just like what Joseph's brothers did when they sold him into slavery. Joseph could see the big picture as he was made second to Pharoah and saved his people and many others through a time of famine. Joseph told his brothers what man meant for evil, God meant for good. Though the enemy meant evil in what they did on September 11th, 2001, it brought those of us who are Watchmen to pay attention, to warn, and also lifted the veil of the unseen."

As Messenger brought up principalities and the devil, I began to think about the Antichrist. I wondered if the Antichrist could be alive at this moment, especially since I knew what Messenger had shared concerning the trumpets. It seems time could be drawing close to the moment Daniel spoke of in his book, the period known as the 70th week, the 7-year tribulation. I looked at Messenger and said, "Do you suppose the Antichrist could be alive and walking among us today?"

Messenger says, "It is interesting that you ask that question now."

"Why is that?"

"Because this is what I had planned to share with you next."

I sat there waiting to hear what Messenger would share on the topic. Somehow, I felt that whatever he was about to share would not be a coincidence as nothing he had shared so far could be left to random coincidence or mere chance. There was too much to be left to chance. I looked back at Messenger and said, "Go on then, share what you know concerning the Antichrist."

Explore this chapter's photos/calendars mentioned by scanning the QR code or visiting the link:

https://www.revealingthetimes.com/chapter15

# CHAPTER 16
# MANY ANTICHRISTS

Messenger reaches into the clay vessel and pulls out a scroll. He opens the scroll and says, "Open your Bible to **1 John 2:18-23**. You may read it aloud to me when you are there."

**1 John 2:18-23** *"Little children, it is the last hour; and as you have heard that the Antichrist is coming, even now many antichrists have come, by which we know that it is the last hour. They went out from us, but they were not of us; for if they had been of us, they would have continued with us; but they went out that they might be made manifest, that none of them were of us. But you have an anointing from the Holy One, and you know all things. I have not written to you because you do not know the truth, but because you know it, and that no lie is of the truth. Who is a liar but he who denies that Jesus is the Christ? He is antichrist who denies the Father and the Son. Whoever denies the Son does not have the Father either; he who acknowledges the Son has the Father also."*

Messenger then says, "In John's Day, even he referred to the time they lived in as the last hour. The last hour is between the time of Jesus' first coming and when Jesus comes again. Even though there has been about 2,000 years between these times, this whole period is still considered the last hour. In his day, there were many antichrists, to say the spirit of antichrist. If they did not believe in Jesus to be the Son of God, if they denied the Son as John says, they do not have the Father either. They are antichrist. If they acknowledge the Son, they have the Father also."

"So, many who did not believe during John's Day, many antichrists as we see from his writings?"

"Yes, that's right. There are also many antichrists in the present times in which you now live." Messenger took a moment to place the scroll back into the clay vessel as he pulled another scroll. As he began to open the scroll, he said, "There is one particular antichrist that I want us to look at though. This particular antichrist is the prefigure of the Antichrist. The Antichrist that John referred to in the scriptures you had just read, the part where John says, 'You have heard that the Antichrist is coming.' That Antichrist with the capital 'A' refers to the final Antichrist of the end times during the 7-year tribulation."

"There is an antichrist in the scriptures that foreshadows the Antichrist of the end times during the 7-year tribulation?"

"Yes, though in the scriptures, we do not see this antichrist mentioned by name. However, we know which antichrist is being referred to because we have the records of history that we can look back on as it shows us."

"So, which book in the bible do I need to go to?"

Messenger then says, "Open your bible to **Daniel 8:3-12**. You may read it aloud to me when you are there."

**Daniel 8:3-12** *"Then I lifted my eyes and saw, and there, standing beside the river, was a ram which had two horns, and the two horns were high; but one was higher than the other, and the higher one came up last. I saw the ram pushing westward, northward, and southward, so that no animal could withstand him; nor was there any that could deliver from his hand, but he did according to his will and became great. And as I was considering, suddenly a male goat came from the west, across the surface of the whole earth, without touching the ground; and the goat had a notable horn between his eyes. Then he came to the ram that had two horns, which I had seen standing beside the river, and ran at him with furious power. And I saw him confronting the ram; he was moved with rage against him, attacked the ram, and broke his two horns. There was no power in the ram to withstand him, but he cast him down to the ground and trampled him; and there was no one that could deliver the ram from his hand. Therefore the male goat grew very great; but when he became strong, the large horn was broken, and in place of it four notable ones came up toward the four winds of heaven. And out of one of them came a little horn which grew exceedingly great toward the south, toward the east, and toward the Glorious Land. And it grew up to the host of heaven; and it cast down some of the host and some of the stars to the ground, and trampled them. He even exalted himself as high as the Prince of the host; and by him the daily sacrifices were taken away, and the place of His* *sanctuary was cast down. Because of transgression, an army was given over to the horn to oppose the daily sacrifices; and he cast truth down to the ground. He did all this and prospered."*

I looked over the scripture I had just read, then said, "So how do we know this vision that Daniel had was history?"

Messenger then said, "Because the Angel Gabriel interprets the vision for Daniel. Keep in mind as well that this vision Daniel had was in the year 551 BC. Well over 200 years before the vision Daniel had would take place."

"How do you know that it was in the year 551 BC when Daniel had the vision?"

"Because the scriptures say that Daniel's vision took place during the third year of the reign of King Belshazzar. The third year of his reign was in the year 551 BC. I would now like you to read **Daniel 8:19-26**."

**Daniel 8:19-26** *"And he said, 'Look, I am making known to you what shall happen in the later time of the indignation; for at the appointed time the end shall be. The ram which you saw, having the two horns—they are the kings of Media and Persia. And the male goat is the kingdom of Greece. The large horn that is between its eyes is the first king. As for the broken horn and the four that stood up in its place, four kingdoms shall arise out of that nation, but not with its power. 'And in the latter time of their kingdom, when the transgressors have reached their fullness, a king shall arise, having fierce features, who understands sinister schemes. His power shall be mighty, but not by his own power; He shall destroy fearfully, and shall prosper and thrive; he shall destroy the mighty, and also the holy people. Through his cunning he shall cause deceit to prosper under his rule; and he shall exalt himself in his heart. He shall destroy many in their prosperity. He shall even rise against the Prince of princes; But he shall be broken without human means. 'And the vision of the evenings and mornings which was told is true; Therefore seal up the vision, for it refers to many days in the future.'"*

Messenger then says, "The male goat was the kingdom of Greece. The large horn was the first king, Alexander the Great. Alexander the Great was the one who conquered Medo-Persia. Alexander the Great had no children, therefore when he died in the year 323 BC at the age of 33, the kingdom split four ways, and each had a king. They were

Cassander, who was over Macedonia. Lysimachus was over Thrace and Asia Minor, Seleusus was over Syria and Babylonia, and Ptolemy was over Egypt and Arabia. The little horn emerged from those four horns and was a king named Antiochus Epiphanes. Antiochus Epiphanes was king over Syria from 175 BC to 164 BC. The little horn is also represented by the final Antichrist. The little horn represents Antiochus Epiphanes and the final Antichrist, though Antiochus is a prefigure. To say that Antiochus Epiphanes foreshadows the final Antichrist. Antiochus Epiphanes is a pattern of the Antichrist."

"What did Antiochus Epiphanes do?"

"He persecuted the Jewish people and caused the abomination of desolation by sacrificing a pig on the altar to Zeus, a false god."

"And you are saying that the final Antichrist would be the fulfillment of this prefigured one?"

"Yes, that's right. Turn to **Daniel 9:24-25** and read aloud to me once you are there."

**Daniel 9:24-25** *"Seventy weeks are determined for your people and for your holy city, to finish the transgression, to make an end of sins, to make reconciliation for iniquity, to bring in everlasting righteousness, to seal up vision and prophecy, and to anoint the Most Holy. 'Know therefore and understand, that from the going forth of the command to restore and build Jerusalem until Messiah the Prince, there shall be seven weeks and sixty-two weeks; The streets shall be built again, and the wall, even in troublesome times."*

Messenger then says, "What you just read was the countdown to Messiah's first coming. The seven weeks and sixty-two weeks is a total of sixty-nine weeks of years totaling 483 years to the first coming of Messiah. The decree of Artaxerxes to rebuild Jerusalem was in the year 445 BC. The countdown then brings us to the time of Jesus Messiah's first coming. You may now read **Daniel 9:26-27**."

**Daniel 9:26-27** *"And after the sixty-two weeks Messiah shall be cut off, but not for Himself; And the people of the prince who is to come shall destroy the city and the sanctuary. The end of it shall be with a flood, and till the end of the war desolations are determined. Then he shall confirm a covenant with many for one week; But in the middle of the week he shall* *bring an end to sacrifice and offering. And on the wing of abominations shall be one who makes desolate, even until the consummation, which is determined, is poured out on the desolate."*

Messenger then says, "When it says, 'Messiah shall be cut off,' this is talking about when Jesus was crucified, His death on the cross. Then it says, 'the people of the prince who is to come shall destroy the city and the sanctuary,' this is talking about when the city of Jerusalem and the temple were destroyed in 70 AD."

"The people of the prince? The 'prince' is the Antichrist, right?"

"Yes, that's right."

"So, does that mean that the Antichrist will be a Roman since the people who destroyed the city of Jerusalem and the temple in 70 AD were the Romans? It says, 'The people of the prince.' That would indicate that the Antichrist would be Roman, right?"

Messenger then says, "And what makes you think the people who destroyed the city of Jerusalem and the Temple in 70 AD were Romans?"

"Well, they were, weren't they?"

Messenger took a moment, then looked at me and said, "It was Rome that gave the order to destroy the City of Jerusalem and the temple in 70 AD. However, there was at that time what you call Roman Provinces, which were considered part of the Roman Republic. Syria was once part of the Roman Empire." 'Roman Syria was an early Roman Province annexed to the Roman Republic in 64 BC by Pompey in the Third Mithridatic War following the defeat of King of Armenia Tigranes the Great.'(RomanSyria-Wikipedia.https://en.wikipedia.org/wiki/Roman_Syria)

Messenger then says, "Interestingly enough, Pompey, after his conquest of Jerusalem in 63 BC, Pompey desecrated the Temple by daring to enter the Holy of Holies." 'Syrian province forces were directly engaged in the First Jewish-Roman War of 66-70AD.'(RomanSyria-Wikipedia.https://en.wikipedia.org/wiki/Roman_Syria)

Messenger continues to say, 'The people of the prince to come' is not referring to the Roman people, but to the Syrian people, the prince to come, this Antichrist would emerge from the Syrian people, the little horn out from the four horns. Antiochus Epiphanes, who was the king of Syria, the leader of Syria, the final Antichrist would be the fulfillment of this."

"So, you are saying that the final Antichrist will be of Syria?"

Messenger then says, "Let us finish looking at what this final Antichrist will do, shall we. The final Antichrist will confirm a covenant with many for one week, meaning for a total of seven years, though in the middle of that seven years, the Antichrist will bring an end to sacrifice and offering. Since the temple was destroyed in 70 AD, this means that a future temple is to be built and sacrifices will continue as they once did. This will happen at the start of the seven-year tribulation. Animal sacrifices will begin again, though in the middle of the seven-year period, the Antichrist will bring a stop to sacrifice and offering. Can you think of why the Antichrist will do this at the midpoint of the seven-year tribulation?"

"Because he is going to declare that he is God."

"That's right."

I took a moment to think about all of this and said, "How do we know for certain that this is something for the future with a final Antichrist?"

Messenger then says, "Open your bible to **Matthew 24:15-16** and please read aloud to me when you are there."

**Matthew 24:15-16** *'Therefore when you see the 'abomination of desolation,' spoken of by Daniel the prophet, standing in the holy place" (whoever reads, let him understand), "then let those who are in Judea flee to the mountains.''*

Messenger says, "The scripture you just read was Jesus talking, which means that this was referring to the future and final Antichrist, not the prefigured one of the past Antiochus Epiphanes. Remember, we are to look at all the different dynamics of the prefigured one to see the final Antichrist in the future. Though the book of Daniel would not be fully understood until the time is close to the end." Messenger took another moment as he continued to be in thought as he then said, "What is another way of saying the seven-year tribulation?"

"I am not sure."

Messenger then says, "You can find it in the book of Jeremiah." **Jeremiah 30:7** *"Alas! For that day is great, so that none is like it; And it is the time of Jacob's trouble, but he shall be saved out of it."*

I then said, "Oh yes, that's right, I remember that the seven-year tribulation was also called the time of 'Jacobs' trouble.'"

"And why do you suppose that is? Why is it called 'Jacobs' trouble?"

"I don't know."

Messenger then says, "Jacob had served seven years for Rachel and received Leah. Jacob then was given Rachel after he had fulfilled Leah's week and served another seven years. Because Jacob had served seven years and the tribulation is seven years, they call it Jacobs' trouble. Though there is another reason this was given to Jeremiah to say such a thing, it is meant to reveal another connection, something that had been concealed, to now being revealed."

"What is it? What is the other reason, the other connection?"

Messenger says, "Where was Jacobs' trouble? Where did he spend that time serving those seven years?"

"At his Uncle Laban's house."

"And where was his Uncle Laban's house?"

"I don't know."

Messenger then says, "Jacob's Uncle Laban's house was in Syria."

"Really? It was in Syria?"

"Yes, now do you see the connection? When he served seven years, Jacobs' trouble was linked with Syria. The time of the seven-year tribulation will be linked with one, the Antichrist from Syria." Messenger then says, "The final Antichrist, the lawless one, is also referred to as a 'beast' or the 'lion' of the North."

I thought about what Messenger has been sharing with me and said, "So if this final Antichrist is alive among us now, do you know who he is?"

Messenger then said, "One can see a pattern by looking back at Antiochus Epiphanes, though to know with 100 percent certainty as to who the Antichrist is, that won't happen until the Antichrist stands in the holy place where he ought not when he declares himself as God. That will be when he is fully revealed, when he shows his true colors."

"I thought the Antichrist would be revealed at the start of the seven-year tribulation?"

Messenger then says, "Think about how many peace treaties have been made with Israel since they have been a nation, since 1948. Were any of those peace treaties made by the final Antichrist? No, they weren't. Even when the final Antichrist confirms a covenant, many will not see the connection because the people have seen many peace treaties made. Again, the final Antichrist will be fully revealed when he shows his true colors as he stands in the holy place, declaring himself to be God. Open your bible to **2 Thessalonians 2:1-4**, and you can read it aloud to me when you are there."

**2 Thessalonians 2:1-4** *"Now, brethren, concerning the coming of our Lord Jesus Christ and our gathering together to Him, we ask you, not to be soon shaken in mind or troubled, either by spirit or by word or by letter, as if from us, as though the day of Christ had come. Let no one deceive you by any means; for that Day will not come unless the falling away comes first, and the man of sin is revealed, the son of perdition, who opposes and exalts himself above all that is called God or that is worshiped, so that he sits as God in the temple of God, showing himself that he is God."*

Messenger then says, "As you have just read, the man of sin is revealed when he sits as God in the temple of God, showing himself that he is God."

"So, there will be another temple?"

"Yes, there will be. As it is built and animal sacrifices continue, there will come a man who will sit in the temple of God, showing himself that he is God. This happens at the midpoint of the seven-year tribulation."

"And you're saying that there is no other way to discover who the final Antichrist is?"

Messenger then says, "Just because one may not fully know until that day comes, does not mean that we have not been given a pattern or clues to follow what had been concealed. Turn back to the book of Daniel and read **Daniel 11:33-35**."

**Daniel 11:33-35** *"And those of the people who understand shall instruct many; yet for many days they shall fall by sword and flame, by captivity and plundering. Now when they fall, they shall be aided with a little help; but many shall join with them by intrigue. And some of those of understanding shall fall, to refine them, purify them, and make them white, until the time of the end; because it is still for the appointed time."*

Messenger then says, "Next, I want you to read **Daniel 12:4-9** and read aloud to me please."

**Daniel 12:4-9** *"But you, Daniel, shut up the words, and seal the book until the time of the end; many shall run to and fro, and knowledge shall increase." Then I, Daniel, looked; and there stood two others, one on this riverbank and the other on that riverbank. And one said to the man clothed in linen, who was above the waters of the river, 'How long shall the fulfillment of these wonders be?' Then I heard the man clothed in linen who was above the waters of the river, when he held up his right hand and his left hand to heaven, and swore by Him who lives forever, that it shall be for a time, times, and half a time; and when the power of the holy people has been completely shattered, all these things shall be finished. Although I heard, I did not understand. Then I said, 'My lord, what shall be the end of these things?' And he said, 'Go your way, Daniel, for the words are closed up and sealed till the time of the end. Many shall be purified, made white, and refined, but the wicked shall do wickedly; and none of the wicked shall understand, but the wise shall understand."*

Messenger then says, "What you just read about the man in linen standing above the waters of the river, remember this is a vision that Daniel is having. He sees the man standing above the waters of the river. The two standing on the side of the riverbank, one on one side and the other on the other side of the riverbank, are the pre-incarnate Two Witnesses who will have a ministry for 1,260 days. When they finish giving their testimony, the Antichrist will kill them. The time, times and half a time is 3 ½ years, referring to the latter half of the seven-year tribulation. The holy people are to mean those who have been 'set apart.' That is what 'holy' means, to be 'set apart.' When the power of those who have been 'set apart' has been completely shattered, all these things will be finished. The mystery will be finished. So, what is this understanding that the book of Daniel is referring to? It refers to those who have searched and who are wise. Those who have been given understanding and will instruct many. They will see the pattern. They will see what had been concealed, and not because they are anyone special, for they could not find this on their own. The time has been set for a time of revealing. As John wrote the book of Revelation, he gives us another piece to look at to help aid in this understanding. Open your bible to **Revelation 13:18** and read aloud to me when you get there, please."

**Revelation 13:18** *"Here is wisdom. Let him who has understanding calculate the number of the beast, for it is the number of a man: His number is 666."*

Messenger then says, "Now read aloud the verse before it, verse 17."

**Revelation 13:17** *"And that no one may buy or sell except one who has the mark or the name of the beast, or the number of his name."*

Messenger looks at me and says, "Even though the Antichrist will not be fully revealed until the midpoint of the seven-year tribulation, John writes out a way for us to identify him, which wasn't John alone, it was the Lord who gave this to John and John wrote in Revelation what he both saw and heard. If those who have the understanding are not meant to know who the Antichrist is until the midpoint of the tribulation, then John would not have taken the time to write this specific part out. John tells us plainly what the number 666 is. John says that 666 is the number of a man's name. John says to calculate the man's name and then says the total will equal 666. Now, John was not saying if there are six letters to the first name, six letters to the middle name and six letters to the last name, it gives you a total of 666. That is not what John meant when he said to calculate it. John was a Jew, and in the Hebrew language, each Hebrew letter has a numerical value. You are to take the name of the person and have the name with each Hebrew letter and then calculate it. Then, add the values of each letter together to come up with the total. It is called Hebrew Gematria. If the person's name does not equal 666 through the Hebrew Gematria known by John, then you don't have to worry because that person is not the Antichrist. Though if the person I am about to show you has a name that equals 666 by the Hebrew Gematria, it is not to say that this person for sure is the Antichrist, because again, one will not fully know until the midpoint of the seven-year tribulation, however by knowing that his name in the Hebrew Gematria does equal 666 along with the other things that very closely connects him to the prefigured antichrist, that of Antiochus Epiphanes, this man is worth watching very closely to see what he does and to see what happens around him. After all, we are watchers, we are watchmen, and that is what we are to do, to be watchful."

I look to Messenger and ask, "So, will you tell me who this person is?"

"Yes. First, allow me to recap a few things. I will do it in a list form:

1. Antiochus Epiphanes prefigured the final Antichrist. Antiochus Epiphanes was the king of Syria.

2. The seven-year tribulation is referred to as Jacobs' trouble because Jacob served a period of seven years. Jacob was at his Uncle Laban's House, which was in Syria.

3. The lawless one, the final Antichrist, is also called the 'lion' from the North. North of Israel is Syria.

4. The lawless one, the final Antichrist, is also called the 'beast.'

5. The Antichrist will be a dictator. He will be a tyrant, though he will appear to be peaceful in the beginning when he confirms the covenant.

Now, are you ready for me to give you the list of the man who relates to each of these I have given you?"

"Yes please."

Messenger then begins to list out the rest as follows:

1. Bashar Al-Assad is the President of Syria. He is the leader and ruler of Syria.

2. Again, there is this link with Syria as that of Jacobs' trouble, the seven-year tribulation.

3. Bashar Al-Assad. The last name 'Assad' means 'lion.' He is in the north of Israel and has even been referred to as 'the lion' because of his name.

4. Bashar Al-Assad's grandfather had the last name 'Wahsh,' though he changed the last name to 'Assad.' The name 'Wahsh' means 'Beast.'

5. Bashar Al-Assad has been a dictator. He has been a tyrant, though he may very well appear to be peaceful to those around him and in the media.

Messenger then says, "Now let's see if his name calculates to 666 as 666 would be the total of the calculation of his name in the Hebrew Gematria as to what John was referring to when he said to calculate the number, the number is the total of his name. Hebrew alphanumeric ciphers were used in biblical times."

"So, my friend, do you see this Chart. I will go over with you letter by letter of the name Bashar Hafez Assad."

*(Note to reader: Chart on next page)*

"Okay."

Messenger then begins writing out each letter and its equivalent in Hebrew this way:

First Name: B=Bet; A=Aleph; SH=Shin; A=Aleph; R=Resh

Middle Name: H=Chket; A=Aleph; FE=PEH; Z=Zain

Last Name: A=Aleph; SS=Samech; A=Aleph; D=Dalet

| | | |
|---|---|---|
| B=Bet=2 | H=Chket=8 | A=Aleph=1 |
| A=Aleph=1 | A=Aleph=1 | SS=Samech=60 |
| SH=Shin=300 | FE=PEH=80 | A=Aleph=1 |
| A=Aleph=1 | Z=Zain=7 | D=Dalet=4 |
| R=Resh=200 | <u>Total: 96</u> | <u>Total: 66</u> |
| <u>Total: 504</u> | | 504+96+66=<u>666</u> |

Explore this chapter's photos/calendars mentioned by scanning the QR code or visiting the link:

https://www.revealingthetimes.com/chapter16

# CHAPTER 17
# THE GENERAL AND THE MAN

Present day, Jeremy is still sitting on the bench with David in the backyard of David's house overlooking the lake. Jeremy had just finished showing David the Hebrew chart Messenger had once shown him, showing the numerical value of each Hebrew letter for the full name of Bashar Hafez Assad and how his name equals 666.

David took the page in his hand, looking over it carefully with each letter and that number on the bottom right corner of the page, number 666. David then looks at Jeremy and says, "Everything you have shared with me, from the dreams to the birth of Jesus, His baptism, and now this. Everything is so precise. All of this is too much to be just a coincidence. Though you said that Messenger had told you that we still would not know with 100 percent certainty that Bashar is the Antichrist until the midpoint of the tribulation?"

"That's right."

"How could that be," said David. "We have all of this information, everything that connects him to the very pattern of what is talked about concerning Antiochus Epiphanes."

"Because David, right now, that is what it is. It is a pattern. The pattern could mean that he indeed is the Antichrist, or the pattern could just mean that the time of the end is drawing closer than we might think and we should be watching for Jesus Messiah's coming. We should be Watchman on a wall. Because Bashar's name does calculate to 666 through the Hebrew Gematria and because he has fit the pattern relating with the prefigured antichrist concerning Antiochus Epiphanes, Bashar is worth watching as Messenger had said."

David says, "So, are there more patterns between Antiochus Epiphanes and Bashar Hafez Assad?"

"There are."

"What are they?"

"Antiochus Epiphanes came into power because of the death of his brother Seleucus, who was to rule. Bashar Al-Assad also came into power because of the death of his brother who was to rule."

"Really? Again, another pattern."

"Yes, and there are a few more as well." Jeremy opens his Bible and reads **Daniel 11:23** *"And after the league is made with him he shall act deceitfully, for he shall come up and become strong with a small number of people."* Jeremy then reaches into his leather case and pulls out a picture as he hands it to David.

David could see that it was a picture of Bashar Al-Assad and a small number of people. "What is this a picture of?" asked David.

"That is a picture taken of Bashar Al-Assad and other Arab officials who visited Damascus on February 26th of this year, 2023, as they are highly considering bringing Bashar Al-Assad's Syria back into the Arab League since Syria's membership had been suspended since late 2011."

David then says, "The league made with him, he becomes strong with a small number of people. You are right. There is a pattern, even more so than one would expect."

Jeremy places the picture back into the leather case and says, "Yes, and even more than that. There is a man alive today with a last name the same last name as one of Antiochus Epiphanes Generals. I call this part, 'The General and the Man.'"

"Why do you call it 'The General and the Man?'"

"I will tell you in a moment." Jeremy then says, "It would be one thing if all they shared was the same last name. However, the reason this is not a coincidence is because of what I am about to share with you. After I share this with you, I will give you the name."

"Okay."

Jeremy then says, "As you know, in the book of Daniel, there is a part that goes over Nebuchadnezzar's first dream. The dream was of a man with a head of gold, the chest and arms of silver, the belly and thighs bronze, the legs were of Iron and the feet and toes were partly Iron and partly clay. Each of these represented an empire. The head of gold was the Babylonian Empire, the chest and arms of silver was the Medo-Persian Empire, the belly and thighs of bronze was the Greek Empire, the legs of Iron was the Roman Empire, and the feet and toes mixed with Iron and clay represents a revived Roman Empire. All of these empires are no more, except the revived Roman Empire represented by the feet with ten toes mixed with Iron and clay. This empire is still future. It will be the last empire prior to the second coming of Christ. The stone represents Christ at His second coming, bringing to nothing all of the previous empires. It would be an end to Gentile power. His second coming will establish His millennial kingdom, which will have no end."

David then says, "Yes, I know about this dream that Nebuchadnezzar had. I remember reading about it. What is your point though?"

Jeremy then says, "Empires are forged by war, wars are fought by soldiers, though Generals plan out the strategies. Therefore, I say to you, 'The General and the Man.' What we need to be looking at is the last empire to come before Christ's second coming, which is the feet with the ten toes of Iron mixed with clay. This will be known as a 'revived Roman empire.'"

"Okay, are you saying that this is soon to come?"

"I am saying that it is in the works, even as I am sitting here talking with you."

"How?"

"Remember, I just told you that Generals plan out strategies?"

"Yes, though how does this pattern relate with Antiochus Epiphanes?"

"Antiochus Epiphanes, as I have shared with you, is the prefigure of the future Antichrist. There was a General who was alive during the time of Antiochus Epiphanes, and this was one of Antiochus Epiphanes Generals. This General would have planned out strategies to advance

Antiochus Epiphanes in his kingdom, just like this one man who is alive today. Like a General, his strategies would be planned out to advance the Antichrist to a greater position of military might and power."

"So, who was Antiochus Epiphanes General?"

Jeremy looks at David and says, "His name was Ptolemy <u>Macron</u>."

David's eyes began to get bigger as he said, "Macron!? Really, Macron. That is the last name of the French President, Emmanuel <u>Macron</u>."

"Exactly."

David then says, "So you are saying there is a pattern because they share the same last name?"

"Not just because they share the same last name, it is because of what Emmanuel Macron has wanted to do. He has talked about bringing together a European Army and initially had discussed this coming out of surrounding nations."

"10 nations!? The 10 toes. A revived Roman empire."

Jeremy then says to David, "That is what this seems to be molding into. During the G7 in the summer of 2022, Emmanuel Macron suggested creating a revived Roman empire. Then Prime Minister Boris Johnson of Great Britain also thought this would be a good idea. Boris Johnson claimed that he had a vision based on the Roman 'Mare Nostrum,' which would be the Mediterranean Sea and the countries around it."

"What does 'Mare Nostrum' mean?"

"The phrase 'Mare Nostrum' means 'Our Sea,' which is about controlling the area and countries surrounding the Mediterranean Sea just as the Roman Empire did, hence a revived Roman Empire."

David then says, "And how are you saying that Antiochus Epiphanes General Ptolemy Macron and French President Emmanuel Macron relate in the pattern other than having the same last name?"

"As I have shared with you, the General plans the strategy for victory which forges empires. Just as Ptolemy Macron was the General for

Antiochus Epiphanes, Antiochus Epiphanes being the prefigure of the final Antichrist, so too is French President Emmanuel Macron planning a strategy for a victory which would forge what will be known as the revived Roman Empire and in the end, this will be of benefit to increase strength and power to the final Antichrist."

"Do you think French President Emmanuel Macron knows that is what he is doing? Do you think he knows his strategy will be strengthening the final Antichrist?"

"Whether President Emmanuel Macron knows this or not is unknown. However, what is known is that Emmanuel Macron was baptized a Catholic at his request at the age of 12, though he is now agnostic. To be agnostic means a person who holds the view that any ultimate reality, such as God, is unknown and possibly unknowable. Therefore, this would mean denying the Son, who is Jesus Messiah. We already know what John says about that. One who denies the Son is an antichrist. So once again, just like in John's Day, there were many antichrists, and so too in the times in which we now live. We are in the last of the last hour."

David then says, "Is there anywhere else in the scripture that connects this?"

"Absolutely. Remember the phrase 'Mare Nostrum' meaning 'Our Sea' about the revived Roman Empire and the Mediterranean Sea?"

"Yes, I remember you mentioning that just a bit ago."

"And you remember me telling you about the stone that will crush that final empire, the stone representing Christ's second coming?"

"Yes, I remember."

Jeremy then opens the Bible and begins to read **Daniel 11:40-45** *"At the time of the end the king of the South shall attack him; and the king of the North shall come against him like a whirlwind, with chariots, horsemen, and with many ships; and he shall enter the countries, overwhelm them, and pass through. He shall also enter the Glorious Land, and many countries shall be overthrown, but these shall escape from his hand: Edom, Moab, and the prominent people of Ammon. He shall stretch out his hand against the countries, and the land of Egypt shall not escape.*

*He shall have power over the treasures of gold and silver, and over the precious things of Egypt; also the Libyans and Ethiopians shall follow at his heels. But news from the east and the north shall trouble him; therefore he shall go out with great fury to destroy and annihilate many. And he shall plant the tents of his palace between the seas and the glorious holy mountain; yet he shall come to his end, and no one will help him."*

David then says, "So, the Antichrist will have many victories and consume some of those surrounding countries?"

"Yes, he will have absorbed what is to be the revived Roman Empire. The part that I shared with you, the phrase 'Mare Nostrum' which means 'Our Sea' at the end of the scripture I had just read to you, see where it says, 'he shall plant the tents of his palace between the seas and the glorious holy mountain.'"

"Yes, I see."

"The tents of his palace between the seas refers to the Mediterranean Sea and also perhaps the Dead Sea or Sea of Galilee, and the holy mountain refers to Jerusalem. Though no one will be able to help him (the Antichrist) at the second coming of Christ, the very stone which will shatter that revived Roman empire. This will occur during the last half of the seven-year tribulation. During the time known as a time, times, and half a time."

David then says, "So, what if Emmanuel Macron doesn't know this is what he is doing?"

"By him being agnostic, to not have Christ, he can be used by the ruler of this world, the ruler of this world is the Devil. He can be used whether he knows that he is or not."

"And if he doesn't know. What can we do about it?"

"We can pray. We can also hope that Emmanuel Macron comes to read this book and pair it with the Bible to search for himself. For as an agnostic to not know for sure whether there is a God or not, we can pray that by reading this book and pairing it with the Bible to search for himself what has been revealed, may he come to realize that all of this is not random coincidence or mere chance, that if he doesn't know, may he open his eyes and come to truly believe in Jesus as the Son of God, that the Father sent Him and be saved. That is our hope. For the Antichrist is not a lover of the things of God, but of fortresses, and what he is doing now is of the things of fortresses. The Antichrist will use those fortresses which will make up the revived Roman Empire, and the Antichrist will become powerful enough to finance wars. With this power, he will attack every stronghold. This will happen during that latter half of the seven-year tribulation."

David then says, "And what if President Emmanuel Macron does know exactly what he is doing and knows this will be for the final Antichrist?"

"All we can do is be Watchmen on a wall and report what we have seen and heard so that others may watch. In hopes that others may come to perceive with their eyes and to understand what they hear with their ears concerning our testimony and come to believe in Jesus, to know that He is the Son of God and that the Father has sent Him and that He is coming again."

David then says, "Back to Bashar Al-Assad, is there any other pattern linking him with the final Antichrist?"

"There is."

"What is it?"

Jeremy then begins to read **2 Thessalonians 2:9-10** *'The coming of the lawless one is according to the working of Satan, with all power, signs, and lying wonders, and with all unrighteous deception among those who perish, because they did not receive the love of the truth, that they might be saved."*

"Okay, I know about this part. What are you saying?"

Jeremy closes the Bible and lays it between them on the bench as he then says, "Remember what I told you that Messenger had said to me, that the Devil knows when Jesus was baptized because the Devil knows the scriptures and the Devil knows that Jesus came into the wilderness that very same day. The Devil knows that Jesus was baptized on September 11th, 26 AD, and the Devil knows that Jesus was born on the Feast of Trumpets on September 11th, 3 BC. The Devil and the unseen principalities war on that day."

"Okay, and what does this have to do with Bashar Al-Assad?"

"Bashar Al-Assad was born on September 11th, 1965. He is the Devil's very counterfeit version. The Anti-messiah."

David then says, "I thought we wouldn't know with 100 percent certainty whether he is the Antichrist until the midpoint of the seven-year tribulation when the Antichrist stands in the holy place declaring himself to be God."

"This is true. All we can do is be watchful. With all the things within the pattern that link him with Antiochus Epiphanes and the other things that have been shared with you, make him worth watching closely."

David then says, "What if it's not him and all the things which have been seen is bait from the Devil to spot those who are the Watchmen on the wall, to spot those who have the understanding."

"That could very well be possible too. To have a decoy in place so one doesn't see the snake, the serpent lurking closely behind for the attack, for the strike. Either way. No matter if he is meant to be a decoy set by the Devil or is to be the final Antichrist to be fully revealed at the midpoint of the seven-year tribulation when the Antichrist stands in the house of God declaring himself to be God, either way, it's for certain."

"What is that?"

"The Devil has shown his hand. We are watching and making known the workings of the Devil. Since this makes the Devil known, you must know that there is a God, and He has a Son whose name is Jesus, Yeshua Messiah, that Jesus is the Son of God and that the Father has sent Him. You see, by those who read this book and search through the scriptures for themselves, many will come to believe that all of this is not coincidence or chance, and many will come to believe that Jesus is truly the Son of God, that He was sent by the Father when many come to be saved. No matter how tricky the Devil may think that he is, through his lying wonders and signs, he has shown his hand and is losing. The Devil's problem is that he doesn't want to acknowledge he has already lost. He knows that his time is short. What he doesn't want is for people to repent, to turn to Jesus for salvation. We who are Watchmen on a wall need to pray and hope they repent and turn to Jesus and be saved."

David then says, "Amen to that brother." David then took a moment to stand up. He walked near the water and began to think about the two men that were standing on either side of the riverbank while the one dressed in linen was standing above the waters. He turns to Jeremy and says, "We have talked much about the Antichrist, though what about the two men, known as the Two Witnesses?"

"What about them?"

"Did Messenger tell you anything about the Two Witnesses?"

"He did."

"Will you share with me what he told you?"

Jeremy stands up and begins to walk toward David. Both of them now stand close to the water's edge as Jeremy says, "That was actually going to be what I was going to share with you next."

"The Two Witnesses?"

"Yes."

David then says with excitement in his voice, "Are the Two Witnesses Moses and Elijah, or how about Elijah and Enoch? I have always believed that the Two Witnesses are Moses and Elijah because of what Revelation 11 says that the Two Witnesses will be able to do. Did Messenger tell you who they are?"

"Messenger shared a lot with me concerning the Two Witnesses, though to start, I should first share the transfer of authority with you."

"The transfer of authority?"

"Yes. That was how Messenger first began to share with me concerning the Two Witnesses of Revelation 11. I will share with you as if I was back there again with Messenger as he shared this with me."

David nodded his head and said, "Okay, that will be just fine." David seemed to be puzzled though. He didn't understand what he meant by transfer of authority, though he would soon understand this mystery as it was about to be revealed.

Explore this chapter's photos/calendars
mentioned by scanning the QR code or
visiting the link:

https://www.revealingthetimes.com/chapter17

# CHAPTER 18
# THE TRANSFER OF AUTHORITY

As Messenger had finished sharing with me things that pertained to the Antichrist, I couldn't help but think of the Two on God's side, the Two Witnesses of Revelation 11. I looked at Messenger and said, "What about the Two Witnesses? They are Moses and Elijah, aren't they?"

Messenger looks back at me as he smiles and says, "You still want to know more?"

"Yes, absolutely."

Messenger then says, "What makes you think the Two Witnesses are Moses and Elijah?"

"Because of what Revelation 11 says about them. They will be able to turn the water to blood and cause it to not rain during the time of their testimony. Their testimony is for 1,260 days. Moses was able to turn the water to blood, and Elijah was able to cause it to not rain for a period of 3 ½ years. Since they can do the same thing, it would be safe to say the Two Witnesses are Moses and Elijah, right?"

Messenger then says, "Did Moses and Elijah always have that authority?"

"Well no, of course not."

"And who gave them that authority?"

"God did."

"That's right, and the authority had always belonged to God. Therefore, God can give that same authority to another, couldn't He?"

"Yes, I suppose He could."

Messenger then says, "Are there any other reasons you would think of the Two Witnesses of Revelation 11 as Moses and Elijah?"

"Yes, there are a couple of other different reasons."

"What are they? Share them with me."

I begin to think of the scripture in the book of Malachi. I open the Bible and begin to read **Malachi 4:4-5** *"Remember the Law of Moses, My servant, which I commanded him in Horeb for all Israel, with the statutes and judgments. Behold, I will send you Elijah the prophet before the coming of the great and dreadful day of the Lord."*

I then said, "See, the scripture here mentions Moses, and then the scripture even says that the Lord will send Elijah the prophet before the coming of the great and dreadful day of the Lord, which is referring to the time of the end. The scripture here mentions Moses and Elijah, so it would be them, wouldn't it?"

Messenger then looks at me and says, "What had we looked at earlier regarding John the Baptist? Remember the scriptures say that Gabriel had told Zacharias that John would go before Him in the spirit and power of Elijah?"

"Yes, I remember that. However, John wasn't Elijah, though he came in the spirit and power of Elijah. In the end times, it would be the actual Elijah, right?"

Messenger then takes the Bible from my hand as he turns back the pages and begins to read **Matthew 17:9-11** *"Now as they came down from the mountain, Jesus commanded them, saying, 'Tell the vision to no one until the Son of Man is risen from the dead.' And His disciples asked Him, saying, 'Why then do the scribes say that Elijah must come first?' Jesus answered and said to them, 'Indeed, Elijah is coming first and will restore all things. But I say to you that Elijah has come already, and they did not know him but did to him whatever they wished. Likewise, the Son of Man is also about to suffer at their hands.' Then the disciples understood that He spoke to them of John the Baptist."*

Messenger then says, "Do you see how Jesus referred to John the Baptist as Elijah?"

"Yes, I see that, though Jesus mentions the actual Elijah coming first before He begins talking about Elijah being John the Baptist."

Messenger then says, "Jesus did not say the actual Elijah. He simply said, Elijah. What I would challenge you to look at is that Jesus calls John the Baptist Elijah. Is it possible that Jesus could have referred to the future person calling him Elijah just as He called John the Baptist Elijah?"

"Okay, yes, I suppose that could be possible."

Messenger then asks, "What other reason do you think the Two Witnesses are Moses and Elijah?"

"It is found just a few verses before what you read. The Transfiguration. It was where Peter, James, and John saw Moses and Elijah appear talking with Jesus."

"Though what happens shortly after that? All they saw was Jesus. Why do you suppose that was?"

"Well, I have been told that Moses and Elijah represent the Law and the Prophets, and Jesus came to fulfill the Law and the Prophets."

Messenger then says, "Jesus did come to fulfill the Law and the Prophets, though there is another reason they no longer saw Moses and Elijah and only saw Jesus."

"What? What is the other reason?"

"One is not to focus on the person of Moses and Elijah, for Moses and Elijah could do nothing without the Lord. Jesus, who is God in the flesh, has the authority. It is about Him, not Moses and Elijah. People fixate on the person of Moses and Elijah when they read Revelation 11 because of what the Two Witnesses will be able to do. In the end, Jesus, who is God in the flesh, has the authority, and just as it was given to Moses and Elijah, it can also be given to two other individuals who will be living during the time of the tribulation." Messenger took a moment and said, "There is something else interesting about this. As you know, during the transfiguration, John was there and saw Moses and Elijah. They even name them by name, though this same John who wrote the book of Revelation, when he wrote about the Two Witnesses, John doesn't name them by name. He doesn't name them by name because the Two Witnesses he saw were not Moses and Elijah."

"So, you are saying that God, who has this authority, will give that authority to two individuals who will be living during the tribulation?"

Messenger then says, "Before I answer your question, I will need to take you to a few other places within the scripture. As you know, in Revelation 11, John calls the Two Witnesses the two olive trees. John does this for a reason. So that we, the reader, go back to the book of Zechariah." Messenger then turns back the pages and begins to read **Zechariah 4:11-14** *"Then I answered and said to him, 'What are these two olive trees—at the right of the lampstand and at its left?' And I further answered and said to him, 'What are these two olive branches that drip into the receptacles of the two gold pipes from which the golden oil drains?' Then he answered me and said, 'Do you not know what these are?' And I said, 'No, my lord.' So he said, 'These are the two anointed ones, who stand beside the Lord of the whole earth.'"*

Messenger then says, "The two olive trees represent the two offices, which are the kingly and priestly offices. The two olive branches are the two men from the kingly and priestly offices. Now, do you remember what I shared with you just a moment ago about Jesus being the one who has the authority?"

"Yes, I remember."

"Good." Messenger then turns through the scriptures and begins to read **John 15:4-5** *"Abide in Me, and I in you. As the branch cannot bear fruit of itself, unless it abides in the vine, neither can you, unless you abide in Me. I am the vine, you are the branches. He who abides in Me, and I in him, bears much fruit; for without Me you can do nothing."*

Messenger then says, "Jesus was saying this to His disciples, and the same can be applied to the church as well as to the Two Witnesses of Revelation 11. They are the branches and can do nothing without Him. Just as the two branches that drip into the receptacles of the two gold pipes from where the golden oil drains, so too the Two Witnesses who will stand beside the Lord of the whole earth must abide in Him, for they can do nothing without Him. Jesus has the authority and will give that authority to the Two Witnesses of Revelation 11."

"Okay, I understand what you are saying here."

"Very good. Since we have talked about this authority, let me now show you a mystery, something that has always been there in the scriptures and has been concealed until now. Though now is the time of revealing."

"What is it? What is this mystery?"

"It is the mystery surrounding the transfer of authority. Before Moses died, he was to lay hands on a man by the name of Joshua, the son of Nun. Moses did so, passing the authority given to him by the Lord onto Joshua. Moses was to look on from Mount Nebo across the Jordan River and into Jericho. Moses was to see all the land of the promised land, though he was not going to go over into that land. When Moses died, Joshua and the people crossed the Jordan River, and the waters parted. The waters parted at the Jordan River for Joshua and the people, just as the waters of the Red Sea had parted for Moses and the people. When Joshua and the people cross the Jordan River, they are now on the other side at Jericho. The authority that was once on Moses was now on Joshua. Do you see this transfer of authority from Moses to Joshua? The transfer of authority took place before crossing the Jordan River into Jericho. Do you see what I am showing you here?"

"Yes, I see what you're showing me."

Messenger then says, "So that was the transfer of authority from Moses onto another. Now let us look at the transfer of authority from Elijah onto Elisha, shall we." Messenger then begins to share with me as he says, "You can read about this in **2 Kings 2:1-15**. Though, what I will do is just highlight to you the main parts of this. Elijah was about to be taken by the Lord up into heaven by a whirlwind. At three different times, as Elijah was journeying, he had told Elisha to stay where he was and not to follow him, though Elisha said to Elijah each of the times, 'As the Lord lives, and as your soul lives, I will not leave you!" The first place they traveled to was from Gilgal to Bethel. The second place they traveled to was from Bethel to Jericho. Then, the third place they traveled was from Jericho to the Jordan River. When they reached the Jordan River, Elijah took his mantle, rolled it up, and struck the water. The waters parted as they crossed the Jordan River on dry ground. Once they reached the other side of the Jordan River, which was on the other side across from Jericho, Elijah asked Elisha, saying, 'Ask! What may I do for you, before I am taken away from you?' Elisha then asked for a double portion of Elijah's spirit to be upon him. This authority was not Elijah's to give but the Lord's alone. Therefore, Elijah's response was this, 'You have asked a hard thing. Nevertheless, if you see me when I am taken from you, it shall be so for you; but if not, it shall not be so.' Elisha did end up seeing Elijah taken up to heaven by a whirlwind. As Elijah went up, Elisha cried out saying, 'My father, my father, the chariot of Israel and its horsemen!' Elisha took the mantle that had fallen from Elijah as he went up. Elisha then stood by the riverbank of the Jordan. Elisha struck the water of the Jordan with the mantle of Elijah. Though Elisha said something very important at this point, Elisha said, 'Where is the Lord God of Elijah?' See, even Elisha knew that nothing could happen without the Lord God, as the authority had always belonged to the Lord God. The authority that the Lord God had placed on Elijah, the Lord God had now placed on Elisha. When Elisha struck the water, the waters of the Jordan divided before him just as they did for Elijah. Elisha crossed back over to the other side on dry ground towards Jericho. Now, there were people from Jericho there on the other side, watching Elisha cross the Jordan River just as Elijah had done. The people were known as the sons of the prophets from Jericho. When they saw Elisha cross the Jordan River, they said, 'The spirit of Elijah rests on Elisha.' Why did they say this? The answer is that they saw the water part before Elisha as he crossed on dry ground. The authority that was once on Elijah was now on Elisha. Now, each time Elijah had traveled where he did, as Elisha had followed him before Elijah was taken up in a whirlwind to heaven, what did Elijah say?"

I then said to Messenger, "Elijah had said to Elisha to stay where he was, that the Lord had sent him to each place where he was traveling to."

"That's right. And why do you suppose the Lord had sent Elijah to travel that route back to the other side of the Jordan River across from Jericho?"

"I am not sure."

Messenger then says, "To deliver a message to those of us who would be reading this now. The transfer of authority from Moses to Joshua and the transfer of authority from Elijah to Elisha happened in the same place. Could the Lord God have taken Elijah up in a whirlwind from anywhere, and the transfer of authority from Elijah onto Elisha happen somewhere else? Absolutely, though the Lord God chose the same place where the authority was transferred from Moses to Joshua for us to one day see that it is not about Moses and Elijah. It is about the authority of God that had been transferred from Moses and Elijah to two other men. The water parting and the crossing on dry ground showed evidence of that transfer of authority."

I looked at Messenger and said, "I had never noticed this before, but you are right. Why hadn't I seen this before?"

Messenger then said, "The words have been there all this time, though you and others read over those words and miss the message that had been concealed, though now has been revealed to you for such a time as this."

"Is there anywhere else that speaks of this mystery? Pointing to a transfer of authority?"

"Yes, there is. How did the people realize that the authority that had once been on Elijah was now on Elisha?"

"When they saw the waters parting, and Elisha had crossed on dry ground."

"That's right, and what are the two called in Revelation 11?"

"They are called or known as the Two Witnesses."

"Exactly right." Messenger then turns through the scriptures and begins to read **<u>Isaiah 43:2</u>** *'When you pass through the waters, I will be with you; And through the rivers, they shall not overflow you. When you walk through the fire, you shall not be burned, nor shall the flame scorch you.'*

Messenger then says, "Do you see from the scripture I just read to you where the Lord says, 'When you pass through the waters, I will be with you.'"

"Yes, I see that."

Messenger then says, "In this same chapter, the Lord also says, 'You are My witnesses.'" Messenger begins to read **Isaiah 43:8-12** *"Bring out the blind people who have eyes, and the deaf who have ears. Let all the nations be gathered together, and let the people be assembled. Who among them can declare this, and show us former things? Let them bring out their witnesses, that they may be justified; Or let them hear and say, 'It is truth.' 'You are My witnesses,' says the Lord, and My servant whom I have chosen, that you may know and believe Me, and understand that I am He. Before Me there was no God formed, nor shall there be after Me. I, even I, am the Lord, and besides Me there is no savior. I have declared and saved, I have proclaimed, and there was no foreign god among you; Therefore you are My witnesses,' says the Lord, 'that I am God.'"*

Messenger then says, "The Lord speaks through Isaiah to the people, the nations that have gathered together, those who had served false gods and worshiped Idols, the Lord tells those who have eyes and yet are blind, those who have ears and are deaf because they have served false gods and worshipped idols to bring out their witnesses to declare and show of the former things. However, they could not do it because the gods they served were false, and only the One True God can proclaim and declare the former things. Only the One True God can tell of things to come. The other set of witnesses mentioned are the ones where the Lord says, 'You are My witnesses.' His witnesses serve Him, the one true God, and because they are His, He shows them things. They proclaim, and they set in order because they are His witnesses. They proclaim that He alone is God, and there is no foreign god among them. Now, these witnesses of His were meant to be the people of Israel as they had witnessed His deliverance from Egypt, His providing for them in the wilderness. Yet, they began serving false gods and worshiping idols at that time long ago. And now, many of those who dwell in Jerusalem, the people of Israel, are meant to be witnesses as it was their ancestors who witnessed the many times of deliverance by God Himself, and it was their ancestors who had witnessed the things Jesus our Lord had done though they have rejected their savior. In the scriptures I have just read to you, the Lord says, 'Besides Me there is no savior.' And who is the

Savior? His name is Jesus our Lord. Jesus said He is in the Father and the Father is in Him. There is God the Father, the Son and the Holy Spirit. One God in three persons. In the scriptures I had just read to you, God also says about those He calls His witnesses, He says, 'My servant whom I have chosen, that you may know and believe Me, and understand that I am He. Before Me there was no God formed, nor shall there be after Me.' The Lord says they are His servants. Do you remember what I had shared with you earlier when Jesus spoke about Himself being the vine and spoke of the branches?"

"Yes, I remember when you shared that with me."

Messenger then says, "This is what Jesus had said after He gives the message that He is the vine, and you are the branches." Messenger then begins to read **John 15:14-17** *"You are My friends if you do whatever I command you. No longer do I call you servants, for a servant does not know what his master is doing; but I have called you friends, for all things that I heard from My Father I have made known to you. You did not choose Me, but I chose you and appointed you that you should go and bear fruit, and that your fruit should remain, that whatever you ask the Father in My name He may give you. These things I command you, that you love one another."*

Messenger then begins to read **John 16:12-15** *"I still have many things to say to you, but you cannot bear them now. However, when He, the Spirit of truth, has come, He will guide you into all truth; for He will not speak on His own authority, but whatever He hears He will speak; and He will tell you things to come. He will glorify Me, for He will take of what is Mine and declare it to you. All things that the Father has are Mine. Therefore I said that He will take of Mine and declare it to you."*

Messenger then says, "Jesus no longer calls them servants, but His friends and says that He has chosen them. The disciples of Jesus were witnesses in Jerusalem, in Judea and Samaria, and to the end of the earth. The disciples had to wait until they had been given the Holy Spirit. The Holy Spirit gave them authority, and by the Holy Spirit, they were able to give us the New Testament that we read today. Also, the Holy Spirit even now continues to guide us into all truth through His word. In the time of tribulation, many of the people of Israel who have yet to believe that Jesus is Lord, that He is Messiah, cannot be witnesses to Him because they have rejected Him. However, God will send them Two

Witnesses to speak and to give testimony. Those Two Witnesses are the ones spoken of in **Revelation 11**."

Messenger hands the Bible back to me. As he handed the Bible to me, I asked him, "Is there anywhere else in the bible you want me to look concerning this authority?"

"Yes, there is one other place. As we have talked about what the Two Witnesses of **Revelation 11** will be able to do, they will have the power to shut the heavens so that it does not rain during the days of their prophecy. They will have power over the waters to turn them to blood, and they will be able to strike the earth with all plagues. This is the authority they will have. Go to **2 Chronicles 7:14** and read this aloud to me once you are there, please."

**2 Chronicles 7:14** *"If My people who are called by My name will humble themselves, and pray and seek My face, and turn from their wicked ways, then I will hear from heaven, and will forgive their sin and heal their land."*

Messenger then says, "The scripture you have just read is well known and has been spoken many times, though read the very verse before it."

I then look and begin to read **2 Chronicles 7:13** *"When I shut up heaven and there is no rain, or command the locusts to devour the land, or send pestilence among My people."*

Messenger then says, "You see, God spoke this to king Solomon during the night after king Solomon had sent the people to their tents after the dedication of the temple. The very same things that God said in **2 Chronicles 7:13** are the very things the Two Witnesses in **Revelation 11** will be able to do because it is God who has that authority, and He gives that authority to them beginning at the start of when their 1,260 days will begin."

I began to think about what Messenger had shared with me earlier about the trumpets and about the Antichrist being alive among us. I then said to Messenger, "Since five of the trumpets have occurred and as you have shared, the Antichrist is alive among us. Would that mean the Two Witnesses of **Revelation 11** are also alive somewhere on this earth among us?"

"Yes, that would seem to be the case."

I then looked at Messenger and said, "Since they are not Moses and Elijah, who are they?"

Messenger then said, "It is not important on who they are but whose they are. They are His. Just as one is not to focus on the man, Moses or Elijah, one must not focus on the men who will be the Two Witnesses of **Revelation 11**. These two men would be able to do nothing without the Lord. The focus is to be on the Lord, always has been and always should be our focus, to be on Him. We should however heed their message when they begin their 1,260 days when they give their testimony, for it will be a message of repentance, to return, to turn the people back to their creator, to know that Jesus is the Son of God and that the Father has sent Him, that they may be saved."

I began to close the Bible on my lap. As I set it down between us on the bench, Messenger says, "Your question of who they are is the wrong question to ask, though I can tell you where they come from."

"Where they come from? What do you mean?"

Messenger then says, "I can tell you what house the Two Witnesses of **Revelation 11** come from. One of the Witnesses will be from one house, and the other Witness will be of another house."

"A house, like a home, where they live? Is that what you mean?"

"No, the house I speak of is the line, what line they are from." Messenger picks up the Bible and places it back on my lap, saying, "You will need this for me to show you the two houses of which I speak. As I said, though it is not I, the scriptures tell us, just as what I have shared with you before that had been concealed, there is now a revealing for such a time as this. Of the Two Witnesses, one will be of one house and the other Witness will be of another house, so let us look at the two houses, shall we."

Explore this chapter's photos/calendars mentioned by scanning the QR code or visiting the link:

https://www.revealingthetimes.com/chapter18

# CHAPTER 19
# THE TWO HOUSES

Messenger looked out at the river and said, "As you know, the Two Witnesses are mentioned in **Revelation 11**, and since I have been here with you, I have shared with you that five of the trumpets have happened. I ask you now, between what trumpets are the Two Witnesses mentioned?"

I opened the Bible and turned to the book of Revelation as I began to look. I then saw the answer to his question as I said, "The Two Witnesses are mentioned between trumpet six and trumpet seven."

"Very good." Said Messenger. "Now, just as we had looked in various places through scripture to bring the pieces together, so are we to do the same here. First, look again at **Revelation 11**, particularly **Revelation 11:4**. You may read it aloud to me when you are there."

**Revelation 11:4** *'These are the two olive trees and the two lampstands standing before the God of the earth.'*

Messenger then said, "We have already discussed how John had placed here in **Revelation 11** that the Two Witnesses, these two men are the two olive trees. We know that John did so for a purpose, so that we, the reader, would know to go back to the book of **Zechariah 4**, where Zechariah has the vision of the lampstand and the two olive trees. As I had shared with you before, the two olive trees represent the two offices of the kingly line and the priestly line. The two olive branches are the two men who hold those two offices. They are the two anointed ones who stand beside the Lord of the whole earth. During the days of Zechariah, the two men who held these two offices were Zerubbabel and Joshua. Zerubbabel was the governor who represented the kingly line, and Joshua was the priest who represented the priestly line. With two offices, each office comes from a certain house, a certain line. Therefore, concerning the Two Witnesses of **Revelation 11**, One witness will come from the kingly line, and One witness will come from the priestly line. Returning to what you have discovered from the book of Revelation, the Two Witnesses are mentioned between trumpet six and trumpet seven. Let us now read how trumpet six ends. You may read aloud **Revelation 9:20-21** when you get there."

**Revelation 9:20-21** *"But the rest of mankind, who were not killed by these plagues, did not repent of the works of their hands, that they should not worship demons, and idols of gold, silver, brass, stone, and wood, which can neither see nor hear nor walk. And they did not repent of their murders of their sorceries or their sexual immorality or their thefts."*

Messenger then says, "As trumpet six ends, is the very way of how a certain Psalm begins. Please read aloud **Psalm 115:1-13**. We will not read the whole Psalm, just those 13 verses as I want you to see how it starts, and the two houses that are mentioned."

I turn back the scriptures and begin to read **Psalm 115:1-13** *"Not unto us, O Lord, not unto us, but to Your name give glory, because of Your mercy, because of Your truth. Why should the Gentiles say, 'So where is their God?' But our God is in heaven; He does whatever He pleases. Their idols are silver and gold, the work of men's hands. They have mouths, but they do not speak; Eyes they have, but they do not see; They have ears, but they do not hear; Noses they have, but they do not smell; They have hands, but they do not handle; Feet they have, but they do not walk; Nor do they mutter through their throat. Those who make them are like them; So is everyone who trusts in them. O Israel, trust in the Lord; He is their help and their shield. O house of Aaron, trust in the Lord; He is their help and their shield. You who fear the Lord, trust in the Lord; He is their help and their shield. The Lord has been mindful of us; He will bless us; He will bless the house of Israel; He will bless the house of Aaron. He will bless those who fear the Lord, both small and great."*

Messenger then says, "Do you see where the scripture you just read mentions the silver, gold, things made with men's hands?"

"Yes, I see it."

"And do you see there is the mention of two houses? There is the mention of the house of Israel and the mention of the house of Aaron. One of the Witnesses will be of the house of Israel, and the other

Witness will be of the house of Aaron. The house of Israel represents the kingly line, and the house of Aaron represents the priestly line."

"What about the part that mentions 'those who fear the Lord, both small and great."

Messenger then says, "The place that mentions 'those who fear the Lord, both small and great.' That represents the church."

I then looked at Messenger and said, "How do we know the mention of these Idols, things of silver and gold, the work of men's hands to then mentioning the two houses are a way of God telling us the Two Witnesses will be from those two houses?"

Messenger looks back at me and says, "Do you remember the place that I had you read in the book of Isaiah, the place where God said He would be with them when they walk through the waters, and how that same chapter in the book of Isaiah mentions God saying through Isaiah 'You are My witnesses.' Do you remember this?"

"Yes, that was Isaiah 43."

"Exactly, and the next chapter mentions God saying through Isaiah, 'You are My witnesses.' Go to **Isaiah 44:7-8**, and you may read aloud to me when you are there."

**Isaiah 44:7-8** *"And who can proclaim as I do? Then let him declare it and set it in order for Me, since I appointed the ancient people. And the things that are coming and shall come, Let them show these to them. 'Do not fear, nor be afraid; Have I not told you from that time, and declared it? You are My witnesses. Is there a God besides Me? Indeed there is no other Rock; I know not one.'"*

Messenger then says, "Here again, God is telling the people who have worshiped false gods and idols to let them be their witnesses. Let them show these to them. Though again, since God is the one who can proclaim and declare it, to set things in order, those who are His witnesses He can guide them into all truth through the Holy Spirit by decerning the signs of the times and by what has been concealed in His word awaiting the times of revealing."

"Okay, I understand what you are saying here, though where is the mention of the idols? As you said, you can see it in the same area of this scripture?"

Messenger then points down to the very next three verses. "Read **Isaiah 44:9-11**."

**Isaiah 44:9-11** *"Those who make an image, all of them are useless, and their precious things shall not profit; They are their own witnesses; They neither see nor know, that they may be ashamed. Who would form a god or mold an image that profits him nothing? Surely all his companions would be ashamed; And the workmen, they are mere men. Let them all be gathered together, let them stand up; Yet they shall fear, they shall be ashamed together."*

Messenger then said, "So, do you see the connections there?"

"Yes, I can see the connections there, though couldn't others say you are just making that fit?"

Messenger then says, "I suppose they could. That is why we cannot just go with this connection to identify that the Two Witnesses do in fact come from the two houses of the house of Israel and the house of Aaron. Just like how I had shared with you the birth of Jesus and the baptism of Jesus, to do so, we need to have all of the pieces."

"So, you are saying there are more pieces that would link the Two Witnesses with the two houses? With the house of Israel and with the house of Aaron?"

"Yes, that's right. Though, as I have shared with you before, it is not I who am saying it. The message has always been concealed within the scriptures awaiting the time of revealing for such a time as this."

"What are the other pieces?"

Messenger then says, "There are several. Regarding Idol worship, under whose leadership did the people of Israel set up and worship the golden calf while in the wilderness?"

"That was Aaron, the brother of Moses. While Moses was up on Mount Sinai receiving the law from God, they were doing that below under Aaron's leadership."

"That's right, so that was one gold calf. Then, who was it that set up two gold calves for the people to worship? This was much later, during the times after the kingdom had divided."

"That was under the leadership of Jeroboam."

"That is exactly right. And what tribe was Jeroboam from?"

"I am not sure."

Messenger then says, "Jeroboam was of the tribe of Ephraim, and he was the first king of the northern kingdom of Israel after the kingdom had divided. The northern kingdom was also known as the house of Israel. So, I have just shared with you that there was idol worship under the leadership of Aaron in the wilderness, and this is the house of Aaron. Then, there is idol worship under the leadership of Jeroboam, who is of the tribe of Ephraim, and this is the house of Israel. Both had to do with golden calves."

"So, there are the two houses again. The house of Israel and the house of Aaron."

"Yes." Said Messenger. "As I have shared, the Two Witnesses of **Revelation 11** will be from two houses. One will be of the house of Israel, and the other will be of the house of Aaron. They will have nothing to do with worshiping a false god or idols. They will serve God and Him alone. And do you remember the vision of Zechariah in **Zechariah 4**, the vision of the two olive trees?"

"Yes, of course I remember."

Messenger then says, "Please read aloud to me **Hosea 14:4-9**."

**Hosea 14:4-9** *"I will heal their backsliding, I will love them freely, for My anger has turned away from him. I will be like the dew to Israel; He shall grow like the lily, and lengthen his roots like Lebanon. His branches shall spread; His beauty shall be like an olive tree, and his fragrance like Lebanon. Those who dwell under his shadow shall return; They shall be* *revived like grain, and grow like a vine. Their scent shall be like the wine of Lebanon. 'Ephraim shall say, 'What have I to do anymore with idols?' I have heard and observed him. I am like a green cypress tree; Your fruit is found in Me.' Who is wise? Let him understand these things. Who is prudent? Let him know them. For the ways of the Lord are right; The righteous walk in them, but transgressors stumble in them."*

Messenger then says, "Do you see how the scripture you just read talks about Ephraim where the Lord says through Hosea that his beauty shall be like an olive tree? Also saying, what will he have to do anymore with Idols? There will be one who comes from the house of Israel, from the line of Ephraim, who will be one of the witnesses of **Revelation 11**. At the time of return, he shall take words with him and offer the sacrifice of his lips, he shall give testimony and speak a message of repentance that will be accompanied with obedience, and it is in the Lord, the Lord who is his green cypress tree, it is in the Lord where he bears fruit, for he shall abide in Him."

"This is amazing. All of what you have said. It is all here in the scriptures. The message had been concealed, though as you have said, the revealing is now, for such a time as this."

Messenger then says, "Yes, and there is one other message concerning the two houses of which the Two Witnesses come from that had been concealed, though the time of revealing has come for such a time as this."

"What is it?"

"Following the death and resurrection of the Two Witnesses, what does John see as the temple of God was opened in heaven?"

"John saw the ark of His covenant."

"Exactly right. And do you remember what I had shared with you while I had talked with you concerning the time when Jesus had been baptized by John the Baptist?"

"That the ark of the covenant made in the wilderness was a shadow of that which is in heaven."

Messenger then says, "Yes, and what was placed in the ark of the covenant?"

"The rod that had budded, the manna and the two stone tablets."

Messenger then says, "And whose rod was that which had budded with the almonds?"

"It was the rod that had belonged to Aaron."

"That's right." Said Messenger. "And once again, we have to look for the concealed message contained within the ark of the covenant. The rod that had budded, which belonged to Aaron, represents the house of Aaron. The manna represents Jesus as Jesus Himself said that He is the true manna that comes down from heaven. The two tablets of stone represent the law that had been given to Moses. In order to see what this represents, we must look to another place in scripture. Open your Bible to **Jeremiah 31:31-34**, and you may read aloud to me when you are there."

**Jeremiah 31:31-34** *'Behold, the days are coming, says the Lord, when I will make a new covenant with the house of Israel and with the house of Judah—not according to the covenant that I made with their fathers in the day that I took them by the hand to lead them out of the land of Egypt, My covenant which they broke, though I was a husband to them, says the Lord. But this is the covenant that I will make with the house of Israel after those days, says the Lord: I will put My law in their minds, and write it on their hearts; and I will be their God, and they shall be My people. No more shall every man teach his neighbor, and every man his brother, saying, 'Know the Lord,' for they all shall know Me, from the least of them to the greatest of them, says the Lord. For I will forgive their iniquity, and their sin I will remember no more.'*

Messenger then says, "The tablets of stone represented the law, though a better covenant that the Lord has made is written in the scriptures you have just read. The reason there is mention of the house of Israel and the house of Judah is because the kingdom had been divided, as I have shared with you earlier. You could read what the Lord says through Jeremiah of the covenant He would make with the house of Israel. His law would be in their minds, and He would write it on their hearts. So, there we have in the ark of the covenant the rod of Aaron that budded, which represents the house of Aaron, the manna, which represents Jesus, and the tablets of stone for the law, which represents the house of Israel. Once again, there are the two houses. The house of

Aaron and the house of Israel. All three together represent something else as well."

"What is that?"

"All three represent Jesus. The rod that had budded belonged to Aaron. The rod is a lifeless piece of wood that once had life in it when it was attached to a tree, though once the rod is no longer attached to the tree, there is no life in it. The rod to bud with almonds was impossible, though nothing is impossible for God. Life came into what was dead only by the power of God, through Jesus. The manna, as I shared with you, represents Jesus and the tablets of stone were written by the finger of God. When the people came to test Jesus in **John chapter 8**, when they brought the woman caught in the act of adultery and said to Jesus that it was written in the law of Moses that such a woman shall be stoned to death, what do the scriptures in **John chapter 8** tell us that Jesus did?"

"Jesus stooped down to the ground and began writing with His finger."

Messenger then said, "That's right. After the people had said to Jesus that it was written in the law of Moses that such a woman shall be stoned to death, Jesus was then telling them without saying it, though by doing what He did at that moment as the law of Moses was written by the finger of God, when Jesus began writing with His finger He was saying without saying, 'I know, I am God, I am the one who wrote the law, I am the one who gave the law to Moses.' The new and better covenant is the one where the law would be on their minds and written on their hearts. This could not be accomplished without Jesus having died on the cross, who now lives forever. **Hebrews chapter 8** in the New Testament talks more about this. I would invite you to read that for yourself at some point."

"So, the rod and the tablets of stone represent the house of Aaron and the house of Israel, though all three also represent Jesus?"

"Yes. As I have shared with you before, Jesus said He is the vine, and you are the branches. The branches can bear no fruit without Him. They can do nothing without Him. It is all about Him. He has the authority. So, all that the Two Witnesses will have the power to do, they could do nothing without the Lord. Jesus is the tree of life. Every branch that is in Him has life and every branch that is not in Him withers and is cast into the fire. The new covenant is for the house of Israel, and those who accept Jesus as their Lord and Savior are grafted into the house of Israel into that olive tree. Remember what I shared with you from **Psalm 115**. There is the house of Israel, the house of Aaron and all who fear the Lord, both small and great. At the time of tribulation, you will have the Two Witnesses. One of the house of Israel, one of the house of Aaron and those who fear the Lord both small and great, which represents the church."

"Is there anything else?"

"Yes. There are just a couple of other things that I can share with you on this. Remember, in **Zechariah chapter 4**, Joshua was the high priest who represented the house of Aaron, Zerubbabel was the governor, and he was of the house of Judah. However, the other witness will be from the house of Israel and also represents the governor. You see, there is the kingly line of the house of Judah and the kingly line of the house of Israel. Remember what I just shared with you concerning the writing of the law on their heart. Here is what is said about the governor. Please read aloud to me **Jeremiah 30:21-22**."

**Jeremiah 30:21-22** *"Their nobles shall be from among them, and their governor shall come from their midst; Then I will cause him to draw near, and he shall approach Me; For who is this who pledged his heart to approach Me? Says the Lord. 'You shall be My people, and I will be your God.'"*

Messenger then says, "And the covenant that you had read concerning the house of Israel regarding that He will put His law on their minds and write it on their hearts. Right after that, the Lord says through Jeremiah, 'And I will be their God, and they shall be My people.' It's the same as what you had just read for me. Do you see?"

"Yes, I see. It all comes together."

Messenger then says, "Speaking of coming together. I should tell you why there is one of the house of Israel to be a witness who shall come from the line of Ephraim."

"Okay, why?"

"As I have shared with you, Zerubbabel is of the house of Judah. There is already one from the house of Judah, and He is the Witness of all Witnesses. The One of the house of Judah is Jesus our Lord. The reason there is to be one witness from the house of Israel is because the kingdoms are still at this time divided. And why did they divide? Do you remember?"

"Because the yoke was made heavy by Rehoboam."

"That's right. However, Jesus says that His yoke is light. Because Jesus has lightened the yoke, because He has removed the yoke from Ephraim's neck, no longer shall the kingdoms be divided. They shall be united once again. Please read aloud to me **Ezekiel 37:15-19**."

**Ezekiel 37:15-19** *"Again the word of the Lord came to me, saying, 'As for you, son of man, take a stick for yourself and write on it: 'For Judah and for the children of Israel, his companions.' Then take another stick and write on it, 'For Joseph, the stick of Ephraim, and for all the house of Israel, his companions.' Then join them one to another for yourself into one stick, and they will become one in your hand. And when the children of your people speak to you, saying, 'Will you not show us what you mean by these?'—say to them, 'Thus says the Lord God: 'Surely I will take the stick of Joseph, which is in the hand of Ephraim, and the tribes of Israel, his companions; and I will join them with it, with the stick of Judah, and make them one stick, and they will be one in My hand.'"*

Messenger then says, "It will be in that moment where there will no longer be two divided kingdoms, but one Kingdom and one King. The King is our Lord Jesus. Now read aloud **Ezekiel 37:23**."

**Ezekiel 37:23** *"They shall not defile themselves anymore with their idols, nor with their detestable things, nor with any of their transgressions; but I will deliver them from all their dwelling places in which they have sinned, and will cleanse them. Then they shall be My people, and I will be their God."*

Messenger then says, "Do you see the part you just read that says, 'And will cleanse them.'"

"Yes, I see it."

"This is also what Jesus says when He talks about Himself being the vine and you the branches." This is **John 15:3-4** *"You are already clean because of the word which I have spoken to you. Abide in Me, and I in you. As the branch cannot bear fruit of itself, unless it abides in the vine, neither can you, unless you abide in Me."*

I began to close the Bible as I said to Messenger, "So, everything you have shared with me makes sense, and you have shown the pieces to bring them together, though I have one question."

"What is that?"

"Why do the Two Witnesses have to be of the house of Aaron and the house of Israel?"

Messenger then says, "A matter is established by the testimony of two or three witnesses. The one from the house of Aaron represents the priestly line, and the one from the house of Israel from the line of Ephraim represents the kingly line. Their testimony will be of Jesus. That Jesus is the High priest, that Jesus is the Priest of all priests, and the kingdoms shall no longer be divided, for Jesus has lightened the yoke of His people, and Jesus is the rightful King. Jesus is King of kings. Though with one who has such a testimony, the testimony of the testator comes into being at their death, the matter is then established. Their resurrection happens right before the sounding of the seventh angel, and look at what the seventh angel proclaims."

I open my Bible and begin to read **Revelation 11:15** *'Then the seventh angel sounded: And there were loud voices in heaven, saying, 'The kingdoms of this world have become the kingdoms of our Lord and of His Christ, and He shall reign forever and ever!'"*

Messenger then says, "Do you see? The kingdoms are then united."

"So, when will the Two Witnesses begin giving their testimony? **Revelation 11** says they will prophecy 1,260 days, clothed in sackcloth."

Messenger has me close the Bible and place it on the bench between us as he pulls out some pages from his leather case. Messenger then says, "I happen to have here in my hand something I have already written out in the event you were to ask me this question." Messenger then hands me the pages as he says, "Please read this, and should you have any further questions, you can ask me after. Some things you will read I may have already mentioned to you, though it will be good for you to go over them again in order to remember what has been shared with you this day. There are other messages that have been concealed within the scriptures, though as I have shared with you, this is the time of revealing."

Looking at the pages in my hand, the top of the first page had a title underlined in dark bold letters that read, 'The Timeline of the Two Witnesses.' I began to read…

Explore this chapter's photos/calendars mentioned by scanning the QR code or visiting the link:

https://www.revealingthetimes.com/chapter19

# CHAPTER 20
# THE TIMELINE OF THE TWO WITNESSES

Before I share with you the timeline of when the Two Witnesses begin their 1,260 days, I want to share with you this: Knowing that Yeshua is the Word in the flesh and knowing that we can look back into the Old Testament and see particular scriptures in the Old Testament that point to Yeshua, for example, **Exodus Chapter 12** is where God tells Moses to take a lamb without blemish and to bring it into your house on the 10th day of the first month which is the month of Nisan. You are to have the lamb in your house for four days, and on the 14th day, you shall take the lamb outside of your gates and sacrifice the lamb at twilight. Twilight is 3 pm. God tells Moses that the people are to do this each year on the same day and at the same time.

The question is, why? Well, now that Yeshua had His first coming, we can answer the "Why." The answer is that the Passover lamb was always pointing to Yeshua, the Son of God who would come as a lamb without blemish to be without sin, that He would go into Jerusalem in the courts of the temple on the 10th day of the month of Nisan, that four days later on the 14th day He would be taken outside of the city gates to be Crucified, and at exactly twilight, at 3 pm He says "It is finished," and gives up the ghost. What was told to Moses on how to bring the lamb in, when to bring the lamb out, and when to sacrifice the lamb, Yeshua fulfilled to the month, day, and hour because it was always pointing to Him. What Moses and the people of Israel did with the Passover Lamb was a shadow of the Substance, the Substance being Yeshua Hamashiach, Jesus.

Sure, it may sound easy to explain the above as those who believe and have studied can easily understand that. Still, I assure you, for the people in Old Testament times, it was a mystery, not fully understanding what this lamb was pointing to for the future until John the Baptist says, "Behold the lamb of God." And even then, some did not yet understand.

Another example is **Psalm 22**, written by David. Psalm 22 starts off by saying, "My God, My God, why hast thou forsaken me." Psalm 22 also says, "They pierced my hands, they pierced my feet, they cast lots for my garments." We know that David died of old age and that David's hands and feet weren't pierced, so again, for the people of the Old Testament times who would have read this Psalm by David, it would have remained a mystery to them. However, a day would come when Our Lord is on the Cross and He says the words that start Psalm 22 "My God, My God, why hast Thou forsaken me." Any of the people who were there looking at Yeshua on the Cross and hearing Him say those words, provided they had studied the Old Testament scriptures, should have thought of Psalm 22 and realized that this same Psalm mentions "They pierced my hands, they pierced my feet, they cast lots for my garments," to then see right before them that this was prophetic, His hands are pierced, His feet are pierced, and look over there, they are casting lots for His garments. The problem though, for the people of that day, their eyes were darkened, meaning they didn't see or even think of the connection to the Psalm David wrote. Instead, they mocked Him and said that He was calling out for Elijah.

Again, we can talk about this, and we can easily understand and see the connection between Psalm 22 and Jesus on the Cross. No longer are those words a mystery of "They Pierced my hands, they pierced my feet, they cast lots for my garments," because we can read about this in the New Testament, in the Gospels of what happened while Jesus was on the Cross. We can now connect the two, and this ah-hah moment becomes easier to connect the two because Jesus being on the Cross with His hands and feet pierced has already happened.

It is interesting to note that many Pastors will say that the reason Jesus said, "My God, My God, why hast Thou forsaken Me," is because God the Father turned His back from Him, turned His face from Him. Many Pastors have given that reason in their attempt to explain it, though if the ones who hold to that reasoning would only read a little further into Psalm 22. You see, we know that God knows the end from the beginning and is all-knowing. God knew there would come a day in the future when some Pastors would tell the Church that God the Father turned His face from His Son. Since God knew some would say that He made sure the reader would know the truth, it is found in the very same Psalm where we read, "They pierced My hands and My feet." **Psalm 22:24** *"For He* *has not despised nor abhorred the affliction of the afflicted; Nor has He hidden His face from Him; But when He cried to Him, He heard."* Did you catch that? "Nor has He (God the Father) hidden His (God the Father) face from Him (the Son Jesus Christ)." Notice the "H" in "He," "His," and "Him" are all capitalized.

So, the question about the Two Witnesses is, (When do they begin their testimony? When does their 1,260 days begin?) If one understands that God is the same yesterday, today, and forever. If one comes to realize that Jesus, The Word in the Flesh, is the key by seeing how things foreshadowed Him and how He fulfilled certain High Holy Days to the month, day, and even hour, we can then come to understand the same foreshadowing and fulfillment that will also come with the timing and start of The Two Witnesses.

How can we find this out though? By reading and looking deeper into God's Word. So that is what I am going to share with you. I was paraphrasing in the previous Scriptures, such as **Exodus Chapter 12** and **Psalm 22**. For the ones I will share with you now, I will give you word for word so that you may see how they are connected. The first Scripture I will share is **Revelation 11:3-4** *"And I will give power to my two witnesses, and they will prophesy one thousand two hundred and sixty days, clothed in sackcloth. These are the two olive trees and the two lampstands standing before the God of the earth."*

God says the two witnesses are the two olive trees and the two lampstands. We have read about two olive trees somewhere else, haven't we? Of course we have. In the book of Zechariah, **Zechariah 4:11-14** *"Then I answered and said to him, 'What are these two olive trees--at the right of the lampstand and at its left? And I further answered and said to him, 'What are these two olive branches that drip into the receptacles of the two gold pipes from which the golden oil drains?' Then he answered me and said, 'Do you not know what these are?' And I said, 'No my lord.' So he said, 'These are the two anointed ones, who stand beside the Lord of the whole earth.'"*

We know that in the book of Zechariah, the two olive trees represented that of Zerubbabel and Joshua. Zerubbabel was governor and represented the "kingly" line, and Joshua was the High Priest representing the "priestly" line. Now, Zerubbabel and Joshua are not the Two Witnesses spoken of in Revelation Chapter 11. They merely are a foreshadow of being the two olive trees. Just as the Passover lamb foreshadowed the substance being Christ, so too the positions of Zerubbabel and Joshua, being the two olive trees in the book of Zechariah, foreshadow the substance being the Two Witnesses spoken of in Revelation Chapter 11.

So, the next question to ask then, if these "Two Olive Trees" spoken of in Zechariah represent Zerubbabel and Joshua and the "Two Olive Trees" are also a foreshadow of the Two Witnesses spoken of in Revelation 11, can we know when they will begin their testimony of 1,260 days? The answer is a big "Yes." How, you ask, by looking at the shadow, "Two Olive Trees" who have already been.... Zerubbabel and Joshua. We need to look at when Zerubbabel and Joshua came onto the scene. Now, Zerubbabel and Joshua came onto the scene during the time of laying the foundation of the temple in 536 BC. However, they are mentioned much more at a later time, and key dates are given at the moment the second temple is being built.

When the people were allowed to go back to Jerusalem after Cyrus issued the decree, the people began building the foundation in 536 BC. However, the construction was halted, and for several years, all that lay there was the foundation. There was no temple yet. It wasn't until the year 520 BC that the second temple started being built, and the building of the second temple was finished in 516 BC.

So, can we know when exactly the building of the second temple started and when the second temple was finished? The answer again is "Yes," and we can discover the exact month and day for both. How, you may ask? By looking at the scriptures.

**Haggai 1:1-5** *"In the second year of King Darius, in the sixth month, on the first day of the month, the word of the Lord came by Haggai the prophet to Zerubbabel the son of Shealtiel, governor of Judah, and to Joshua the son of Jehozadok, the high priest, saying, 'Thus speaks the Lord of hosts, saying: 'This people says, 'The time has not come, the time that the Lord's house should be built.' Then the word of the Lord came by Haggai the prophet, saying, 'Is it time for you yourselves to dwell in your paneled houses, and this temple to lie in ruins?' Now therefore, thus says the Lord of hosts: "Consider your ways!"*

Then we see the day they began building the second temple by reading **Haggai 1:14-15** *"So the Lord stirred up the spirit of Zerubbabel the son of Shealtiel, governor of Judah, and the spirit of Joshua the son of Jehozadok, the high priest, and the spirit of all the remnant of the people; and they came and worked on the house of the Lord of hosts, their God, on the twenty-fourth day of the sixth month, in the second year of King Darius."*

So now that we have the day the building of the second temple started, how about us finding out the day, month and year the second temple was finished.

**Ezra 6:15** *"Now the temple was finished on the third day of the month of Adar, which was in the sixth year of the reign of King Darius."*

The month of Adar is the 12th month.

The sixth month spoken of in Haggai is the month of Elul.

So, the starting of the building of the temple was the 24th day of the Month of Elul in 520 BC, which was the 2nd year of the reign of King Darius.

The temple was finished on the 3rd day in the Month of Adar in 516 BC, which was the 6th year of the reign of King Darius.

Elul 24, 520 BC, corresponds to September 21st, 520 BC.

The word of the Lord comes to Haggai the Prophet, to tell them to consider their ways and to build the temple for the first time on Elul 1, 520 BC, corresponding to August 29th, 520 BC.

Adar 3, 516 BC, corresponds to February 21st, 516 BC.

You discover that the time it took from the going forth on building the temple in 520 BC to the time the temple was finished in 516 BC was a total of 3 1/2 years. The two olive trees, Zerubbabel and Joshua, came on the scene at the start of its building, which took 3 1/2 years to build.

This foreshadows the timeline of when the Two Witnesses spoken of in Revelation Chapter 11 begin their 1,260 days where they give their testimony, which lasts for 3 1/2 years.

Just as Zerubbabel and Joshua began at the starting of the building of the second temple, the Two Witnesses of Revelation 11 will begin their 1,260-day testimony as the Third Temple begins to be built.

Since we know the Antichrist walks into the Holy of Holies, declaring himself to be God at the midpoint of the tribulation, we know that at the midpoint of the 7-year tribulation, the temple has been built. If we just calculate from the midpoint to the start of the seven-year tribulation, that gives us 1,260 days, which is the time of the two witnesses. Therefore, the Two Witnesses begin their testimony at the start of the seven-year tribulation. They give their testimony for the first 3 1/2 years as the third temple is being built. The Antichrist then kills them, and at this midpoint, the Antichrist goes into the built temple of the Holy of Holies, declaring himself to be God. For the remaining 42 months, the last 3 1/2 year period, the Antichrist brings on the Mark of the Beast, and his true colors show during those 42 months. During the first half of the seven years, he will act as a peacekeeper and will confirm the covenant, which will pave the way for the Third Temple to begin being built. The Antichrist then causes all sacrifices to stop at the midpoint, as it is written in the book of Daniel.

I hope you do well in reading this. Remember also, just as Zerubbabel and Joshua represent the kingly and priestly line, their positions and symbolizing Two Olive Trees foreshadow The Two Witnesses of Revelation 11, which will also represent the kingly and priestly line. One will represent the "kingly" line of the house of Israel, and the other will represent the "priestly" line of the house of Aaron. Since the Kingdoms have not been united and are still divided, one of the Witnesses who represents the "kingly" line of the house of Israel will be a descendant of Ephraim, the other Witness who represents the "priestly" line of the house of Aaron will be a descendant of Aaron. Jesus is of the Tribe of Judah and represents both King and Priest. Though the Coronation has not yet taken place. The very declaration doesn't happen until the seventh angel sounds, and the seventh angel doesn't sound until after the Two Witnesses are called up by God.

This is also what is meant by **Ezekiel 37:15-19** which is titled "One Kingdom, One King." It reads, *"Again the word of the Lord came to me, saying, 'As for you, son of man, take a stick for yourself and write on it: 'For Judah and for the children of Israel, his companions.' Then take* *another stick and write on it, 'For Joseph, the stick of Ephraim, and all the house of Israel, his companions.' Then join them one to another for yourself into one stick, and they will become one in your hand. And when the children of your people speak to you, saying, 'Will you not show us what you mean by these?' Say to them, thus says the Lord God: "Surely I will take the stick of Joseph, which is in the hand of Ephraim, and the tribes of Israel, his companions; and I will join them with it, with the stick of Judah, and make them one stick, and they will be one in My hand."*

I had finished reading the pages Messenger had handed me concerning the timeline of the Two Witnesses and could see what he was talking about. It made sense. All we can see from the Old Testament scriptures that foreshadowed Jesus' first coming could be applied the same way in the foreshadowing of the two olive trees from the past in the Old Testament to help us better understand the substance of the Two Witnesses of Revelation 11. I handed the pages back to Messenger and said, "This is all very interesting. So does this mean the two witnesses would begin their testimony on the 24th day of the 6th month on the Hebrew calendar?"

Messenger then says, "It doesn't mean the two witnesses of Revelation 11 will begin on the 24th day of the 6th month of the Hebrew calendar. Looking at the shadow would mean that the two witnesses will begin their 1,260 days at some point as the third temple begins to be built, and we do not know when that day would be."

"I thought about another connection concerning the two houses. The house of Aaron being of the line of Aaron and the house of Israel being of the line of Ephraim."

Messenger then says, "Go on."

"The two witnesses will be able to do the same things as Moses and Elijah. John the Baptist was in the power and spirit of Elijah. John the Baptist's mother Elizabeth was of the daughters of Aaron, meaning that John the Baptist was of the house of Aaron. Then, before Moses died, the authority that had been given to him by God was transferred to Joshua the son of Nun. Joshua was from the tribe of Ephraim, which represents the house of Israel."

Messenger then says, "Very good. Well done. You have seen well."

"I only thought of this because I had thought back to what you had shared about the time when Jesus was baptized by John the Baptist. I remember you saying that John the Baptist was of the house of Aaron. I then thought about how scripture had said that John the Baptist was in the spirit and power of Elijah. After you had shared with me that one of the witnesses would be of the house of Aaron, I couldn't help but think about Joshua the son of Nun and what tribe he was from. Once I had remembered that he was of the tribe of Ephraim and you saying that the other witness would be from the house of Israel of the line of Ephraim, I was just able at that point to make the connection."

Messenger smiles and says, "I am glad you have been paying attention."

I then stood up from the bench and began to pace back and forth while thinking about something else. Still, while pacing back and forth, I looked at Messenger and said, "Does this mean that the witness of the house of Aaron will be in the spirit and power of Elijah and the witness of the house of Israel will be in the spirit and power of Moses?"

Messenger then stands up and walks towards me as he places his hand on my shoulder, saying, "You are beginning to understand, though this is not by your power, but by His Spirit as the Spirit is guiding you into truth. As I have shared with you, the tablets of stone in the Ark of the Covenant represent the law. The law was given to Moses. The new covenant was made with the house of Israel to write the law on their hearts. So, to answer your question, the answer is yes, the one of the house of Israel will be in the spirit and power of Moses."

"And what about the rod that budded? I know that the rod belonged to Aaron and would represent the house of Aaron as you said, though how does this relate to Elijah?"

Messenger then says, "What happened to Elijah?"

"He was caught up into a whirlwind into heaven."

"That's right, it was a rapture. What did I tell you about the rod?"

"You said that it was dead, that it had no life in it."

Messenger then says, "Though it was dead, suddenly life happened, and it produced almonds. What was impossible was made possible by God. Elijah was raptured. In the future, at the time of the rapture, the dead in Christ will rise, and those who are alive and remain in Christ will be changed in a moment, in the twinkling of an eye. What was once dead, has life. What you see in the rod is a sudden change as it budded. So too, there will be a sudden change for those in Christ who are changed in a moment, in the twinkling of an eye. What would be impossible is made possible by God."

"So, when is the rapture?"

Messenger then looks at me and says, "Do you truly want to know my thoughts on this?"

"Yes, of course, that is why I had asked."

Messenger then says, "Truly, my thoughts are that too many become divisive over this subject. Does the rapture happen at pre-tribulation? Does the rapture happen at mid-tribulation? Does the rapture happen after the tribulation? Is there a rapture at all? These are the questions that are asked. And the answers others give on these questions have caused so much division, though there should not be division."

"I agree, there shouldn't be division within the church. What do you think though?"

Messenger says, "I can tell you that there truly will be a rapture. I can tell you that the rapture will not happen at the end of the tribulation because those who are in Christ are not appointed to God's wrath. Those who think there will not be a rapture say that because they say the word 'rapture' is not found in the Bible. The word 'rapture' isn't in the Bible. However, those who hold to the thought there is no rapture need to understand why there truly will be a rapture." Messenger walks back towards the bench and says, "Come, sit down beside me and open the bible to **1 Thessalonians 4:16-18** and read aloud to me when you are there."

**1 Thessalonians 4:16-18** *"For the Lord Himself will descend from heaven with a shout, with the voice of an archangel, and with the trumpet of God. And the dead in Christ will rise first. Then we who are alive and* *remain shall be caught up together with them in the clouds to meet the Lord in the air. And thus we shall always be with the Lord. Therefore comfort one another with these words."*

"The word 'caught up' in the Greek is the word 'harpazo,' which means 'caught up, to snatch away, to bring to oneself.' The Latin word for 'harpazo' is 'Rapturo,' where we get the word 'Rapture' from. So, when others say that the word 'rapture' is not there, it is there, just not in the way they would expect to see it." Messenger then says, "Now turn to **1 Corinthians 15:51-52** and read aloud to me please when you are there."

**1 Corinthians 15:51-52** *"Behold, I tell you a mystery: We shall not all sleep, but we shall all be changed—in a moment, in the twinkling of an eye, at the last trumpet. For the trumpet will sound, and the dead will be raised incorruptible, and we shall be changed."*

Messenger then says, "Paul speaks of this rapture as a mystery, something yet to be revealed, though the rapture remains to be truth. Paul says this will occur at the last trumpet. Now read aloud to me **Revelation 10:7**."

**Revelation 10:7** *"But in the days of the sounding of the seventh angel, when he is about to sound, the mystery of God would be finished, as He declared to His servants the prophets."*

Messenger then says, "So you see, Paul had spoken of the mystery which was the mystery concerning the rapture, and the place you have just read says that when the seventh angel is about to sound, the mystery of God would be finished. And what is this mystery?"

"The mystery of the rapture?" Asked Jeremy.

"Yes." Said Messenger.

"So, you have said the rapture will not be at the end of the tribulation because we who believe are not appointed to His wrath. That would leave either a pre-tribulation rapture or a mid-tribulation rapture. From what you have just shared with me, it sounds like you hold that the rapture will be at the mid-point of the seven-year tribulation. Is that what you think?"

Messenger then says, "I do lean more towards that it would be in the mid-point of the seven-year tribulation. Though, as I have shared with you before, it has been concealed within the scriptures."

"If the rapture happens during the mid-point of the seven-year tribulation, would that mean we would know the day and the hour? Scripture tells us that no one knows the day and the hour but the Father only."

Messenger then says, "Just because the rapture would be at the mid-point of the seven-year tribulation does not mean you know the day and hour. You still would not know the day and the hour. Only the Father knows. I am beginning to think that you believe the rapture of the church and the second coming of Christ are the same thing."

"Aren't they?"

Messenger then says, "No, they are two separate events. The rapture of the church is where those who are in Him go up to meet Him in the clouds. They are caught up to Him. The second coming of Christ is when He steps foot again on the Mount of Olives."

"Okay, I understand that now. Though there are many who hold to the rapture being before the seven-year tribulation starts."

Messenger then says, "I know that. And I know which scriptures they will use that make them think so. They use Revelation chapter 4. Go on and read aloud to me **Revelation 4:1**."

**Revelation 4:1** *"After these things I looked, and behold, a door standing open in heaven. And the first voice which I heard was like a trumpet speaking with me, saying, 'Come up here, and I will show you things which must take place after this.'"*

Messenger then says, "People who believe in a pre-trib rapture before the seven-year tribulation begins, they look at the scripture you had just read, and they say things like, 'The church is never mentioned again after this point, so this must be the rapture.' They will associate John going up with the time when the church also goes up, though John was the only one who went up in order that he be shown what would take place. What happened to John is no different than what happened to Paul. Please read aloud to me **2 Corinthians 12:1-4**."

**2 Corinthians 12:1-4** *"It is doubtless not profitable for me to boast. I will come to visions and revelations of the Lord: I know a man in Christ who fourteen years ago—whether in the body I do not know, or whether out of the body I do not know, God knows—such a one was caught up to the third heaven. And I know such a man—whether in the body or out of the body I do not know, God knows—how he was caught up into Paradise and heard inexpressible words, which it is not lawful for a man to utter."*

Messenger then says, "So you see. Paul too, was caught up in the third heaven, into Paradise, though whether in the body or out of the body, he didn't know. While there, he heard inexpressible words. While John was there, he was shown things that would happen. Paul also says that he would come to visions and revelations of the Lord. This makes Paul also a prophet, though one would not think of him as a prophet, yet the very things Paul wrote about concerning the rapture of the church is a future event, and he wrote that this will happen. He says it is a mystery and would happen at the sounding of the last trump. Revelation 4 is not the last trump. Revelation 10:7 says the mystery of God would be finished at about the sounding of the seventh angel as He declared to His servants the prophets. Paul was one of those servants and prophets who wrote about that very mystery. Now, do you see?"

"Yes, I see what you are saying here. I can see your point, though the church isn't mentioned anymore after Revelation 4, are they?"

Messenger then says, "They are, just not in the way you would think of them to be mentioned. Remember when I shared with you about the two houses, the house of Aaron and the house of Israel? Of the two witnesses of Revelation 11, one of the witnesses will be of the house of Israel, and one witness will be of the house of Aaron. In Psalm 115, I had shared with you before, after the mention of the house of Israel and the house of Aaron, there is the saying, 'those who fear the Lord both small and great.' When the scriptures say, 'those who fear the Lord both small and great,' that is the mention of the Church. Please now read aloud to me **Psalm 115:17-18**."

**Psalm 115:17-18** *"The dead do not praise the Lord, nor any who go down into silence. But we will bless the Lord from this time forth and forevermore. Praise the Lord!"*

Messenger says, "What you had just read, concealed within the message, is the very proclamation of a resurrection of the dead."

"How is that?"

"The scripture there says the dead do not praise the Lord, nor any who go down into silence. The scripture then says, 'We will bless the Lord from this time forth and forevermore,' that is saying that after the dead in Christ are raised to life, from that time forth and forevermore, we will bless the Lord. Forevermore is just what it means, 'forevermore.' And we know that from Paul, the dead in Christ rise first and those of us who are alive and remain that are in Christ, we will be changed in a moment, in the twinkling of an eye, and we will be caught up together with them in the clouds to meet the Lord in the air." Messenger then looks to me and says, "There are just a few more things I can share with you on this."

"Okay, I am all ears."

"As you know, we who are in Christ are not appointed to God's wrath. Others take that and then say that we will be raptured before the seven-year tribulation begins as we are not appointed to God's wrath. They are right when they say that we would be raptured before God's wrath. However, God's wrath happens during the latter half of the seven-year tribulation, the last 3 ½ year period. So even with the rapture occurring at the mid-point of the seven-year tribulation, the same is true, we are being raptured before God's wrath is poured out. God's wrath happens during the seven bowl judgments and during the final 3 ½ years of the seven-year tribulation."

"Yes, I remember reading about the seven bowl Judgements. You are right about that. I had never considered that God's wrath happens during the latter half. I had always assumed the whole seven years from start to finish was God's wrath."

Messenger then says, "Please read aloud to me **Daniel 12:1**."

**Daniel 12:1** *"At that time Michael shall stand up, the great prince who stands watch over the sons of your people; And there shall be a time of trouble, such as never was since there was a nation, even to that time. And* *at that time your people shall be delivered, every one who is found written in the book."*

Messenger then says, "The time of trouble, such as never was since there was a nation, refers to the latter half of the seven-year tribulation. It then goes on to say that at that time, meaning that as that time is about to start, your people shall be delivered, and the scriptures you have just read say 'everyone who is found written in the book.' When you read further in Daniel 12, the man clothed in linen who stands above the waters is asked, 'How long shall the fulfillment of these wonders be?' The man clothed in linen answers, saying, 'It shall be for a time, times, and half a time.' There, we have the total time being 3 ½ years."

"The book of Daniel even refers to the rapture, in what you just had shared with me, what you just had me read. I had never thought about the timing it was giving either, though what you said makes sense, that it would be at the midpoint, during mid-trib."

Messenger then says, "There is one final piece I will share with you that many have never considered before, though once I have shared this with you, this will make sense to you as well."

"Okay, what is that?"

"As I have shown and shared with you, the two witnesses begin their testimony during the first half of the seven-year tribulation as the third temple begins to be built. The two witnesses are then killed at the midpoint of the seven-year tribulation. After the 3 ½ days, when a voice from heaven says, 'Come up here,' those who see it and recognize what had just happened, the scripture says the people were afraid and gave glory to the God of heaven. Now I will ask you, suppose any decent size Church you ever go to, if you ask those in attendance, 'by a show of hands, how many of you have ever been to Jerusalem?' You are bound to see some hands go up. It is no secret that Christians from all over the world tour Jerusalem year after year. Many go on tours with their church."

"Okay, yes this is true."

Messenger says, "And did you know that right there in Jerusalem, there is a cemetery called 'Protestant cemetery.' There are many

Christians who have passed away and paid a lot of money to have their bodies shipped to Jerusalem to be buried in 'Protestant cemetery.' Though a believer in Christ has died, we know from scripture that such a one is absent from the body and present with the Lord. When the Lord comes on the clouds, the dead in Christ will rise first. Their bodies will go up from the graves to be joined with their spirit with the Lord in the air as they will be given glorified bodies. Those of us who are alive and remain in the Lord will be changed in a moment in the twinkling of an eye as we too, will go up to meet the Lord in the air."

"Okay, yes, you have shared this with me before. What is your point?"

"My point is, believers in Christ travel to Jerusalem year after year, and there is even a Christian cemetery there in Jerusalem, which means when the rapture happens, when the dead in Christ go up first, those who are in Jerusalem will see it, they will witness it as they have bodies of believers in Christ buried right there in Jerusalem."

"Yes, that's right. Though, I still do not understand your point."

Messenger then says, "After the two witnesses are killed, the two witnesses are truly dead in Christ. When they rise, the scriptures say that the people feared and gave glory to the God of heaven. This is the first time they see it. If the rapture happens before the seven-year tribulation begins, that would mean those who are in Jerusalem at the time when the two witnesses go up would have seen the rapture 3 ½ years before that with the church. I have already shared with you that Christians tour there in Jerusalem year after year, and there are dead in Christ buried there in Jerusalem as well. Though, they don't see the rapture happen 3 ½ years before that because it doesn't happen 3 ½ years before that. The people fear and give glory to God because this is when they first see it. Paul says, 'I speak to you a mystery,' that mystery is concerning the rapture. Revelation 10:7, as we have discussed here today, says the mystery will be finished at about the sounding of the seventh angel, and it is here where you see people who are in fear and give glory to God as they saw the two witnesses stand on their feet and go up as the voice says 'Come up here.' People may say, 'The church is not mentioned with the two witnesses though.' I will say to them, 'The church is not mentioned with John as he went up in Revelation chapter 4 either, though so many associate that with the rapture of the church. Even there, it is said to John in Revelation chapter 4, 'Come up here,' though as I have shared with you earlier, that was only concerning John, not the church. I have already shared with you, however, that the church is mentioned with the two witnesses. One just needs to know where to look. One must bring all the pieces together as we have already, concerning the other things I have shared with you today."

"All of what you have just shared with me makes sense, and I can understand that perfectly. The people fear and give glory to God in that moment because this will be the first time they witness the rapture. If the people had witnessed the rapture 3 ½ years before, then the two witnesses' resurrection would be of no surprise or shock to them."

Messenger then says, "That's right. There are a couple of other things I would like to share with you concerning the two witnesses and the church, though for now, I would like to share something else with you."

"Okay, that's fine. What is it?"

"It is another mystery, something that involves a particular book in the Bible, of a particular time in history, something that requires one to look here and there in the scriptures, something that involves an eclipse as we know God created the sun, moon and stars to be for signs and seasons. There is a mystery that has been concealed. Though, as I have been sharing with you today, the time of revealing is now, for such a time as this."

"What is the mystery?"

Messenger begins pulling out some pages from his leather case as he says, "I call it…..the Esther Connection."

Explore this chapter's photos/calendars mentioned by scanning the QR code or visiting the link:

https://www.revealingthetimes.com/chapter20

# CHAPTER 21
# THE ESTHER CONNECTION

The Esther connection?"

Messenger then says, "Yes. The Esther connection. I call it the Esther connection because what I am about to share with you has many concealed messages within it. See, although the book of Esther does not mention God once in that particular book, there is evidence of His presence throughout the book of Esther. I have shared some of that with you before, though what I haven't shared with you is the concealed parts that require one to look here and there throughout the scriptures and some things that couldn't have its revealing until now."

I couldn't imagine what Messenger would begin sharing regarding this with me. I thought too, about what he had said regarding an eclipse. I was filled with anticipation as I sat there beside him, waiting with my bible in hand, ready to open to any scripture he would have me to go to, ready to look at any pages he would hand me to look at. I was ready. I looked at Messenger and said, "Are you wanting me to look at those pages you have in your hand?"

Messenger says, "Soon, though first I want you to open your bible to **Haggai 2:23** and read aloud to me when you are there."

**Haggai 2:23** *"In that day,' says the Lord of hosts, 'I will take you, Zerubbabel My servant, the son of Shealtiel,' says the Lord, 'and will make you like a signet ring; for I have chosen you,' says the Lord of hosts."*

Messenger then says, "The signet ring was a symbol of authority, used by one who represented the king. The one who wore that signet ring could stamp a seal with it after writing a document because the seal would have the stamping of the king's signet ring. It would stand as if the very document bared the words of the king himself. Just like Joseph had the signet ring of Pharaoh, Joseph was second to Pharaoh in all the land. In the book of Esther, there is a man by the name of Haman who has the signet ring of the king. Haman is second to the king, having the signet ring. Go to **Esther 3:8-12** and read this aloud to me when you are there."

**Esther 3:8-12** *"Then Haman said to king Ahasuerus, 'There is a certain people scattered and dispersed among the people in all the provinces of your kingdom; their laws are different from all other people's, and they do not keep the king's laws. Therefore it is not fitting for the king to let them remain. If it pleases the king, let a decree be written that they be destroyed, and I will pay ten thousand talents of silver into the hands of those who do the work, to bring it into the king's treasuries.' So the king took his signet ring from his hand and gave it to Haman, the son of Hammedatha the Agagite, the enemy of the Jews. And the king said to Haman, 'The money and the people are given to you, to do with them as seems good to you.' Then the king's scribes were called on the thirteenth day of the first month, and a decree was written according to all that Haman commanded—to the king's satraps, to the governors who were over each province, to the officials of all people, to every province according to its script, and to every people in their language. In the name of king Ahasuerus it was written, and sealed with the king's signet ring."*

Messenger then says, "When Mordecai saw this decree that had been written on the 13th day of the 1st Month, he tore his clothes and put on sackcloth. Neither Mordecai nor anyone was permitted to go into the king's gate wearing sackcloth, so Queen Esther sent clothes for him to change into so she could speak to him directly. However, Mordecai refused to change out of his sackcloth because he was in mourning for the plot that Haman was plotting to destroy him and all his people. Mordecai learned of this when he read the decree in Shushan. The Greek word for Shushan is 'Susa.' This decree was created on the 13th day of the 1st Month on the Hebrew calendar, known as the month of Nisan." Messenger then hands one of the pages to me. It was a calendar. Messenger then says, "The year the decree was given was in the year 474 BC. Look at the 13th day of the 1st Month for that year and tell me what you see."

I began to look at the calendar. In the top left corner, I could see the number 1 representing the 1st month of the Hebrew calendar. I then looked at the 13th day. As I looked at the 13th day, I saw the day it corresponded to on our calendar underneath that. Knowing everything

Messenger had shared with me earlier, I was amazed by what I had just seen. I looked at Messenger and said, "The 16th of April. The 13th day of the 1st Month on the Hebrew calendar in the year 474 BC corresponded with April 16th."

Messenger then says, "That's right, and what have I told you about April 16th?"

"That just so happened to be the day on our calendar when Moses and the people had reached the other side of the Red Sea and when Joshua and the people had crossed the Jordan."

"That's right, and what did Moses say to the people on that day that corresponded to April 16th? Do you remember?"

I thought about it, though couldn't remember. I asked Messenger, "Can I go back to the book of Exodus and look?"

"Of course."

I turned back to the book of Exodus and then read **Exodus 14:13-14** *"And Moses said to the people, 'Do not be afraid. Stand still, and see the salvation of the Lord, which He will accomplish for you today. For the Egyptians whom you see today, you shall see again no more forever. The Lord will fight for you, and you shall hold your peace.'"*

Messenger then says, "As the Egyptians were pursuing the people to destroy them, so too was Haman's plot, his decree to destroy them, both the decree to destroy them and the Egyptians going after them to destroy them corresponds to the same day on your calendar, April 16th. The message that Moses told the people that day because of their fear of the Egyptians is the same message that can be applied to Haman's decree. As Mordecai was in mourning wearing sackcloth, so too could be said, 'Do not be afraid, Mordecai. See the salvation of the Lord. The Lord will fight for you, and you shall hold your peace.' We know that in the book of Esther, God is not mentioned, though we can see the evidence of His presence as He fights for His people and brings deliverance."

"I can't believe this. This too, happens to fall on the day that corresponds to April 16th. This cannot be a coincidence."

Messenger then says, "There is more to share concerning what has been concealed. There is more to reveal that must be given to you for such a time as this." Messenger takes the page back from me and says, "What you had read earlier was saying that Zerubbabel would be as a signet ring, and what I have shared with you earlier is that Zerubbabel was a foreshadow of one of the witnesses of Revelation 11. In the book of Esther, Haman is killed by order of the king as his plot is uncovered. In the end, Mordecai, who once wore sackcloth at the king's gate, was given new garments, and the signet ring that was once on the hand of Haman was given to Mordecai. Please read aloud to me **Esther 8:2**."

**Esther 8:2** *"So the king took off his signet ring, which he had taken from Haman, and gave it to Mordecai; and Esther appointed Mordecai over the house of Haman."*

Messenger then says, "So, here is the pattern I wish to show you. Haman was also like a prefigure of the Antichrist, one seeking to kill and annihilate the Jewish people. Haman had 10 sons. The Antichrist and the 10 kings. Haman and his 10 sons were killed. The Antichrist and the 10 kings will be no more. Mordecai wore sackcloth outside of the king's gate, refusing to change out of his sackcloth because he was in mourning for what Haman was plotting to do. The Witnesses will be in sackcloth in mourning for the people as they know the time of the Antichrist and plot to destroy and annihilate is near, so they will warn the people, telling them to repent of their ways. One of the witnesses I have shared with you will be of the house of Israel from the line of Ephraim. When Haman was no more, the signet ring passed onto Mordecai, the one who had been wearing sackcloth. Haman and his 10 sons are no more. In the future, the Antichrist and the 10 kings will be no more. There will then be the one from the house of Israel of the line of Ephraim and the 10 lost tribes who will be restored and reunited with Judah, and the kingdom shall be one. The house of Haman was given to Mordecai. In the end, the place we know as earth, where the Antichrist will rule for a short time, will be his no more, and our King, Jesus Messiah, will reign on earth for a thousand years during the millennial reign. Jesus and His people. Mordecai, who once wore sackcloth outside the king's gate, was later changed into royal garments as he entered the king's court and was given the signet ring, being second to the king. After the death of the two witnesses, 3 ½ days later, when life enters them and they stand on their feet, a voice from heaven will say, 'Come up here.' As they go up into the King of kings' court, they will be changed out of their sackcloth and given glorified bodies. They will be changed. There is still yet more to what is concealed, and the revealing is now for such a time as this."

"What? What is it? Please show me."

Messenger then hands me another page. It is another calendar. Messenger then says, "This is a calendar from the year 520 BC for the 6th Month of the Hebrew calendar known as the Month of Elul. Remember what I shared with you concerning the timeline of the two witnesses? That we are to look at the shadow in order to see the substance of what shall be?"

"Yes, I remember."

Messenger then says, "As was written in the book of Haggai, it was on the 24th day of the 6th month known as the Month of Elul when the spirit of Zerubbabel, Joshua and the remnant of the people were stirred up. The 24th day of the 6th month was the day the second temple began to be built. The 24th day of the 6th month on the Hebrew calendar of the year 520 BC corresponded to September 21st on your calendar. Do you remember me sharing this with you when you had read my letter on the timeline of the two witnesses?"

"Yes, I remember."

Messenger then hands me another page. It was another calendar. Messenger then says, "Keep the other calendar in your hand as you look at this one. The calendar I have just given you is the calendar of the 12th Month on the Hebrew calendar, known as the month of Adar. This is the calendar for the year 516 BC. As I had shared with you concerning the timeline of the two witnesses, the shadow is that of Zerubbabel, the governor and Joshua, the high priest. The book of **Ezra 6:15** reads, *'Now the temple was finished on the third day of the month of Adar, which was in the sixth year of the reign of king Darius.' The sixth year of king Darius's reign was 516 BC. The calendar you now have in your hand is the calendar that shows the day the temple was finished. Look at the third day of the month of Adar and tell me what you see. What day does it correspond to?"*

I began to look at the third day of the 12th Month of the Hebrew calendar, the Month known as the Month of Adar. When I came to the third day, I looked at Messenger and said, "The third day of the Month of Adar in the year 516 BC corresponded to February 21ˢᵗ on our calendar." I then said to Messenger, "I don't understand why you are showing me this. I had already read about these days in your letter as you talked about the timeline of the two witnesses."

Messenger then says, "Patience, my friend, you will soon see why I am showing you these calendars." Messenger then begins to point to a particular day on the calendar that was for 516 BC. The day Messenger was pointing to had an orb on the very day. The orb was a Lunar Eclipse."

I then said, "Okay, there is a Lunar Eclipse. What are you saying?"

Messenger then says, "It is not what I am saying. What have I told you that is in the book of Genesis? God created the sun, moon and stars for signs and seasons. As I have shared with you, the Lunar Eclipse was, at times, God's sign for warning for the Jewish people and the solar eclipse, a warning for all nations."

"Okay, I am not following though. Why is this one important?"

Messenger then says, "Look at the day the Lunar eclipse fell on."

When it finally registered, I opened my eyes widely as I looked at the day. I then said, "The 13ᵗʰ day of the Month of Adar. The lunar eclipse was on the 13ᵗʰ day of the Month of Adar in the year 516 BC, the same month the second temple had finished being built."

Messenger then says, "That's right."

"So, years before the Jews set day of destruction on the 13ᵗʰ day of the Month of Adar in the year 473 BC, God had placed His sign, His marker in the heavens, marking that day in the year 516 BC."

Messenger then says, "That's right, though you are missing an important piece. God wasn't marking the day in 516 BC to tell the people of their destruction. God was marking the 13ᵗʰ day in the year 516 BC, years before 473 BC, to proclaim the day of their deliverance, that He would bring them deliverance." Messenger then handed another page to me. It was a list showing the days from significant years of the past and how they corresponded with our calendar. Messenger then says, "Do you remember what I had shared with you concerning the Exodus out of Egypt, taking place in the year 1445 BC?"

"Yes, I remember."

Messenger then says, "The following year was the year 1444 BC. This list I have handed you shows you the 12th Month of Adar in the year 1444 BC along with the years 516 BC. I then also have here on this list the 1st Month of the Month of Nisan in the year 1445 BC, the year of the Exodus and the year of 474 BC for the day Haman had set the decree."

I was amazed as I began to read the list:

--1445 BC, the 1st Month Nisan (The crossing of the Red Sea) happened on that day that corresponded with **April 16th**.

--474 BC, the 1st Month Nisan the 13th day (When Haman had set the decree) was the day that corresponded with **April 16th**.

--1444 BC, the 12th Month Adar, the 3rd day of the Month of Adar, fell on what corresponded to **February 21st**.

--1444 BC, the 12th Month Adar, the 13th day of the Month of Adar, fell on what corresponded to **March 3rd**.

--516 BC, the year the temple was finished on the 3rd day of the 12th Month of the Month of Adar fell on what corresponded to **February 21st**.

--516 BC, the year the temple was finished, in the 12th Month of the Month of Adar, there was a Lunar Eclipse that occurred 10 days after the temple had been finished. The 13th day of the Month of Adar fell on what corresponded to **March 3rd**.

The list had all the days that corresponded to our calendar in dark bold as they were underlined to stand out among the list of the years. I looked at Messenger and said, "Of all the years for these to match like this. There is no way this is just some random coincidence or chance."

Messenger then says, "Has anything I have shown you been coincidence or mere chance? What I have shown you here is like what I have shown you concerning the significant years of deliverance. We can see God's hand through the history of the past, though there is still more that I must show you. More of the message has been concealed, though now is the time for revealing for such a time as this."

"Okay, what is it?"

Messenger then says, "What did the people do at the end of the book of Esther? What does it say the people did when they had defeated their enemies on the 13th day of the Month of Adar?"

"They celebrated and gave gifts to one another following the deaths of those who had tormented them."

Messenger then says, "That's right. Now, remember all I had shown you concerning the shadow we were to look at concerning the two witnesses of Revelation 11? We had to look at Zerubbabel and Joshua as those two were the Two Olive Trees in Zechariah's time. They are a shadow. The two witnesses of Revelation 11 will be the substance, just like the Passover Lamb was the shadow and Jesus Messiah is the substance."

"Yes, I remember."

Messenger then says, "Very good." Messenger then hands me another page. The page was another list. I was astonished by what I began reading.

--Zerubbabel and Joshua (shadow of the substance, the substance being the two witnesses of Revelation 11) spirit stirred on the 24th Day of the 6th Month in the year 520 BC. The Month, Day and Year the second temple began to be built.

--The 13th day of Adar, the 12th Month of the Hebrew Calendar in the year 516 BC, had the Lunar Eclipse. The Month and year the second temple was finished.

--The 13th day of Adar, which is the 12th Month of the Hebrew Calendar in the year 473 BC, was the day and year of the Jews deliverance, and that day and the following two days, they had sent gifts one to another to celebrate the death of those who had tormented them.

--The 24th day of the 6th Month, known as the Month of Elul in 520 BC, to the 13th day of the 12th Month, known as the Month of Adar in the year 516 BC. The days between them total 1,260 days.

Messenger then says, "So, even though God is not mentioned in the book of Esther, His very presence and guiding hand is throughout it. And the evidence that God is truly the One who inspired what was written is also evidenced by what we read in the book of Esther as we can also read of something that is yet future in Revelation 11."

"What is that?"

Messenger says, "What I have told you. Zerubbabel and Joshua their spirits are stirred as the building of the second temple begins. This was on the 24th day of the 6th month, known as the month of Elul, in the year 520 BC. That day to the 13th day of Adar in the year 516 BC is a total of 1,260 days. On the 13th day of Adar in the year 473 BC, the Jewish people give gifts one to another for the next couple days in celebration of the death of those who had tormented them." Messenger then takes the bible from me and opens to Revelation 11. He points to a certain verse and has me read.

**Revelation 11:10** *"And those who dwell on the earth will rejoice over them, make merry, and send gifts to one another, because these two prophets tormented those who dwell on the earth."*

Messenger then says, "Do you see now? The Jews at the end of the Book of Esther gave gifts to one another because of the death of those who had tormented them. The death of those who had tormented them was on the 13th day of the month of Adar and they celebrated the following two days. As I have shared with you, Zerubbabel and Joshua represent the two olive trees, and they represent the shadow of the substance, the substance being the two witnesses of Revelation 11. Their spirits are stirred on the 24th day of the 6th month in the year 520 BC, and exactly 1,260 days later, on the 13th of Adar in the year 516 BC, there is a Lunar Eclipse that happens, and God uses it to be for a sign for His people. The two witnesses of Revelation 11 will give their testimony for exactly 1,260 days, and at their death, people all over the world will send gifts one to another as they will celebrate the death of those two prophets because these two prophets, these two witnesses tormented those who dwell on the earth."

This was all a lot to take in. Everything that Messenger was showing me was spot on, piece by piece. Messenger was now revealing what had been concealed within the scriptures for such a time as this. I gave the pages to Messenger, though he handed them back to me as he said, "Keep them."

Messenger then took the leather case from beside him and handed it to me. He then said, "Take this leather case and place the pages inside it. I am giving this to you for safekeeping." Messenger then took the shofar with the leather strap with the five markings on it and began to hand it to me as he said, "Take this shofar and keep watch. Be watchful, as I have shared with you what these five markings represent. Be watchful for the starting of the sixth. When that time comes, be watchful for what follows after. Sound the shofar and proclaim what you see and hear. You will be guided. You may plan in your heart, though the Lord will direct your steps. The Spirit will guide you into all truth. Be watchful and be ready."

"Are you leaving?"

Messenger then says, "There will be more to share with you, though not today. I will see you again on a day you will not know, though it will be the day appointed for us to meet again."

"I have so many other questions though. You had said you would share more concerning the two witnesses and the church, the Lord coming on the clouds. I have questions about Zerubbabel and Joshua, the remnant, their spirits being stirred as they began building the second temple. You had said the shadow doesn't mean the two witnesses of Revelation 11 have to begin their 1,260 days on the 24th day of the 6th Month, that by looking at the shadow, the two witnesses will begin giving their testimony as the third temple is being built. Why though?"

Messenger says, "I will answer your last question, and then I must go. Zerubbabel, Joshua and the remnant had their spirits stirred as they began to build the second temple. In the future, as the third temple is beginning to be built, the two witnesses and a remnant will have their spirits stirred up, though not to build the third temple. Their spirits will be stirred up because they know the truth; they are the temple, not a temple built with hands, a temple built without hands." Messenger then turned to a scripture in the bible as he began to read **John 14:23** *'Jesus* *answered and said to him, 'If anyone loves Me, he will keep My word; and My Father will love him, and We will come to him and make Our home with him.'"* Messenger then says, "Those who are truly the Lord's will understand this, that He lives inside them, that the Holy Spirit is in them who believe that Jesus is the Son of God and that the Father sent Him. The Holy Spirit that lives within their heart will stir up the Two Witnesses and a remnant as the third temple begins to go up, the temple built by man's hands." Messenger then closes the bible, hands it to me, and says, "You will also need this. Remember to always test what you see and hear with what is written. Follow what is said, meditate on His word, and allow Him to guide you. I will see you again. Until then…keep watch."

I watched as Messenger stood up and picked up the clay vessel with the scrolls. He began to walk away as he turned to look back at me and said, "There is no need to say goodbye, for we will see each other again."

All I could do at that moment was nod to him in agreement. I placed the bible into the leather case along with the pages. I walked away from the bench towards the river with the leather case on one shoulder and the shofar on the other. The straps crossed over on my back. As I approached the riverbank facing the east, I pressed the shofar to my lips and began to sound it at the water's edge. They were long and deep blasts. I then turned around, looked to the west, and wondered if anyone had heard…the sound of the shofar…the sound of warning.

Explore this chapter's photos/calendars mentioned by scanning the QR code or visiting the link:

https://www.revealingthetimes.com/chapter21

# CHAPTER 22
# THE SIXTH TRUMPET

Present day. David had just finished asking the questions that related to all that Jeremy had shared with him concerning the Two Witnesses. The matter of the two houses, that of Israel and Aaron, the timeline of when the two witnesses will begin their testimony as the third temple begins to be built. David thought all of it was amazing. Everything that had been concealed, Messenger as it seems, had brought revealing to it, even the Esther Connection, as Messenger called it. There was only one question that still lingered on David's mind. One question that he hadn't asked yet. David now knew how Jeremy wound up with the leather case and the Shofar. Messenger gave them to him, including the bible with the red templar cross on its center. The question that came to David's mind related to those markings on the shofar, or as it should be said, 'The marking that has yet to be on the shofar.' David's question lingered on his mind about the sixth trumpet as he remembered Jeremy sharing that the Two Witnesses of Revelation 11 are talked about between trumpet six and trumpet seven.

David stands up from the bench as he walks up to the edge of the lake. He then turns around and says to Jeremy, "So, since Messenger had told you to keep watch, to be watchful for the starting of trumpet six, my question to you is, have you seen anything that would indicate the starting of trumpet six?"

Jeremy stands up as he walks towards the covered gazebo that had the table there. He sits at the table with his bible and leather case. He looks at David and says, "Sit with me, and I will share with you what I have seen and heard."

David walks over to the table to sit down across from Jeremy, as Jeremy then lays the bible at the table's center. Jeremy then says, "To answer your question, we must first look to the scriptures as Messenger had said, 'You will also need this. Remember to always test what you see and hear with what is written. Follow what is said, meditate on His word and allow Him to guide you.'"

David then says, "Yes, of course. Is there someplace in the bible you want me to look at? To read from?"

Jeremy then says, "Open the bible to **Revelation 9:13-19** and you may read aloud to me once you are there."

**Revelation 9:13-19** *"Then the sixth angel sounded: And I heard a voice from the four horns of the golden altar which is before God, saying to the sixth angel who had the trumpet, 'Release the four angels who are bound at the great river Euphrates.' So the four angels, who had been prepared for the hour and day and month and year, were released to kill a third of mankind. Now the number of the army of the horsemen was two hundred million; I heard the number of them. And thus I saw the horses in the vision: those who sat on them had breastplates of fiery red, hyacinth blue, and sulfur yellow; and the heads of the horses were like the heads of lions; and out of their mouths came fire, smoke, and brimstone. By these three plagues a third of mankind was killed—by the fire and the smoke and the brimstone which came out of their mouths. For their power is in their mouth and in their tails; for their tails are like serpents, having heads; and with them they do harm."*

Jeremy then says, "To answer your question, I do believe we have seen the starting of the sixth trumpet, though before I go into that with you, we need to be mindful of a few things."

"Okay, what's that?"

"We need to be mindful of what Messenger had shared concerning a few of the previous trumpets. Remember that a third does not mean the whole world. A third, like the times before, could mean that general area or a third of those involved in the conflict/war mentioned above. Next, we need to remember that Messenger had said that 'angel' in the Greek is the word 'Angelos,' which means 'Messenger.' When the word 'angel' is used, it does not mean that this is always a heavenly being. It is simply sometimes a messenger."

"Okay, yes, I remember this as you had shared with me what Messenger had told you concerning this. Is there anything else?"

Jeremy then says, "Yes, there is something else. When John is describing horses used in this future war, we must remember that John is trying to describe things as best as he can from what he is seeing. When he describes war, he may use the word 'horses' because that is how wars were fought back in his day. They were fought on horses. I assure you, we are not going back to fighting like we did during the Revolutionary War, where we are all riding on horses again. John is describing as best as he can from what he is seeing. He sees there is war, and the best way for him to describe it is by describing how wars were fought in his day, on horses."

David then says, "So, I had heard in the past that this army of two hundred million was going to be some demonic army. Is that what it is?"

Jeremy then says, "No, that is not what it is. People of the past had associated this army of two hundred million with a demonic army because no one had heard of such a number to describe such a massive army. When John had written the book of Revelation, there were only about two hundred million people worldwide, so for people to think of a two hundred million-person army would have been impossible. However, it is possible today, with the size of our population on the earth, to have such an army of two hundred million. What was impossible back then is now possible today."

"So, the army of two hundred million is of people then?"

"Yes, it will be made up of people."

David then says, "I hadn't figured these were actual horses either, as John describes them as having heads like lions, and smoke, fire and brimstone coming out of their mouths. You are saying that John is describing the machinery being used?"

"Yes David. John is describing as best as he could, something he had never seen before."

David then says, "What kind of machinery do we have that has a head like a lion, with fire, smoke and brimstone coming out of its mouth and their tails being serpents, having heads? I have never seen any machinery used in war that looks like that."

Jeremy says, "Yes you have, though you would possibly not give it this description because you know what it is, they exist in your day, though place something like this back in John's Day, and this would be how he would describe it." Jeremy then reaches into the leather carrying case and pulls out a page that he hands David.

David couldn't believe what he saw as he looked at the picture. He could see exactly how John would say it had a head like a lion. The front of it was branched out like the mane on a lion's head. What was branched out like a mane was the shield used to protect the people in the back of it who were firing it. David looked at Jeremy and said, "What is this called again?"

Jeremy says, "This is a Howitzer Cannon." Jeremy then pulls out another page from the leather case and hands it to David.

David looks at the next picture. It was a picture someone took at the tail of the Howitzer Cannon as men were standing behind it, firing it. David could see from the picture there was fire, smoke and brimstone coming out of the mouth of the Howitzer Cannon, and at the tail of it, there were men. David then says to Jeremy, "What about the serpents having heads? Where are they?"

Jeremy then points at each head of every man standing behind the Howitzer Cannon and says to David, "These are the serpents having heads that John saw."

David then says, "Why would John call these men serpents if they are not truly serpents?"

Jeremy says, "Is it too hard to believe that John would call these men serpents? What does John the Baptist call those who came out to him while he was baptizing?"

David then says, "John the Baptist calls them a 'Brood of Vipers.'"

Jeremy says, "And were those men actually Vipers?"

"No, of course not."

"Though, nonetheless, that is what John the Baptist calls them. Who were some of these people who came to John the Baptist while he was baptizing?"

David then says, "Some of them were Pharisees and Sadducees, even tax collectors and soldiers, I think."

"Ah, tax collectors and soldiers. And what does a Viper do? It constricts, squeezes and kills. What did the tax collectors and soldiers of John the Baptist's day do? They would constrict, squeeze, oppress and kill. Now do you see why John the Baptist called these people the offspring of Vipers? They were not literal Vipers, though John the Baptist describes them as such. This is no different than what John did when he wrote that their tails were serpents having heads. John also said, 'With them they do harm.' Here is my question to you, David. How much harm is caused by war, and how many dead? You see, these machines don't operate on their own. They operate from man. With man, these machines do harm. Now do you see?"

"Yes. I see." David took a moment to think about something, then looked at Jeremy and said, "Even though I have never met Messenger, from what you have shared with me about him, about how he revealed things to you, you sure are sounding a lot like Messenger."

Jeremy then says, "It is not I. I would not be able to find what I have found or discover what I have discovered without the Lord. His Spirit guides me, as I am sure Messenger could say the same thing if he was here with us now."

David then says, "So, you were saying that you believe we are beginning to see the starting of the sixth trumpet? Can you explain?"

Jeremy says, "I began to see the starting of it in February 2022, and I came across some of the pieces a week before it began. Remember what Messenger has said, 'You need to have all the pieces in order to see the full picture.'"

"What did you see?"

Jeremy says, "As I have shared with you, the horses John wrote about are not actual horses in trumpet six. They are of machinery that I have just shown you pictures of. Though how does John describe the riders on them?"

David looked at the scripture and found the answer in part of Revelation 9:17. David then says, "The scripture says they have breastplates of fiery red, hyacinth blue, and sulfur yellow."

Jeremy then says, "That's right. Even though John did his best to describe the machinery that was being used that he saw, he described the soldiers who were fighting in this future war, and he saw on the soldiers' breastplates, certain colors. He saw the colors of fiery red, hyacinth blue and sulfur yellow."

David then says, "And you saw this piece a week before it began? Before what began?"

Jeremy says, "I saw the colors on breastplates a week before Russia invaded Ukraine on February 24th, 2022."

David became stunned by what Jeremy just said. David then says, "When? How?"

Jeremy pulls out another page from the leather case. Before he hands the page to David, Jeremy says, "A week before Russia invaded Ukraine, the Ukrainian Soldiers were conducting training exercises in Chernobyl. There was video coverage of this training on CNN. As I watched, I then saw it. At the center, on the very front of the Ukrainian Soldier, on the front of his breastplate was the colors of his flag." Jeremy then hands the picture to David as Jeremy points to the colors on the front of the soldiers' breastplate and says, "Do you see it? Hyacinth blue over sulfur yellow. They are the very colors that John describes seeing on the soldiers in the time of the sixth trumpet."

David looks at the picture in awe of what he is seeing. David then thinks about what Jeremy had just said concerning where they were having their training exercises and says, "Chernobyl!!! The very place of the third trumpet. You see the colors on the breastplate of a soldier, the very colors described by John concerning the sixth trumpet and the time you first see this is while these soldiers are standing in the very place where the third trumpet occurred."

Jeremy then says, "Yes. You are beginning to see well."

David then says, "What about the fiery red color? Where is that one?"

Jeremy then pulls out another picture from the leather case and hands the picture to David. The picture shows Vladimir Putin shaking hands with a Chinese soldier. Standing on the other side, facing the picture, is a Russian Soldier in his dress uniform. The dress uniform of the Russian Soldier had what looked like a breastplate that covered the entire chest. The color was fiery red.

David then says, "Where was this taken? When?"

Jeremy says, "This picture was published on September 25th, 2018. Though if you want to know when this was, it was during the very first live military exercise condoned between Russia and China. This was the first military exercise China and Russia had ever done together. Would you like to know the first day Russia and China got together to have this military exercise?"

"Yes. When was it?"

"The first day that Russia and China came together for their live military exercise was on the Feast of Trumpets that year. The Feast of Trumpets in 2018 fell on the day that corresponds to September 11th."

David's eyes began to open bigger as he said, "Are you serious? September 11th?"

Jeremy then says, "Yes, now do you think that is just coincidence? You see, this is the very thing that Messenger was saying. If we know the true day when Jesus was born, we can better understand the unseen principalities that war against that day. The Devil and the unseen principalities know when Jesus Messiah was born, and they know when He was baptized by John the Baptist. This military exercise wasn't just on September 11th, 2018. It also happened to be the Feast of Trumpets. As you look at this picture David, remember this from scripture."

Jeremy turns to the book of Ephesians and begins to read **Ephesians 6:12** *'For we do not wrestle against flesh and blood, but against principalities, against powers, against the rulers of the darkness of this age, against spiritual hosts of wickedness in the heavenly places."*

Jeremy then pulls out two more pages from the leather case. He hands one of them to David. The picture was a lineup of Russian Soldiers in their dress uniform. All of them in the lineup had what looked like a breastplate that covered the entire chest. It was in the color fiery red. Jeremy then handed the other picture to David. The picture was of Russian Soldiers in another dress uniform. The dress uniform had what looked like a breastplate that covered the entire chest. It was in the color hyacinth blue.

David said, "And how do you know for sure this was what John was seeing?"

Jeremy then says, "I suppose one would need to take this on faith. As Messenger would say, 'Should you choose to accept it.' There is more to this, however. Again, we cannot just look at one thing to say this is it. As Messenger said, we need all the pieces to see the full picture. We cannot rely on our own abilities. Messenger had said that we would need the bible in order to test both what we see and hear and that we would need the Holy Spirit to guide us."

David then says, "Yes, that's true. So, what else did you see? How else were you guided for you to know this was what you thought it was?"

Jeremy then says, "The very sabbath following the invasion by Russia into Ukraine, there was a Torah Portion that was read all over the world. It had been assigned since ancient times. This part, I call 'The Torah Portion and the Geographical Measurement.'"

## The Torah Portion & The Geographical Measurement

Jeremy pulls out another page from the leather case. Before he hands the page to David, he says to David, "Part of the Torah portion that was read on the Sabbath following the invasion into Ukraine was this."

Jeremy turns through the scriptures and begins to read **Exodus 38:26** *"A bekah for each man (that is, half a shekel, according to the shekel of the sanctuary), for everyone included in the numbering from twenty years old and above, for six hundred and three thousand, five hundred and fifty men."*

Jeremy then says, "The number **603,550** men represented all men who were 20 years old and above who would be able to go to war. This number we read in the Torah portion relates to war as it is the total of men who would be able to fight in one, should there be war."

David says, "Okay, and what does this have to do with Ukraine?"

Jeremy then says, "Later that evening, that Sabbath following after Russia had invaded Ukraine, after I had already read the Torah portion, I was lying in bed, and suddenly this thought comes over me, this feeling within me that said, 'You need to go to Google search and type in the Google search 'What is the Geographical measurement of the country of Ukraine?' I got up from bed, walked over to my computer, and typed in the Google search 'What is the Geographical measurement of the country of Ukraine?' This was the answer that came up on (Worlddata.info)." Jeremy then handed the page to David so he could see for himself.

David looks at the page from (Worlddata.info). The Geographical measurement of the country of Ukraine is a total of **603,550** km2

David could not believe it; it was the exact same number. David thought to himself, 'What are the odds that Russia invades Ukraine when it does, the Torah portion containing the very number that also happens to be **603,550**?' David just couldn't believe this to be a random chance. David then says, "And you just found this connection because of a thought you had?"

Jeremy says, "Yes, though this could not have been by me alone. It was the Holy Spirit that spoke to my heart that guided me to it. This is not all though. There is more."

David then says, "What is it? Please tell me."

Jeremy says, "As I have told you of the connection with the discovery of the color on the breastplates during this time as Russia was getting ready to invade Ukraine, look here with me." Jeremy points down to the next section of the scriptures being read. He tells David to then read aloud **Exodus 39:2-7**.

**Exodus 39:2-7** *"He made the ephod of gold, blue, purple, and scarlet thread, and of fine woven linen. And they beat the gold into thin sheets* *and cut it into threads, to work it in with blue, purple, and scarlet thread, and the fine linen, into artistic designs. They made shoulder straps for it to couple it together; it was coupled together at its two edges. And the intricately woven band of his ephod that was on it was of the same workmanship, woven of gold, blue, purple, and scarlet thread, and of fine woven linen, as the Lord had commanded Moses. And they set onyx stones, enclosed in settings of gold; they were engraved, as signets are engraved, with the names of the sons of Israel. He put them on the shoulders of the ephod as memorial stones for the sons of Israel, as the Lord had commanded Moses."*

Jeremy then says, "The scriptures you have just read are regarding the making of the ephod. The ephod was what held the breastplate in place. The breastplate of the high priest was worn by Aaron and his descendants after him. The scriptures that follow what you had just read talk about making the breastplate. The breastplate and the ephod were then connected, making what would be like one piece."

David then says, "So, you are telling me that you had discovered the very colors on the breastplates before Russia invaded Ukraine, to then reading the Torah portion that following Sabbath, which has the number 603,550 in it, to then be guided with the thought you had in discovering that the Geographical measurement of the country of Ukraine is 603,550 km2, to then reading the very next thing that follows in the Torah portion is regarding the making of the breastplate. It is impossible to find this on your own."

"I didn't find this on my own. The glory goes to God. Nothing is impossible for Him. What is impossible for man, God makes possible."

David then says, "Is there more regarding the colors on the breastplates?"

Jeremy pulls out two more pages from the leather case, and as he holds onto them, he says to David, "What has been the other conflict that had made news headlines following Russia invading Ukraine?"

David says, "The rising threat of China invading Taiwan."

"That's right." Jeremy then hands one of the pages to David. It was a picture of Chinese soldiers in formation. In the center, on the top of their breastplate, were the colors of fiery red. Jeremy then hands the next page to David. It was a picture of Taiwan soldiers gathered in a group. In the center, on the top of their breastplate, were the colors of hyacinth blue.

David then says, "Are these actually breastplates though?"

"Yes, they are. We call them flak vests, though what makes this vest to protect soldiers from shrapnel is the solid breastplate that is within it. John seeing this, would have known what it was because breastplates existed even in his day. These are the colors he saw. This was part of what he saw, should you choose to accept it."

David then says, "What about the Euphrates though, and the four angels that are bound at the Euphrates, are they going to be loosed soon?"

Jeremy then says, "Is that what you think? Do you think they are four angelic beings?"

David then says, "That is what I have heard before."

Jeremy then says, "Remember what Messenger had said, that just because the word angel is there does not mean it is an angelic being. The Greek word is 'angelos,' meaning 'messenger.' I will ask you this question. How can a river bind or contain something to keep it in its place?"

"I am not sure, perhaps keeping them chained under the water."

Jeremy takes another page from the leather case and hands the page to David. It was a picture of the Euphrates River with four different colors around the Euphrates river. David then asked, "What are these?"

"Those are the four countries that are bound by the Euphrates River. What have you heard in the summer of 2022, even at the time while still hearing about Russia and Ukraine, along with China and Taiwan?"

David then says, "News reports have gone out that the Euphrates River is drying up."

Jeremy then says, "That is exactly right." Jeremy points to the picture of the Euphrates River with four colors around it and says, "These are the four countries. They are Syria, Iraq, Iran and Turkey. You have heard of these countries in your news headlines for a few years now. The Euphrates River binds these four. Their borders are contained, bound by the Euphrates River. As the Euphrates River continues to dry up, and when it does, these four countries will no longer be bound by it, and they are messengers who have a message to give in the future, the message is 'war.'"

David could see it as he laid all of the pages out across the table that Jeremy had given him. All the pieces were there. He then asked Jeremy, "How were you able to find this? To put all of this together?"

Jeremy began to pick up the pages David had laid across the table. He places the pages back into the leather case and says, "I have done what Messenger told me to do. Remember what I told you? What Messenger said to me? When Messenger handed the bible to me, he said, 'You will also need this. Remember to always test what you see and hear with what is written. Follow what is said, meditate on His word and allow Him to guide you.' That is what I did. I tested what I saw and heard with the scriptures. He told me to be watchful for the start of the sixth trumpet. Everything else, the Holy Spirit guiding me along the way."

David then says, "So this is the starting of it? It is not in full force at this point?"

"That's right. Think of it as a domino effect. What we are seeing, what is happening is what will lead into it."

David says, "Is there anything more concerning Russia and Ukraine and China and Taiwan?"

"There is. The very message of Jesus Himself." Jeremy then turns through the scriptures and begins to read **Matthew 24:6** *"And you will hear of wars and rumors of wars. See that you are not troubled; for all these things must come to pass, but the end is not yet."*

Jeremy then says, "What you are hearing of between Russia and Ukraine is war, and what you are hearing of between China and Taiwan is rumors of war. You are hearing of both right now. We need to heed the rest of that message Jesus gave concerning this, and that is to not be troubled. These things must come to pass. The end is not yet."

David stands up from the table and walks out from the gazebo. He looks over at the fountain beside the lake. It was of a seal lying on its back, spitting water out from its mouth. Seeing this made David think about the seals of Revelation. He turns to Jeremy and says, "What about the seals? Don't get me wrong. You know that I believe that five of the trumpets have happened, though so many have said or taught that the seals must happen before the trumpets. Can you share anything concerning any of the seals?"

Jeremy picks up the leather case to close it and places it on the seat beside him. He then says, "You will need to come back to the table if I am to show you." Jeremy then placed his hand on the bible after saying that.

David walks back to the table to sit down and says, "What are you going to share with me?"

"How about the first four seals? You know them as the four horsemen…."

Explore this chapter's photos/calendars mentioned by scanning the QR code or visiting the link:

https://www.revealingthetimes.com/chapter22

# CHAPTER 23
# THE FOUR SEALS

Jeremy looks across the table and asks David, "What do you know about the first four seals?"

"I know that many call them the four horsemen of the Apocalypse."

"That's right, and 'Apocalypse' means 'revelation' to reveal, to pop the lid off something and make it known. That is what I am going to do with you here today."

"Okay." David then smiles as he says, "So far, everything you have shared with me, everything Messenger had shared with you, has been popping the lid off something, making it known and understood. Everything has been a revealing."

Jeremy smiles back, though he gives no response. He then turns the bible to himself as he turns to **Revelation 6:1-2**. Jeremy then says, "Before we get into what I am going to share with you, let us first look at what the scriptures have to say about these four seals, or four horsemen if you will." Jeremy then turns the bible back toward David and says to him, "Please read aloud to me **Revelation 6:1-2**."

**Revelation 6:1-2** *"Now I saw when the Lamb opened one of the seals; and I heard one of the four living creatures saying with a voice like thunder, 'Come and see.' And I looked, and behold, a white horse. He who sat on it had a bow; and a crown was given to him, and he went out conquering and to conquer."*

Jeremy then says, "Now please read aloud to me the second seal. I want us to have read these four seals, then I will go over them with you."

**Revelation 6:3-4** *"When He opened the second seal, I heard the second living creature saying, 'Come and see.' Another horse, fiery red, went out. And it was granted to the one who sat on it to take peace from the earth,* *and the people should kill one another; and there was given to him a great sword."*

"Okay, and the next one. Please continue."

**Revelation 6:5-6** *"When He opened the third seal, I heard the third living creature say, 'Come and see.' So I looked, and behold, a black horse, and he who sat on it had a pair of scales in his hand. And I heard a voice in the midst of the four living creatures saying, 'A quart of wheat for a denarius, and three quarts of barley for a denarius; and do not harm the oil and the wine."*

David says, "And now, you want me to read the 4th seal?"

"Yes. Please continue."

**Revelation 6:7-8** *"When He opened the fourth seal, I heard the voice of the fourth living creature saying, 'Come and see.' So I looked, and behold, a pale horse. And the name of him who sat on it was Death, and Hades followed with him. And power was given to them over a fourth of the earth, to kill with sword, with hunger, with death, and by the beasts of the earth."*

Jeremy then says, "Do you remember what I shared about many antichrists? About what Messenger had shared with me?"

"Yes, I remember."

"Even during John's Day, there were many antichrists, and John even said, referring to the time, that they were living in the last hour. Regarding the four horsemen, they are four spirits. Remember, we must have all the pieces in order to see the full picture. We cannot just look in one place in the scriptures to say, 'This is it.' We must also look to other places within scripture to find our answer in identifying just what these four horsemen are." Jeremy then turns through the scriptures and says to David, "Read aloud to me **Zechariah 6:1-8**."

**Zechariah 6:1-8** *"Then I turned and raised my eyes and looked, and behold, four chariots were coming from between two mountains, and the mountains were mountains of bronze. With the first chariot were red horses, with the second chariot black horses, with the third chariot white horses, and with the fourth chariot dappled horses—strong steeds. Then I* *answered and said to the angel who talked with me, 'What are these, my lord?' And the angel answered and said to me, 'These are four spirits of heaven, who go out from their station before the Lord of all the earth. The one with the black horses is going to the north country, the white are going after them, and the dappled are going toward the south country.' Then the strong steeds went out, eager to go, that they might walk to and fro throughout the earth. And He said, 'Go, walk to and fro throughout the earth.' So they walked to and fro throughout the earth. And He called to me, and spoke to me, saying, 'See, those who go toward the north country have given rest to My Spirit in the north country.''*

Jeremy then says, "See, what you have just read tells us what these colored horses are. They are spirits that go to and fro throughout the earth."

David then says, "I can see that three of them in the book of Zechariah and three of the horses in the first three seals are the same color, though in Zechariah, one horse is dappled, and in Revelation, the horse is pale. So, this couldn't be referring to the same, could it?"

"You are right. Three are the same, and the dappled one and the pale one seem to be different, don't they? In order to understand this is the same horse, we need to understand what it means when a horse is dappled, do you know?"

"No, I am not sure."

Jeremy then says, "When a horse is dappled such as, say, a gray horse, the gray horse may be born a base color, though as it ages, white hairs begin to appear here and there, then becomes more prevalent as the horse continues to age. Seeing the dappled horse in the book of Zechariah shows the horse is aging though not dead yet, meaning that even in Zachariah's time, the clock of time is winding down, though the end is not yet. In Revelation, however, the horse is no longer dappled, no longer aging, the horse itself being pale to represent death and represents we are in the time of the end. Both the dappled horse and the pale horse represent the same horse. Both relate to death and dying. Think of yourself as you age. What happens to your hair?"

"It becomes gray."

"Yes, and not just all gray at first. You may have gray hair here and there that is dappled. And why does your hair begin to turn gray and dappled? Because your body is slowly dying until one day, as the body is dying, there is then death. Now do you see how the dappled and pale horse is the same horse, just at a different stage in time?"

"Yes, I understand. So, the angel tells Zachariah that these are spirits?"

"Yes, they are spirits. The white horse represents the spirit of antichrist, the spirit of one who may start out seeming to go about peacefully, until you then begin to see this one going out conquering and to conquer, taking what does not belong to them, perhaps land, all because they want more and more power. These four spirits have happened throughout the course of history. We saw an example of this with Adolf Hitler. He had met with the British prime minister at a time, speaking words of peace. Adolf Hitler was given land called Sudetenland in acts of peace words of peace. He didn't even have to fire a shot. He wanted this land because there were 3 million Germans in that land, and he said that he wanted to unite the Germans. After some time, Adolf Hitler took over Czechoslovakia, and no one was really doing anything to stop him, so he wanted to see how much further he could go with the whole conquering and to conquer spirit, so Adolf Hitler then invaded Poland. It wasn't but a couple of days after Adolf Hitler invaded Poland when Great Britain then declared war."

David then says, "So that was the spirit of the white horse?"

"Yes. Then, Great Britain declared war. What emerges from this is what we know in history as World War II. This was the spirit of the Red Horse. The Red Horse is war. During World War II, you then saw famine of biblical proportions. Millions died from famine, famine which was the aftermath, the effect of war. The Black Horse is famine. Then, the final horse, the pale horse which is death. The pale horse is the result of war and famine. Both war and famine lead to death. We were able to see the spirits of the four horsemen during World War II. We are starting to see them appear again even as we speak, and throughout the past couple of years."

"How is that? How are they beginning to appear again?"

Jeremy then says, "In Russia, you have a man by the name of Vladimir Putin who has crossed borders into other land in attempts of conquering and to conquer, taking what doesn't belong to him, what isn't his. He wants to unite them, not much different than the very claims Adolf Hitler had in saying that he wanted to unite the Germans. Because of this spirit of conquering and to conquer, it has now led to war between Russia and Ukraine. As you know, the Red Horse is war. Do you remember me sharing with you how the word a third is used many times?"

"Yes, I remember how you talked about a third and what you said on what Messenger had shared with you."

"So, Ukraine is considered to be the breadbasket for much of Europe as Ukraine covers about a third of the grain for parts of Europe. So, there we have a third being mentioned. Not a third of the whole earth, but a third of that area of Europe. Due to the aftermath of the war in Ukraine, the grain had ceased to be shipped out. Many had pleaded with Vladimir Putin to open the ports and allow the grain to be shipped out. Famine will result. There will be higher costs for grain as a result as well. This is the spirit of the Black Horse. Then ultimately, what follows war and famine is death. We are seeing all of this again. As I have shared, think of this as a domino effect leading to a much bigger war and famine. In the end, you will see this antichrist spirit of the white horse have its full fulfillment in the final Antichrist, who will confirm a covenant, appearing peaceful, to then showing his true colors at the midpoint of the seven-year tribulation and will be followed by war and famine of biblical proportions. On top of the famine in the end, this final Antichrist will also have a mark that all are to have in order to buy or sell. Much of the grain that had been loaded on ships during the war between Russia and Ukraine, where Russia controlled the ports, do you know where those grain ships wound up?"

"No, where?"

"They wound up in Syria. And you remember what I have told you concerning Syria and the one who is President of Syria."

"Yes, I remember."

Jeremy then says, "Now, just like Messenger had said when he shared with me about the many antichrists, this is what I will say concerning Vladimir Putin and even Bashar Al-Assad. I am not here to accuse them. I will share with you again what I have shared from scripture." Jeremy then begins to read **Ephesians 6:12** *"For we do not wrestle against flesh and blood, but against principalities, against powers, against the rulers of the darkness of this age, against spiritual hosts of wickedness in the heavenly places."* Jeremy then says, "Vladimir Putin and Bashar Al-Assad may fully know who they are working for and what they are doing. If they do know, all the more reason to watch them closely in what they do and continue to do. Though if they are not aware, if they don't realize that they are being used as puppets by the unseen principalities, by the rulers of the darkness of this age, by the spiritual hosts of wickedness in the heavenly places, if they are not aware they are being used, then they are strongly encouraged to cease what they are doing and consider their ways, to know that all of what has been shared here is not a coincidence or mere chance."

David could see and understand all Jeremy was sharing with him. He looked at Jeremy and said, "So, the first four seals have happened many times over, though they will have their final fulfillment with the final Antichrist?"

"That's right, and what John is seeing concerning these doesn't imply that they happen before the trumpets can ever start. John sees what has always happened with the first four seals, though they will reach their final fulfillment at the time of the final Antichrist. The trumpets however, as I have shared with you, have happened, the first five, and we are now seeing the starting of the sixth trumpet. As I have shared with you before, trumpets are meant to be a warning, to wake up, to be alert, to be watchful. The trumpets are to do just that, to alert those of us who are watching so that we may proclaim in the hopes that others may come to believe that Jesus is the Son of God and that the Father has sent Him, that He is coming again, for He told of these things before they had ever happened. What I have been sharing with you, He revealed to His servants, and do you remember what I have shared with you concerning His servants?"

"What is that? Please remind me."

Jeremy begins to read **John 15:14-17** *"You are My friends if you do whatever I command you. No longer do I call you servants, for a servant does not know what his master is doing; but I have called you friends, for all things that I heard from My Father I have made known to you. You did not choose Me, but I chose you and appointed you that you should go and bear fruit, and that your fruit should remain, that whatever you ask the Father in My name He may give you. These things I command you, that you love one another."*

David then says, "Amen to that." David began to look at the leather case and the shofar, remembering what Jeremy had shared with him concerning Messengers' final words to Jeremy before he had left. David then asks, "Do you remember sharing what Messenger said to you before he left? You said that Messenger had said, 'Be watchful for the starting of the sixth. When that time comes, be watchful for what follows after.' Do you remember that?"

"Yes, I remember Messenger saying that to me. Why do you ask?"

David then says, "You have shared with me that what we have been seeing is the starting of the sixth trumpet. Messenger had not only told you to be watchful of the starting of the sixth, Messenger also told you to be watchful for what comes after. I was just Wondering if you have continued to be watchful and if there have been things that have come after?"

"Yes, I have continued to keep watch, and there have been things that have followed after."

"Really? Like what?"

Jeremy then says, "Messenger had shared that the two witnesses are mentioned between trumpet six and trumpet seven. Messenger also said that the Two Witnesses of Revelation 11 will begin giving their testimony as the third temple begins to be built. There have been recent developments over the past several months that, as it stands right now, looks to be paving the way for a soon rebuilt third temple."

"What is it? What developments?"

"Something that the Jewish people in Jerusalem have looked for and not found for almost 2,000 years. Something they require to have in their possession that will then pave the way for them to one day build the third temple."

"What have they not had for 2,000 years? What do they require to have in their possession?"

Jeremy opens the straps from the leather case as he opens it. He pulls out a page and hands the page to David. It was a picture of a red cow. David looks at Jeremy after looking at the picture and says, "What is this?"

Jeremy then says, "What you are looking at there….is a red heifer."

# CHAPTER 24
# THE RED HEIFER & THE POOL OF SILOAM

A red heifer? What is that for?" asked David.

"A sacrifice. It will be used as a sacrifice."

David then says, "I thought there was no more need for the blood of lambs, bulls or goats because of what Jesus had done for us on the cross?"

"You are right. There is no more need for the blood of lambs, bulls or goats, though some of the Jewish people who have yet to believe that Jesus is the Messiah, they still hold to the Law, and for them to worship God is to have animal sacrifice."

"What do you mean by saying, 'Some of the Jewish people?'"

"There are other Jewish people who do believe Jesus is Messiah. They are known as Messianic Jews."

David then looked at the picture of the red heifer again, saying, "Why is the red heifer important if we who are in Christ know that there is no more need for animal sacrifice, for the blood of lambs, bulls or goats?"

Jeremy then says, "To us, it is not important. However, at the same time, the red heifer is something important for us to pay attention to precisely because of the Jews who have yet to believe in Jesus as Messiah, to those who still follow the law."

David seemed confused as he said, "I don't understand. The red heifer is not important to us who believe, though it is important for us to pay attention to, what do you mean?"

Jeremy pulls out a page from the leather case. Before he hands the page to David, he says, "The scriptures tell us that the Antichrist will stand in the house of God claiming to be God. The Antichrist will stand in the holy place where he ought not. This tells us that there will be a rebuilt temple when this happens. The book of Daniel says that the Antichrist will confirm a covenant for one week. As you know, the one week represents a period of seven years. The book of Daniel tells us that in the middle of that week, the Antichrist will put an end to all sacrifices. What I have just shared with you tells us that there will be a rebuilt temple and that animal sacrifices will resume during the first 3 ½ years of the seven-year tribulation. For the temple to be rebuilt and in order to have animal sacrifices again, the Jewish people who follow the law first need a red heifer. Not just any red heifer. They need a pure red heifer." Jeremy, still holding onto the page, turns through the scriptures and says to David, "Here, please read aloud **Numbers 19:1-3**."

**Numbers 19:1-3** *'Now the Lord spoke to Moses and Aaron, saying, "This is the ordinance of the law which the Lord has commanded, saying: 'Speak to the children of Israel, that they bring you a red heifer without blemish, in which there is no defect and on which a yoke has never come. You shall give it to Eleazar the priest, that he may take it outside the camp, and it shall be slaughtered before him."*

Jeremy then says, "Those who follow the Law, scripture tells them they must have a red heifer without blemish, to mean without spot. The red heifer cannot have more than two white hairs or two black hairs. If it does, then it will be disqualified. The red heifer to be used must have never had a yoke upon it. If it has, it will be disqualified. Should the red heifer meet all the required specifications, they must wait until it is in its third year. Once the red heifer reaches its third year, if it is still considered pure and still meets all the qualifications, the red heifer is then taken outside the camp, outside from the temple mount, and the red heifer is taken to the mount of olives where they will take scarlet, hyssop and cedar wood. They will burn this, along with the pure red heifer, in the fire out on the mount of olives in a designated place where they can look in the direction of where the temple would be."

David then says, "And why would they do this?"

"In order for the high priest they select to be able to do sacrifices, to be able to enter the holy of holies on the day of atonement, their high priest and their other priests must be ritually pure. In order for them to be ritually pure, they would take the ashes of the red heifer and mix the ashes of the red heifer with water three days after the red heifer would be burned. They would then sprinkle the water with the ashes of the red heifer mixed with it onto the high priest, and the high priest would be ceremonially clean, ritually pure. The high priest would also wash himself and his clothes in water. So, because they follow the Law, their selected high priest cannot go into the holy of holies on the day of atonement, and they cannot offer animal sacrifices because they would be considered unclean unless they had the ashes of a pure red heifer that had been mixed with water to sprinkle themself with."

David then says, "So, do they have a pure red heifer?"

Jeremy then hands the page to David. It was a picture of five red heifers. Jeremy says, "This is a picture of five pure red heifers flown to Israel from Texas in September of 2022. The five pure red heifers landed in Israel on September 15th, 2022. The people who brought them to Israel paid more than $250,000 to have these five pure red heifers flown to Israel. So, you can see they are serious about this. This is how important this is to them."

"Why did they ship five? Why not just one?"

Jeremy then says, "Because these five red heifers are pure, though one thing still is needed for them to qualify. They must be in their third year of age to qualify, and they are not in their third year yet. The reason they brought five is in case any of the five ever develops more than two white hairs or two black hairs, that would then disqualify it. Their hope is that at least one of the five will stay pure until it reaches its third year. All they need is one to stay pure until it reaches its third year, and once it reaches its third year, it then can be sacrificed and burned on the altar out on the mount of olives at a place they designate."

"When will they be in their third year?"

"They will be in their third year right around the time of Passover in 2024."

"That is only a year away."

"That's right. And by the time this book goes out for all to read, it will only be about a month away."

As Jeremy took a drink of his water, David thought about the water aspect of this and said to Jeremy, "you said that they would mix the ashes of the red heifer with water. Where would they do this?"

"They would do this at the Pool of Siloam."

"The Pool of Siloam? Isn't that the pool where Jesus had healed the man who was born blind?"

"It is. The Pool of Siloam, which means 'sent.' Jesus took dirt mixed with some of His spittle and rubbed it on the man's eyes, telling the man to go and wash at the Pool of Siloam. When the man born blind had washed at the Pool of Siloam, he could then see. You can read more about this at another time in **<u>John chapter 9</u>**."

David then says, "The Pool of Siloam doesn't exist anymore though, does it?"

"The Pool of Siloam has existed since king Hezekiah had built it, though it was lost, buried under the ground, but as of 2004, the lost Pool of Siloam had been found."

"So, they now also have the Pool of Siloam?"

Jeremy says, "Yes, and there has been another development concerning the Pool of Siloam."

"What is that? What other development?"

"Since 2004, the Pool of Siloam has been found, though only a small sliver of the Pool of Siloam has been uncovered. There is water in this small sliver of the Pool of Siloam that had been uncovered. Just this year, they announced that they would begin excavating the rest of the Pool of Siloam, making it the size it originally was, which was much bigger. They have already started the work to excavate the rest of the Pool of Siloam. They had a water libation ceremony this past year in 2022 during the Feast of Tabernacles there. This was like a practice run for them, as they will do this during the Feast of Tabernacles when the third temple is built."

"Why are they excavating the rest of the Pool of Siloam?"

Jeremy then says, "They are doing this as this will be another attraction for people to come see, to restore things that once were. Even though that is their intention, the Pool of Siloam being made the size it originally was will also make the water purification for the people who gather there take less time. The small sliver of water that is there now would take too much time for all who would gather there for the water purification."

"And you said the water purification was done with the ashes of the red heifer? The priests would do the water purification to sacrifice at the temple?"

"Yes, and people from all nations would gather there. Some would wash at the Pool of Siloam for water purification. They would then walk up the steps that would take them right up to the temple on the temple mount. They will be doing this again when the temple is rebuilt."

David then says, "So, you are saying that around the time of Passover next year in 2024, they will take one of the red heifers and burn it out on the mount of olives?"

"Yes, provided that at least one is still pure and meets all the requirements. There is no designated day, no designated feast day where the burning of the red heifer is required. The burning of the red heifer can happen at any time throughout the year. They just need to wait until the red heifer reaches its third year. Once it has reached its third year, I can tell you they will not wait long to burn it out on the mount of olives as they would not want to take the chance for it to become disqualified because of a blemish, because of more than two white hairs or two black hairs appearing on it."

"This will for sure be done out on the Mount of Olives?"

"Yes. They have already made the preparations. They have already purchased a plot of land on the Mount of Olives to perform the burning of the red heifer. They will take cedar wood, scarlet and hyssop with one of their pure red heifers that will then be in its third year and burn it on the mount of olives in a place they already have prepared that is facing the temple mount. Three days after they do this, they will take the ashes of the red heifer and mix it with the water of the Pool of Siloam to sprinkle those they have selected as their priests and high priest to make them ritually clean. This will pave the way for a rebuilt temple and sacrifices to resume."

David then says, "In order for them to begin building the third temple, the Antichrist will confirm the covenant for one week, for seven years."

"Yes. However, it will not be a new covenant. The book of Daniel says the Antichrist will confirm it, meaning that the covenant is something that is already in place. The Antichrist will simply confirm it, meaning to be in agreement with it. That time will mark the start of the seven-year tribulation. The third temple will begin to be built, sacrifices will continue, and 3 ½ years into that seven-year period, the Antichrist will then walk into the Holy of Holies to declare himself as God. Remember, even when confirming the covenant, the Antichrist is not fully revealed at this point. As it has been shared with you, there have been many peace agreements made with Israel since Israel became a nation in 1948, and none of them were the Antichrist. When the confirmation of the covenant takes place, even then, he will not be revealed. The revealing of the final Antichrist will not happen until he stands in the place where he ought not and declares himself to be God, where he then puts a stop to all sacrifices. This is when his true colors show. This will be at the midpoint. For the remaining 3 ½ years, he will put in place the mark of the beast. This will be a period of 42 months. Those who do not take his mark will not be able to buy or sell, and he will persecute and kill those who do not take his mark or worship him. During that time, there will be tribulation saints. Many who witness and see the rapture of the church will instantly believe, fear, and give glory to God. They will be the tribulation saints. However, there will still be many others who will not believe and will then be given over to the strong delusion that they should believe the lie, that they may be condemned, who will not believe the truth. The strong delusion, the lie, will be the Antichrist claiming to be God. Those who have pleasure in unrighteousness who do not believe the truth, the truth being that Jesus is Messiah, that Jesus is the Son of God, and the Father sent Him, that He is coming again. Those who take pleasure in unrighteousness, who believe the lie, will take the mark of the beast and they will be condemned."

David then says, "Is the covenant in place now? You said that the covenant will already be in place, that the Antichrist will simply confirm it."

"Yes, it is possible the covenant is already in place. You know it by the name, 'The Abraham Accords.'"

"The Abraham Accords? How would we know that it will be the Abraham Accords that the Antichrist will confirm?"

Jeremy then says, "We know that it is possible it could be the Abraham Accords that the Antichrist will confirm because of what has been concealed for us as watchmen to find."

"What is that? What has been concealed?"

"When I say concealed, what I mean is that not many have seen or realized what I am about to tell you. As you know, the Abraham Accords were first signed between leaders from Bahrain, Israel and the United Arab Emirates. The signing took place on September 15th, 2020. The five pure Red Heifers arrived in Israel two years later to the day. They arrived in Israel on September 15th, 2022. Let us look for a moment at the Covenant that was made with Abraham, between God and Abraham, shall we." Jeremy then turns through the scriptures and says to David, "Please read aloud to me **Genesis 15:9**."

**Genesis 15:9** *"So He said to him, 'Bring Me a three-year-old heifer, a three-year-old female goat, a three-year-old ram, a turtledove, and a young pigeon."*

Jeremy then says, "The scripture you just read is the Covenant God made with Abraham. Notice the first animal the Lord mentions for Abraham to bring."

"A three-year-old heifer. A heifer in its third year."

"That's right. And further in that chapter, **Genesis 15:17** reads, *"And it came to pass, when the sun went down and it was dark, that behold, there appeared a smoking oven and a burning torch that passed between those pieces."*

Jeremy then says, "It was on that same day that God made the covenant with Abraham, who had the name Abram at that time. The pieces the torch had passed between were of the animals that had been sacrificed."

David then says, "So, the signing of the Abraham Accords was on September 15th, 2020, and the five pure Red Heifers arrived in Israel on September 15th, 2022, two years later, on the exact same day? Is there anything else that leads you to believe that the Abraham Accords will be the covenant that the Antichrist will confirm?"

"Yes. When the Red Heifers are in their third year, when one of the Red Heifers will be sacrificed on the mount of olives, it will be 3 ½ years since the Abraham Accords were first signed. That is not to say that was when the seven-year tribulation began. It is simply something for us as watchmen to notice, to pay attention to, that this very well could be the covenant that the Antichrist will confirm. There are still a couple of other pieces that let us know this may be the covenant the Antichrist will confirm."

"What are the other pieces?"

Jeremy then says, "I will paraphrase this. The Abraham Accords states that people shall worship God in their own way. For the Jews who have yet to believe that Jesus is the Messiah, since they still follow the law, for them to truly worship in their own way, they are to have animal sacrifices and need their temple rebuilt. Provided that the Abraham Accords will be the covenant confirmed by the Antichrist, because of what is written in the Abraham Accords, this will allow the Jewish people to rebuild their third temple and resume animal sacrifice. And before the temple is rebuilt and animal sacrifices resume by their designated high priest, they first burn the red heifer on the mount of olives."

"And the other piece? What is the other piece?"

"The other piece is the one who mostly worked to make this Abraham Accord possible. That person was Jared Kushner. Now, please hear what I am saying. I am by no means saying that Jared Kushner is the Antichrist, nor am I saying that Jared Kushner is an antichrist. I am saying that he was the main person who made the Abraham Accords possible. There is a trail for the watchmen to keep watch, something that was seen, and that is the address of the tower that Jared Kushner owned. The address of the tower is 666. That is not to say that Jared Kushner bought that tower because he liked the number of the building. That to Jared Kushner was just mere coincidence and chance, though it was not chance in the aspects of the unseen principalities. You see, the number of that building, 666, was meant to tell us that the man who owned that building would be the front man to make a covenant possible that would be called the Abraham Accords. This covenant in the future would be confirmed by the final Antichrist, who will have the name that calculates to 666."

David then says, "I am not sure about that. This part could be just a coincidence, right?"

Jeremy says, "This is no more coincidence than what happened almost 2000 years ago when Jesus was before Pontius Pilot. During Passover in the year 30 AD, Pontius Pilot had told the people that it was custom that one be released to them. Pontius Pilot gave the people a choice to choose which man they wanted to release. A man by the name of Barabbas, or Jesus, who is Messiah. The people asked for Barabbas to be released. They wanted Jesus to be crucified because they said He commits blasphemy by saying that He is the Son of God, the Son of the Father. At that moment, the two who were standing there for the people to choose on which to be released was a hidden message. Though it was not a coincidence. It happened by divine ordinance in hopes that the people would see and say, 'This could not be a coincidence' though they didn't see because their eyes were darkened, meaning they did not have the understanding. They had unbelief. Though the evidence is still recorded in the scriptures for those who do see, who understand and believe."

"What is it? What was there before them that they didn't see?"

Jeremy then says, "The people wanted Jesus crucified, charging Him with blasphemy, saying that He has said that He is the Son of God, the Son of the Father. Standing on the other side was a man whose name was Barabbas." Jeremy then turns through the scriptures and says to David, "Please read aloud to me **Mark 10:46**."

**Mark 10:46** *"Now they came to Jericho. As He went out of Jericho with His disciples and a great multitude, blind **Bar**timaeus, the **son** of Timaeus, sat by the road begging."*

"The word 'Bar' is the word that means 'son.'" Jeremy then says, "Now please read aloud to me **Romans 8:14-15**."

**Romans 8:14-15** *"For as many as are led by the Spirit of God, these are sons of God. For you did not receive the spirit of bondage again to fear, but you received the Spirit of adoption by whom we cry out, '**Abba, Father**.'"*

Jeremy then says, "The word 'Abba' is the word that means 'Father.' When you take the word 'Bar' and join it with the word 'Abba,' you get Barabba. The name Barabbas means 'Son of Father.'"

David then says, "So, the people who wanted Jesus to be crucified, charging Him with blasphemy because He said He is the Son of God, the Son of the Father, the very man who stood on the other side they had released had the name that means 'Son of Father.'"

"Yes, that is right. The people had a choice. To choose the true Son of the Father or to release the false son of father. They chose the other. The same will be true when they sacrifice the Red Heifer. At some point, when the covenant is confirmed and the third temple starts to be built, while animal sacrifices resume, their eyes will be darkened, to mean they will not see, they will not have the understanding, and many of them will believe the lie and still reject the truth. The Truth that Jesus is the Son of God and that the Father sent Him, that He is coming again."

David then says, "All of these things are happening, and so many people are unaware."

"That's right, all the more reason for this book to go out to the people so that others may come to believe that Jesus truly is the Son of God and that He is coming again." Jeremy took the pages and placed them back into the leather case. He then looked at David and said, "Since I have told you about the sacrifice that will be made by those who hold to the Law, how about now I share with you of the true Sacrifice and the One who took our sins upon Himself on the cross, the One who has made us who believe clean already, by the washing of His word."

David then says, "Yes, please tell me. This needs to be in the book. The people need to know."

# CHAPTER 25
# THE TRUE SACRIFICE

Jeremy turns through the scriptures and asks David, "Did you know that in the New Testament, there is mention of the ashes of a heifer?"

"No, I didn't know. So does that mean the ashes of the heifer are required then?"

Jeremy then says, "I have shared with you that those who follow the law and have yet to believe in Jesus as Messiah, as the Son of God, will follow through with the burning of the heifer to gather its ashes. I suppose the best I can do at this point regarding this is to have you read what is written for yourself." Jeremy turns the bible back towards David and says, "Please read aloud to me from the book of **Hebrews 9:13-15**."

**Hebrews 9:13-15** *"For if the blood of bulls and goats and the ashes of a heifer, sprinkling the unclean, sanctifies for the purifying of the flesh, how much more shall the blood of Christ, who through the eternal Spirit offered Himself without spot to God, cleanse your conscience from dead works to serve the living God? And for this reason He is the Mediator of the new covenant, by means of death, for the redemption of the transgressions under the first covenant, that those who are called may receive the promise of the eternal inheritance."*

Jeremy then says, "Do you see the part that you had just read mentions the ashes of the heifer?"

"Yes, I see it."

"The need for the ashes of a heifer is obsolete because of the perfect and true sacrifice that was done by Jesus Himself with His own body, with His own blood. As I have shared with you concerning those who follow the law and have yet to believe that Jesus is Messiah, this is what can be shared with them." Jeremy then turns the page and says to David, "Please read aloud to me **Hebrews 10:1-9**."

**Hebrews 10:1-9** *"For the law, having a shadow of the good things to come, and not the very image of the things, can never with these same sacrifices, which they offer continually year by year, make those who approach perfect. For then would they not have ceased to be offered? For the worshipers, once purified, would have had no more consciousness of sins. But in those sacrifices there is a reminder of sins every year. For it is not possible that the blood of bulls and goats could take away sins. Therefore, when He came into the world, He said: 'Sacrifice and offering You did not desire, but a body You have prepared for Me. In burnt offerings and sacrifices for sin You had no pleasure. Then I said, 'Behold, I have come—in the volume of the book it is written of Me—to do Your will, O God.'" Previously saying, 'Sacrifice and offering, burnt offerings, and offerings for sin You did not desire, nor had pleasure in them' (which are offered according to the law), then He said, 'Behold, I have come to do Your will, O God.' He takes away the first that He may establish the second."*

Jeremy then says, "As you can see from what you just read, 'sacrifice and offering' God did not desire. These things were offered according to the law. Jesus' death on the cross was the true living sacrifice."

David looks across the table to Jeremy and says, "I know this. Though how can you convince the Jews who have yet to believe that Jesus truly is the Son of God, that the Father had sent Him? Those who follow the law, who have yet to believe in Jesus as their Messiah, don't read the New Testament. They only look at the Old Testament scriptures. If you were to somehow show them from the Old Testament that Jesus was and is the one and final sacrifice, maybe they would come to faith and believe in Him for salvation. Is there any place in the Old Testament we could look at? Provided they read this book, where could we take them to in the Old Testament, where they could ponder and consider that this truly was accomplished through the sacrifice of Jesus our Lord?"

Jeremy thinks about what David had just asked him and says, "Well, there are the scriptures in the Old Testament that many know of, even the Jews who have yet to believe that Jesus is Messiah. They know this is one of the scriptures we look to." Jeremy then turns through the scriptures and begins to read from the book of **Isaiah 53:5-6** *"But He was wounded for our transgressions, He was bruised for our iniquities; The chastisement for our peace was upon Him, and by His stripes we are healed. All we like sheep have gone astray; We have turned, every one, to* *his own way; And the Lord has laid on Him the iniquity of us all. He was oppressed and He was afflicted, Yet He opened not His mouth; He was led as a lamb to the slaughter, and as a sheep before its shearers is silent, so He opened not His mouth. He was taken from prison and from judgment, and who will declare His generation? For He was cut off from the land of the living; For the transgressions of My people He was stricken. And they made His grave with the wicked—but with the rich at His death, because He had done no violence, nor was any deceit in His mouth."*

David then says, "Yes. This is one of the scriptures that even the Jews know we use in attempts to show them that what you just read is talking about Jesus. Jesus was that lamb, the Lamb of God. When going before His oppressors, He opened not His mouth. He was hung on the cross, numbered with the transgressors. He died with the wicked, though He was given the tomb that had belonged to Joseph of Arimathea. Joseph of Arimathea, a wealthy man, gave his tomb for Jesus' burial. He was placed in a tomb with the rich. It is evident that the scripture you had just read was fulfilled in Jesus our Lord, though they don't believe even with this scripture. Are there any other scriptures we can also share with them? Not just to the Jews who have yet to believe but anyone who has had doubt or disbelief. What else can we share with them concerning the one true living sacrifice of Jesus our Lord?"

Jeremy then says, "I have already shared with you concerning **Psalm 22**, when Messenger had shared about the timeline of the Two Witnesses. Do you remember?"

"Yes, I remember. This was what Jesus had said while on the cross, *'My God, My God, why have You forsaken Me?'* That was how **Psalm 22** began, written by David, and in that same Psalm was written, *They pierced My hands and My feet; I can count all My bones. They look and stare at Me. They divide My garments among them, and for My clothing they cast lots."*

Jeremy then says, "That's right, and as we know, Jesus' hands and feet were pierced while on the cross, and while on the cross, the people were dividing His garments among them and casting lots for His clothing." Jeremy then reaches into his leather case and pulls out several pages. While holding the pages in his hand, he says to David, "There is something else that the Lord says about Himself in **Psalm 22**." Jeremy then begins to read **Psalm 22:6** *"But I am a worm, and no man; A reproach of men, and despised by the people."*

"A worm? Like an earthworm? The kind you would have on a fishing hook?"

"No." Says Jeremy, "Not that kind of worm. The worm He is referring to is a crimson worm."

"A crimson worm? What is a crimson worm?" asked David.

Jeremy then says, "More importantly, the question to be asked is 'What was a crimson worm used for?'"

"Okay then. What was a crimson worm used for?"

"The ink or dye from a crimson worm was used to dye the tent of the tabernacle, to dye the priestly robes, used for sacrifice and rituals, and for making scarlet threads and cords. Even more amazing is what happens when a mother crimson worm gives birth to her young."

"What happens when she gives birth?"

"The mother is on a tree when giving birth. When the mother gives birth to her young, the baby crimson worms eat the flesh of their mother. She sacrifices herself for her children. They eat the flesh, and her ink and blood cover her young and are forever stained with it." Jeremy then hands one of the pages to David and says, "This is the aftermath of what happens after the mother gives birth and sacrifices herself for her young."

David looks at the picture. It was a picture of a tree that was stained blood red in the spot where the mother crimson worm had sacrificed herself for her young. Next to that picture was another picture that showed the cross with the blood-red stain after Jesus had sacrificed Himself for us.

Jeremy then said, "Now let me show you a particular scripture that has a concealed message for us who keep His word. Those who keep His word should make this known and proclaim it to those who have doubts or unbelief. The scripture is towards the beginning of the book of Isaiah. I will read this one aloud to you David." Jeremy then turns through the scriptures and begins to read **<u>Isaiah 1:11-18</u>** *"To what purpose is the multitude of your sacrifices to Me?" Says the Lord. "I have had enough of burnt offerings of rams and the fat of fed cattle. I do not delight in the blood of bulls, or of lambs or goats. When you come to appear before Me, who has required this from your hand, to trample My courts? Bring no more futile sacrifices; incense is an abomination to Me. The New Moons, the Sabbaths, and the calling of assemblies—I cannot endure iniquity and the sacred meeting. Your New Moons and your appointed feasts My soul hates; They are trouble to Me, I am weary of bearing them. When you spread out your hands, I will hide My eyes from you; Even though you make many prayers, I will not hear. Your hands are full of blood. Wash yourselves, make yourselves clean; Put away the evil of your doings from before My eyes. Cease to do evil, learn to do good; Seek justice, rebuke the oppressor; Defend the fatherless, plead for the widow. Come now, and let us reason together, Says the Lord, 'Though your sins are like scarlet, they shall be as white as snow; Though they are red like crimson, they shall be as wool.'"*

David then says, "Yes. I know about this scripture. Especially the part at the end that says, 'Though your sins are like scarlet, they shall be as white as snow; Though they are red like crimson, thcy shall be as wool.'"

Jeremy then says, "I am glad you know of this verse, though there is a message concealed in it."

"What is it? What is the message concealed in it?"

Jeremy says, "In the scripture I had just read to you, God is saying that He cannot stand their sacrifices. What is the purpose of them? He speaks through Isaiah as Isaiah writes, saying, 'Come now, and let us reason together,' Says the Lord.' What God was saying to the people then through Isaiah is also to be meant for the people of today and for those soon that will begin to do animal sacrifices again once the third temple begins to be built and even before that when they take the red heifer to burn it on the mount of olives. God is telling them that He cannot stand their sacrifices. There is no more need of the blood of lambs, bulls and goats. When God says, 'Come, let us reason together,' what follows that is where He mentions the part of your sins being like scarlet, they shall be white as snow. He is referring to the crimson worm when mentioning this."

Jeremy then hands the other page to David. It was a picture of a crimson worm after it had died. The crimson worm was white as snow and looked like wool.

David looks at the picture and says, "When does the crimson worm begin to look like this after it has died?"

Jeremy then says, "The crimson worm begins to look white as snow and like wool three days after it has died."

"Three days?"

"Yes. Three days."

David says, "Just like Jesus, when He died, three days later, He rose again."

Jeremy says, "That's right. You see, what God is saying is though your sins are red, meaning alive in you, they shall be as white as snow, to mean 'dead, no more, done away with.' Though your sins are red like crimson, also to mean 'alive in you,' they shall be as wool to also mean 'dead, no more, done away with.' What God was saying here was, 'Come and let us reason together, all of those sacrifices you have done before, all of those animal sacrifices, let me show you the true living sacrifice, which is the sacrifice of My Son on the Cross.'"

David then says, "Why wouldn't God just spell it out for us here? Why does it have to be concealed?"

"God gives you enough to know the truth, though He also does it in such a way that also requires you to have faith at the same time. God, who created all that we see in nature, created the crimson worm to be a silent messenger of the very sacrifice His Son would accomplish on the cross. The crimson worm gives birth the way that it does, on a tree, to sacrifice herself for her young, to leave the tree-stained blood red, to then die. Three days later, the mother who sacrificed herself becomes white as snow and as like wool. **Psalm 22** is the picture of Jesus when He is on the cross. He says that He is a worm. He was on a cross, on a tree. He sacrificed Himself for you, for His children. Those who are His are washed, made clean by the shedding of His blood. He died on the cross. The cross is stained blood red. Three days later, He rose again to life, giving us who are His, the hope that we too will have eternal life, our sins are no more, He has forgiven us, those of us who believe, who have faith in Him, who wait eagerly for His return, for He is coming back with salvation for those who are His."

"This is amazing," says David. "Even here at the beginning part of Isaiah is the message of Jesus' sacrifice and the fact that God, the creator of all we see in creation, made the crimson worm to function in this way as it is, as you said, the silent messenger to what Jesus would do for His people."

Jeremy says, "Yes. And there is more." Jeremy then turns through the scriptures and begins to read **John 6:50-58** *'This is the bread which comes down from heaven, that one may eat of it and not die. I am the living bread which came down from heaven. If anyone eats of this bread, he will live forever; and the bread that I shall give is My flesh, which I shall give for the life of the world.' The Jews therefore quarreled among themselves, saying, 'How can this Man give us His flesh to eat?' Then Jesus said to them, 'Most assuredly, I say to you, unless you eat the flesh of the Son of Man and drink His blood, you have no life in you. Whoever eats My flesh and drinks My blood has eternal life, and I will raise him up at the last day. For My flesh is food indeed, and My blood is drink indeed. He who eats My flesh and drinks My blood abides in Me, and I in him. As the living Father sent Me, and I live because of the Father, so he who feeds on Me will live because of Me. This is the bread which came down from heaven—not as your fathers ate the manna, and are dead. He who eats this bread will live forever."*

David then says, "Jesus mentions the eating of His flesh. It is just like the crimson worm. The young of the crimson worm eat the flesh of their mother. The mother sacrifices herself for her children. Those who eat her flesh and drink her blood are forever stained with the blood of her sacrifice. Jesus was referring to the crimson worm without saying it wasn't He?"

"He was. He was talking about His death, His sacrifice for us. It requires those who keep His word to seek and find. We find Him everywhere throughout the scriptures. You also see that He refers to Himself as the manna. Remember what I have shared with you about what is in the ark of the covenant?"

David says, "Yes. I remember."

Jeremy then says, "Now, the last part of the scripture I am about to share with you, pay close attention to. Pay close attention to all of the scripture I am about to share with you, though especially the end part of the scripture."

"Okay. I will."

Jeremy begins to read **Hebrews 10:19-25** *'Therefore, brethren, having boldness to enter the Holiest by the blood of Jesus, by a new and living way which He consecrated for us, through the veil, that is, His flesh, and having a High Priest over the house of God, let us draw near with a true heart in full assurance of faith, having our hearts sprinkled from an evil conscience and our bodies washed with pure water. Let us hold fast the confession of our hope without wavering, for He who promised is faithful. And let us consider one another in order to stir up love and good works, not forsaking the assembling of ourselves together, as is the manner of some, but exhorting one another, as so much the more as you see the Day approaching. "*

David then says, "Okay. I was paying attention to the last part, as you said. That means we, as believers, are to continue coming together, right? That is what it is saying, isn't it?"

Jeremy says, "Yes. That is what it is saying, though there is more. Just like what I have shared with you regarding the concealed message concerning the crimson worm. There is also a concealed message within these verses. We need to remember that though Paul wrote the book of Hebrews, the words are still inspired by the Holy Spirit. All scripture is inspired by the Holy Spirit as if God is writing with His own hand."

"Yes. I know that. So, what is the concealed message?"

Jeremy then says, "What did I share with you earlier when the people would burn the red heifer? I told you they would then, three days later, take the ashes and mix it with the water of the Pool of Siloam. They would sprinkle on the priest. They would also sprinkle towards the doorway of the temple seven times. What does the scripture say that I had just read to you? It says, 'Having your hearts sprinkled from an evil conscience and our bodies washed with pure water.' What does Jesus say? 'Behold, I stand at the door and knock. If anyone hears My voice and opens the door, I will come into him and dine with him, and he with

Me.' That is from **<u>Revelation 3:20</u>**. Though He is talking to the church, He is referring to the heart of the believer, not a building. The door to your heart where He wants to come and live within you. The picture of the scripture has concealed within it the element of the red heifer sacrifice by the sprinkling and the water for purification. When the warning and encouragement to not forsake the assembling of ourselves together, to exhort one another, so much the more as you see the Day approaching, this message was meant for the people in the time when it was written and is also for us today. For those of us who are watching, as I have shared with you earlier, we shall soon see the red heifer burning that will lead to the sprinkling at the Pool of Siloam to pave the way closer to the building of the third temple. We who are watchmen see the Day approaching. The Day approaching is referring to the soon coming of Christ Jesus our Messiah."

David then says, "And as you have said, they will take the red heifer up on the Mount of Olives in the year 2024 around spring, once they have reached their third year?"

"Yes. That's right."

David hands the pages back to Jeremy. As Jeremy places the pages back into the leather case, David says, "Have you ever been to Israel? To Jerusalem?"

"Yes, I have. I went to Israel for the first time last November of 2022."

"Really!? That is amazing!! What was it like?"

"It was beautiful. Absolutely beautiful. The best trip and one of the best decisions I had ever made in my life was going on that trip."

"Did you make or meet any new friends on that trip?"

"Oh yes, several. I also happened to meet Messenger there, or should I say that he met me."

"How did that happen?"

Jeremy then says, "I don't know. It was like he had said before he left the first time. I wouldn't know the day, though we would meet again at the time appointed, so I suppose that was the appointed time."

"Did Messenger share anything more with you while you were in Israel?"

"He did. He shared with me a couple of mysteries. Mysteries that were to have their revealing for such a time as this. He shared what he called the 'Tent Mystery,' and he shared what he called 'The Mystery of the Sixth Month,' he also shared what it means to be 'Anointed.'" Jeremy could tell from the look on David's face that he wanted to know what Messenger had shared with him. Jeremy looks at his watch for the time, then looks at David and says, "I suppose I will start sharing with you from the time I was there with Messenger as he began sharing with me the mystery of the tent."

Explore this chapter's photos/calendars mentioned by scanning the QR code or visiting the link:

https://www.revealingthetimes.com/chapter25

# CHAPTER 26
# THE TENT MYSTERY

I had been on the Israel tour for a few days now. It was the month of November 2022. We had traveled to a hotel that was off the shore of the Dead Sea. All who would want to, who were on the tour, would be able to float on the Dead Sea the next morning. Before that morning, I walked to the back of the hotel, across the road to the Dead Sea, just to get a look at the water, the light from the moon glistening on its surface. We had just returned from being out in the Wilderness that evening, where we had spent time singing praise and worship. We also had time to ask questions while in the Wilderness. It had been a couple of hours since that time. While standing at the edge of the Dead Sea, pondering the question I had asked in the Wilderness, given a chance to answer my own question, I stood there Wondering if I had explained it well enough for everyone to understand.

It wasn't long after this thought came to mind while looking across the waters of the Dead Sea that the voice of a man who stood behind me said, "Though this water is heavy with salt, do you suppose it would part before you?" The voice sounded very familiar, and the question was almost Identical to the question that was asked of me about a year and a half before when I was standing near the bank of the Mississippi River. I thought to myself, "No, it couldn't be. Could it?" I slowly turned around to look at the man who stood behind me. I couldn't believe it. It was Messenger. He still was dressed in all black, wearing a long black coat. From the looks of him, he was wearing the same clothes I had seen him in a year and a half ago. After I had turned around, Messenger said, "Though if these waters do part before you, I must advise you to wear shoes, for the salt at the bottom is very rough on your feet." Messenger smiles.

"What are you doing here?" I asked.

Messenger then said, "I come here from time to time."

"Where? Here at the Dead Sea?"

"Here in Israel, to the Sea of Galilee, the Wilderness, Jerusalem, all over," Messenger says.

I then asked, "How did you know I was here?"

Messenger then said, "I had told you that we would see each other again, that you would not know what day, though it would be the time appointed for us to see each other again. It is not that I knew where you would be at the appointed time, though at the time appointed, which is now, seeing that we are here together, now I know."

"I don't understand."

Messenger then said, "Remember what I had shared with you from scripture? That man plans in his heart, though the Lord directs his steps. The Lord guides us. I knew there was more to share with you at some point, though even I did not know when that day would be. I knew however, that we would see each other again, and when that time would come, it would be the time appointed."

"Okay. I think I understand now. How did you know that it was me standing here though?"

Messenger smiles and says, "I could see the side of you as I walked towards you." Messenger could see that I did not have the Shofar or the leather carrying case with me. Messenger asked me, saying, "Where is the leather case?"

"I left it at home. Though I brought the Bible with me."

"What about the Shofar?"

"I have the Shofar in the room. I have had it with me at times while here on the tour. I sounded the Shofar on the shores of the Mediterranean Sea the second day we were here."

"Did others take the time to hear its sounding?"

"I believe so."

Messenger then said, "That's good." Messenger then begins to walk closer to me. Both of us then looked back in the direction of the waters of the Dead Sea. Messenger then says to me, "So, tell me about today. What had you all done before coming here tonight?"

"Before coming to the hotel, we spent some time in the Wilderness. We sang praise and worship songs there. We were also given time to ask questions."

"Did you ask any?"

"I did. I asked one question."

"What question did you ask?"

"I asked a question first by saying, 'Seeing that we are in the Wilderness, I was Wondering if you could share the Mystery of when the people of Israel had encamped around the Tabernacle in the Wilderness, and then looking forward to the time when Jesus had ascended from the Mount of Olives to the people then gathered together in the Upper Room?'"

Messenger said, "Did the tour guide answer the question?"

"The tour guide said it would take some time to answer that question."

Messenger smiled, saying, "Yes, I suppose it would, seeing that you had asked a pretty lengthy question."

"Yes, that was what I was thinking about before you came up to me tonight. I wondered if I had answered the question in such a way that everyone had understood."

"The tour guide let you answer your own question? What was your answer? What did you say?"

I looked at Messenger and said, "I had shared with the tour guide and the people in the wilderness that the people of Israel, during their wilderness Wandering, when they set up camp, would pitch their tents 2,000 cubits from the Tabernacle. They would do this each time they set up camp. We know from scripture that the glory of the Lord descended and ascended onto the Holy of Holies at the Tabernacle during the wilderness Wanderings. Fast forward to when Jesus ascended from the Mount of Olives to heaven. Scripture says that Jesus will one-day step foot on the Mount of Olives when He returns. Jesus is God in the flesh. He ascended from the Mount of Olives and will descend onto the Mount of Olives. The Glory of God ascending and descending from the Mount of Olives. When Jesus had ascended from the Mount of Olives, **Acts 1:12** reads,' *Then they returned to Jerusalem from the mount called Olivet, which is near Jerusalem, a Sabbath day's journey.*"

Messenger then says, "Okay, and did you share the significance of that fact?"

"I did. They were there in the upper room. It was there where they were staying. It was there where they had received the Holy Spirit. They were a sabbath day's journey from where the Lord had ascended. The Holy Spirit enters them where they are. A sabbath day's journey is 2,000 cubits. It is the same distance as when the Israelites would pitch their tents around the Tabernacle during their 40 years in the wilderness. Peter hints by giving a clue to this mystery when he writes in **2 Peter 1:13-14** *Yes, I think it is right, as long as I am in this tent, to stir you up by reminding you, knowing that shortly I must put off my tent, just as our Lord Jesus Christ showed me.*"

Messenger then said, "Very good. And did you tell them what Peter meant by saying this?"

"Yes. I had shared with them that Peter was referring to his 'body' as the 'tent' and so the clue to the mystery is that during the wilderness wanderings, they had pitched a tent 2,000 cubits, a sabbath day's journey from the Tabernacle, where the glory of God ascended and descended on the holy of holies. A new and greater covenant would be made in that the Lord would write the law on their minds and in their hearts, which would be accomplished by the Lord's sacrifice on the cross and the promise of the Holy Spirit given to them. Jesus ascends from the Mount of Olives, where He will descend on the Mount of Olives when He returns. The people traveled 2,000 cubits, a sabbath day's journey to Jerusalem from the Mount of Olives, and they were in the upper room as the Holy Spirit, the glory of God, enters their tents, which is their body as Peter describes his body as the tent. All of this is the evidence of the better promise the Lord has given to those who are His."

Messenger said, "And you are Wondering if the people understood your answer in this? Did anyone come to you after?"

"Yes. The tour guide did."

"And what were his words to you?"

"He said, 'Thanks for asking your question and for sharing, I would like to hear more about this.'"

Messenger then says, "It sounds to me that your tour guide understood the answer you gave. I am sure others who were there understood as well."

"Yes. I suppose you are right."

Messenger then looks up at the night sky and says, " There is more to this mystery with the tent, however. When I say tent, I am referring to the Tabernacle."

"Oh, and what is that?"

Messenger then looks at me and says, "The glory of the Lord ascended and descended on the holy of holies as the holy of holies was where the ark of the covenant was placed. I have already shared with you the significance of the Ark of the Covenant and what each item in the Ark of the Covenant represented. You remember right?"

"Yes. I remember."

Messenger then says, "Do you have your phone on you?"

"Yes."

"Good. Take out your phone and look up the book of __Joshua 3:4__. You may read it aloud to me when you are there."

__Joshua 3:4__ *"Yet there shall be a space between you and it, about two thousand cubits by measure. Do not come near it, that you may know the way by which you must go, for you have not passed this way before."*

Messenger then says, "Do you see? They were to keep 2,000 cubits away from the ark of the covenant as the priests and the ark crossed the

Jordan River. The Jordan River parted before them. The ark of the covenant led the way, though more than the ark of the covenant, it was the glory of God that led the way. Jesus told the people that He is what?"

"Jesus is 'The Way, The Truth and The Life.'"

"That's right, and no one goes to the Father except through Him." Messenger then says, "Now please read aloud to me **John 14:4-7** as this is where we see Jesus saying this to His disciples."

**John 14:4-7** *"And where I go you know, and the way you know.' Thomas said to Him, 'Lord, we do not know where You are going, and how can we know the way?' Jesus said to him, 'I am the way, the truth, and the life. No one comes to the Father except through Me. If you had known Me, you would have known My Father also; and from now on you know Him and have seen Him.'"*

Messenger then says, "The crossing of the Jordan to the promised land was a shadow of what will be in the future. The crossing from where we are here, to be raptured up with the Lord in the air. To be where He is. The dead in Christ rise first, then those of us who are alive and remain who are in Christ will be changed in a moment, in the twinkling of an eye. We will be caught up to meet Him in the air. Before they crossed the Jordan, they were told to stay 2,000 cubits, a sabbath day's journey from the ark of the covenant, as the ark of the covenant was to go before them, for they did not know the way as they had not passed that way before. As Jesus talks to His disciples, He tells them, 'Where I go you know, and the way you know.' It is then by Jesus going to the Father, that the Helper, which is the Holy Spirit, will be sent to them to live within their 'tent,' which is their 'body.'"

"This is amazing! How both things connect. From the Old Testament to the place we had just read in **John 14:4-7**."

Messenger then says, "Yes. And yet, there is one more thing I must show you concerning camping their tents in the wilderness wanderings when the people of Israel pitched their tents around the Tabernacle. It can be found in the Book of **Numbers 2:1-34**, though I will share the numbers of the tribes and which tribes had camped on the east side, south side, west side and north side and will share with you their total on each side. I have a piece of paper with me. Do you happen to have something to write with?"

I began reaching into my pockets, then said, "Yes. I do. Here is a pen." I then handed the pen to Messenger and watched him begin to write.

This is what he wrote:

| **East Side** | **South Side** |
|---|---|
| Judah (74,600) | Reuben (46,500) |
| Issachar (54,400) | Simeon (59,300) |
| Zebulun (57,400) | Gad (45,650) |
| Total: 186,400 | Total: 151,450 |
| **West Side** | **North Side** |
| Ephraim (40,500) | Dan (62,700) |
| Manasseh (32,200) | Asher (41,500) |
| Benjamin (35,400) | Naphtali (53,400) |
| Total: 108,100 | Total: 157,600 |

Messenger then says, "Look closely at the totals for each. Where and how they were camped around the Tabernacle in the Wilderness wanderings gave the very Image of the Cross. On land, they may not have known or realized, though, from the air, that is what it would have been. The very image of the Cross."

"Really? That is amazing."

"Yes. And when you add up the total of each, the total is **603,550**."

I then looked to Messenger and said, "**603,550**? I came across this number in the spring when Russia invaded Ukraine. It not only was the number read in the Torah portion following when Russia had invaded Ukraine, that number also happens to be the very number of the geographical measurement of the country of Ukraine."

Messenger then says, "And how were you able to discover this was the geographical measurement of the country of Ukraine?"

"I was laying in bed the same night I had read the Torah portion, and this feeling, this thought came to me as if saying, 'Go to your computer and search on Google, 'What is the geographical measurement of the country of Ukraine?' Then, sure enough, that happened to be the total."

Messenger looks back up to the night sky, saying, "It sounds to me that you have been keeping watch, looking for the starting of the sixth trumpet and things that follow. You could not have discovered that without the Holy Spirit guiding you." Messenger then looks at me and says, "The Tabernacle going through its time in the wilderness for 40 years, the people who had been camped around it, who had failed many times during their time in the wilderness, created the image of the cross by how they were camped. This, in the future, would be Jesus Himself, who is the Tabernacle. He spent 40 days and nights in the wilderness to be tempted in all ways that we were, yet He was without sin. Because He is the spotless lamb of God who is to take away the sin of the world, He was going to one day, at the end of His Ministry, be crucified on a cross. Though He died on the cross. We know that He is now risen. By His resurrection, we who believe in Him hold to this truth, the hope of our salvation."

"Amen to that." I then looked up at the sky as well. Looking at the light of the moon. Though the moon is not light, the moon is only lit as it reflects the light from the sun. The moon bears witness to the light. I thought to myself at that moment, 'This is how we are who are in Christ. We are not the light. Jesus is the true light. We bear witness of His light.' I then thought about what Messenger said regarding Jesus being the Tabernacle. While looking up at the sky, I said, "You had said that Jesus is the Tabernacle, though He had referred to Himself as the Temple."

"That's right," said Messenger. "In the Old Testament, you had the Tabernacle. Until then, during the reign of king Solomon, you had a temple. After that temple was destroyed, you then have the second temple that began to be built by Zerubbabel and Joshua on the 24th day of the sixth month of the Hebrew Calendar, known as the month of Elul. This second temple was the one king Herod refurbished, which took 46 years, from 20 BC to 26 AD. This was the temple Jesus was standing in when He said He would tear down the temple and build again in three days, talking about His body. The building of the temple that Jesus was standing in was the one that had started being built by Zerubbabel and Joshua in the year 520 BC. As I had shared with you before, from the year 536 BC to 520 BC, all that laid there was the foundation. Though in the future, Jesus refers to His body as the temple."

"Yes. That's right. I remember this. Why are you now talking about the temple though?"

Messenger then says, "Peter had referred to his body as a tent. Jesus refers to His body as the temple. There is however another reason I am sharing with you the message that Jesus gave when He said He would tear down this temple and in three days He would build again."

"What is the reason?"

"It goes back to the 24th Day of the sixth month, the day when the second temple began to be built. There was a reason that God stirred up the spirit of Zerubbabel, Joshua and the remnant on that day to begin building the second temple. Though to find out this mystery, it will require us looking at other years in order to bring about the revealing of this mystery."

"What mystery?"

"I call it…. 'The Mystery of the Sixth Month.'"

# CHAPTER 27
# THE MYSTERY OF THE SIXTH MONTH

The Mystery of the Sixth Month?" I asked.

"Yes. The Mystery of the Sixth Month." Said Messenger.

I then looked at Messenger and said, "You had already shared the mystery of the sixth month with me, remember? You had told me about when Zerubbabel and Joshua's spirits were stirred up on the 24th day of the sixth month to begin building the second temple, that 1,260 days later would just so happen to fall on the 13th day of the twelfth month known as the month of Adar. You had shared that the 13th day of the month of Adar and the couple days that followed happened to be celebrated and known as the Feast of Purim towards the end of the book of Esther in the year 473 BC. You mentioned that during that time, the people gave gifts one to another to celebrate the death of those who had tormented them. You then shared about how the two witnesses of Revelation 11 will give their testimony for 1,260 days and after they finish giving their testimony, that the beast, the Antichrist, will kill them and people from all over the world will give gifts one to another to celebrate their deaths as they had tormented them."

Messenger then says, "Yes, that's right. There is more to the Mystery of the 24th day of the sixth month though."

"More than what you have already shared?"

"Yes." Said Messenger.

"Okay. I am all ears. I am ready to listen to all you would have to share with me."

"Very good." Said Messenger. "What I share with you concerning the mystery of the 24th day of the sixth month should not take very long. To reveal this mystery to you, we must look at a couple of scriptures, and we will also need to look at a few significant years in history."

"Okay. What scripture would you like me to read on my phone first?"

Messenger looked at my phone in my hand, then said, "I will have you read Jesus' reply after the Jews had asked Him for a sign to show that He had the authority to turn over the tables of the money changers in the temple. Read aloud to me **John 2:18-21**."

**John 2:18-21** *"So the Jews answered and said to Him, 'What sign do You show to us, since You do these things?' Jesus answered and said to them, 'Destroy this temple, and in three days I will raise it up.' Then the Jews said, 'It has taken forty-six years to build this temple, and will You raise it up in three days?' But He was speaking of the temple of His body."*

Messenger then says, "So we see from the scripture that you had just read, Jesus was referring to His body as the temple."

"Yes. I knew this part. Many others know about this part as well. This isn't much of a revealing so far."

"Patience my friend, patience." Messenger then begins to pull out a few pages from within his long black coat. He hands them to me. They were Calendars. The very same type of Calendars that Messenger used to show me before. At the top left corner of the page was the number 6, representing the Hebrew sixth month known as the month of Elul. Under the days of the Calendar, I could see that this Calendar was for the year 1884 BC.

I then looked at Messenger and said, "1884 BC. This was one of the years of deliverance you shared with me before."

"That's right." Said Messenger. "Now look at the 24th day and tell me what that day corresponded to on your Calendar."

I began to look at the 24th day. I looked at the day it corresponded to on our calendar. I then looked up towards Messenger and said, "September 11th. The 24th Day of the 6th Month in the year 1884 BC corresponded to September 11th."

"Yes." Said Messenger. Messenger then handed another Calendar to me. It was for the year 538 BC and was a Calendar of the sixth month.

I looked at the 24th day of the sixth month of the year 538 BC. The 24th day corresponded to September 11th in the year 538 BC.

Messenger says, "Do you see the day the 24th day of the sixth month corresponds to in the year 538 BC?"

"Yes. I see it. It is September 11th, 538 BC."

"Very good." Messenger then hands the next Calendar to me. This Calendar was also for the sixth month, and the year was for 473 BC.

I looked at the 24th day of the sixth month for the year 473 BC. The 24th day corresponded to September 11th in the year 473 BC.

Messenger then says, "And you see this one? The day that the 24th of the sixth month corresponded to in the year 473 BC?"

"Yes. It is also September 11th."

Messenger smiles as he hands me the Calendar from 30 AD. It was also for the sixth Hebrew month, the month of Elul.

I looked at the 24th day of the sixth month for the year 30 AD. The 24th day corresponded to September 11th in the year 30 AD.

I then looked at Messenger and said, "These are the years you had shown me before, representing a year of deliverance. You had shown me how the Calendars matched during those years of deliverance."

Messenger then says, "That's right. And now you see for each of those years that represented a year of deliverance, the 24th day of the 6th month fell on what corresponded to September 11th on your Calendar."

"Why is this significant?"

Messenger takes the pages back from me and places them in the inside pocket of his long black coat as he says, "The Lord stirred up the spirit of Zerubbabel, Joshua and the remnant on the 24th day of the sixth month in the year 520 BC. Now, in the year 520 BC, the 24th day of the sixth month fell on what corresponded to September 21st, though what matters is that the day their spirit was stirred, the day they began building the second temple, was on the 24th day of the sixth month. We then see that the 24th day of the sixth month during each of those years of deliverance corresponds to September 11th, which represents Jesus Messiah, as I have already shown you the significance of September 11th regarding Jesus, His birth, His Baptism."

"This is amazing. So, you are saying the Lord chose the 24th day of the sixth month to stir the spirit of Zerubbabel, Joshua and the remnant for the very purpose to one day bring to light a message that has been concealed all this time?"

"Yes." Said Messenger. "Should you choose to accept it."

"What is the message?"

"The message is that it points to Jesus. He is the true living temple, not a temple built with hands, a temple built without hands." Messenger then looks at me and says, "Concerning Zerubbabel and Joshua. You remember me sharing with you that they represent the shadow of the Two Witnesses of Revelation 11. One the 'kingly' line and the other the 'priestly' line."

"Yes, I remember."

Messenger then says, "Then there is also the remnant. Now, remember what I shared with you earlier when Jesus answered the Jews, saying that He would destroy the temple and raise it up again in three days. We know that he was talking about His body being the temple."

"Yes, I remember. Are you about to reveal something else to me?"

"Yes." Said Messenger. "There is more to this concealed message, which can be found in two scriptures. One of the places is when Jesus is being brought in secretly to be questioned. The other is found in the book of Revelation. We will look at the place in scripture where Jesus is being questioned by Caiaphas first. Please read aloud to me **Matthew 26:59-66**."

**Matthew 26:59-66** *'Now the chief priests, the elders, and all the council sought false testimony against Jesus to put Him to death, but found none. Even though many false witnesses came forward, they found none.*

*But at last two false witnesses came forward and said, 'This fellow said, 'I am able to destroy the temple of God and to build it in three days.' And the high priest arose and said to Him, 'Do You answer nothing? What is it these men testify against You?' But Jesus kept silent. And the high priest answered and said to Him, 'I put You under oath by the living God: Tell us if You are the Christ, the Son of God!' Jesus said to him, 'It is as you said. Nevertheless, I say to you, hereafter you will see the Son of Man sitting at the right hand of the Power, and coming on the clouds of heaven.' Then the high priest tore his clothes, saying, 'He has spoken blasphemy! What further need do we have of witnesses? Look, now you have heard His blasphemy! What do you think?' They answered and said, 'He is deserving of death.'''*

Messenger then says, "The scriptures you just read show that two false witnesses came forward and spoke about what Jesus had said before when He said He would destroy the temple and build it in three days. The next part to note is Jesus' reply. He says, 'You will see the Son of Man sitting at the right hand of the Power and coming on the clouds.'"

I then looked at Messenger and said, "Okay, and why is that a part to note?"

Messenger said, "Remember I had shared with you that the Two Witnesses of Revelation 11 will represent the 'kingly' and 'priestly' lines?"

"Yes. I remember."

"It is not just one from the house of Israel and one from the house of Aaron. Even though one of the Two Witnesses will be from the house of Israel, and one will be from the house of Aaron, there are also those who fear the Lord, both small and great, which represents the church. Even though the Two Witnesses spoken of in Revelation 11 represent 'king' and 'priest.' The church also represents both 'kings' and 'priests.' Now remember what I said. We should note what Jesus had said in His response from the scripture you had just read. Read aloud to me now **Revelation 1:5-7**."

**Revelation 1:5-7** *"And from Jesus Christ, the faithful witness, the firstborn from the dead, and the ruler over the kings of the earth. To Him who loved us and washed us from our sins in His own blood, and has made us kings and priests to His God and Father, to Him be glory and dominion forever and ever. Amen. Behold, He is coming with clouds, and every eye* *will see Him, even they who pierced Him. And all the tribes of the earth will mourn because of Him. Even so, Amen."*

Messenger then says, "Do you see what you had just read? There is the mention of 'kings' and 'priests,' then the very mention of Him coming with the clouds, just as He said after He was questioned. After Jesus had responded, answering their question, they then charged Him with blasphemy. Remember what was said?"

"What? What was said?"

"The priest said, 'What more need is there of witnesses?' Well, I can tell you what more need there is of witnesses. You see, they had two false witnesses who spoke against Him regarding what He had said about destroying the temple and building it up in three days. We know that Jesus was talking about His body. At that time, there were two false witnesses. Though at the time of the end, there will be two true witnesses that will stand boldly, they will not speak against Him. The two true witnesses will speak for Him in favor of Him, and they will do so until they finish their testimony after 1,260 days, and their temple, which is their body, will be destroyed, killed by the Antichrist, though the Antichrist will not have the final say, three-and-a-half days later the breath of God will enter them, and they will stand on their feet, and a voice from heaven will say, 'Come up here.' They shall be built up again. They will be given their glorified body, transformed out of their black sackcloth and wearing kingly and priestly garments. Can you see that it is all there? What had been concealed is now revealed for such a time as this."

"Yes. Amen. I can see it. The connection. This is not a coincidence or chance. It is evident that the concealed message is found here and there, just like all of what you have shared up to this point."

Messenger then says, "Amen. I have just shared with you the mystery of the 24$^{th}$ day of the 6$^{th}$ Month, though there is also a mystery concerning what follows one month later."

"A month later? Are you talking about the Feast of Trumpets or the Day of Atonement?"

"No, I am not referring to that."

"The Feast of Tabernacles then?"

"No, not that either. I am referring to exactly one month following the 24th day of the 6th Month. It is the mystery of the 24th day of the 7th Month."

"There is a mystery regarding the 24th day of the 7th Month?"

"Yes. There is."

"What is it?" I asked.

Messenger then says, "The 24th day of the 7th Month is known as the day 'Israel is Set Apart.'"

"Set Apart?"

"Yes." Said Messenger. "To be considered 'holy' is to be 'set apart.' To be 'consecrated' is to be 'set apart.' To be 'anointed' is to be 'set apart.' Do you remember when Zechariah asked the angel what the two olive trees were that stood on the right and the left of the lampstand, that had the two olive branches that drip into the two gold pipes where the golden oil drains?"

"Yes. I remember."

"And you remember after the angel said to Zechariah, 'Do you not know what these are?' When Zechariah told the angel that he didn't know, what was the angel's answer to Zechariah's question?"

"He said, 'These are the two anointed ones, who stand beside the Lord of the whole earth.' As I have shared with you, these are a shadow of the Two Witnesses of Revelation 11. The Two Witnesses are the two anointed ones. They are the two 'set apart' ones."

"Set apart for what?"

Messenger then says, "Set apart to God for His glory."

"And you are saying there is something concealed? A mystery concerning the 24th day of the 7th month?"

"Yes." Said Messenger. "We will look at this day. We will even look at some scriptures related to the 24th day of the 7th Month, known as the Month of Tishrei. We will also look at some of the scriptures that speak of being set apart, being consecrated."

"Okay. And you are saying this is important?"

"Oh, very important." Said Messenger. "One who is to be 'set apart' is one who is to be anointed. So, we will look at that. We will look at…. The 'Anointing.'"

Explore this chapter's photos/calendars mentioned by scanning the QR code or visiting the link:

https://www.revealingthetimes.com/chapter27

# CHAPTER 28
# THE ANOINTING

Messenger pulls out from his coat pocket a vial. The vial had some kind of liquid in it. I looked at it intently and asked Messenger, "What is that?"

Messenger then said, "This is anointing oil. Anointing oil was used to sanctify, to set apart, to make holy. Take out your phone and look up **Exodus 30:30** and read aloud to me what it says please."

**Exodus 30:30** *"And you shall anoint Aaron and his sons, and consecrate them, that they may minister to Me as priests."*

Messenger says, "You see, the anointing oil was used on Aaron and his sons. They served as priests to the Lord. They were set apart. Read now **Exodus 40:12-15** aloud to me please."

**Exodus 40:12-15** *"Then you shall bring Aaron and his sons to the door of the tabernacle of meeting and wash them with water. You shall put the holy garments on Aaron, and anoint him and consecrate him, that he may minister to Me as priest. And you shall bring his sons and clothe them with tunics. You shall anoint them, as you anointed their father, that they may minister to Me as priests; for their anointing shall surely be an everlasting priesthood throughout their generations."*

Messenger then says, "Those of the house of Aaron were to be set apart at the age of twenty and above. Set apart to God for His service."

"Twenty and above? That is the same as those who were numbered who were to be of age to go to war."

"That is exactly right." Said Messenger. "Though there is more than a war to be fought from what one can see with their eyes. Remember, we do not wrestle with flesh and blood."

"But with principalities."

"That's right." Said Messenger. "The anointing oil was not only for the priests however. The anointing oil was also used to anoint kings. The prophet Samuel anointed Saul with the anointing oil. Saul, who was to be king. Samuel also anoints David with the anointing oil as well. The Lord sent Samuel to find one to be king in place of Saul, as Saul had disobeyed the word of the Lord. David was the youngest of his brothers, though the Lord chose him and sanctified him. The Lord was not interested in the appearance of the man. The Lord was interested in what was in his heart. Go to **1 Samuel 16:11-13** and read aloud to me when you are there please."

**1 Samuel 16:11-13** *"And Samuel said to Jesse, 'Are all the young men here?' Then he said, 'There remains yet the youngest, and there he is, keeping the sheep.' And Samuel said to Jesse, 'Send and bring him. For we will not sit down till he comes here.' So he sent and brought him in. Now he was ruddy, with bright eyes, and good-looking. And the Lord said, 'Arise, anoint him; for this is the one!' Then Samuel took the horn of oil and anointed him in the midst of his brothers; and the Spirit of the Lord came upon David from that day forward. So Samuel arose and went to Ramah."*

After reading the scripture, a thought came to mind as I looked at Messenger and said, "Priest and king. Both the priest and king were anointed with the anointing oil. I think about what you shared concerning the Two Witnesses of Revelation 11. You said one will be from the House of Israel representing the 'kingly' line, and the other will be from the House of Aaron representing the 'priestly' line."

"That's right." Said Messenger. "They are also referred to in the book of Zechariah as the two anointed ones." Messenger paused a moment and then said, "Remember what I shared with you from the book of Revelation concerning 'kings' and 'priests' the church, those who fear the Lord both small and great will be 'kings' and 'priests.' The two witnesses of Revelation 11 will each represent the office of 'priest' and 'king.' These will be two men."

I looked at Messenger, then said, "So, what about the 24th day of the 7th Month? You said this day has meaning, is known as Israel being set apart?"

"Yes, that's right." Said Messenger. "You can read about what happened on this specific day in the book of Nehemiah. The scripture read is **Nehemiah 9:1-38** though I will not have you read all of **Nehemiah 9:1-38**. I will instead have you read just the first part, and then I will have you read how it ends. Start first with reading **Nehemiah 9:1-3** aloud to me when you are there."

**Nehemiah 9:1-3** *"Now on the twenty-fourth day of this month the children of Israel were assembled with fasting, in sackcloth, and with dust on their heads. Then those of Israelite lineage separated themselves from all foreigners; and they stood and confessed their sins and the iniquities of their fathers. And they stood up in their place and read from the Book of the Law of the Lord their God for one-fourth of the day; and for another fourth they confessed and worshiped the Lord their God."*

Messenger then says, "Do you see what scripture says they are wearing?"

"They are wearing sackcloth."

"That's right." Said Messenger. "Now read aloud to me **Nehemiah 9:38**."

**Nehemiah 9:38** *"And because of all this, we make a sure covenant and write it; Our leaders, our Levites, and our priests seal it."*

Messenger then says, "What you just read says their 'leaders,' as in a 'governor.' What was Zerubbabel? He was a 'governor.' Then you read their Levites, their priests seal it. What was Joshua? He was 'high priest.' This was a covenant that man made with God rather than a covenant God had made with man. They seal the covenant. Just as a covenant that God made with Israel, to seal it was to be done by the shedding of blood, by sacrifice. So, at the beginning, you see they wear sackcloth, and the sealing of the covenant was by those who held the office of 'governor' and 'priest.' As I have shared with you before, Zerubbabel and Joshua are a shadow of the substance. The substance will be the Two Witnesses of Revelation 11. What do the Two Witnesses wear? They wear sackcloth. They will be 'Set Apart' 'Two Anointed Ones' and will seal the testimony they give by their death, which will be the shedding of their blood when the Antichrist kills them. This will not happen until they have finished giving their testimony after their 1,260 days. Go to **Hebrews 9:16-17** and read aloud to me when you are there, please."

**Hebrews 9:16-17** *"For where there is a testament, there must also of necessity be the death of the testator. For a testament is in force after men are dead, since it has no power at all while the testator lives."*

Messenger then says, "The word 'testament' is the Greek word translated 'Covenant.' Think of this as a 'Will' that one writes up. When your loved one writes up a 'Will,' they list their wishes and the names of those who will receive an inheritance. Before the person who wrote the 'Will' dies, the words within the 'Will' are only promises. Once the one who wrote the 'Will' dies, then what was written in the 'Will' takes effect, and the inheritance is given to those written in the 'Will.' The same applies to what Jesus did for us on the Cross. Before Jesus' death on the cross, our inheritance was at that time a promise, though once He died on the cross for us, the New Covenant was signed and sealed with His blood. Those found written in His 'Will' in the Lambs book of life will receive their inheritance, eternal life, present with the Lord."

I then looked at Messenger and said, "So why is the testimony and death of the Two Witnesses necessary, since the covenant has already been made complete by what Christ did for us on the cross?"

Messenger then said, "Remember, Jesus was rejected by many during His first coming. They brought out two false witnesses who spoke against Him. In the future, there will be two true witnesses who will speak of the truth that He is the Son of God, and the Father sent Him, that He is coming again. People will have a choice to either heed the word of the Two Witnesses and the remnant of believers, or the people will choose to follow the Antichrist and the false prophet. Choosing one will lead to eternal life in the presence of our Lord and Savior, Jesus Messiah, our King, King of kings and Lord of lords. Choosing the other will lead to forever condemnation, and their part will be in the lake of fire, separated from God for all eternity, where they will be with the Antichrist and the false prophet."

"Is there more of a connection with the 24th day of the 7th month?"

"Yes, there is." Said Messenger. "Though the message is concealed, as many read over this, it doesn't occur to the reader that this was the

24th day of the 7th month. The Lord Himself even mentions the word 'consecrate' as to reveal this day even well before the people had made that covenant with Him found in **Nehemiah 9:1-38**. God was affirming a covenant He would make with Israel, and it happened on the same day, on the 24th day of the 7th month hundreds of years before. Go to **2 Chronicles 7:14-18** and read aloud to me when you are there."

**2 Chronicles 7:14-18** *"If My people who are called by My name will humble themselves, and pray and seek My face, and turn from their wicked ways, then I will hear from heaven, and will forgive their sin and heal their land. Now My eyes will be open and My ears attentive to prayer made in this place. For now I have chosen and sanctified this house, that My name may be there forever; and My eyes and My heart will be there perpetually. As for you, if you walk before Me as your father David walked, and do according to all that I have commanded you, and if you keep My statutes and My judgments, then I will establish the throne of your kingdom, as I covenanted with David your father, saying, 'You shall not fail to have a man as ruler in Israel.'"*

Messenger then says, "You read the word 'sanctified' in the scripture you just read. Again, the word 'sanctified' means to 'Set Apart.' During the time of king Solomon, what was being sanctified in that moment was the Temple Solomon had built. However, as I have shared with you, we know the true temple is Jesus Himself, and we too are the temple as both He and His Father live in us and make their home in us, as the scriptures say. He takes away the first that He may establish the second."

I looked at Messenger and said, "How do we know this was on the 24th day of the 7th month?"

Messenger then says, "I have shared this with you before, though you may not remember. Read aloud **2 Chronicles 7:10**."

**2 Chronicles 7:10** *"On the twenty-third day of the seventh month he sent the people away to their tents, joyful and glad of heart for the good that the Lord had done for David, for Solomon, and for His people Israel."*

Messenger then says, "The scripture you just read tells us that Solomon sent the people away back to their tents on the 23rd day of the 7th month. It was later that evening when the Lord came to Solomon. The Jewish custom is that the day starts when the sun sets in the evening.

As the book of Genesis says, 'There was evening and there was day and that was the first day.' Because evening was mentioned first before 'day,' a new day begins in the evening. Since the Lord met with Solomon in the evening, it had now become a new day, the 24th day of the 7th month."

"Very interesting."

"There is more that is interesting about this day as well." Said Messenger. "Remember before I had shared with you what can be read just before verse 14. Read aloud to me **2 Chronicles 7:13** please."

**2 Chronicles 7:13** *"When I shut up heaven and there is no rain, or command the locusts to devour the land, or send pestilence among My people."*

Messenger then says, "What you just read are the very things the Two Witnesses of Revelation 11 will have the authority to do as it will be given to them by the Lord. Again, even here, we can see the relation bringing us back to the Two Witnesses of Revelation 11, just as the other scriptures I have had you read. There is more to this, however. It requires us to look at a few places in the New Testament. I will tell you one at a time for each one to read. First, read aloud **John 17:17-19**."

**John 17:17-19** *"Sanctify them by Your truth. Your word is truth. As You sent Me into the world, I also have sent them into the world. And for their sakes I sanctify Myself, that they also may be sanctified by the truth."*

"Read now **Acts 26:18**."

**Acts 26:18** *"To open their eyes, in order to turn them from darkness to light, and from the power of Satan to God, that they may receive forgiveness of sins and an inheritance among those who are sanctified by faith in Me."*

"Now read **Hebrews 2:10-11**."

**Hebrews 2:10-11** *"For it was fitting for Him, for whom are all things and by whom are all things, in bringing many sons to glory, to make the captain of their salvation perfect through sufferings. For both He who sanctifies and those who are being sanctified are all of one, for which reason He is not ashamed to call them brethren."*

Messenger then says, "Next read **Hebrews 10:8-10**."

**Hebrews 10:8-10** *"Previously saying, 'Sacrifice and offering, burnt offerings, and offerings for sin You did not desire, nor had pleasure in them' (which are offered according to the law), then He said, 'Behold, I have come to do Your will, O God.' He takes away the first that He may establish the second. By that will we have been sanctified through the offering of the body of Jesus Christ once for all."*

"The last one I will have you read on being sanctified is <u>Hebrews 10:14</u>. Please read that aloud to me."

**Hebrews 10:14** *"For by one offering He has perfected forever those who are being sanctified."*

Messenger then says, "As I have shared with you, to be sanctified is to be 'Set Apart.'" Messenger then looks behind us for a moment and then at me and says, "Because one is then 'set apart' this is what the believer who is sure in his faith, sure in his salvation is able to do...read aloud **Hebrews 10:19-22**."

**Hebrews 10:19-22** *"Therefore, brethren, having boldness to enter the Holiest by the blood of Jesus, by a new and living way which He consecrated for us, through the veil, that is, His flesh, and having a High Priest over the house of God, let us draw near with a true heart in full assurance of faith, having our hearts sprinkled from an evil conscience and our bodies washed with pure water."*

Messenger then says, "Would you like me to share the mystery now with what you just read?"

"Yes, please do."

"What you had read earlier from the book of Exodus, about taking the anointing oil to place on Aaron and his sons. Before the anointing oil was placed on Aaron and his sons, the anointing oil was placed on the tabernacle and the door of meeting. They were also to wash with water. Remember, I have shared with you that Jesus is the true Tabernacle, He is the true Temple and He is also the door. We are washed by the water, which is the water of the word. He is the word in the flesh, God in the flesh, God is Spirit. To be born again, we must be born again by water and the Spirit. We can now enter boldly into the door of meeting because we who believe in Him have been washed in His blood and are forever His."

"Amen. Truly, we are saved through faith in Him, through Jesus our Lord, our Rock and Shield."

Messenger then says, "Amen, my friend." Messenger then takes a moment to untie his sandals as he begins to take them off to feel the sand under his feet. He then says, "So, what are the plans for you all tomorrow?"

"We are going to a Bedouin camp tomorrow and having a service there."

Messenger then says, "Oh, that will be nice. Before you leave on the bus tomorrow, you should sound the Shofar."

"Okay, I can do that."

Messenger also says, "And following the service tomorrow, you should share with the host of the tour a message about when he dedicated his life to God. He did this at the age of twenty, and as is written in the scriptures, those who are of the sons of Aaron for all generations shall be 'set apart' to God at the age of twenty and above. Do this and see what he says to you."

"Okay, I will. Will I see you again while I am here?"

Messenger begins to walk away, leaving his footprints in the sand as he turns back and says, "We will see each other again the day after tomorrow when you are in Jerusalem. I will be waiting for you that evening as you walk out from the 'Dung Gate.' There, as I walk with you, I will have one final message to share with you."

"And what message is that?"

Messenger then says, "As I have shared with you what had been concealed, though no longer a mystery, it is now the time for the revealing for such a time as this. There are a few things left to reveal to you that will be revealed to you during our walk together the day after tomorrow. What I have left to reveal to you will end with what I like to call.... 'The Writing on the Wall.'"

I watch Messenger continue to walk away, seeing more of his footprints in the sand leading to the road. I said to Messenger as he walked further away, "The Writing on the Wall? What writing on the wall? On what wall?"

Messenger then says while walking away, "The day after tomorrow, I will show you. You shall see. Until then, peace to you, my friend."

# CHAPTER 29
# THE HANDWRITING ON THE WALL

I began walking towards the Dung gate. The sun was beginning to set. As I got closer, I could see Messenger standing beside the stone wall under the archway of the gate. Once he saw me, he started to walk in my direction as we both walked out from under the arch-way together.

"So, my friend, how did yesterday go? Did you end up going to the Bedouin camp for the service?"

"I did. The place was amazing, and the service was great as well. I did what you asked. I told him what you wanted me to say."

"And… What did he say when you told him that?"

"He told me that he knows that now, though he didn't know that was in the scripture when he decided to dedicate his life to God on his twentieth birthday. He then tells me that I have been the only person he knows who had ever picked up on that."

"Was that all he said?"

"No, he also asked me if I had ever written a book and said that if I haven't, I should. He then asked me if I was published, and I told him I wasn't. That's when he said with a smile, 'In case you didn't know, I am published. When you finish your book, send it to me and I will give it to my publisher.'"

"And so, it begins." Said Messenger with a smile. "Did anything else happen yesterday?"

"Yes. People from the tour who heard us both talking as we walked out of the Bedouin camp together laughed as they said, 'Hearing the two of you talk, it sounds like we are listening to the same person.' Yesterday, we also went to Susa to this ancient synagogue."

"You don't say. It is very interesting that he asks you if you have written a book, then mentions sending it to the publisher when you finish it and then going to Susa. You remember what I told you about Susa?"

"Yes, I remember. The place also known as Bashan, where Mordecai was when he saw the decree that had been given out by Haman sealed with the king's signet ring."

"Do you remember what I had told you about that day? It fell on the same day that corresponded to April 16th. Remember what I had told you, that when Mordecai saw and read what was there, what Moses said to the people could very well be said to Mordecai during that time."

"Yes. I remember. Be still and see your salvation. The Lord will fight for you. Something like that, right?"

"That's right." Said Messenger. "Was there anything your tour host said while there at the ancient synagogue in Susa?"

"Yes. He shared with us a writing that was part of the ancient mosaic flooring that says, 'Remember Yeshua.'"

"Yeshua." Says Messenger. "Yeshua is the word that means 'Salvation.' So the message is 'Remember Salvation.' I told you that what happened during the time of Esther was an amazing testimony of deliverance. Even though God was not mentioned once in the book of Esther, He was still very much present as He fought for them and guided them through to deliverance."

"Yes. So amazing. So beautiful."

"Did anything else happen yesterday, or how about today before you came here?"

"Today, we went up on the temple mount. It was beautiful to be up there, walking where Jesus had walked. What happened after was amazing too. It was divine."

"What happened?" Asked Messenger.

"We were going to take a tour on our bus through Bethlehem. I was on the Red bus, the last bus at the end of our convoy. The tour host was on the white bus at the front of the convoy. Throughout the whole tour, I always sat in the same seat when I was on our bus. Before we traveled through Bethlehem, we were told that we would have a special guest join us on our bus. It was the tour host. The tour host got on our bus and sat in the seat directly in front of me, though he didn't know I would be sitting there. We had more than 300 people on our tour. What are the odds that he would be sitting right in front of me as we travel through Bethlehem."

"That is amazing. Yes, definitely divine. Only God could have brought the two of you together so well. So, did you both talk?"

"Yes. Of course we talked. We pretty well talked through most of the drive through Bethlehem. I shared with him some of the dreams I had and the connection with the years of the division of the kingdom of Israel as well as the year when the northern kingdom of Israel went into Assyrian captivity. I shared with him that in the years 931 BC and 722 BC, the feast of trumpets fell on the day that corresponded to September 11th. I also shared with him the dream I had about Capitol Hill and the man wearing Pope's clothing. There was much we talked about as we traveled through Bethlehem."

Messenger then says, "Sounds to me that the Lord chose a perfect place for such a divine gathering. This provided time for you both to get a chance to talk more, as I am sure it would be very busy throughout the tour. As you traveled through Bethlehem together, the place of Messiah's birth, the Lord chose that place for the both of you to also give birth to something… a beautiful message… a testimony." Messenger then says, "So, was it busy at other times once you would get off the bus and on the tour?"

"Yes. Busy, though relaxed at the same time. So beautiful. For three nights so far, I have taught in different conference rooms at each of the hotels we have stayed at. I would do this after our dinner and would not finish with the message until almost Midnight. I was amazed that even though I had to wake up early the next day, I felt rested. I felt energized and rested throughout this entire trip. It's been great. Everything has been beautiful."

While Messenger and I continued to walk along the road along the outer wall of the City of Jerusalem, Messenger looked at me and said, "What was the message you shared in the conference room at the hotel?"

"Do you remember telling me before you had left, not this last time, the time when you gave me the shofar, the leather case and the bible?"

"Yes. I remember. I told you to keep watch for the starting of the sixth trumpet and what follows after. Have you done that?"

"I have."

"And what have you seen?"

In that moment, I had shared with Messenger all that I had observed leading up to Russia invading Ukraine and what followed. I shared with Messenger how I was guided to discover what was read in part of the Torah portion that following sabbath and then being guided to look up the geographical measurement of Ukraine. All to find out that the geographical measurement and the number read in the Torah portion during that Sabbath was the exact number 603,550. I shared with Messenger the colors on the breastplates. I shared about China and Taiwan being the rumors of war and the colors on their breastplates. I even talked about the five red heifers that had been shipped to Israel.

Messenger then says, "You have done well, my friend. You have been gifted with sight, the ability to perceive what you have seen and to understand what you have heard. However, this gift is not because of you. It is not you. It is who lives within you. The Holy Spirit guides you. Let Him continue to do so and pray that others may also see and perceive, to hear, and understand. The Lord gifts His children with different gifts. It is important that you all use those gifts to work together for the greater good. To bring many to the Lord in hopes they may come to be saved. For those who have fallen away, in hopes they return, to remember their salvation. You all should work together for His glory."

"Yes. Amen. I pray for this all the time. That we work together for His glory."

Messenger then says, "As you have said, we are not fully in the sixth trumpet, though what we are seeing is the starting of it. The mention of the 200 million that John heard when he wrote about the sixth trumpet, let me share something with you." Messenger brings out a page from inside his coat and hands it to me. It was a report that had been written on October 2nd, 1998.

This was what part of the report said:

*"The Peoples Republic of China PRC is seen by many as an economic powerhouse with the worlds largest standing military that has the potential to translate economic power into the military sphere. As one of the elements of power, a nations military potential is based not only on its capability to defeat an adversary, but also its ability to coerce and exercise influence. Chinas standing armed force of some 2.8 million active soldiers in uniform is the largest military force in the world. Approximately 1 million reservists and some 15 million militia back them up. With a population of over 1.2 billion people, China also has a potential manpower base of another 200 million males fit for military service available at any time…."* (Larry M. Wortzel) China's Military Potential (dtic.mil)

After reading what Messenger handed me, I handed the page back to Messenger and said, "Why did you have this with you? Did you know I would talk about the sixth trumpet with you?"

Messenger then says, "I had hoped that you would be watchful as I had asked you to, and you have. I had this with me in the event you would mention what you have both seen and heard. Did you notice the mention of 200 million males fit for military service available at any time?"

"Yes. I noticed that."

"I assure you, my friend. He was not quoting the book of Revelation regarding trumpet six when he wrote about 200 million males. He is a leading expert in China warfare, reporting facts that just so happens to be the same number. Do you think that is just a coincidence?"

"No. I have found there is too much that comes together for all of this to be a coincidence, from the dreams to how we have been guided to find what we find. Not knowing where to look or where to begin to find anything, and yet here we are talking about all of this now. All of this piece by piece. As you have said before, we need to have all the pieces to see the full picture. The Lord, by the Holy Spirit, has been the one who has helped us find those pieces. Guiding us into all truth."

"Yes. Amen, my friend."

"I do have one question though. This mention of China and 200 million males. China is not mentioned in trumpet six, though 200 million is mentioned. Can you help me understand this?"

Messenger then says, "It goes back to what I have shared with you before. Remember when I told you about what would really bake your noodle? John reported what he saw and heard. He wrote it down. When it comes to the 200 million in trumpet six, we read that John heard the number of them. John heard those who would be living during that time mention the number 200 million, and some of the people mention the 200 million during this time because John is the one who wrote it. Yet, at the same time, there is a leading expert on China warfare who also confirmed this number back in 1998, not because he was reading what John wrote almost 2000 years ago, but because this was factual information that the military expert in China warfare was reporting."

"So, it is like when the people mentioned Chernobyl when it happened. The very word that means 'Wormwood.' During the time of Chernobyl, the third trumpet, as people mention the word 'Chernobyl' and the mention of 'Wormwood,' John was writing down what he heard almost 2000 years ago before it happened. He heard the name, and he wrote it down. Though the scriptures say that John heard the name of the star was Wormwood."

"That's right." Said Messenger. "What we must keep in mind, however, is that John was seeing and hearing these things that were happening at this specific period of time. He saw what looked like a star falling, burning like a torch. The comet I showed you that happened to be closest to the earth and could be seen by the naked eye on April 10th, 1986, to then just 16 days later, Chernobyl happening and hearing its name, 'Wormwood.' John was seeing and hearing these things at the same time. I have shared all of this with you."

"Yes. I remember. So, you are saying the same applies to this with trumpet six? What about the timespan? How long will this go on for if we are seeing the starting of trumpet six?"

"The timespan cannot be measured in a way that would satisfy some who want exact dates. However, I can help you to understand how it was when John wrote it down. Again, remember John wrote what he saw and heard. Remember when I had shared the fifth trumpet with you?"

"Yes. I remember."

"Remember when I shared with you what Saddam had done by lighting all of those oil wells on fire in 1991? It brought back news of what he had done to a particular oil refinery and city in Iran back in 1980. What Saddam did to that City in Iran and that oil refinery happened more than 10 years prior. However, it was brought back up in the news during the time of trumpet five, and John heard the name 'Abaddon.' As I have shared with you before, the spelling of 'Abadan,' the city of Iran, and Abaddon in trumpet five are spelled differently, though the pronunciation is the exact same, and we need to remember that John wrote down what he heard. The space of time from 1980 to 1991 was more than 10 years. What happened in 1980 was not Trumpet Five, though because what happened in 1980 came back into the news during the time of Trumpet Five, caused it to become part of what John wrote when he heard the name Abaddon associated with this leader who brought destruction and whose name also means 'Destroyer.' So, Trumpet Five happened during a particular span of time, though there were elements written in it that happened years before, though written for that same time because there was mention of both at that time. It is also interesting to note when speaking of the city and refinery of Iran that bears the name 'Abadan,' guess who came to their aid to renovate and build it back up again?"

"Was it China?"

"Yes. It was China. Do you understand what I am sharing with you here?"

"Yes. I understand. And you are saying the same can be applied to trumpet six? As we are watching the starting of it, the timespan of when it comes to fullness is unknown to us, though still all of it is written as if happening all together at once, as you just mentioned by your example with the city of Iran and the time of trumpet five, is that right?"

"Yes. That's right." Said Messenger. "Trumpet six mentions the Euphrates River and the four bound at the Euphrates River. As you have shared with me, there are four countries bound by the Euphrates River, and as you see now, the Euphrates River is drying up. These four will no longer be bound by it. You have done well to mention this, though keep in mind that we do not wrestle with flesh and blood but with Principalities. There is an unseen force, an angel bound at each of these countries as well. So, in the natural, you are right. These are the four bound at the Euphrates River, though to the unseen principalities, there are four angels bound here as well."

"And you are saying that China will also be part of this concerning the Euphrates River?"

Messenger then says, "The kings of the east will cross on dry ground because the river Euphrates will be dried up. The way will be prepared for them. This happens later, though what you see now with the river Euphrates drying up along with what you have seen concerning the colors on their breastplates, you are seeing the starting of it. Take out your phone and go to the book of Daniel. Read aloud to me **Daniel 11:43-45**."

**Daniel 11:43-45** *"He shall have power over the treasures of gold and silver, and over all the precious things of Egypt; also the Libyans and Ethiopians shall follow at his heels. But news from the east and the north shall trouble him; therefore he shall go out with great fury to destroy and annihilate many. And he shall plant the tents of his palace between the seas and the glorious holy mountain; yet he shall come to his end, and no one will help him."*

Messenger then says, "Notice what you have just read. Though this happened in ancient times concerning Antiochus Epiphanes, the same will happen and has been happening even now. The starting of it. Things are being prepared as they lead to that coming end. The end times fulfillment of this is the lawless one. The Antichrist will have power over the treasures of gold and silver. He will have power over money, buying and selling, and he will have power over the precious things of Egypt. The precious things of Egypt is their natural gas, and even now, the natural gas from Egypt passes through Syria and Jordan to Lebanon. Notice what I just said to you, Syria and Jordan. Who controls the temple mount?"

"Jordan controls the temple mount."

"That's right." Said Messenger. "There have also been the conflicts in Lybia, and the War you have seen between Russia and Ukraine has not been the deadliest war this year of 2022. It has been the war in Ethiopia. Both of the conflicts and wars you have been hearing of in your news. All of these things are paving the way to what will lead to what is spoken in the scriptures you just read." Messenger took a moment as I looked at him while we were still walking around the outer wall of Jerusalem. Messenger looks at me and says, "Speaking of Ethiopia, do you happen to know when the new year in Ethiopia is celebrated? The day it falls on with your calendar?"

"No. When?"

Messenger says, "The Ethiopian new year is called 'Enkutatash,' which means 'gift of jewels.' People say it refers to when the Queen of Sheba had returned from visiting king Solomon here in Jerusalem. The Ethiopian New Year every year, unless it is a leap year, falls on September 11th."

"Really!? September 11th!?"

"Yes. September 11th." Said Messenger. "Going back to the scripture you had read. Part of those who come from the east will be China. When the 'beast' which is the Antichrist, comes to show his true colors at the midpoint of the seven-year tribulation, when he has control over who may buy or sell, China, who was so close to being the dominating world power, will make an attempt to war against the Antichrist in an attempt to try and become the dominating power. This time of war will be the time spoken of when the way has been prepared for the kings of the east to travel across dry ground as the river Euphrates will be dried up. Before that time comes and before the midpoint of the seven-year tribulation begins, there shall be a great deliverance, the deliverance you know as the Rapture of the church. Please read aloud **Daniel 12:1-3**."

**Daniel 12:1-3** *"At that time Michael shall stand up, the great prince who stands watch over the sons of your people; And there shall be a time of trouble, such as never was since there was a nation, even to that time. And at that time your people shall be delivered, every one who is found written in the book. And many of those who sleep in the dust of the earth shall awake, some to everlasting life, some to shame and everlasting contempt. Those who are wise shall shine like the brightness of the* *firmament, and those who turn many to righteousness like the stars forever and ever."*

Messenger then says, "And the very scriptures that follow what you just read mention the amount of time remaining, which will be a time, times and half a time. There will be 3 ½ years that will remain. That will be the latter half, known as the great tribulation, where God's wrath is poured out, and we who are in Christ are not appointed to God's wrath. As I have shared with you before, the rapture and the Lord's second coming are two different things. There will be those who are of Christ during the latter half of the tribulation. They are the tribulation saints. They are those who instantly believe and fear and give glory to God when the two witnesses go up, and the earthquake happens in that same hour. Remember what I have shared with you? They give fear and glory to God because when they see the two witnesses stand to their feet who were once dead and go up to heaven raptured before them, this will be the first time they had ever seen it, and many will know exactly what this was and will believe. They will be tribulation saints. Others will still have doubt and unbelief while still holding to the ways of the world, and they will follow the ways of the Antichrist. Now concerning those kings of the east who travel on dry ground across the dried-up Euphrates river to battle against the Antichrist in hopes they gain world dominance. The Lord is the one who leads them there to that battle to bring them to a swift end and pay attention to what follows. Read aloud to me **Revelation 16:15-16**."

**Revelation 16:15-16** *'Behold, I am coming as a thief. Blessed is he who watches, and keeps his garments, lest he walk naked and they see his shame.' And they gathered them together to the place called in Hebrew, Armageddon."*

Messenger then says, "This will be at the time of the Lord's Return. Known as His second coming. Please read aloud to me **Revelation 16:17-18**."

**Revelation 16:17-18** *'Then the seventh angel poured out his bowl into the air, and a loud voice came out of the temple of heaven, from the throne, saying, "It is done!" And there were noises and thunderings and lightnings; and there was a great earthquake, such a mighty and great earthquake as has not occurred since men were on the earth."*

Messenger then says, "This is during the seventh bowl judgment, the finality of God's wrath at the end of the remaining 3 ½ years of the great tribulation. Following this is when the Lord returns. His second coming is when He comes to rule and reign for a thousand years, and we who are His will rule and reign with Him. There will also be one final judgment, following the last brief rebellion at the end of the Millennial reign when Lucifer is loosed for a final and short time."

I can see the Mount of Olives in front of me as we walk around the outer wall. I think about the five red heifers that had been shipped to Israel just a couple of months before I had left for Israel. I thought about how one of them will be burned out there on the Mount of Olives once it reaches its third year of age. I looked at Messenger and said, "What about the red heifer? Is there anything you can tell me about this?"

Messenger then says, "You mean, is there anything more I can share with you on the red heifer other than what you have shared with me?"

"Yes. Is there anything else?"

"There is." Said Messenger. "Though the message has remained concealed, it is a mystery, though now is the time for the revealing for such a time as this."

"What is it?"

Messenger then says to me, "Go to the book of Samuel. Read aloud to me **1 Samuel 16:2-5**."

**1 Samuel 16:2-5** *"And Samuel said, 'How can I go? If Saul hears it, he will kill me.' But the Lord said, 'Take a heifer with you, and say, 'I have come to sacrifice to the Lord.' Then invite Jesse to the sacrifice, and I will show you what you shall do; you shall anoint for Me the one I name to you.' So Samuel did what the Lord said, and went to Bethlehem. And the elders of the town trembled at his coming, and said, 'Do you come peaceably?' And he said, 'Peaceably; I have come to sacrifice to the Lord. Sanctify yourselves, and come with me to the sacrifice.' Then he consecrated Jesse and his sons, and invited them to the sacrifice."*

Messenger then says, "You see, what you had just read was the truth. This was what Samuel was told to do by the Lord as Samuel went to Jesse and his sons. Notice Samuel brings a heifer and comes peaceably, and he truly came peaceably. What followed this was Samuel anointed the youngest, who was not there with them. He anoints David and confirms him secretly as the new king. What you read is the truth, though in the near future, there will be one who comes to power known as the willful king, who is the Antichrist. There will be a sacrifice of a red heifer. There will be a confirmation of the covenant. The Antichrist will not be there at the burning of the red heifer, though what will follow at some point is one who comes peaceably. The devil himself will empower him and will be the anti-messiah, not of king David. He will be a willful king. He will come in peaceably only for half of the time that he confirms with many for one week of seven years, and in the middle of that seven years, he will fully be revealed as to who he is, still many who are of the world will believe the lie and follow him and take his mark. We must pray for others to be watchful of the times and stand ready. To bear witness and proclaim that Jesus is the Son of God, the Father sent Him and He is coming again."

"I suppose the red heifer sacrifice and the confirming of the covenant will pave the way for the third temple to be built. Since from what you have shared about the two witnesses giving their testimony as the third temple begins to go up, we should watch for the third temple when it starts to be built, and we should watch for Two men who will be able to have fire proceed out of their mouth right?"

Messenger then says, "The red heifer sacrifice is one of the steps that pave the way closer to a third temple being built. Once a covenant is confirmed, that will then allow the Jews to build the third temple. You should be watchful of this, yes. Though to be watching for two men who will be able to have fire proceed out of their mouth, is that what you think the Two witnesses will be able to do?"

"That is what Revelation 11 says. The Two Witnesses will have fire proceed out of their mouth to devour their enemies who try to harm them."

Messenger then says, "You have been watching too many movies. However, this is no fault of those who have put such things in a movie showing the Two witnesses to show fire proceeding out of their mouth. They are only taking that to be literal, just as you are. Remember what I have shared with you. We must have all the pieces to see the full picture. Please read aloud to me **Jeremiah 5:14**."

**Jeremiah 5:14** *'Therefore thus says the Lord God of hosts: 'Because you speak this word, behold, I will make My words in your mouth fire, and this people wood, and It shall devour them.'''*

Messenger then says, "You see, even in the book of Jeremiah, we read that the people will be as wood. Now, we don't take that literally, do we? Were the people really going to be wood? No, yet that is what is said. We then see in the book of Jeremiah what the fire in his mouth actually represents. The 'fire' is the word they speak. Consider also where we read in the book of Revelation when it says that a sword will be protruding from the Lord's mouth. One doesn't think an actual sword will come out of His mouth. Everyone knows the sword represents the word. The same applies to the Two Witnesses of Revelation 11. It is not literal fire that will be proceeding out of their mouth. It will be the word they speak when they begin giving their testimony, it will spark a revival, though there will still be those of the world that seek to do them harm, yet the words they speak will even bring some to die to self and return to the Lord having salvation." Messenger then looked at me and said, "Speaking of the book of Jeremiah. You should go by the name Jeremiah rather than Jeremy. You do know what the name Jeremiah means, don't you?"

"Yes. The name Jeremiah means 'YHWH will raise' or 'God is high."

Messenger then says, "That is right. Now, one last thing about the book of Jeremiah. You see, even within the book of Jeremiah, there is a concealed message concerning the Two Witnesses of Revelation 11. One I have already shared with you concerning the fire being the word they speak. The other is this, please read aloud to me **Jeremiah 1:11-12**."

**Jeremiah 1:11-12** *'Moreover the word of the Lord came to me, saying, 'Jeremiah, what do you see?' And I said, 'I see a branch of an almond tree.' Then the Lord said to me, 'You have seen well, for I am ready to perform My word.'''*

Messenger then says, "What have I shared with you concerning the rod that budded with almonds placed in the Ark of the Covenant?"

"You have said the rod that budded with almonds was Aaron's rod and represents the house of Aaron."

"That's right. And just like in the days of Jeremiah when the Lord was ready to perform His word, so too will He perform His word through the Two witnesses when they give testimony in the days of their testimony of 1,260 days. The book of Jeremiah is also the book that mentions the New Covenant that I have shared with you before in **Jeremiah 31:31-33**, which speaks of the house of Israel. So in the book of Jeremiah, you find concealed within it the object that represents the house of Aaron, the substance in the New Covenant in the house of Israel, and even the mention of the word in the mouth being fire. Lastly, the meaning of the name of the very book (Jeremiah), where it is written, means 'YHWH will raise' 'God is high.' The Two Witnesses of Revelation 11, God will raise to life 3 ½ days after their death, and they will stand on their feet and go up to Him who calls when He says, 'Come up here.' They will go to God who is high and to be lifted up, worthy of our praise."

"Amen. Truly Amen."

As Messenger and I walked along the Eastern wall, coming towards the Eastern gate, Messenger said, "This is what I wanted to show you. The writing on the wall."

I looked at the place Messenger pointed to on the Eastern wall. It was plant vines growing out from the stones on the Eastern wall. The vines that grew out were Hebrew letters. I looked at Messenger and said, "How did these get here? Did someone put them this way to make these Hebrew letters?"

Messenger then says, "No man made these vines to form into these Hebrew letters. They happened this way on their own, though should you choose to accept it, God formed them to grow the way they did."

"Why would God do such a thing?"

"To deliver a message."

"What kind of message?"

Messenger then says, "Well, you see, there are some Jews who have come to see this, and they believe that God is writing His most holy name on the Eastern wall. Three of the Hebrew letters are here, and they are waiting for the fourth letter to appear."

"What is the name?"

"YHWH," Messenger said. "Though the fourth letter is not going to appear because the message has already been written. The writing is already on the wall."

"What is the message?"

Messenger then says, "The message is concealed within the meaning of each Hebrew letter. You have the 'Y' that is the 'Yod,' you then have the 'H' that is the 'Heh,' and last you have the 'W' that is the 'Vav.' The 'Yod' means 'hand,' the 'Heh' means 'behold,' and the 'Vav' means 'Nail.' When you put all three letters together as they are here written on this Eastern wall, it bears the message, 'Hand beholds nail.'"

"Hand beholds nail!? As in the hand that beholds the nail."

"That's right," said Messenger. "There is a reason the message is on this Eastern wall. Do you see over there?" Messenger begins pointing towards what looks like a closed stone walled gate that is part of the Eastern wall. Messenger then says, "That Eastern gate that is closed off is the very gate that Jesus will come through at His second coming. Before He comes through the Eastern gate, He will first do something else."

"What will He do?"

Messenger turns me around as we look to the Mount of Olives.

Messenger then says, "The Lord will step foot upon the Mount of Olives at His second coming. Read aloud to me **Zechariah 14:1-5**."

**Zechariah 14:1-5** *"Behold, the day of the Lord is coming, and your spoil will be divided in your midst. For I will gather all the nations to battle against Jerusalem; The city shall be taken, the houses rifled, and the women ravished. Half the city shall go into captivity, but the remnant of the people shall not be cut off from the city. Then the Lord will go forth and fight against those nations, as He fights in the day of battle. And in that day His feet will stand on the Mount of Olives, which faces Jerusalem on the east. And the Mount of Olives shall be split in two, from east to west, making a very large valley; Half of the mountain shall move toward the north and half of it toward the south. Then you shall flee through My* *mountain valley, for the mountain valley shall reach to Azal. Yes, you shall flee as you fled from the earthquake in the days of Uzziah king of Judah. Thus the Lord my God will come, and all the saints with You."*

Messenger then says, "So, you see. The Lord when He returns. He will step foot on the Mount of Olives facing this Eastern wall. Every eye will see Him, even those who pierced Him. The one whose hands beheld the nails will return here and there will be a violent earthquake, and the Mount of Olives will split in two. He will then pass through the Eastern gate that is shut. The message is already there. The writing is on the wall. He is coming soon. We do not know the day or the hour, only the Father knows, yet we stand and keep watch."

"Do you think the Jews who have seen this on the wall, instead of them waiting for another letter to appear, if they knew the message is already there, do you think they would come to believe that Jesus is truly the Son of God and that He is coming again?"

"Some of them may, though there will still be others who will still not believe."

"I pray all may come to believe that Jesus is the Son of God, that the Father sent Him and He is coming again. I pray they turn to Him and believe in faith, that they may have salvation."

"Amen." Says Messenger. "I pray that too." Messenger then says, "So, my friend. What are you all doing after this?"

"Tonight, we are actually going up to the Mount of Olives, where we will praise and worship. We will also have communion there."

Messenger then says, "When you are up there on the Mount of Olives tonight, take your shofar that I have given you, press it to your lips while facing this Eastern wall and sound it with long blasts. May those who are here take notice of its sounding and give ear to stand ready, to keep watch for the return of the Lord, our King."

"I will do that."

Messenger then says, "Good. I have given you these things that you may be a Watchman. Stand ready, keep watch, give warning and proclaim the good news."

"What if they won't hear? What if they won't listen and still won't believe?"

"Do not worry about those who mock in unbelief. Do not worry about those who will still not hear or listen. Many will come to believe, many more will have eyes and perceive, and many will have ears and understand what has been shared with you for others to know. Never cease to pray. May those who have ears to hear and eyes to see come to know and believe that Jesus is the Son of God, the Father has sent Him and He is coming again. May those who have had doubt believe that He is who He is and be saved. Because of the message you have been given, many will hear and come to believe in the Lord. The message you have been given is not to replace the scriptures. The message is to act as a companion with the scriptures for those who have still had doubt and unbelief. May they be like the Bereans in Paul's day. May they search through the scriptures for themselves concerning our report. May they test what is said here and come to believe that Jesus truly is the Son of God. He is Messiah, King of kings and Lord of lords. He is the Way, the Truth and the Life. No one goes to the Father except through Him. Amen and Amen."

"Amen."

Messenger then says, "And what will you be doing tomorrow?"

"At some point tomorrow, we will be back on the Mount of Olives, where the host of the tour will do an anointing for those of us who were on the tour."

Messenger then says, "This will be tomorrow?"

"Yes."

"Are you aware that tomorrow will be the day of a lunar eclipse and tomorrow is also the day when elections will be held in your country? This too, what will happen tomorrow by the anointing service, will be a confirmation, though there is more to what will happen tomorrow. Those who organized this tour did not do this for this reason. They did not choose this day tomorrow because the elections are being held in your country tomorrow. Here is the message. Read aloud to me **2 Peter 1:10-11**."

**<u>2 Peter 1:10-11</u>** *"Therefore, brethren, be even more diligent to make your call and election sure, for if you do these things you will never stumble; for so an entrance will be supplied to you abundantly into the everlasting kingdom of our Lord and Savior Jesus Christ."*

Messenger then says, "Remember that you have been cleansed from your old sins. Though, there will be those who will attempt to silence the message you have been given. There will be those who attempt to discredit you because of the reproach of your youth. Though, for those who give attention to the reproach of your youth they forget to hold to grace and mercy that comes from the Lord. Read aloud to me **<u>1 Corinthians 1:26-31</u>**."

**<u>1 Corinthians 1:26-31</u>** *"For you see your calling, brethren, that not many wise according to the flesh, not many mighty, not many noble, are called. But God has chosen the foolish things of the world to put to shame the wise, and God has chosen the weak things of the world to put to shame the things which are mighty; and the base things of the world and the things which are despised God has chosen, and the things which are not, to bring to nothing the things that are, that no flesh should glory in His presence. But of Him you are in Christ Jesus, who became for us wisdom from God—and righteousness and sanctification and redemption—that, as it is written, 'He who glories, let him glory in the Lord.'"*

Messenger then says, "Always remember that. Though you are weak, in Christ, you have been made strong."

"I will remember. Will I see you again?"

"If it is the Lord's will, we shall see each other again. If so, it will be at a time unknown to us, though it will be at a time appointed by the Lord should He choose for us to come together again."

"Is there anything else you would like to say before you go?"

Messenger then says, "Yes. As I have said, you have seen well as you have seen the starting of the sixth trumpet and what has followed after. Be mindful of what the Lord has said concerning what we will hear in these days. Read aloud to me **<u>Matthew 24:6-8</u>**."

**<u>Matthew 24:6-8</u>** *"And you will hear of wars and rumors of wars. See that you are not troubled; for all these things must come to pass, but the* *end is not yet. For nation will rise against nation, and kingdom against kingdom. And there will be famines, pestilences, and earthquakes in various places. All these are the beginning of sorrows."*

Messenger then says, "What has been happening is the beginning of sorrows. Right before a woman goes into labor, her contractions begin to come closer together before the time that is set for her to give birth. The reason you are seeing all of these things happening all at once is because the contractions are getting closer together. What has happened in Ethiopia, what has happened with Libya, what has happened with Russia and Ukraine, that is war. What you have been hearing with China and Taiwan is the rumors of war. The earthquakes in various places as you know, there have been many in various places, though there is something for you to know. The place where the rumors of war are being heard, during the height of this a few months ago, there was a 6.6 earthquake that hit Taiwan on September 17th, 2022. Also, on the very day that Vladimir Putin officially announced he would send more Russians to fight in Ukraine, even after months of the war already taking place. The day Vladimir Putin made this announcement was on September 21st, 2022. That very day, there was a 6.0 earthquake in Russia. So, in the places where war and rumors of war are being heard, you are also seeing and hearing of earthquakes happening in those places. Though Jesus said this would happen, He also said, 'See that you are not troubled; for all these things must come to pass, but the end is not yet.'"

"I don't believe it was a coincidence that these earthquakes happened here at these specific times. The very ground is shaking in order to wake us up, so we are aware of the times. Yet still, many do not believe. Jesus said these things would happen beforehand, and yet still so many have yet to believe that He is Lord."

Messenger then says, "That's right. It is as Peter said in **2 Peter 3:3-4** *'knowing this first: that scoffers will come in the last days, walking according to their own lusts, and saying, 'Where is the promise of His coming? For since the fathers fell asleep, all things continue as they were from the beginning of creation.'"*

Messenger then begins to look back at the Mount of Olives and says, "Remember what I had shared with you from the book of Zechariah. When the Lord returns, when He stands on the Mount of Olives, they will split, making a deep valley. Keep watch, my friend, for there is much that is yet to happen. When you see and hear, search the scriptures and proclaim. For the Lord has told of these things before they come to pass, so when they do come to pass, one may believe that Jesus is the Son of God, that the Father has sent Him and He is coming again. Truly, truly, Amen and Amen."

"Amen, my friend. I will keep watch and proclaim in the hopes they repent and be saved by faith in Jesus our Lord and King."

Explore this chapter's photos/calendars mentioned by scanning the QR code or visiting the link:

https://www.revealingthetimes.com/chapter29

# CHAPTER 30
# THE SHAKING

Monday morning. Present day, back in David's office. It had been an interesting couple of days as Jeremy and David finished reviewing all Messenger had shared with Jeremy. The two of them were ready for this message, this book, to reach those around the world. They had a few more things to finish before they could officially say, 'We are ready to print.' Jeremy had a couple more things to share, and David had a question that had been lingering on his mind since Jeremy had ended with the last thing Messenger had told him concerning when Jesus steps foot on the Mount of Olives, that the Mount of Olives would split in two with a deep valley between them.

David stands at his desk, picks up his phone, and dials Penny.

"Yes 007."

"Penny, of those rescheduled appointments. Will you call them today and let them know we can plan for Wednesday and the following days if that works for them."

"Okay. I can do that. What time should I schedule them if they are available?"

"Anytime from Wednesday to Friday this week will be fine."

"Okay, I will call them and let them know. How was your weekend?"

"It was eye-opening, jaw-dropping and awe-inspiring the whole weekend since Friday."

"That's nice. I take it Jeremy was with you over the weekend?"

"He was, and he is still here with us. He is here in the office with me now."

"So, I take it we are going to publish his book then? I hope so. I would like to know more. Don't keep what was shared with you to yourself."

"There are a couple of things left to do Penny, though trust that you will soon know all that has been shared Friday and through this weekend, even what will be shared today."

"That's great. I look forward to it. Tell Jeremy I said hello."

"Will do." David gets off the phone and says to Jeremy, "Penny says 'hello.'"

"That's nice. I will be sure to wish her well before I leave here today."

David walks around to the front of his desk, sits across from Jeremy, and says, "So, there has been a question I have wanted to ask since this weekend. It is related to the last thing Messenger shared with you. The part about Jesus, when He returns and stands on the Mount of Olives, that the Mount of Olives will be split in two with a deep valley between them."

"Okay. What is your question?"

"Do you think there is anything prophetic concerning the earthquake that happened on February 6th this year in Turkey and Syria? I can't help but think about what Messenger had shared with you, almost as if he knew this would happen. He said to you to search the scriptures when you see and hear. Before he says that to you, he tells you about the Mount of Olives splitting in two, leaving a deep valley between them. He tells you to search the scriptures, for the Lord has told us these things before they come to pass so that when they do come to pass, one may believe that Jesus is who He is, the Son of God and the Father sent Him. I can't help but think about that Olive grove in Turkey that split in two during that earthquake, leaving a large, deep valley between them. You have seen it right?"

"Of course, I have seen it."

"So, do you think it is prophetic?"

"By prophetic, do you mean can it be found within the scriptures?"

"Yes. That is what I mean." Says David.

Jeremy reaches down to pick up his leather case on the floor beside him. He opens it up and pulls out a page from it. He then opens his Bible and says to David, "Yes. It can be found within the scriptures, though it does not say the word 'earthquake' in the particular scripture I will read to you. There is however a message that is concealed that one must know why the Lord says what He says in a certain scripture the way He says it."

"Like a parable?"

"Not necessarily a parable. Sometimes, the Lord will have something within His word that is enough to reveal it, though still written in such a way that requires one to still have faith. So, I will share it with you, and it will be up to you if you choose to accept it or not."

"Okay." Says David. "You can tell me."

Jeremy first opens his Bible and begins to read aloud **Zechariah 14:5** *'Then you shall flee through My mountain valley, for the mountain valley shall reach to Azal. Yes, you shall flee as you fled from the earthquake in the days of Uzziah king of Judah.'*

Jeremy then says, "The first clue we have is here within the scriptures of **Zechariah 14:5**. There is the mention of the word 'earthquake' and before that, is where we read of the Mount of Olives being split in two with a deep valley between them. This happens when the Lord returns and steps foot on the Mount of Olives. What we saw in Turkey in the aftermath of the earthquake that happened on February 6th, with the Olive grove splitting in two with a long deep valley between them, is only a preview of how it will be when the Lord returns on the Mount of Olives and the Mount of Olives splits in two. Though one may say this is a coincidence and that I am just making this fit. That is why I cannot just stop there. As Messenger had shared before, we need all the pieces. We need to test what is mentioned within the scriptures with what is being said and with what is happening around us. So let us find the other pieces, shall we."

"Yes. Please show me." Says David.

Jeremy then takes the Bible and hands it to David as he says, "I will have you read for yourself these next scriptures. Read aloud to me **Isaiah 17:1**."

**Isaiah 17:1** *"The burden against Damascus. 'Behold, Damascus will cease from being a city, and it will be a ruinous heap.'"*

Jeremy then says, "This is the scripture that talks about how in the latter days, Damascus will be no more. It will cease from being a city. Damascus is one of the oldest cities that has existed since ancient times, though in the later days, before the return of the Lord, it will cease to be a city. Read aloud now **Isaiah 17:6**."

**Isaiah 17:6** *"Yet gleaning grapes will be left in it, like the shaking of an olive tree, two or three olives at the top of the uppermost bough, four or five in its most fruitful branches," Says the Lord God of Israel."*

Jeremy then says, "This was referring to the judgment that fell upon the northern kingdom of Israel in 722 BC, often referred to as Ephraim. The judgment was so great, as evidenced by the parable given about the olive tree, saying that by its shaking, two or three olives are left at the top of the uppermost bough and only four or five in its most fruitful branches. This was a way of saying that the judgment of the Lord was so great that the shaking was so strong that it pretty well made the northern kingdom of Israel as if it was no more, yet to say there are two or three olives in the uppermost bough and four or five on its most fruitful branches was a way of saying that God would leave a remnant from each of the tribes of Israel. They may be thought of as the 10 lost tribes of Israel, though in the book of Revelation, there is mention there will be 12,000 from each tribe, which tells us they may seem lost to us. Still, they are not lost to the Lord. There will still be that remnant that will bear fruit as they abide in the Lord. Now read aloud **Isaiah 17:7-8**."

**Isaiah 17:7-8** *"In that day a man will look to his Maker, and his eyes will have respect for the Holy One of Israel. He will not look to the altars, the work of his hands; He will not respect what his fingers have made, nor the wooden images nor the incense altars."*

Jeremy then says, "You remember what has been shared with you concerning the Two Witnesses. They are the two olive trees, the two olive branches. You remember what has been shared with you concerning the way Trumpet six ends is how Psalm 115 begins. Psalm 115 mentions the two houses. One who will be from the house of Israel and one from the house of Aaron. These two whose very ancestors from long ago worshipped false gods and idols, things made with their hands, though in the later days, those who remain in the branch, those who bear fruit and abide in the Lord shall respect Him and not look anymore to things made by their hands, not giving themselves over anymore to Idols and false gods. Read aloud now **Isaiah 17:9**."

**Isaiah 17:9** *"In that day his strong cities will be as a forsaken bough and an uppermost branch, which they left because of the children of Israel; And there will be desolation."*

Jeremy then says, "Just as it was for the northern kingdom of Israel in 722 BC, so too can this be seen when one looks at Damascus. This once strong city is like an uppermost branch left on its own pretty well leafless, and all the branches below are withered with no life in them, bearing no fruit. The surrounding towns of Damascus are rubble, a ruinous heap, a heap of ruins. Read aloud now what follows in **Isaiah 17:10-11**."

**Isaiah 17:10-11** *"Because you have forgotten the God of your salvation, and have not been mindful of the Rock of your stronghold, therefore you will plant pleasant plants and set out foreign seedlings; In that day you will make your plant to grow, and in the morning you will make your seed to flourish; but the harvest will be a heap of ruins in the day of grief and desperate sorrow."*

Jeremy then says, "Now, what I am about to share with you is very important to pay attention to. In the scripture you just read, there is talk of planting pleasant plants. They would plant pleasant plants, and a year later, from the time they had planted them, they would expect a good harvest, though the Lord says that it will be a heap of ruins, a day of grief and desperate sorrow. The heap of ruins mentioned in this chapter is a clue for us to look back to the place referred to as a ruinous heap in the latter days, which was talking of Damascus."

Jeremy then takes the page that he had pulled from the leather case and he hands the page to David. It was a picture of a father planting a pleasant plant with his son. Below the picture, there were words that read, 'Planting trees for Tu Bishvat 1945.'

David looks at Jeremy and says, "What is Tu Bishvat?"

"Tu Bishvat is a Jewish holiday that occurs on the 15th day of the Hebrew month of Shevat. It is also called 'Rosh HaShanah La'ilanot,' which means 'New Year of the Trees. Each year, on that day, the people of Israel will plant trees and pleasant plants. It is custom that they take of the fruits that had ripened from Tu BiShvat and were to be counted for the following year's tithes. In other words, a harvest would be done."

David then says, "Okay, and what does this have to do with what happened with the earthquake on February 6th."

Jeremy pulls out another page from the leather case and hands the page to David. David was able to read what was on the page. The page informed David what day of the month on our calendar corresponded with the 15th day of Shevat on the Hebrew calendar this year. The day was February 5th, 2023.

Jeremy then says, "Do you see? This year, on February 5th, the people of Israel were planting trees and pleasant plants, though literally, the very next day, there would be grief and desperate sorrow that occurred on the morning of February 6th."

David was stunned by what he had just seen here. He thought to himself, 'What are the odds, of all the years where the 15th of Shevat falls on a different day in our calendar each year, that this year, it happens to land on what corresponds to February 5th this year where the very next morning would be grief and desperate sorrow.'

David looks at Jeremy and says, "So, is this judgment?"

Jeremy then says, "Because this has been written within the scriptures well before it would happen, it is something of far more importance."

"What is that?"

"Mercy." Says Jeremy. "You see, God who sees the end from the beginning, knew this day would happen. He knew the earthquake that would cause the Olive trees to shake violently would happen the day after the people of Israel would be planting pleasant plants. So, because He knew this day would happen long in the future, in the latter days. He inspired Isaiah to write about the shaking of the Olive tree and having the people plant pleasant plants only to see the next morning a day of grief and desperate sorrow. The Olive trees on the Olive grove in Turkey shook so violently that the very ground was altered as the Olive grove split in two, making a large, deep valley between them. This is why God inspired Zechariah to mention the word 'earthquake' after Zechariah writes about the Day when the Lord returns and steps foot on the Mount of Olives that the Mount of Olives will be split in two with a deep valley between them. God loves His people, even those who have yet to believe. He loves them and tells them of things before they come to pass. They are found in His word, in the scriptures, so that when they do come to pass, one may come to believe that Jesus is the Son of God, that the Father sent Him and that He is coming again. The dividing of the Olive grove in Turkey is a warning, a picture of the future day when the Lord returns, for when the Lord returns, it will not be a day of mercy on the unbeliever. It will be a day of Judgment. Did you know there were also reports of children who had been trapped under the rubble for days? One cannot survive without water for more than 3 days. The body starts to shut down, yet some of these children who had been trapped under the rubble came out looking well nourished. Multiple accounts from different children who were trapped alone under the rubble of various sites give testimony that they were not alone while under the rubble, that one dressed all in white with white hair and a white beard gave them food and drink. The adults didn't see this. Though children who were not together bear witness and share the same message, they were not alone. God gives enough for you to know that He is who He is, though He does it in a way that requires you to still have faith in believing."

"This is amazing." Says David. "Though I pray for all those families there in Turkey and Syria that lost a loved one. I pray for their well-being. That they may be cared for and looked after."

"As do I," said Jeremy. "I have prayed for their well-being since the day it happened. I saw pictures of men who went through the rubble, men who had children in their arms with shouts of joy and smiles on their faces as they had just saved another life. Seeing these pictures of them shows they have 'love.' Seeing the picture of them holding a child in their arms is like seeing a picture of one of our firefighters rescuing a child from a burning building. There is 'love' there. The people in Syria and Turkey have Mothers and Fathers, just as we have Mothers and Fathers. They love, and we love. So why do we fight? Why do we war with each other? God does not want this. The warring and fighting are not of flesh and blood. It is spiritual. We wrestle not with flesh and blood but with principalities. If one is not in the Lord, they are more prone to be oppressed and controlled by principalities they don't see. It is enough. Pray and love one another. This is the greatest commandment. That you love one another."

"Amen." Says David. "What about the verses that follow after what I had read? What about **Isaiah 17:12-14**?"

Jeremy says, "Go ahead and read it."

**Isaiah 17:12-14** *"Woe to the multitude of many people who make a noise like the roar of the seas, and to the rushing of nations that make a rushing like the rushing of mighty waters! The nations will rush like the rushing of many waters; But God will rebuke them and they will flee far away, and be chased like the chaff of the mountains before the wind, like a rolling thing before the whirlwind. Then behold, at eventide, trouble! And before the morning, he is no more. This is the portion of those who plunder us, and the lot of those who rob us."*

Jeremy says, "This is yet future. The woe mentioned concerns the future woe. The third woe is the judgments that God will do on all the nations that come against Jerusalem. The book of Zechariah talks about what will happen to those who fight against Jerusalem. Read aloud what is written in **Zechariah 14:12-15**."

**Zechariah 14:12-15** *"And this shall be the plague with which the Lord will strike all the people who fought against Jerusalem: Their flesh shall dissolve while they stand on their feet, their eyes shall dissolve in their sockets, and their tongues shall dissolve in their mouths. It shall come to pass in that day that a great panic from the Lord will be among them. Everyone will seize the hand of his neighbor, and raise his hand against his neighbor's hand; Judah also will fight at Jerusalem. And the wealth of all the surrounding nations shall be gathered together: Gold, silver, and apparel in great abundance. Such also shall be the plague on the horse and the mule, on the camel and the donkey, and on all the cattle that will be in those camps. So shall this plague be."*

Jeremy then says, "The warning here is real, the plagues written here and the judgment of those who will gather to fight against Jerusalem are real, yet in the last days, still there will be those nations that will surround

Jerusalem to fight against her. Upon the Lord's return, they will have a swift end, and His wrath will be poured out on the desolate."

David then says, "I hope we are not here to see or experience that day. It will be a time in the history of man that has never been before."

Jeremy then says, "If we are in Christ the Lord before the rapture of the Church happens, we won't be here as we are not appointed to God's Wrath. We will be raptured. The dead in Christ will rise first, and those who are alive and remain who are in Christ will be changed in a moment, in the twinkling of an eye, we will be caught up to meet the Lord in the air, and we will forever be with the Lord and will be 'kings' and 'priests.'"

"Amen to that, my friend." David then says, "So, what are your hopes for this book?"

Jeremy then says, "My hope and prayer is that this book brings a person to open their Bible, to look for themselves and test what is said here in this book. To pay attention to what has happened in their history and what is currently happening around them. Those who have had doubts or unbelief may come to know the truth. The Bible is not just stories. These things happened, and evidence is being uncovered all the time. We hope they come to know that Jesus spoke of things almost 2000 years ago that would come to pass beforehand so that when they would come to pass, one may believe that Jesus truly is the Son of God, that the Father sent Him and He is coming back again. If they truly come to believe in Jesus as their Lord and Savior before the rapture of the church, then they will be part of that rapture. For those who will be left behind, my hope is that they come across this book and learn the truth, that they don't follow the beast or take his mark. Suppose they are left behind and come to believe once they see the rapture, and they give glory to God. In that case, my words to those who will be tribulation saints are this: Know that you will be hunted down and many of you will be persecuted. Some of you will be beheaded for your witness and because you would not take the mark or worship the beast or his image. Some of you will pass of hunger as you will no longer be able to buy or sell, though here is what I pray that you hold onto: Hold onto hope in the Lord. You witnessed the rapture of the church. Know that if you are one of those tribulation saints, death is only a moment. Though it is not forever, your life will go on, and you will take part in the blessings of the first resurrection. You will have eternal life and be with us and our Lord and Savior, Jesus Christ. Don't lose heart. Love one another, find fellow believers and work together in love, encourage one another. I love you and will hopefully see you one day."

David then says, "Amen brother."

Jeremy hands the device that had been recording everything to David.

David then says, "Is all of it on here?"

"It should be." Says Jeremy.

David stands up, walks back to his desk, and picks up the phone as he dials Penny.

"Hello again 007."

"Penny, can you come in here to the office? I have something I need to give to you."

"Sure thing."

Jeremy pulls out pages from his leather case. He stands up and walks to David's desk as he hands the pages to David.

David then says, "What are these?"

"Those are all the pictures and Calendars that you will need to have as part of the book so that others can see the pictures and Calendars for themselves. There are some who read and learn better with visual aids. This is for them. The other pages here are two bonus chapters to be included in the book. I wrote them beforehand, so they are not part of this recording."

"What are the two bonus chapters called?"

"Chapter 31 is titled: Leapt from The Womb Mystery."

"And the other chapter? What is it titled?"

"Chapter 32 is titled: The Letter to the Church."

"Very well." Says David. "When would you hope to see this book released?"

"My hope and prayer is that this book will be released on the Day of Atonement this year."

David then says, "And why the Day of Atonement?"

"Because the people will have a choice to make. To believe in Jesus, that He is truly the Son of God, the Father sent Him and He truly is coming again, or they will choose to continue in unbelief. More than 30 years have passed from trumpet five to where we are now, though only four years had passed between trumpet three and trumpet five. We do not know the day or the hour of the Lord's return. Only the Father knows. It could still be 30 or more years away or sooner than we think. I like what a Pastor once said, 'Plan as if the Lord isn't coming for another 100 years, though live your life as if He could be coming today.'"

David says, "That is a good way to look at it since we don't know the day or the hour. It keeps us watching as we should. To get the book out by the Day of Atonement, I am sorry to say there is not enough time to get the book out by then. A lot goes into the preparation before a book is released."

"I understand David. When do you think the book could be available?"

"With the time it takes, we would be looking at sometime early this coming year in 2024. Is there a date in 2024 you would prefer?"

"I would like to see the book released and available before the Solar Eclipse on April 8th, 2024. Is that possible?"

"Oh yes," says David. "We can release the book well before that."

Jeremy thought to himself of the perfect day. He looks at David and says, "How about March 6th, 2024."

"We could do March 6th. Is there something revealing about that day?"

Jeremy smiles as he thinks back to the day of floating on the water, out on a swan paddle boat. It was such a beautiful day. So many beautiful days with his Esther, though that day was extra special. A day of laying her foundation with Sapphires. How beautiful is the word of the Lord to her, to them both. Jeremy looks at David and says, "March 6th was the original day of Purim established by Queen Esther in 473 BC. It was a day to celebrate deliverance from their enemies who tried to destroy them. I am sure the enemy will do all they can to keep this book from being released, though to have it released on March 6th will also celebrate deliverance and the hope of deliverance and return for those who may come to read it."

"Yes Jeremy. Absolutely. I also want you to know that just because the book would not be released on the Day of Atonement, those who read this book will still have a choice to make, as you said earlier. May those who have had doubts come to believe that Jesus is the Son of God, the Father sent Him and He is coming again. May the believer be the light they were meant to be for such a time as this."

"Yes David. Amen."

"So we will set the release day for March 6th, 2024."

"Thank you David."

"No Jeremy, thank you."

"Thank God." Said Jeremy. "All glory goes to Him."

Penny walks into David's office and says, "Okay, what have you got for me?"

David motions to Penny, asking her to wait outside the office for a moment. David then looks at Jeremy and says, "I have one other question. Do you think the one you mentioned the other day could possibly be the Antichrist, as in the final Antichrist?"

Jeremy then says to David, "As I had shared with you before, it is possible, though the Antichrist will not be revealed until he stands in the house of God declaring himself to be God. Until then, we will not know for sure, though he is worth watching closely. It is possible that he could be a decoy set up by the enemy. Think of it like Air Force One. When Air Force One is in flight, they send off another one just like it that is also in flight. One contains the President of the United States, whereas the other is a decoy. The same could be possible with the person I have shared with you. This person could be a decoy, whereas somewhere else, there will be that one who has the devil himself inside the man.

Nevertheless, there is too much to be a coincidence that connects with the man I mentioned. Either way, whether he is the Antichrist or made to be a decoy, the enemy, the principalities behind this man have shown their hand since there is so much that connects with this man, there is too much that gives evidence of the working of the unseen principalities."

David then says, "Yes, I can understand that. I suppose we just keep watch."

"Yes, that is what we should do. Keep watch, my brother."

David then motions for Penny to come into the office. He hands Penny the device with everything recorded, including the pictures and the two bonus chapters.

Penny then says, "What is this?"

"That is the book." Said David. "The book was created as we spoke these last few days. I need you to take this to our team to print and edit, along with these pictures and two bonus chapters. We have a book to print and get out to the people."

Jeremy then said, "Why did you not schedule any appointments for tomorrow since we finished today?"

"Because I have a lot of calls to make in order to get everything set up for this book to go out in as many places around the world as it possibly can."

With everything in hand, Penny looks at David before she walks out of his office and says, "007, is this going to be a mission impossible?"

David looks at Jeremy. He then looks at the Shofar with the markings, the leather case and the Bible that was on the table in front of him.

David looks at Penny and says, "No Penny. I believe all things are possible with God."

Explore this chapter's photos/calendars mentioned by scanning the QR code or visiting the link:

https://www.revealingthetimes.com/chapter30

# BONUS CHAPTER I
# CHAPTER 31
# LEAPT IN THE WOMB MYSTERY

I hope you, the reader, have been blessed by reading this book. I pray that this book has sparked a fire in you to open your Bible and start reading for yourself the great wonders of His word. If you have read this far through the book, I ask that you read through this chapter and the ones to follow. This chapter is meant for my brother or sister who has that hunger to learn more, who wants to dive further into the hidden mysteries concealed within the scriptures, though the time for their revealing is now. This chapter is also meant for the reader who has had doubt, those who have asked the question: (Is God Real?) (Are the scriptures truly inspired by God?) (Am I just here today and gone tomorrow?) (Is there truly life after death?). If these are some of your questions, I pray that if you have read this far through the book and begun to search the scriptures for yourself, that you have come to find the answers to these questions. If you still may have doubt, pray for the Holy Spirit to guide you, to open your eyes and your heart to receive the truth. To answer those questions you may have asked, I will tell you that (Yes, God is very much real.) (Yes, the scriptures are truly inspired by God.) (No, you are not just here today and gone tomorrow.) (Yes, there truly is life after death, and where you spend it is up to you.)

This chapter is also meant for that one out there who has felt alone in this world, or maybe you have felt pressured to make a decision, doing something you really don't want to do. Know this, at no point in this chapter will I judge you. I love you. If I love you, having never met you, how much more does God love you? A whole lot, I can tell you that. No matter the storm, no matter what situation you may be in, you are not alone. There is always someone you can call or reach out to. It may be a friend, a family member, or someone you just met. You never know who God may bring in your path at just the right moment or time for such a time as this in your life. Maybe that moment is right now as you read these words meant for you. I hope these words speak to you and that you rest in the love Jesus has for you. Shall we continue?

God has always been with us. We see Him in everything. From every flower to every blade of grass, the stars in the sky, the sun and the moon, how do they hang up there and not fall on us? When I say that God has always been with us, I am also saying that we can see the evidence right before our eyes of the existence of God. If we can't see, then we have a sense of smell and a sense of touch. Those in the field of science or chemistry, even those who study biology, will spend hours researching and studying to answer some of the tough questions about how the sun, moon and stars hang up there on nothing. Some of them have done well in answering these questions, though I can share the answer with you to all of them. Do you want to know the answer? It is this: God designed it to be so.

Some are in the field of science who believe in God. Many are Christians, though there are others in the field of science who have used the answers they have come up with to attempt to disprove the existence of God. They discover so many material answers to what they can see and touch that they miss the spiritual. There is evidence of God's fingerprint, His intelligent design in all life that we see around us. For those who thought the world was flat, all they needed to do was read the Bible, and the answer was there all along. The earth is round, the circle of the earth.

I could spend hours talking about astronomy or physics, though there is something even more special that I would like to talk about…. You. You were created for a purpose; you were not an accident. Some in the field of science may hold to the (Here today, gone tomorrow) philosophy. We can see the evidence of that mentality in what they do. When a life is created in the womb, what brought life is God. However, we see clinics around us everywhere that take the precious life that was growing in you today and make it to be gone tomorrow. I have stood outside some of those clinics, not to point the finger, not to judge those who walk inside them. I just sing praise and worship. What I can tell you is that something happens to those who hear the words of the songs we sing. They feel it. Many times, there have been those who have walked into those clinics, and before they follow through with what they went there to do, they suddenly walk out and walk towards us. They chose a different way, giving the life growing inside them a chance to live. Maybe that person did not want to be a parent, though they chose to give their child up for adoption to a family that may not be able to have children. They choose life. If you are in this position in your life and you are unsure what to do and feel you have nowhere else to turn to, know that you are not alone. There is always someone who can help.

You may have heard others preach to you or at you. That is not what I am doing here with you today. I want to talk to you and the life that is growing inside you right now. Allow me to share a few scriptures with you that talk about you. Will you permit me to have this time with you? Okay good. Here are just a few scriptures that talk about you:

**Psalm 139:13-18** *"For You formed my inward parts; You covered me in my mother's womb. I will praise You, for I am fearfully and wonderfully made; Marvelous are your works, and that my soul knows very well. My frame was not hidden from You. When I was made in secret, and skillfully wrought in the lowest parts of the earth. Your eyes saw my substance, being yet unformed. And in Your book they were written, the days fashioned for me, when as yet there were none of them. How precious also are Your thoughts to me, O God! How great is the sum of them! If I should count them, they would be more in number than the sand; When I awake, I am still with You."*

God was there with you even when you were in your mother's womb, which also means that God is there with the life growing inside you now. He is knitting that life together. He is working. We have heard it said, "My body, my choice." I guess one does have a choice in what they do, though I want you to take a moment to step back and think about the choice of the life that is growing inside you now. Are you giving them a choice? Are you giving them a chance at life? Do they have a choice? Will you speak for those who cannot speak for themself? Will you be their voice? If God saw it fit to get to work and begin knitting us together in our mother's womb, that means we are special. We have a purpose. Who are they to stop His work?

The title of this chapter is: Leapt in the Womb Mystery. There is a mystery that has always been there within the scriptures, the answer to a question that science had only just discovered over the years. Allow me to reveal this mystery to you. It goes back to the time when the Angel Gabriel visited Mary. Gabriel had come to tell her that she was highly favored and that she would conceive and give birth to a Son. The Holy Spirit would overshadow her. She would become pregnant, having not laid with a man. She was a virgin. The child within her would be the Son of the most high God. His name is Jesus or in the Hebrew… Yeshua. While Gabriel was with Mary, he told her that her cousin Elizabeth was with child, even in her old age. He tells Mary that Elizabeth is in her sixth month. You can read about this in the Gospel of

**Luke 1:24-45**. Through these verses, we read that Elizabeth, after having conceived, hid herself for five months, then we read that in the sixth month was when Gabriel visited Mary, then Gabriel himself tells Mary that this is Elizabeth's sixth month. Why so many times in just a few verses do we, the reader, need to know what month Elizabeth was in her pregnancy? I will tell you why. Here is the mystery, the message that has been concealed, though always there for us to discover. When Gabriel left Mary, the scriptures say that in those days, Mary went with haste into the hill country to visit her cousin Elizabeth. Elizabeth was six months pregnant at this time. When Mary spoke, this is what happened found in **Luke 1:41-44** *"And it happened, when Elizabeth heard the greeting of Mary, that the babe leaped in her womb; and Elizabeth was filled with the Holy Spirit. Then she spoke out with a loud voice and said, 'Blessed are you among women, and blessed is the fruit of your womb! But why is this granted to me, that the mother of my Lord should come to me? For indeed, as soon as the voice of your greeting sounded in my ears, the babe leaped in my womb with joy. Blessed is she who believed, for there will be a fulfillment of those things which were told her from the Lord."*

A clue to this mystery is not only given in knowing what month it was for Elizabeth's pregnancy. The clue was also in what the scriptures say. There is the word 'heard,' and then there is the word 'ear' when Elizabeth said, 'As soon as the voice of your greeting sounded in my ears.' Elizabeth then bears witness to what the child in her womb had done. The babe leaped. The babe in her womb reacted to the sound from outside the womb. Elizabeth was six months pregnant. Science has discovered that during the stages of development of the babe in the womb, it is at six months when the babe is able to hear sounds outside of the womb and react to those sounds. Science has discovered it, though the answer has always been there in the scriptures. The very moment Mary went to visit Elizabeth it was the exact time when the babe in Elizabeth's womb could hear the voice of Mary and react to it. And so he did. He leaped. Had Gabriel visited Mary and given her the news one month earlier and had Mary visited Elizabeth one month earlier, the babe in Elizabeth's womb would not have heard Mary's voice. Gabriel was sent by God to Mary at exactly the right time because He has always known when the babe can hear sounds from outside the womb and react to them. He knows because He is the One who knit you together in your mother's womb. He chose that time so that even before John was born, he would bear testimony to the truth. John would be the silent voice, the silent witness to the truth from within the womb to help us unfold the concealed message, the mystery. John would have a part to play from the womb in revealing that mystery, that the answer was always there even before science discovered it.

I hope this has inspired you. If you are reading this now and perhaps last week, last month, or even a few years ago, you had made the choice and went through with your decision at the clinic of the (here today, gone tomorrow) thought. Perhaps you have felt remorse from that decision, from that choice. Know this, the babe that was in your womb is now present with the Lord, and know that you are fearfully and wonderfully made. God loves you.

I know someone who was adopted. Luckily, abortion was not passed into law at this time. The mother was 18 and still lived at home. Her parents told her that she could not have the child and still live at home, so the mother gave the child up for adoption once the child was born. The child was brought into the home of a loving family who were unable to get pregnant. That child grew, and once an adult, that person got married and had two sons and two daughters. One of the sons had a child of their own, so now they have a grandson. All of that life, all the special memories shared with family, experienced all because the mother gave the baby up for adoption. Had abortion been law at that time, the mother may have gone the route of abortion. Had that happened, look at all the life that would have been missed and lives that would not be. You may make the choice thinking (My body, my choice) and think it is only you in the picture here, though God knows the end from the beginning. He sees all. When you make the decision to end a life, He grieves for all the lives that could have been, that could have come just from your one child. If you have already gone through with it, know that God loves you, and should you go to Him and pray, know that He has forgiven you. His mercy and grace is with you.

If you have chosen to follow Jesus, to accept Him as your Lord and Savior, you have chosen life. Choose life....

# BONUS CHAPTER II
# CHAPTER 32
# THE LETTER TO THE CHURCH

My fellow brothers and sisters in Christ. I hope and pray you found this book to be a blessing. Know that this book on its own is no blessing at all if we didn't have the Bible. If we didn't have His word. This book you have read is not meant to stand on its own. It is meant to bring the reader to open up their Bible and search through the scriptures for themselves. This book is meant to wake up the church for any who may have been sleeping and who have not been keeping watch. Jesus has wanted all of those who are His to keep watch. It is no secret many out there have had doubt and unbelief as to whether there is a God, and if so, is Jesus His Son? You happen to know the truth. You know that Jesus truly is the Son of God, that the Father sent Him, and you know that He is coming again.

Perhaps you gave your life to the Lord at a young age or came to believe later in your life. Regardless of when you made that choice, rest easy in knowing that if you are truly His, you will be with Him where He is and have not been appointed to God's wrath. Though maybe there is someone you know, it may be your Mother, Father, brother, sister, cousin or a close friend that you know is not a believer and has had doubts. Maybe you have tried to witness to them in the past, though you couldn't find the words. That's okay. At least you have tried. Though while they still have unbelief, while they are still not convinced of the truth, while they still have breath and their heart still beats, you still have opportunity to witness to them in hopes they come to be saved. Maybe you still don't have the words to say, though if this book touched you, if it moved you, I encourage you to give this book to that one you know who has struggled with unbelief and doubt.

When I say to give them this book, I don't mean to give them yours. This book is to be a resource book for you, to be a companion alongside your Bible as you read through the scriptures for yourself. Perhaps buy this book for your loved one or close friend as a gift. That way, you have one and they have one. If you have a bible study group in your church or in your home, I encourage you to get this book for those in your study group or tell them where they can get a copy.

If you have read through the entirety of this book, perhaps some of what you have thought or believed before has been challenged. Things like (Who are the two witnesses?) (When was Jesus Born?) (When is the Rapture?) (Is there a Rapture?)

My prayer for you and hope for you is that you search through the scriptures for yourself and see all of the connections that have been given concerning the two witnesses of Revelation 11.

The dialogue in this book is fictional, though all the connections are real. The dreams written within this book are not made up. I actually had them. As you read through this book, you know by now that I mentioned things like the 'Timeline of the Two Witnesses' and 'What house they will be from.' I mention the 'Birth of Jesus' and 'His Baptism by John.' There are also the trumpets of Revelation. There have been others who have also come to realize that some of the trumpets of Revelation have already happened. The article shared in this book concerning Trumpet Three, written on July 26th, 1986, is a real article, and many who live in Ukraine do in fact believe Chernobyl was Trumpet Three. In this book, I go into a little more detail as to what the star burning as a torch actually was and connect things such as what John heard when he wrote down the word 'Abaddon' in trumpet five.

I didn't find this on my own. I would not have known where to begin to look. I would have a feeling that suddenly I was to look here or look there and come to find out, I was being led, guided into truth that I had no idea was there, yet it was.

The reason for including the trumpets in the book is because in the spring of 2022, having already known that five of the trumpets have already happened, the one I was watching for next was the starting of trumpet six. I came across that when I first saw a news clip from CNN showing Ukrainian soldiers training in Chernobyl a week before Russia invaded Ukraine. As I watched, suddenly, the video crossed by a Ukrainian soldier who had the colors of Hyacinth blue and sulfur yellow on his breastplate. I knew this was one of the descriptions that John gave in what he saw when he wrote out trumpet six. The fact they were training in Chernobyl of all places, the very place of trumpet three, was also eye-opening to me.

I continued to search and follow as I felt I was being led along the way. I then came across the colors of the breastplate on the Russian dress uniform. One is fiery red, the other hyacinth blue. Then, when I read the Torah portion of that very Sabbath following when Russia invaded Ukraine, I came across a number that was in part of that Torah portion. The number 603,550. It was later that same night while laying in bed, a thought came over me, not an audible voice, just a thought that I was to go to Google search and type in the Google search:

(What is the geographical measurement of the Country of Ukraine?) I was the first to be wowed as it was the exact same number 603,550 km2

You can find this on Worlddata.info

I then began to look more into what John was describing in trumpet six. The horse having a head like a lion, with fire, smoke and brimstone coming out of its mouth. I had already known that John was simply trying to describe what didn't exist in his day. Wars were fought on horses in his day, so that is how he described the machinery being used. He described them as horses. No horse has a head like a lion, and no horse has fire, smoke and brimstone coming out of its mouth. I then came upon a picture showing the men who were fighting in Ukraine. The picture showed the men standing behind a Howitzer cannon. Fire, smoke and brimstone was seen coming out of the mouth of the cannon. The shield was branched out like the mane on a lion, and standing at the tail of this were the men. Their heads could be seen. The Howitzer cannon does not fire on its own. They are operated by man, and with man, they do harm.

A few months later, news reports came out of the Euphrates River drying up, the very mention of the Euphrates River also being in trumpet six. I knew there were four countries that surrounded the Euphrates River. They were bound by it. With the Euphrates River drying up, those four countries would no longer be bound once it is dried up. In the natural realm, we see the four countries of Iraq, Iran, Turkey and Syria. In the spiritual, there are also unseen principalities at work in those countries.

I was convinced, having already known that five trumpets had already happened, that I was seeing the starting of trumpet six. We are not in the fullness of trumpet six however. We are only seeing the starting of it. Because this is currently happening, I knew this needed to be known to the people and wanted to get this out to you.

The connections of the Antichrist, the number of his name, the prefigure of the Antichrist in Antiochus Epiphanes to his General Ptolemy Macron to the people I mention who are alive today, all of those connections are real. I am not saying that Bashar Al-Assad is in fact the Antichrist, though he is worth keeping an eye on. Every generation has that one who is waiting in the wings who would be used by the devil because the devil does not know God's time of when the rapture will be. Only the Father knows the day and the hour. Though, when the rapture happens, and the church is taken out of the way, the restrainer is the Holy Spirit. When the restrainer is taken out of the way, then at that time, the Antichrist will show his true colors and be revealed.

There is a rapture of the Church. I want you to know that. Some believe it will be a pre-trib rapture. Others believe in a mid-trib rapture. Some believe we will be here through the whole seven years, while some believe there is no rapture at all.

Brothers and sisters in Christ, there will be a rapture, and though we do not know when that day or hour will be, it is closer than we may think. Tomorrow is just one day closer. The rapture is nothing to be frightened of, for those of us who are in Christ. We will be meeting the Lord in the air and will forever be with the Lord when that time comes. This will be a great day for us who are in Christ. However, for those who will be left behind, it will be a world unlike mankind has ever seen or experienced since there has been mankind. It will be a time of great darkness.

More than 30 years stand between trumpet five and where we are now. So, is it possible that we may have 30 or more years before the rapture? It's possible. Though there are only four years between trumpet three and trumpet five. So, is it possible that we may have only four years before the rapture? It's possible. I am not setting dates. No one knows the day or the hour. Only the Father knows. All I am saying is that it's possible. It could be another 100 years, highly unlikely, though is it possible, it's possible.

As a church, we are a family. I pray that we not be divided over when the rapture happens. Is it pre-trib, or is it mid-trib? What matters is that there will be a rapture. I would love for it to be pre-trib and get out of here with you all before things begin to really get ugly down here. Though I say this to you, if it happens to be mid-trib and you begin to see the third temple going up in Jerusalem, I pray that your spirits be stirred and share the gospel with as many as you can, all those you know who have struggled with unbelief, witness to them, get them this book and any other book you think may help them. Buy them a bible if they don't have one, or get one from your local church and give it to those in need because if you are here and you begin to see the third temple going up, know that we, the church, will not be here much longer. We can be caught up to meet the Lord in the air at any time. If it is pre-trib, that also means it could be at any time. It could be tomorrow or next weekend while you are on your family vacation. Not knowing when the rapture will take place means all the more reason to go out and witness to those you may know or come across who have not believed.

Let us not debate and become divided over when Jesus was born. Was He born in the spring? Was He born in the fall? The fact is that He was born, and that is what matters most. Jesus was born of a virgin. Her name is Mary. He is the Son of God, The Father sent Him, and He is coming again. Before things came to pass, He told us of them so that when they do come to pass, we may believe.

I encourage you, as the scriptures say in **Hebrews 10:23-25** *"Let us hold fast the confession of our hope without wavering, for He who promised is faithful. And let us consider one another in order to stir up love and good works, not forsaking the assembling of ourselves together, as is the manner of some, but exhorting one another, and so much the more as you see the Day approaching."*

If you have stopped going to Church, maybe because you have felt too busy or perhaps because COVID had you leave and you haven't been back since that time. I encourage you to come back and gather with your church family. If you don't have a church, I encourage you to find one, especially as we see the Day approaching.

Brothers and sisters in Christ, you know that you are the light. Jesus said in **Matthew 5:14-16** *"You are the light of the world. A city that is set on a hill cannot be hidden. Nor do they light a lamp and put it under a basket, but on a lampstand, and it gives light to all who are in the house. Let your light so shine before men, that they may see your good works and glorify your Father in heaven."*

Also, I encourage you to keep this scripture in mind as well.

**Mark 4:21-25** *"Also He said to them, 'Is a lamp brought to be put under a basket or under a bed? Is it not to be set on a lampstand? For there is nothing hidden which will not be revealed, nor has anything been kept secret but that it should come to light. If anyone has ears to hear, let him hear.' Then He said to them, 'Take heed what you hear. With the same measure you use, it will be measured to you; and to you who hear, more will be given. For whoever has, to him more will be given; but whoever does not have, even what he has will be taken away from him."*

I share the above scriptures with you to say this. If you are in Christ, you are indeed a light that is to be on a hill. Do not hide your light under a basket or place it under your bed. Set your light up on a lampstand. We are not to forsake the assembling of ourselves together, especially as we see the Day approaching. Though if all we do is go to Church on Sunday, then go on with the rest of our lives Monday through Saturday, and we are not sharing the gospel with others then the Church building has become your basket. You all who are in Christ are light, the light of the world. If all of your light is only being shown within the church building, the church building has become the basket. Still go to church, though let your light shine when you leave out from service and witness to someone, bring them to church, invite them.

When Jesus fed the 5,000, He told his disciples to gather up the pieces left over, not to waste a bit. How much more the food that lasts for eternal life? When you are in church, and you are being spiritually fed, remember to gather up the pieces with you, not to waste a bit. Share the spiritual food of Him our Lord with others. Share the good news!!

I love you all, and I look forward to one day seeing you either here or when we are gathered with the Lord.

To those who Pastor a church, to those who have been called into ministry, may we always strive to fight the good fight, to run the race well. To count on each other for encouragement, to lift each other up in the Lord always. Remember to always love one another. I thank you for your service and what you do. Though you may plan in your heart, may the Lord continue to guide your steps.

May God bless you and yours,

I Love you my friend.

P.S. For those of you who want more. I have included another bonus chapter for such a time as this…. I hope you have scanned the QR codes or typed in the links at the end of the Chapters to view the pictures and calendars. At the end of this book, another QR code/link will take you to a Chapter titled: (Messenger's Epilogue). You will want to read Messenger's Epilogue as it continues to reveal current events and leaves you with a profound message of hope amidst all that has been happening.

This book is interactive with the QR codes and links, allowing you to have more information through reading and visual aids. There is also one last QR code titled: (Bonus Content) where videos and messages will be included as they come. You can scan the QR code for Bonus Content as long as you have this book. Things continue to be revealed for such a time as this, and we want you to have access to that information as it comes.

Now, onto CHAPTER 33: THE REVEALING

# BONUS CHAPTER III
# CHAPTER 33
# THE REVEALING

Jeremy walked outside by the street at the front entrance of the Publisher's office. He could hear the sound of the wind, though he didn't know where it had come from or where it was going. He looks across the street and can see the leaves blowing in a direction straight ahead. The leaves were carried by the wind towards a bench in the distance. Jeremy could see there was a man sitting on the bench, though he could not see who the man was as the bench was facing the other direction. All Jeremy could see was the man's back.

Jeremy decides to cross the street, following the direction of the leaves toward the bench. As he walked closer, he could see the man sitting on the bench was dressed all in black, and beside the bench was a clay vessel. Jeremy thought to himself, "Could this be Messenger?"

The man sitting on the bench began speaking as Jeremy approached. Without turning around, the man says, "So, my friend, how were the last few days? Did they accept the message? Do they have the book?"

Jeremy continued walking ahead to where he was, facing the man sitting on the bench. It was Messenger.

He looks at Messenger and says, "How did you know it was me when your back was to me?"

Messenger looks up to Jeremy and says with a smile, "After all I have shared with you and all the time spent with you, are you surprised at this? That I would know it was you before seeing you?"

"I suppose there is nothing that would surprise you. Though, since you knew it was me, I would assume you already know the answer to the questions you had just asked me."

Messenger smiles again as he says, "I suppose I should tell you why I have been sitting here waiting for you then, shouldn't I?"

"Yes. Why are you here?"

"Have a seat my friend." Messenger motions his hand towards the place beside him. As Jeremy sits down, Messenger reaches into his clay vessel beside him and pulls out a thin leather casing with leather ties around it. The leather casing looked to not be able to hold much of whatever could be inside it.

"What is that?" Jeremy asked.

"This is the reason I am here with you now. There is one more thing for you to share with the publishers. One more thing to go out to those around the world before the time."

"Before the time?"

"Yes, before the time of the gathering."

"What gathering?"

Messenger opens the leather casing as he pulls out a single page. The page had an image on it. It was a Solar Eclipse.

Messenger then says, "As you and others from all over the world were there in Southern Illinois to see the Solar Eclipse that happened August 21st, 2017. So too, hundreds of thousands from all over the country and around the world will come to Southern Illinois to witness the Solar Eclipse of April 8th, 2024."

"Okay. I am sure everyone knows about this Solar Eclipse happening on April 8th, 2024."

Messenger then pulls out another page. Before handing it to Jeremy, he says, "Remember the dreams you had concerning the eclipses? What has been discovered? How the name 'Marion' means 'of the child of Mary' and 'Wished for child.'"

"Yes, I remember. I also remember that the places of 'Marion' was named after 'Francis Marion' who fought in the Revolutionary War. All of this is in the book to go out. The reader will already be able to read about this, including the information about the relative of 'Francis Marion' the poet, 'Julia Rush Cutler.'"

"That's right. I know this is to be in the book, including part of the poem written by 'Julia Rush Cutler' that mentions 'Sun of Righteousness.' As you have shared in the book, 'Sun of Righteousness' is mentioned in **Malachi 4:2** which also says, 'with healing in His wings.'"

Messenger then shows Jeremy the page. It was a picture of a Sun disk with wings around it.

He looks at Jeremy and says, "Have you seen this image before?"

"Yes, I have seen it before. This is an ancient image from Egypt, isn't it?"

"It is. Though there is also the image of the sun disk with wings around it in other ancient civilizations, including that of the Aztecs."

"How is that possible, since these ancient civilizations had never met? How could they come up with the same image?"

Messenger places the picture back in the leather casing, saying, "I suppose I should tell you of Egyptian mythology."

"Mythology is false though, isn't it?"

"Yes, mythology is false. However, I can show you something about it. In Egyptian mythology, they wrote of a goddess by the name of 'Naunet' who was depicted as a creating force. Her husband was known as the god who had the name 'Nun,' and when they came together, 'Naunet' gave birth to 'Ra' the 'Sun god.' This however, is false, though I will show you something else."

Messenger then pulls out another page from the leather casing. Before he shows the page to Jeremy, he says, "Do you know what type of writing existed before the Hebrew letters?"

"Yes. They were pictographs, right?"

"That's right. Just as God inspired man to write the scriptures of the Bible, God also inspired the ancient Hebrew pictographs as well." Messenger hands the page to Jeremy. He was able to see the Hebrew word for 'Nun' and the pictograph that was beside it, along with the meaning of it. The meaning was: 'Seed, fish, life.' As Jeremy looks at the pictograph for 'Nun,' he hands the page back to Messenger as Jeremy points to it, saying, "What is this?"

"That is a sperm."

"A sperm? How would the people in ancient times ever have known what a sperm looked like? They didn't have microscopes back then."

Messenger then says, "As I just shared with you, the Hebrew pictographs were inspired by God. God knows what a sperm looks like, as He is the One who created all things. God inspired the pictograph for the Hebrew word 'Nun' that was a picture of a 'sperm' and the Hebrew word 'Nun' means 'seed, fish and life.'"

"What does this have to do with what you shared with me concerning the Solar Eclipse and what you shared from Egyptian mythology?"

Messenger then says, "I will tell you and show you in a moment, though first let me ask you, do you remember reading in the scriptures where God had told Abraham that He would visit Sarah at the time of life, and she would have a son?"

"Yes, I remember reading this in the Bible."

Messenger says, "People of science have asked the question of 'when is the time of life in the womb?' They have asked, 'Is it the time of conception?' 'Is it the time of the heartbeat?' They ask this question, though if they would just look to God's word, they would discover the answer to their question."

"How would they find the answer there?"

"God gives the answer to the time of life in the womb. He tells Abraham that He will visit Sarah at the time of life. Do you have your Bible with you?"

"I do."

"Open your Bible to **Genesis 18:10** and read it aloud to me when you are there."

**Genesis 18:10** *"I will certainly return to you according to the time of life, and behold, Sarah your wife shall have a son."*

Messenger then says, "Now go to **Genesis 18:13** and read that aloud to me."

**Genesis 18:13** *"And the Lord said to Abraham, 'Why did Sarah laugh, saying, 'Shall I surely bear a child, since I am old?' Is anything too hard for the Lord? At the appointed time I will return to you, according to the time of life, and Sarah shall have a son."*

Then Messenger says, "Now let's look at what happened at the time of life when the Lord visited Sarah. Please read aloud to me **Genesis 21:1-2**."

**Genesis 21:1-2** *"And the Lord visited Sarah as He had said, and the Lord did for Sarah as He had spoken. For Sarah conceived and bore Abraham a son in his old age, at the set time of which God had spoken to him."*

Messenger then says, "You see the answer there? The time of life in the womb was when Sarah conceived. The time of conception."

"Okay. Yes, I can see that."

"Why do you suppose the Lord asked the question, 'Is anything too hard for the Lord?'"

Jeremy looks at Messenger and says, "Because Sarah and Abraham were both old in age and her womb was dead, there was no life in her womb, though because of the Lord's promise, because of His word, Sarah's dead womb would have life."

"That is exactly right." Said Messenger. "Can you think of anything else of where there was once death, though because of the Lord's word, because of His promise, there is life?"

"Yes. The day of the resurrection of Jesus, the Son of God. The day He rose again from death to life."

"Very good Jeremy. What would seem to be impossible. God made possible because of His word, because of His promise and there was life." Messenger then says, "Go now to **John 1:1-5** and read this aloud to me when you are there."

**John 1:1-5** *"In the beginning was the Word, and the Word was with God, and the Word was God. He was in the beginning with God. All things were made through Him, and without Him nothing was made that was made. In Him was life, and the life was the light of men. And the light shines in the darkness, and the darkness did not overcome it."*

Messenger then says, "Remember this: there is 'life' and 'light,' and you remember the parable Jesus gave of the sowing of the seed right?"

"Yes, I remember."

"What was the 'seed' in the parable Jesus gave?"

"The 'seed' was the 'word.'"

"That's right. The Lord gives you the natural so you will understand the spiritual."

"What do you mean, He gives the natural to understand the spiritual?"

Messenger then says, "Sarah's old womb represented death, Abraham was old in age as good as dead, though at the time of life in Sarah's womb, at the time of conception, life began according to the Lord's promise, according to His word. You then have the tomb where the Lord Jesus, Yeshua, was buried. In that place, there was death, though in that place of death, life began three days later at His resurrection."

"Okay. I understand what you mean. Though what about what you had just shared a bit ago with the Egyptian mythology about 'Naunet' and 'Nun' when they come together to give birth to 'Ra' 'The Sun?' I don't understand this connection, especially since Egyptian mythology is false."

Messenger then says, "Imagine, if you will, at the time of creation, when God makes it possible for a woman to bear a child, imagine that God shows this time of life to His Angels. The scriptures tell us that we do not wrestle with flesh and blood but with principalities. Those principalities are 'fallen angels'. The 'fallen angels' include Lucifer, 'the devil.' They take the truth and twist that truth to form in ancient cultures what you see with the sun disk and the wings, along with 'Naunet' and 'Nun' coming together to give birth to 'Ra' 'the Sun.'"

"So then what is the truth, the principalities twist?"

Messenger pulls out another page from the leather case, saying, "Think of 'Naunet,' the creation force as the 'egg' in a womb, and 'Nun' is the 'seed' the 'sperm.' When the two come together, this is what happens."

Messenger then hands the page to Jeremy. It was a picture of what looked like a 'Solar Eclipse.'

"What is this? Is this a Solar Eclipse?" Jeremy asked.

"This is not a Solar Eclipse. What you are looking at is an image of what happens at the time of conception, the time of life. Light shines in the darkness, and life happens. In that moment, it does look like a Solar Eclipse, like giving birth to the image of the Sun."

"This is amazing. I can see how principalities would have taken this truth to give a twisted version to the ancient Egyptians they have in their mythology."

Messenger then says, "And remember what I have also shared with you. The Hebrew pictograph for 'Nun' looks like a 'sperm,' and back then, they had no microscopes to have known what a 'sperm' would have looked like. 'Nun' means 'seed, fish and life.' Also, remember Joshua the son of Nun. The one who was given authority after Moses. Joshua is the Hebrew Yeshua. Yeshua means 'Salvation.' When you put it together, you get, 'Salvation son of seed, or Salvation son of life.'"

"Though Jesus was not born of a human father, He was born of a virgin, there was no 'sperm' there was no 'seed' right?"

Messenger then looks at Jeremy and says, "You are right, there was no 'sperm,' though remember what is the other 'seed' that is mentioned when Jesus gives the parable of the sowing of the 'seed?'"

"The 'seed' is the 'word.'"

Messenger then says, "That's right, and Jesus is the Word in the flesh, He is the Word, God in the flesh, born of a virgin."

"This is amazing."

"There is more though. Do you remember what Jesus said to Martha before He raised Lazarus from the dead?"

"Jesus told Martha that He is 'The resurrection and the life.'"

"Exactly." Messenger took the page from Jeremy as he placed it into the leather case, then pulled out one other page. He hands the page to Jeremy. It was a picture of the round stone covering the tomb. The round stone had a ring of light around it while covering the tomb. Messenger then says, "Should you and others choose to accept this, imagine at the time of Jesus' resurrection, at the time of life, light shines in the darkness, the darkness was not able to overcome it, and life begins. And what does the image look like?"

"It looks like a Solar Eclipse. I mentioned earlier in the book that at the time of Jesus' resurrection, light around the round stone would have looked like a Solar Eclipse. I also mention that as April 8th, 2024, is the time of the Solar Eclipse, April 8th in the year 30 AD was the time of Jesus' resurrection."

"Yes, though the Eclipse of the Sun is only meant to be a 'sign,' what I am sharing with you is something that has been concealed, hidden for thousands of years. It bears the same image as it does at the time of life in the womb. Jesus is the Way, the Truth and the Life."

"And no one goes to the Father, except through Him."

"That's right. Jesus is the only way. Believing that He is the Son of God, the Father sent Him, that He is coming again. Believing in your heart and confessing with your mouth that He is Lord."

Jeremy hands the page back to Messenger.

Messenger places the page back into the leather case. He then hands the leather case to Jeremy containing the pictures. He then says, "Take this across the street, hand it to the publisher. I encourage you all to look into the scriptures concerning the natural 'seed' at the time of conception and that of the spiritual 'seed,' may you all have ears to hear and eyes to perceive and see the connection."

Jeremy stands up from the bench and asks Messenger, "Is there anything else?"

"There are three additional pages in the leather case. You can pull them out and look at them if you wish."

Jeremy pulls out the last three remaining pages from the leather case. Two of the pages were calendars. One calendar was for the year 2024, at the time of the Solar Eclipse of April 8th, 2024. The other calendar was for the year 2024 BC. Jeremy was able to see the Solar globe showing a Solar Eclipse that fell in the year 2024 BC and could not believe what he was seeing. Both 2024 and 2024 BC had the Solar eclipse happening on the day that was the 29th day of the Hebrew month and corresponding with April 8th. The last page was the Parashah. The Torah portion has been assigned since ancient times and is set to be read on the Sabbath following the Solar Eclipse of April 8th, 2024. The Parashah in the Hebrew is 'Tazria,' which means 'Conceived Seed.'

Jeremy then says, "Really? This is the Parashah for the sabbath following the Solar Eclipse of April 8th, 2024? You just finished sharing with me of the time of conception, conceived seed, the time of life."

Messenger then says, "That is the Parashah set since ancient times that is to be read on sabbath following the Solar Eclipse of April 8th, 2024."

"Do you think anything will happen that day?"

Messenger stands up from the bench and says, "A revival could happen that day should the people accept and receive the message. Imagine the image of the time of life, the time of conception, that looks like a Solar Eclipse being on a shirt with the words 'You are fearfully and wonderfully made.' Imagine the impact that could make on all who come from all over the country and around the world. Not only could that impact save a life in the womb, others could be saved by accepting Jesus as their Lord and Savior. That He truly is the Son of God, the Father sent Him and He is truly coming again. A revival could spark. Share the message with the people in hopes that they hear and turn. May the people open their Bible and search for themselves. If they do not have a bible, may they get one."

Jeremy pulls his phone out of his pocket. He shows the phone to Messenger and says, "I am glad that I have recorded our conversation just now. This is how David and I did this since Friday and through the weekend. This is how the book was to be made, so it is fitting that this last chapter would be done the same way. What do you suppose I should title the last chapter?"

Messenger smiles as he then says, "Every chapter within the book is about 'revealing.' The title of the book is 'The Revealing.' Since this last chapter addresses something that had been hidden for thousands of years, though is revealed for such a time as this, you should title the very last chapter of the book 'The Revealing.'"

"I like that. I will do that."

"Remember Jeremy, set your light up on a lampstand, for there is nothing hidden that will not be revealed. Set the shofar to your lips and blow. Let the sound be heard."

"When will I see you again?"

Messenger picks up the clay vessel and begins to walk the other way in the direction of the wind as he says, "The time is set, though unknown to us. However, there will be more given to you. It will be at precisely the time appointed. Until then, keep watch my friend."

Jeremy begins to walk across the street. Once he crossed to the other side, he could hear Messenger say one last thing to him. "When you can, read **John chapter 3**, where Jesus had met with Nicodemus at night, pay attention to what Jesus says to Nicodemus concerning the wind, then go to **Ecclesiastes 11:5-8**. May you have ears to hear and eyes to perceive, for the light is sweet. Light is life. He is the light of the world, and His word is the seed. Go in peace my friend." Messenger then turned and continued to walk in the direction of the wind.

Jeremy walks back up to David's office. He couldn't see Penny anywhere, though as David saw Jeremy, he motioned for Jeremy to come in.

"Did you forget something?" Asked David.

Jeremy hands David his phone as he says, "Push play."

"What is this?" David asked.

"We have one other chapter to write."

David smiled as he said, "Is this going to be a mission impossible?"

"Is anything too hard for the Lord?"

"What shall we title the chapter?"

Jeremy hands the thin leather case to David that contains the last remaining images, then says, "The Revealing. Call it 'The Revealing.'"

Explore this chapter's photos/calendars mentioned by scanning the QR code or visiting the link:

https://www.revealingthetimes.com/chapter33

**Explore More! - Messenger's Epilogue**

Congratulations on reaching the end of this incredible journey through the pages of The Revealing. We hope you've gained important insight through every moment of this adventure. But wait, there's more!

Receive more insight into the mystery of Isaiah 9:10 as well as the connection of September 11th and October 7th in more ways than one! As a special for our dedicated readers, we have an exclusive chapter waiting for you called: Messenger's Epilogue.

Messenger's Epilogue delves deeper into the story, provides extra insights on current events from Israel and Hamas, to Russia and Ukraine as well as China and Taiwan. It offers a unique perspective that complements the main narrative and in the end opens a concealed mystery that gives a profound message of hope in the midst of what's been happening. To access Messenger's Epilogue, simply scan the QR code below or visit our website page at:
https://www.revealingthetimes.com/MessengersEpilogue

**Here's how to unlock the content for Messenger's Epilogue:**

1. Use your smartphone or tablet to open the camera app or a QR code scanner app.
2. Align your device's camera with the QR code below.
3. Your device will automatically recognize the code and lead you to Messenger's Epilogue on our website.

This additional chapter is our way of saying thank you for your dedication to The Revealing and Revealing The Times. We believe you'll find this to be a must needed extension of the book you've just read.

# BONUS CONTENT

The Journey doesn't end here! Our website is also home to exclusive content and insights. A network hub to connect with fellow readers. It's a place where the revealing continues.

So, what are you waiting for? Scan the QR code or visit the website link at www.revealingthetimes.com/BonusContent to access and explore the world beyond the book's pages. We can't wait to continue this journey with you.

Thank you for choosing The Revealing as your reading companion. We hope you'll visit us online soon for such a time as this.

We invite you to check out our Store/Shop at Revealing The Times Called: Christ & Me  Christian & More

From Bonus Content to receiving our Newsletter. Find out how you are able to get the full experience by scanning the QR code.

May God continue to bless you and yours in the name above every other name Yeshua Jesus.

Your brother and friend,

Jeffrey Rush

# ABOUT THE AUTHOR

**Jeffrey Rush** has been mentioned by many as having the gift of sight. Revealing hidden mysteries that had been concealed within the scriptures. Being able to dive into the ancient text of the Bible and bring to light certain events that have taken place in times past to include ancient times, to events that have happened 100 years ago to current events happening now. He holds a degree in Religious Studies and completed 8 units of Clinical Pastoral Education. He has served as a Ministry Leader where he worked with young adults within a non-denominational congregation and local community. During  that time Jeffrey had also served as a Chaplain serving in hospitals, assisted living centers and nursing homes. He has also been a guest speaker at various congregations in the United States. Those who have heard his messages to include some who have been recognized as prophetic voices of our time encouraged Jeffrey that if he hadn't written a book, that he should for such a time as this. Others who have said his messages are profound have ranked him among those very prophetic voices. His messages are not just a warning to the United States, but a warning to those all over the world. Jeffrey is also the founder of Revealing The Times. A network hub designed for the remnant of those around the world who are doing what Jesus told us to do, to watch and proclaim. For that remnant who are watching, for those living in places all over the world where things are happening before their very eyes, they too have a voice and should be heard. Jeffrey's hope is for those who read The Revealing, to also search the scriptures for themself. To bring the doubter to believe and the believer to be the light they are meant to be for such a time as this. Go to www.revealingthetimes.com to join the mailing list and get connected with the remnant of fellow watchers around the world. May we sound our voice as a trumpet in hopes that others may hear and believe.